Inquire of the Dead

a novel

K.E. Sanderson

This is a work of fiction. Names, characters, places, and incidents either are the product of the author's imagination or are used fictitiously. Any resemblance to actual persons, living or dead, events, or locales is entirely coincidental.

Copyright © 2021 by K.E. Sanderson

All rights reserved. No part of this book may be reproduced in any form on by an electronic or mechanical means, including information storage and retrieval systems, without permission in writing from the publisher, except by a reviewer who may quote brief passages in a review.

First Edition 2021

Book Design by K.E. Sanderson

Cover Design by K.E. Sanderson

Cover photography by Getty Images

ISBN 978-1-7368177-1-1 (paperback)

ISBN 978-1-7368177-0-4 (ebook)

Published by Invizion International, Inc.

For my mother,
who finally learned how to curse.

That Night

A Pack of Hounds

Monstrous red eyes and a low growl preceded an enormous shaggy head emerging from the surrounding darkness. "Nice doggie," she said as it stalked closer, but it didn't look like any dog she'd ever seen. The distant howling stopped, replaced by loud barking nearby. More animals seemed headed her way.

Adam jumped out of his truck. "What are you doing?"

The huge animal snarled and crept even closer to Greer. She threw her hands out protectively in front of herself, the heavy camera banging against her sternum. When several more pairs of scarlet eyes appeared in the pitch-black yard, Greer turned and ran, bolting away from the church and across the dimly lit street. Greer had never been a runner, but now she moved faster than she thought possible. In between rabid barks and growls, she could faintly hear Adam calling her name. Guilt slackened her pace when she realized she'd just abandoned him to a pack of wild dogs, until another bark spurred her on. She made a quick right turn, searching for shelter, only to find a few mom-and-pop businesses shuttered for the night under broken streetlights. Greer squinted at street signs, frantic to recall anything useful about this area, but nothing was familiar, so she kept running.

The camera bounced hard against her chest. She put a hand up to steady it as she stole a glance over her shoulder, only to find the pack gaining on her. A dark figure ran behind them. *Maybe Adam?* She couldn't stop to find out.

Each breath was becoming a struggle. They must be wolves, she thought desperately, to be so big. Yet, Providence had never been known for its wolves. Ever. The space in front of her suddenly opened; one of the small parks scattered throughout the city. A fountain and mounted statue lay half hidden in the gloom. Greer briefly considered the fountain, then aimed for the higher ground of the horse and rider. She heard snarls and splashing. *Too close!* When she reached the low steps of the monument, Greer bounded up and launched herself toward the statue, reaching for the nearest metal hoof. Wrapping both hands around the cool bronze, she pulled hard, raising herself high enough to hook a foot over the top of the stone base.

The wolves were jumping, snapping razor sharp teeth inches from her, their breath hot and foul. Before she could climb any higher, one of the beasts clamped its jaws around her left thigh. She screamed and looked down, finding herself eye to eye with one of the creatures.

Greer beat at the revolting muzzle with her free hand, but the wolf bit down even harder. Blood and scalding saliva mixed and streamed down her leg. She cried out in pain and fear, before striking it again and again, aiming for its crimson eyes.

As the other animals circled the monument, barking frantically, the stench of burning oil inflamed her throat until she began coughing uncontrollably. Spots formed before her eyes, and she felt her grip slipping from the statue.

Cruel laughter split the air.

Just as she almost lost her grip, an unexpected, quiet voice prodded at the back of her mind encouraging her to hang on. She strained, grabbing tighter to the statue, fighting to rise above the wolves.

A bright light pierced the darkness, casting a silver glow over the pack churning around her. As she heard a low voice begin speaking in a language she didn't recognize. The surging mass of fur at her feet abruptly turned toward the dazzling glow. Crouching low, the creatures bared their teeth. As the light drew near, they gradually slunk away from the monument, vanishing in the shadows.

As the silver light arrived at the steps, Greer saw it was held by Adam, his hand aloft and ablaze. He called out to the wolf still latched onto her. The animal rolled its eyes toward the light but snarled and renewed its hold on her thigh. She gasped and almost lost her grip as its teeth dug deeper. The edge of her vision began closing in. Adam spoke faster, louder and his sweat-soaked face drew tighter in concentration. The beast darted its eyes between the two of them. Adam closed the distance to press the brilliant light into the dark fur. With a piercing yelp, the wolf abruptly broke free and disappeared after its pack.

The charm Adam held gradually lost its radiance as he let it fall to his chest. He then grasped her forearm, attempting to unwrap her from around the horse's hoof. When she didn't budge, he tugged again gently and said, "They are gone. Come down."

Every muscle in her body immediately turned from steel wire to elastic string. Without any grace whatsoever, she slid down the stone into a heap against the monument, her breath coming in great gasps. Acrid fumes from the animals still hung in the air. As darkness overtook her, she was sure she'd never feel right again.

Greer vaguely realized she was being carried. When a shiver ran through her, a low voice said, "You are safe." Streetlights flickered overhead. A car rushed by. She moaned. "I have you," faintly penetrated her mind as everything started fading to black again.

She struggled against the darkness, trying to recall where she was and how she got here.

Earlier

The Days are Coming

Greer knew the dead and believed their stories. Kneeling in the empty churchyard, she listened for one now.

The morning dew cooled her fingertips as she pressed them deeper into the grass. Scents and sounds from long ago teased at the edge of her consciousness. Greer was accustomed to such sensations, and they elevated her work above that of other students. Focusing deeper, she caught a hint of acrid smoke, followed by grunting, deep and guttural. Alarm prickled from her scalp down to her worn work boots, and the feeling of being watched bristled the hairs on the back of her neck.

Greer's pulse quickened.

"Good morning, Ms. Dixon."

"Damn it," she said, muttering at the loss of the developing impression. She quickly bit her tongue at the sight of Adam Walker, the tall, dark and tousled assistant professor leading the excavation. She had agreed to be his teaching assistant, satisfying one part of her master's requirement.

He dropped a roll of canvas where he stood and slid several sawhorses off his shoulder with a clatter. "You are here early," Adam said, a hint of Rhode Island accent cutting through his cultured baritone.

She shrugged. "Getting a feel for the place. It seems to be quite the graveyard."

"No, actually, and I am not expecting to find any bodies this summer. My hope is this little dig will allow the freshman great hands-on experience. Mind helping me carry the rest of the equipment over?" She broke into long strides to keep pace as he continued, "If I recall from your application, you have only worked on a few East Coast excavations?"

"Right. Most of my field work has been out West, plus one *incredible* site in Bulgaria."

"Digging up a Rhode Island churchyard may be boring by comparison. In fact, I was rather surprised when you agreed to join my project. You really had your pick of summer placements."

"There's no such thing as a boring excavation. I always learn something new and..." she paused to scan the low skyline of Providence, "I don't know. I felt like I should be close to home for a while."

"I am confident you will be a great TA. Still, let me know if you have any concerns." He punctuated the last part with an appraising look.

Greer was intrigued once again by the intensity of his blue eyes. "I'm sure you had a lot of applicants," she said, recalling his classroom and a few females vying for the attention of the freshly minted instructor. As far as Greer knew, he'd never acknowledged their advances; otherwise, she never would've chosen to work with him. "I was glad this worked out for both of us."

"I'm sure it was the right choice," he agreed with a cautious smile as he pulled a large piece of plywood from his truck and tucked it easily under his arm. "What did you think of your first year of grad school?"

A myriad of experiences crowded to the forefront of her mind, as jumbled as the wooden stakes and bright string in the box she now held. "It was absolutely fascinating and exhausting. But don't worry, I can't wait to break ground. I could hardly sleep last night thinking about it."

Adam's quick laugh matched her own as they set back across the brightening yard.

St. Agatha's Cathedral, an old church in the middle of town, had been declared an official historical site, so the diocese needed the city's approval to break ground in the adjoining yard. City planners were correct in demanding a formal survey, and the mayor, a congregant himself, had twisted a few arms at the university to get the work done for free.

They were about to excavate a patch of grass stretched between the cathedral and the brick office building next door. Greer wasn't surprised the diocese wanted to build here. This was a lot of prime real estate to leave undeveloped in an old, coastal town. Still, she hoped the new builder would save the large oak trees lining the sidewalk.

Adam built a makeshift table out of the plywood laid across sawhorses, typical for this outdoor work. He towered over it as he began sorting stacks of papers on top.

Greer carefully walked the area again, noting the density of the soil underfoot, the shadows and moss playing over the cathedral wall, the sweet scent of growing things in the middle of a bustling city.

She was soon smiling stiffly at each of the students as they arrived.

Once all four students were accounted for, Adam hustled the class over to the red-brown wall looming over the yard and began his lesson. "Here you can see where the west transept once held a second doorway." He traced the faint color variation on the wall. "Just here. The stone has been expertly matched but, if you look closely, you can see it is not original. It was also completely plastered over on the inside, making this difficult to spot."

"Was it the door for poor people?" asked a gangly boy who kept brushing wild hair out of his eyes.

"No, it likely led to the parsonage," said a short, square girl wearing cargo pants and a fishing hat. Her eyes were almost lost under the brim; yet a sense of determination emanated from its shadows.

Greer said, "Actually, parsonage is a term used by Presbyterian churches. Catholics built rectories or vicarages for their residing clergy." The correction earned her a dirty look from underneath the hat.

"True," Adam said with a nod toward Greer before drawing them back into the lecture. "However, there is no record of a rectory here. We all know that historical records are often incomplete, so we should focus on this pre-existing entrance as we begin."

Greer scanned the young faces in front of her and anticipated their required handholding. She was more worried about their slow pace than not being able to meet their questions. *You learn by teaching,* she reminded herself. When she turned back, Adam was leaning against the wall, brow furrowed.

"One more thing. I know you all expected a leisurely dig this summer," he said. "Unfortunately, it appears the church holds sway over the mayor as well as the dean. We have been asked to fast-track our evaluation as the city prematurely approved the new construction last night. They plan to start building in mid-July instead of late August."

"Do we still get full credit for the class?" asked the lanky kid.

"Certainly, Mr. Rigsby. However, it will mean working quickly and putting in some long days. Set up the grid so we can start digging right away."

The boys moved off, muttering to each other as Ms. Fishing Hat told anyone who'd listen that she was ready to put in as many hours as needed.

Greer hung back to talk to Adam. "You didn't mention the accelerated schedule this morning. I'm concerned given the team's lack of experience."

"I hate to share bad news first thing in the morning. Anyway, I trust you will help keep a close eye on their work."

Only partially convinced, Greer set about helping Rigsby and a kid named Jones. She was pleased when Jones mentioned he had a little previous field experience, and she approved of the profoundly serious expression he wore.

Greer supplied directions and verified measurements as the students hammered stakes into the earth, running bright string between them to establish the formal excavation grid. She was starting to enjoy the instruction; however, she was itching to get her hands into the dirt below.

They weren't quite done when Adam clapped loudly for attention. "You each need to claim a section of the grid and write your initial journal entry. Then we can start the fun stuff ... turf removal!" He chuckled in answer to several loud groans.

Everyone grabbed a shovel and began the tedious work of peeling up grass. Greer concentrated on her section which was dead center in front of the walled-up doorway. This spot had her nerves tingling with promise. Making good progress, she'd just driven the shovel into the top layer of soil again when she heard a shout and felt a sharp blow to the back of her head.

Visions of the Night

The Christmas tree stood sentinel next to her mother in the watery moonlight.

"Mom, why are you here?" twelve-year-old Greer asked.

"I had to see you."

Greer was confused by the tears shimmering on her mother's pale cheeks. It'd been a full day. Dad, Grandma, and Grandpa all said so. Though, hard as she tried, Greer couldn't remember where Mom sat as they ate dinner and opened presents.

Greer rushed in for a hug, only to skid to a halt when she recalled the funeral, mere days before. "No! Mom!"

"I know, Sunshine. I've been so worried." The woman looked unexpectedly young in her white nightgown trimmed in ribbon. It billowed around her legs, caught in an impossible breeze in the small living room.

Greer waited, motionless until her mother stretched out an imploring hand. As Greer boldly stepped forward to meet it, the room brightened, and the sudden gust of a warm spring day tugged at her own gown. Just as fingertips brushed Greer's cheek, her mom vanished.

The room was suddenly empty, cold. Alone, Greer curled up under the tree and fell asleep.

...

A soft beeping dripped in her ear as she tried to pry open heavy eyes.

"Hey, Kiddo."

She recognized her father's voice.

Her vision and mind slowly came into focus as she took in the institutional green curtains and IV drip attached to her arm. "Is everyone ok?" Greer said, stammering slightly as she tried to sit up. A throbbing behind her eyes overtook her; the fluorescent hospital lights flickered.

"They're fine. You're fine." He softly shushed her as he encouraged her retreat to the pillow. He tried presenting a reassuring smile, but bloodshot eyes betrayed him. "When Robert called, I drove here as fast as possible."

"How long have I been out of it?" she asked hoarsely.

"It's after midnight now ... so about fourteen hours." He steadied a glass while she took a sip of water, coughed then took another timid sip. "The doctor said if you didn't wake up within twenty-four hours that we'd have reason to worry. You can imagine I'm *extremely* glad to see those beautiful eyes." He peered down his nose, examining her through bifocals. "Hmm, must be the concussion. They look a little odd."

"A concussion?" She gingerly probed the especially sore spot on the back of her head. Fingers tickled against a few stitches buried in her thick auburn hair. "Thank God no one shaved my hair."

Laughter relaxed his shoulders and the line on his brow. "Robert told them you'd be extremely upset if you couldn't pull your hair up for work. Apparently, the doctor believes in professional courtesy."

"Do you know what happened? I remember pulling up turf, and someone shouting, and then ... nothing."

"One of your students accidentally hit you with a shovel," he said, one eyebrow raised.

Certain his accusing tone had been a joke; Greer barked a short laugh. *Ouch*. Then she sorted through possible scenarios in her befuddled mind.

"How exactly does that happen?"

He answered with a perplexed shrug. Then, squeezing her hand tightly, he held on and silently studied every inch of her face. Greer let him have his moment while she scrutinized him less conspicuously. The last time they spoke, he'd been elbow-deep in a book project at his small Vermont college. The extra room inside his button-down shirt attested to his dedication. She was always reminding him to eat.

As she patted his hand limply, she did her best to sound better than she felt, "You said everyone at the site is ok?"

"I would assume so, but Robert is the one who has spoken to your professor each time he called. He's been here all night, you know, Robert. I just sent him home a bit ago for a shower and some food." He leaned in to whisper conspiratorially, "His fidgeting was putting me on edge."

They sat in silence for a time, listening to the beeping of the machines and the voices in the hall. Occasionally he squeezed her hand or offered another sip of water.

He perked up with a sudden thought. "Oh, I hear you two are finally making wedding plans."

Greer looked at him sideways. "Not really. But I'll let you know what day to show up."

"I'd like to be more help with these things."

She picked at a thread on the hospital blanket while a pang of regret plucked at her heart. "Don't be. I'd feel the same way even if Mom was here. It's just too much fuss to make over a single day." Aiming to distract him, she adopted a mischievous grin and said, "Now if I had only one day to dig under the Sphinx then that would be worth the fuss!"

"Just like your mother." He let out a small sigh. "I was always fighting her dusty, old beaus for attention."

They laughed at the shared memory. Her mom lost herself for hours on end among the bounty of ancient artifacts crammed into her university and home offices. Yet she tirelessly answered every one of Greer's questions about them. Mom was so proud when, at the age of nine, Greer wanted to learn ancient Greek to read original inscriptions on her own.

She debated her next words carefully then decided to plow forward. "Dad, I had that dream again. About Mom."

He straightened, blinking slowly. "I thought you'd outgrown those. Did it upset you?"

"No, that's the thing. This one was different."

"How?"

"She was more *there*. You know?" She hugged herself, trying to remember every detail. "The dreams, well, they were always the same before. But I actually talked to her this time. And she talked too." She reached for his slender hand. "I hope I remembered her voice right. There's no other way to explain it, except that it felt real. Mom touched my cheek." Greer scanned his face to see if he followed her meaning.

It had been years since they discussed a dream of her mother. They were frequent at first, slowly tapering off over the years. At some point she'd finally realized hearing about the dreams took a toll on him, so she'd stopped reporting them. But this one was unique enough that she needed to share.

His eyes slipped out of focus. When his answer came, it sounded detached from his thoughts. "Well, that's a good thing, isn't it? Maybe you're finally coming to terms with what happened."

Greer read the familiar sadness settling over his face. They rarely spoke of her mother, especially how she died. No one could ever truly come to terms with the manner of her death.

"I envy you, you know." He removed his glasses to clean an imaginary spot with his sleeve. "What I wouldn't give to see her, talk to her. Even if only in my dreams." He turned away, slowly replacing his glasses and clearing his throat. She heard him swallow hard before asking, "Should I stick around town for a few days?"

She recognized his stamina was flagging and felt guilty for keeping him up all night with worry. "Nah, Robert will take good care of me."

He offered a vague smile which she took as possible disappointment or relief.

A nurse stepped through the curtain. "Well, looks who's awake," she said with a too-bright smile. "Let's just get your vitals, Sweetie, so we can get you settled into a real bed."

It was actually a few hours before Greer was settled into a private room on the third floor, the promise of a real bed unfulfilled. Despite the thin mattress and scratchy pillow, she kept dozing off.

Her dad gently shook her arm. "Hey. Remember you're supposed to stay awake for a while now."

Fighting to stay alert, she imagined her escape from the tubes and paper gown. "Let's get together soon. July Fourth. Ok?"

He spoke through a cavernous yawn, "It's a date."

When he glanced toward the door, then his watch, she closed her eyes with a long sigh. "Yeah, I thought Robert would be back by now."

She woke again soon to find her dad asleep with a newspaper open in his lap while a gloomy old man watched her intently from the door. His face was sallow; one eye and the corner of his mouth melting into the sparse whiskers. Stains decorated a wrinkled robe, and one of his bright yellow hospital socks was missing.

He jabbed a crooked finger at her. Taken aback, Greer opened her mouth to ask whether he was lost. Before she could speak, he turned away to watch a gurney roll by. Its burly attendant bobbed his head to the beat in his headphones, seemingly unconcerned by the corpse he was transporting, the sheet indiscreetly slipping. The grizzled head dipped as he slowly shuffled after them.

He was out of sight by the time Greer realized the drooping sheet had exposed two feet, only one of which wore a yellow non-slip sock.

She glanced quickly at her father, but he was still asleep, glasses inching down his nose. Rubbing her eyes, Greer brushed the moment off to exhaustion and a splitting headache. Against doctor's orders, she decided a little rest was in order and fell asleep as the gurney's wheels still squeaked down the hall.

Witness

She was bored and grumpy. After days of resting on the couch, her headache was still severe, and she was stewing over missed work. Eager for any distraction, Greer dressed early for lunch with Robert's parents, Richard and Carol Cole. She'd even managed to scrounge up a skirt and silky blouse for the occasion.

When Robert came in from his daily run, already sporting a nice tan, she realized just how much she longed for the sunshine. He brushed a stray hair aside to plant a sweaty kiss on her cheek. "Hungry? Of course, you are," he answered for her, knowing she was always famished. "Let me shower and we'll go."

As they drove, she watched campus slip by. Brown University had been her first and only choice for grad school. In addition to its world-renowned archaeology program, it was close to home and her dad. Living so far away in Utah, while earning her undergraduate degree, had been hard on him, even if he'd never admit it.

Robert scrutinized her out of the corner of his eye. "Mother will want to discuss the wedding. I told her we're finally going to pick a date."

"Yeah, that's what I heard," she said, not in the least bit sorry for her tone. It bothered her that he'd made it sound official to her dad. "We agreed to finish school first."

"Why wait?"

She slumped in the seat, not ready for this discussion again. "Because we need to focus. *I* need to focus." Greer stared out the window as she cracked a knuckle against her thigh.

He deftly caught her hand, giving it a squeeze. "Come on. It's the perfect time with you working in town this summer. Aren't you ready to start our life together?"

Life with Robert was familiar, easy, and sensible. Planning a wedding was sure to be none of those things. Plus, she'd never liked being the center of attention, and she was sure his family wanted an elaborate ceremony.

"Parties aren't my forte. Ask me to manage an excavation and I'm all in. But plan a wedding?" She shook her head. "No. The whole idea puts me on edge."

"Mother will help with all that."

She returned to cracking her knuckles, this time in irritation.

They found his parents already seated outside on a fenced, garden patio. Greer would've bet real money that the mimosa Carol brandished wasn't her first of the day. Others would never have suspected given the older woman's conservative style. Carol worked hard to maintain her wardrobe and figure, all the better to fit in with the neighborhood wives. When Greer began dating Robert in high school, she was blissfully unaware of his family's social climbing. Now that she knew, she wasn't sure she could or should keep up.

"Glad you two could join us," Richard said, smiling his perfect smile which never failed to put others at ease. Robert had inherited the same open, authentic nature, and it was his best attribute in her opinion.

Carol darted out a bejeweled hand to clutch Greer's arm. "How are you, dear girl?"

"Just fine. I'm so glad you asked, Carol," Greer replied flatly. She gently withdrew her arm to place the napkin across her lap. Robert's mother had failed to visit or call the hospital, even once, to check on her.

The woman's hand wobbled as she set her glass down. "I've told you, dear. You must call me Mother now."

Greer quickly lost herself in her glass, wishing it held more than water.

They chatted about harmless topics such as the weather, the stock market, and Robert's legal internship. His parents were happy to hear he'd spent every spare minute studying cases, making up for time lost while she was in the hospital. He was ready to wow the partners on Monday morning.

Greer only half-listened as she allowed the warm breeze and sunlight dancing on the water work to improve her mood. The traffic passing just outside the patio faded to a dull thump at the back of her mind. In fact, the meal had progressed so agreeably, that when Carol mentioned a wedding planner was on his way, Greer choked on the last of her lunch. She threw a pleading look at Robert who, misreading the true source of her distress, helpfully thumped her on the back. Greer coughed while her mind raced through potential responses. None of them made her look good.

Carol spotted someone at the hostess stand and waved her over.

"The wedding planner is here. Richard, dear, take Robert home so we girls can talk."

The men didn't hesitate. They pushed in their chairs and gave each woman a peck on her cheek. Greer quickly stood to block Robert's exit.

"I'm not doing this today," she said through gritted teeth, angry he'd helped ambush her.

He pulled her aside and spoke over the increasing traffic outside the fence. "You can't keep putting this off, Greer. Just get it done. It'll make Mother happy."

The dull throb behind her eyes sharpened. She was about to respond when a car barreled into the intersection only a few yards away; it was moving at an excessive speed and on the wrong side of the road. At the same time, a motorcycle zoomed in from the opposite direction.

In the space of a heartbeat, the car struck the motorcycle, sending the cyclist over the handlebars, bouncing off the hood, then up over the roof of the car. The rider landed with a sickening thud in the middle of the street a few seconds before the car screeched to a halt.

Unmoving, not even breathing, Greer watched.

Several bystanders rushed to the motionless rider whose legs and neck were splayed at all the wrong angles to his body. A man exiting their restaurant pulled his mobile from his suit pocket and dialed furiously. One woman, attempting to check on the driver, was hesitantly approaching the car. The rest just stood ogling, slack-jawed.

Robert helped to dismiss the wedding planner and sat back down with his parents. He occasionally glanced over at Greer who still stood, hugging herself tightly, staring at the body littering the street.

After an ambulance pulled up, medics quickly confirmed the cyclist was dead before checking on the driver in the car. She figured he must've been fine as he was promptly loaded into the back of a police cruiser.

The remaining officers canvassed the crowd asking witnesses for statements. As she followed the activity, Greer was caught off guard by a young woman who was leaning against a light post across the street. She wasn't viewing the carnage but was focused intently on Greer. The girl looked out of time and place, dressed in a long skirt and peasant blouse. Her too-long face was made longer yet by sandy hair that flowed down to her waist.

Greer's discomfort grew under her gaze.

An officer finally approached the fence and spoke to Greer. He was short and broad with a friendly face and apologetic smile that implied tragedy was unavoidable, even manageable.

He asked her name.

"Greer Dixon... sir."

He jotted it down in his little notebook.

"Did you see what happened here today, ma'am?"

She nodded and looked back to the mangled glass and metal glittering on the pavement. The spilled blood hadn't yet begun to dry; it glistened and seemed to pulse in the sharp sunlight. The metallic tang of it caught at the back of her throat. She stared, transfixed, as a tremor passed through the thick gore, swelling and bulging upward. From the blood rose the motorcyclist in his dented helmet and torn leather jacket.

Greer reeled back in horror.

"Ma'am, are you alright?"

She gaped at the figure standing in the street as he pulled off his helmet. He was young with a baby face topped by a shock of red hair. He turned to look straight at her, and with a finger to his lips, slowly shook his head no.

Greer couldn't stop screaming, even as she realized she must be hallucinating.

...

After she'd made a spectacle of herself, Robert and his parents had quickly rushed her out of the restaurant apologizing and explaining her recent head injury. Her fiancé had dropped her off at home after lunch and left again without a word.

Greer was working on her second glass of white wine, alone, unsettled. When the door finally opened, Robert tossed his keys on the counter and pulled her close. She let herself relax against his familiar frame.

"What happened today? Mother was embarrassed."

Her head started spinning but it wasn't from the wine.

Her voice rose in disbelief. "I upset your mother? I saw a dead body today, but that's what you're worried about?"

"We all saw the body, Greer," he said, completely dismissing her concern.

A cold knot twisted to life in her gut. Abandoning her glass, she sulked to the bedroom.

Later, when the mattress shifted as he settled next to her, Greer found she lacked the energy to remain angry. Adrift, she merely stared out the window, watching the shadows lengthen on the houses across the street. But when he tried to snuggle in next to her, she dodged him and locked herself in the bathroom. Greer cranked the shower on as hot as it would go, studying herself in the mirror until it steamed over.

Behold a Door

Hustling toward her spot at the dig the next morning, Greer was interrupted by Rigsby who was tripping all over himself, offering apologies.

"Accidents happen," Greer said, testy but retaining an air of professionalism. She put a hand on his shoulder to stop his bobbing. "Hey, I don't really remember anything. What exactly caused it? The accident?"

"I tripped over Jones' friggin' shovel. And then I kind of ... hit you in the head." He studied his shoes, properly mortified.

Squeezing his shoulder, she said, "I'm going to be fine, but be more careful. Yeah?"

He perked up. Twirling a trowel in circles around one finger, he happily reported passing the safety test Professor Walker made the class take because of the accident.

"Good to know." She gave him a tight smile and pointed him back to his work.

She caught Adam observing them. He nodded in approval and bent back to assisting the tall kid from Ohio. She searched her memory for his name but came up blank.

She was terrible with the names of the living.

A quick survey revealed each section of the grid had been excavated several feet in her absence. The slight flicker of resentment grew when she overheard students complaining that the artifacts they'd found consisted of only a handful of coins and buttons from the early twentieth century. She explained this was typical for the beginning of any dig. Society's scraps somehow made their way into every quiet corner of the world. These ordinary items would be properly catalogued, then tossed in a box at the university library, no more than a brief footnote on the building report.

Adam had removed the remaining turf in her area and excavated a few inches as time allowed. Still, she planned to work late all week to get caught up. The day was pleasantly warm, and her headache receded as she happily dug in the loamy earth.

Greer got on well with most of the undergrads. They came to her with questions when Adam was busy and included her in coffee break chatter. The only exception was the girl with the awful hat who, Greer had been surprised to learn, was Liz Bingham of the infamous local Bingham family. Their patriarch was currently serving time for insider trading. To be fair, Liz didn't seem to like anyone on the team, but she absolutely refused to acknowledge Greer's expertise in any way.

As the students packed up for the day, Greer was grateful for the chance to fully concentrate on her grid. She had a sixth sense for finding the best spots on a dig and had called dibs on this section against the cathedral wall. Greer loved old buildings and planned to specialize in ancient architecture for her doctorate. According to her research, the foundation of the old rectory should be located just another foot or so deeper, if one had indeed existed. It was slow and steady going until then.

The cathedral was built on top of an earlier Catholic church after its congregation outgrew the first structure. Or it may have burned down. No record had been found. The builder was likely a skilled craftsman working without the benefit of formal architectural drawings. However, he and the bishop would've consulted each other often as they sourced local materials and craftsmen to minimize costs. The result was a stunning Gothic Revival structure done in Connecticut Brownstone with two matching bell towers.

The shadows grew as Greer labored with shovel and trowel, finding only rocks since lunch. Every time the five-gallon bucket filled with dirt she hauled it out of her grid and over to the sifting screen. The screen was a rough wood-frame with a fine mesh nailed across the bottom. It was suspended from a tripod by thin chains. She slowly poured the contents of the bucket onto the screen then shook it to force the dirt through and reveal any small artifacts she'd missed. She wiped her brow against her shoulder before turning on the work lights to sift the next pail.

The headache had returned. Greer, sweating and panting, dumped the examined dirt onto the spoil heap. Bending at the waist, she inhaled slowly while a few stars sparked behind her eyelids.

Adam ducked his head from under the canvas tent now sheltering the worktable. He was tagging and cataloging the day's finds.

"Are you staying any later?"

She quickly straightened; worried he'd seen her discomfort.

"Absolutely."

She wiped sweat from her forehead with a sleeve then wandered over to inspect the objects he'd laid out on the trestle table. She gently poked at a few and inquired after the day's haul.

Adam opened his palm to display the cracked bowl of a wooden pipe. "A beautiful piece. I laughed when Rigsby found it and started whooping around the site." She plucked it from his hand, and he chuckled at the memory before regaining his composure. "I really should not laugh at the students."

"I can't fault the kid for his enthusiasm. But he did knock an entire bucket of tools into Liz's section. He might get some unexpected payback."

"Really? I have had no trouble from her."

"No, *you* wouldn't." Greer said with a smirk as she handed the pipe back.

Adam looked bemused; one eye squinting shut. "Well, let me know if I need to have a talk with her."

"Nah, I'm sure she'll be ok." Greer set off with the empty pail.

Adam called after her, "Tell me when you are ready to go."

Scanning the growing darkness, punctuated only by a few work lights and faint streetlamps at the edge of the yard, she hollered back, "I'll be ok. You can leave."

Adam ignored her dismissal and continued working at his steady pace. Greer found she didn't mind his quiet company at all.

When her stomach later growled, she decided to finish one last bucket.

The foundation for the cathedral, where the brown brick rested on large slabs of granite, had peeked through a few inches ago. Scraping the trowel along the edge of the granite, she scooped more dirt into the sieve resting on top of the bucket. Nothing had materialized on its rusty screen in a while.

She pushed into the dirt once more and struck something hard. Probably another rock. Greer carefully scraped more earth away. *Bingo!* The flat stone in front of her must be the foundation they were seeking.

"Adam! I've got it!"

He hurried over, easily clearing the maze of strings and holes, and broke into a wide smile at her revelation. "Great job, Greer. The students are going to be very jealous tomorrow."

"Yes. Yes, they are." She grinned back. Tapping the bucket with her trowel, she asked, "Would you mind emptying this so I can keep going a while longer?"

"Ayuh. Right back."

He grasped the handle, hoisting it as if it was filled with cotton candy and not five gallons of dirt. Greer paused, appreciating his strength before retrieving a soft brush from her tool bag.

Adam returned with the empty pail and the school's camera. Greer stretched a measuring tape in place and snapped a few pictures, then pulled out her notebook to record the depth of the foundation, its composition, and how it was situated in the grid.

"This should make the next few days very interesting," Adam said.

"I wonder if the foundation is complete. Could we be that lucky?" Greer chewed on her pencil, imagining what remained to be found.

Adam flipped the bucket, using it as a seat. He scanned the wall towering over them as he rubbed the back of his neck. "There is every chance most stones were scavenged for other purposes," he said in caution.

"Good evening," said a gravelly voice from the darkness.

Startled, Adam and Greer jumped to their feet. A silhouette slowly entered the hazy light skimming the boundary of the grid.

"Sorry. I'm interrupting," the man said as he stepped closer. "I'm Father Doyle."

The priest's cassock rippled around his ankles in a sudden chill wind.

"How may we help you, Father?" Adam asked. He rolled down his sleeves as the breeze continued to swirl around the yard.

"I've been assigned to oversee this project on behalf of the church. I would've been here earlier today but had many things to attend to."

Adam tensed. "I was not aware anyone would be supervising onsite. Regular reports have been promised to all interested parties."

Greer watched the two men size each other up. Doyle was average height with silver hair and hard eyes that now scrutinized Adam and the organized jumble around him. Even with her professor's height, it felt as if the priest had the upper hand.

She tried interjecting, diplomatically sharing a little information with Doyle while corroborating Adam's process. "We've just now uncovered an old foundation. I'm sure full details will be in the next report."

Adam tilted his chin, throwing her a sideways glance that suggested he'd take it from here.

The priest clasped his hands behind his back. "Please don't let me impede. I'll just observe for a bit. Thank you."

Not caring for an audience, she threw a darting glace between Adam and the priest. "Actually, I think we're done for the night. It'll take some time to dig out the next stone." Still, hating to pause when she was on to something, Greer knelt to run her hand over the exposed foundation. It was unusually warm given the cool night. The heat intensified until she snatched her hand away, smarting as if she'd touched a hot stove. She shook her wrist to dispel the feeling.

"What is it?" Adam asked.

"I don't know. It felt really hot." She studied her hand under one of the work lights. "That doesn't make any sense," she mumbled, running a thumb over the reddened palm.

Taking her hand, Adam gently blew away the dirt to examine the tender skin. Goosebumps rushed up Greer's arm.

"Are you alright?"

"Fine." *Not true.* Flushed, she reclaimed her hand and stood to brush dirt from her knees. "I should get going."

Adam looked about to say something but changed his mind and, climbing up to the grassy yard at the edge of the grid, he reached back to help her. Greer handed up the tools then accepted his offered hand which was almost as warm as the rock.

The priest had wandered away without a word.

They cleaned up the site for the night, placing the lights, tools, and artifacts in the back of Adam's truck. Then he escorted her the short distance to her car.

Closing the door for her, he leaned on the edge of the open window. "See you in the morning?"

"Of course."

She saw him in the rearview, watching her drive away.

. . .

Greer arrived shortly after dawn only to find Adam already set up for the day. He smiled a warm greeting and bent back over the reports spread over the trestle table.

She jumped down into her section and immediately set to work, shivering in the weak light. The stone of the cathedral further chilled the air near it. It took over an hour of digging before she finally felt warm. As she paused to wrap her flannel around her waist, Greer realized she'd avoided touching the foundation stone all morning. Exasperated with herself, she squatted and stretched one finger to the rock. It was cool.

The students were motivated by the new development. Everyone was plugging away inside their own grids to clear down to the same level, racing. She worried they'd miss something in their haste.

Rigsby popped his head up over the edge of his section, looking like a deranged gopher. "I think I'm almost there. You're so lucky you stayed late!"

Even Liz offered reluctant looks of approval this morning.

As they worked late into the afternoon, the students were able to find their way down to the foundation in their sections, and it appeared the structure was intact. Greer had completely leveled her own area to expose the top of the foundation. It was composed of regular one-foot-wide, three-feet-long hewn granite bars and ran at a true right degree angle to the cathedral wall. After helping the undergrads with their sections and supervising their cataloging techniques, Greer eagerly began digging inside the foundation boundary hoping for artifacts deposited by the inhabitants of the presumed refectory. She dug a few inches down into the softer soil. An iron nail, shards of ceramic, and stained glass came to light in her sieve.

At the start of a new pass near the wall, her trowel met with resistance. Greer swallowed the urge to celebrate and instead began the painstaking work of fleshing out the new discovery. Heavy oak boards, worm eaten and moldy from the damp earth, slowly emerged. An iron ring was fitted into a depression in the middle. It looked like an archetypal trap door.

Her heart did a little dance of joy as she sat in the dirt and finally called out, "Got something!"

When the students jumped into her section, someone stepped on her hand. "Back up before you destroy the provenience." She stared at Rigsby, the most likely culprit.

Adam cleared his throat and the students immediately cleared a path. He'd had the foresight to bring the camera.

"You've done it again," he said. Greer squinted up at him, wondering at his lack of enthusiasm. "Please step back everyone. Ms. Dixon and I will finish."

Greer and Adam cleaned around the edges of the door and prepared tools for the next step. The students watched so quietly that her world temporarily compressed down to the door, the steady rhythm of her brush, and Adam working beside her.

A familiar excitement deep in her gut had been mounting since she first glimpsed the oak boards. Trap doors weren't a normal feature for this time period. Cellars inside the city were usually accessed via narrow stairs. They may yet find a set of stairs in another corner of the foundation, but then, Greer thought, that'd make the trap door redundant.

Adam ran a crowbar around the bottom edge of the door then carefully worked the rust covered ring free.

"On the count of three. Ms. Dixon, be ready to slide that two-by-four under the leading edge in case I cannot lift it all the way open."

Adam settled into a wide stance, giving his boots a small twist in the dirt to ensure his footing. Grasping the heavy ring, he counted to himself, "One. Two. Three!" The muscles in his forearms tightened, but the wood didn't budge, only creaking and groaning at the strain. He released his grip, widened his stance and tried again. His biceps flexed, and a vein popped out at his temple. Greer was about to call a halt when the door suddenly broke away from its encrusted mooring. After that, it lifted rather easily. Adam pulled it all the way to a ninety-degree angle, and Greer slid a two-by-four up against the far edge where old iron hinges connected the door to the wooden frame.

Dust and the distinct smell of decay swirled around the opening. The students coughed and gagged.

"Got to love it," Greer joked, waving futilely at the miasma.

"You certainly do get used to it," Adam said, seeming unaffected by the stench. "Liz, please hand me the flashlight."

Greer and Adam knelt to peer into the opening. The dirt floor was a good eight feet down. This was no typical root cellar. Adam trained the light around, allowing glimpses of rough stone walls creating a rectangular room. He stood and shared his first impressions of the space with the students. Their excitement was palpable.

"Wicked cool, Greer!" Rigsby broke into a giant grin.

"Wicked," she said under her breath.

Even the normally cool-headed Jones was twitching in anticipation. "Let's get a ladder and get started."

Adam motioned for quiet and the jumble of conversations tapered off. "Alright now. This is exciting, but we need to let the space air out overnight. Gases have built up down there."

"Can't we even get a look?" Liz said. She'd removed her hat in anticipation of poking her head through the door. Greer realized the girl had been hiding a lovely face under that old thing.

Adam shook his head. "No. Right now, we need to get a barrier set up around the door. We do not want any curious kids falling in overnight."

But one inquisitive student had been trying to get a peek. Even after she'd waved him back, Jones, who was on hands and knees at the opening, leaned in again. His palms slid in the loose dirt, and, with a cry, he tumbled awkwardly down into the darkness.

As the students shouted in panic, Adam sprinted to his truck, while Greer ran to the trestle table to grab a coil of rope and a work lamp. They hollered at students to move out of the way, meeting back at the open doorway, panting.

Greer flicked the light on and trained it down the hole. Adam carefully lowered a ladder to rest beside Jones who was curled up in the fetal position. He hurried down and knelt over the student. Greer gave up trying to shoo the others away as they watched breathlessly. She shivered despite the warm, heavy air exhaled by the room.

They could hear Adam speaking softly as the student slowly rolled onto his back and blinked at the faces hovering above. With sighs of relief, they all fell back from the door, talking animatedly to each other about who'd seen him fall in.

When Jones cleared the doorway a few minutes later, coughing and pallid, he assured everyone he was fine, aside from a few bumps and a giant bruise to his ego.

Adam gave a stern safety reminder to all while Greer rummaged in his truck. She came back hauling a tripod which she placed over the door. By throwing a tarp over it and weighing that down with buckets filled with dirt, they hoped to prevent anyone else from trying to take a peek or a tumble. Tomorrow a pulley and bucket would be attached to the tripod to assist in hauling equipment in and out of the room.

Satisfied with the state of the site, Adam dismissed the students who were running high on adrenalin. They were loudly making plans to grab a few beers in celebration of the safe return of Jones.

"They have the right idea." Adam jabbed a thumb at the receding students. "Would you like to grab a drink? We can talk over a strategy for tomorrow."

He was plainly keyed up. She was still feeling the rush too.

"Sure. We'd better have a clear plan if we're going to keep those kids in line."

A deep chuckle rumbled up from his chest. "Kids? You are not much older. And I only have a few years on you."

"Well, I sure feel older right now. All but Jones are brand new to fieldwork. I'm constantly afraid they're going to goof up and contaminate the whole dig."

"Not to worry." He touched her elbow, steering her down the sidewalk. "Since this is not a historically significant project, it is the perfect learning field for them."

Greer felt that every dig was important but chose not to argue. "Let's get that beer. It's been a long day."

They slid into a sticky booth at the nearest bar. The waitress hurried over and seemed to be offering more than a drink when she asked if Adam wanted 'his usual.' He nodded, giving her only a lukewarm smile in return.

"She seems to like you," Greer said, flashing a knowing grin.

He shrugged. "We went to parochial school together."

Their beers were delivered along with a playful hair tousling for Adam. As the dark waves tumbled over each other, Greer imagined him waking up looking that way every morning. She hastily redirected her thoughts as he smoothed it down and launched into plans for the next day.

They were on their second beer and had a list of needed equipment scribbled on a napkin, when a woman strode up to their table.

Greer peered up out of the corner of her eye as she quietly took another sip. Tightly pursed lips pulled the woman's high cheek bones into sharp relief. Adam kept talking, unaware, but eventually followed the direction of Greer's gaze. Breaking into a huge smile, he slid over to make room.

He waved his bottle in each direction, making introductions. "Greer, this is Cahya. Cahya, this is my TA, Greer."

Greer reached across the table to shake hands. Cahya ignored it, instead using her own hand to capture the jet tresses that'd fallen across her face, tying them into a loose knot at the nape of her neck. Greer absently touched her own hair which was adorned with baked-in dirt and sweat from the day's work.

"I'm his girlfriend," Cahya said as she slipped out of her worn leather jacket. Greer heard the warning in the woman's voice and did her best to look uninterested, bored even. Cahya took a long pull of Adam's beer and continued to stare pointedly across the table.

Seemingly oblivious to the silent exchange happening between the two women, Adam excitedly recounted the day, sounding like a little boy describing a lost treasure. Feeling like a third wheel, Greer excused herself for the night.

"I should walk you back to your car," said Adam.

Clutching her bag, Greer hurried out of the booth. "Thanks, but I'm fine. I'll let you two enjoy your night." She offered her hand once more to the unfriendly woman. "Nice meeting you."

This time Cahya did shake her hand then smiled coolly as she slid that same hand into Adam's lap.

The Heat Consumed

The sound that woke her had been no more than a whisper. It felt like the deepest part of the night, yet moonlight reflecting off snow in the yard brightened the bedroom. With her head still heavy with dreams only half remembered, she threw back the covers and hurried to peek around the doorframe. The hem of a white nightgown disappeared around the corner. Small, bare feet chased it.

She found the living room cluttered with abandoned Christmas presents. A rustling drew her attention to the tree. Its scent was still strong, having been cut down only two days before. Daddy always turned off the tree's lights at bedtime. But now it was glowing.

The soft glow rapidly coalesced into a distinct and awfully familiar outline.

. . .

Greer awoke with a start. Her mother's voice and a lingering whiff of pine tempted her back to the dream, back to her younger self, until the familiar grip of loss constricted her heart.

Like ticking off items on a checklist, she reminded herself that she was a grown woman, a grad student, and engaged to the snoring lump beside her. Tear-filled eyes struggled to focus as Greer eased back into reality.

A loud fart from the other side of the bed broke her reverie. Sighing heavily, she left Robert to his dreams and padded across the thin carpet to the bathroom. After an indulgent shower, she threw on jeans and the last shirt from the dresser. Then, satchel in hand, Greer rushed out of the apartment, ponytail swinging with each hurried step.

It was unreasonably early, but Adam had once again beaten her to the site and was already pulling gear from his truck when she parked. After a quick hello, she helped move equipment into place. He'd remembered everything they discussed last night: a large fan, flexible ductwork, a generator, and extra work lights.

"Now we can explore safely," Greer said, rushing as she carried the work lights across the yard two at a time.

"I want to get the door open and start cycling the air out before the kids get here."

Adam pulled the trap door open in one swift motion. Greer fed the ductwork into the hole. Once it was connected to the fan, which was being powered by a very rusty generator, they sat back to rest.

"Where'd you get that thing? It looks practically antique," she said.

"Knock it, but it has seen me through plenty of digs and a few New England storms."

Nudging the grumbling hunk with her boot, she said, "I just thought Brown could afford newer equipment given what they charge in tuition."

"It will do. Besides, I like old things." His attention was drawn to the edge of the yard where students were arriving. "Looks like everyone wants to get an early start today."

The students argued over who'd be the first down the hole. Rigsby positively couldn't hold still to the point that Greer began to worry about his mental state. In the end, Adam determined he'd go down first, followed by the two tallest boys. He wanted help securing ceiling supports before the rest would be allowed in.

Greer and Liz settled the tripod over the entrance and hooked a rope and pulley to the center. They used the pulley to carefully lower work lights down.

As she waited patiently up top, Greer could only see a few feet into the room. She felt the buzz of anticipation and realized she was almost as excited as the kids.

Adam climbed back into the sunshine and pulled himself up to sit on the edge of the doorway beside her. "You must be dying to get down there. Thank you for being so patient."

"How does it look?"

He gladly accepted the water bottle she offered, gulping half before wiping the back of his hand across his mouth. He considered the open doorway. "Rather boring, actually. No treasure." She heard the edge of disappointment in his voice. "It appears to be empty; however, I am interested in your first impressions."

Eager to get started, Greer methodically swept stray tendrils into a fresh ponytail as she said, "Let's get the tykes fed and busy up here. I want some time to take it all in first."

Adam held the ladder as she descended. When her feet were firmly planted on the dirt floor, Greer flicked her flashlight on and began sharing her observations. In her opinion, the single point of access, rather small dimensions, and lack of visible artifacts offered no immediate clues to its purpose. Yet, just by being void of artifacts, it indicates the occupants didn't leave in a hurry.

Adam brushed his hand across the wall, studying the loose dirt that came away on his fingers. "And that certainly makes our job harder."

She ran an appraising hand over the rough stones of the closest wall. They were dry-stacked walls—without mortar—and rather beautiful. This building style required a good eye for geometry and a lot of patience on the part of the builder.

"The craftsmanship is primitive yet extremely well done," she said. "I don't see anything yet that lets us confirm the building period. But we know this technique lost favor to mortar and cement in the early 1900's."

Greer followed the wall, trailing her fingers lightly. She turned the corner and worked her way down the second one. The stones jutted a few inches here and there due to their rough nature. One shifted slightly under hand. She bent to give it a test wiggle.

An unexpected spark flared in her gut, and she knelt to investigate.

"What do you have there?" Adam crouched down beside her and added his light to her own.

"This one's loose. Get the camera."

Greer pulled the tape measure along the floor and wall while he snapped pictures. She took notes of the stone's exact location.

Finally, Greer gently worried at the edges, patiently drawing the loose piece out while keeping a wary eye for any movement in the surrounding stones.

"Help me with this," she said.

Adam supported the weight of the stone as she tugged it the last few inches. A blast of hot, acrid air slapped her in the face, knocking her back on her heels. She turned her head away, coughing. Unaffected, Adam stuck his face right up to the hole and trained his light inside.

"Nice! There is certainly a small cavity back there. Let me collect the students and some buckets."

Greer took a deep breath before peering into the opening. The odor was revolting, but she managed to spot a second wall, visible a few feet ahead.

"Ok." She called after him belatedly. "And turn the fan back on, would you? It's getting warm down here."

The room was oven-like and pungent. Greer waved a hand in front of her face trying to stir a breeze as she sluggishly tested the wall for more loose stones. Her stomach soured, her head ached, and she broke into a sweat. When a harsh laugh echoed in her mind, she worried the concussion was impairing her faculties.

Adam found her sitting slumped against the wall when he returned. He rushed to kneel beside her.

"What happened? Ms. Dixon?" He shook her shoulder. "Greer!"

Greer lifted her chin and fluttered open her eyes. Her head still ached, but the nausea was passing. Holding her head, Greer said, "I was overheated."

Two students, each armed with buckets and trowels finished banging their way down the ladder. "It's not hot down here," Liz said. She dropped her tools to aim her flashlight at the new hole in the wall. "I wonder how we all missed it this morning." She poked at the surrounding stones, testing them.

"Ms. Bingham, wait for me," Adam said. He turned back to Greer, obviously trying to evaluate her condition. "Maybe you should get some fresh air. We can handle things down here."

Greer waved him away. "No, I'm fine. Give me a second," she said, feeling uncertain.

Adam supervised the students as they carefully began removing the stones around the opening. They were fit tightly, but, since no mortar held them together, it was simply a matter of not letting too many pieces move at once.

Greer pressed the back of a hand to her forehead, willing the stomach-churning headache away. Worse was her mortification at students catching her literally laying down on the job. Using the wall to steady herself, she slowly stood. The room felt off kilter as she made her way over to the group. Yet, once they filled each bucket, she insisted on lugging it to the bottom of the ladder to be hauled up and examined in the daylight.

When the entire opening was clear, Adam called for the work lights to be moved closer. Greer helped, pushing herself despite the headache.

As the hidden cavity flooded with light, the students clapped in excitement. The space was roughly four feet wide and five feet deep with an arched ceiling standing not more than six feet high. The curved ceiling and smooth walls inside were unexpected considering the rough build of the larger room. The real surprise was the intricately painted plaster which lined each wall.

"Remarkable," Adam said. He crossed his arms, settling in to study the space. "Mr. Jones, would you like to walk us through your observations?"

Jones took a deep breath then began in the monotone Greer had come to expect from him. "These walls are constructed of smaller stones which have been mortared together, unlike the rest of the dungeon…"

Adam interrupted, cross. "Excuse me?"

Jones reddened under the scrutiny. "That's what some of us started calling it, professor."

Adam threw him his academic, one-eyebrow-raised glare. Clad in jeans and grime, the effect was more reminiscent of a dusty pirate in Greer's mind. However, it has its desired effect on Jones who looked to his classmates for help.

"You know. The trap door and all ..." he said. Finally, aware that no excuse was going to improve the situation, he stuffed his hands in his pockets, clenched his jaw shut, and waited for the official reprimand.

Adam sighed. "We will obviously need to discuss the project's nomenclature later. Ms. Bingham, would you please continue for us?"

Liz hurried closer. "The plaster is a bit lumpy. Definitely an amateur job." She pointed to the figures depicted in multiple scenes playing out across the walls. "The paintings. They're amateur too, but I think someone really took their time with them."

The tall kid from the Midwest, Greer was searching for his name, jumped in at this point. "The religious themes of these paintings support our theory that the building was a rectory, right? Maybe this was a private altar for the local bishop?"

Adam said, "Good hypothesis, Mr. Malcolm."

Greer stepped in front of a beaming Malcolm, disregarding the heat emanating from the cavity. She agreed with the students' findings; however, no one had commented on the faint rectangular outline visible on the floor of the cavity. She pointed to a large stone inlaid in the center of the otherwise dirt floor.

"What about that?" Greer said.

Adam crouched and tapped the area with a trowel. Malcolm handed him a brush and he quickly cleared away the dust.

Adam said, "Looks like granite. No inscriptions." He tapped the stone again as he mumbled to himself.

Greer knelt and traced the rectangle with her fingers, feeling for irregularities. The stone was just shy of two feet on its longest side.

"It could a base for a small altar," she said, thoughtfully probing the ground with her fingers. "Look at this track of softer dirt encircling it. That suggests something else, don't you think?" She looked to Adam for agreement.

"You believe it may be a capstone?"

She nodded.

Adam ran the trowel around the perimeter, scraping away earth, revealing that the stone was indeed resting on a matching granite box. They dug together to locate the bottom edge.

"What is it?" Malcolm asked peering over Adam's shoulder.

"An ossuary. A stone coffin." Jones said.

From the frightened look on Jones' face Greer thought maybe he'd chosen the wrong field of study.

"Wow! Is this like a first?" asked Liz. She'd turned the brim of her hat up and now her whole face betrayed true glee.

"Not entirely," Adam said. "It is common to find unmarked graves in Providence given its age and the lack of burial laws throughout its early history."

Liz's smile faltered.

Greer cleared more dirt away from the box as she listened to the exchange. The moment she'd touched the granite a general uneasiness struck her. Her nerves jittered; her bones ached. It took effort to ignore, but she refused to let it grow into anything substantial. Superstition on a dig was the killer of scientific method.

"How're we going to lift it out?" Jones asked as his every muscle contracted with anticipation.

Adam pulled a thin, nylon climbing rope from his bag. "A good archaeologist will have several of these available at all times." He helped Jones slip it under the far end of the box. "If I lift from inside the alcove, then, Jones, you can get the shovel under the other end and slowly lever your side. Once it is even with the floor, Malcolm, put your shovel under the middle for support. Then I will slowly push it out into the room."

The plan was flawless. Adam slid the box across the dirt floor just outside of the niche.

"Great work…"

His next words were cut off by several sharp cracks from the alcove. Greer heard a strangled howl. Several large pieces of plaster and a few small stones fell from the ceiling into the hole they had just left in the alcove floor.

"Out! Now!" she shouted, pushing students toward the ladder.

They made it outside safely, hearts pounding.

"That was fantastic!" Liz said, again grinning ear to ear.

"What was that noise?" Jones asked.

Greer shot him a questioning look, surprised someone else might have heard the howl too.

Adam quieted the class with a gesture. "I think it stopped. Ms. Dixon and I will go back down to inspect the damage."

Greer didn't waste any time climbing back down into a lingering haze of dust. A few major cracks had developed in the alcove ceiling, half of the plaster mural was now in pieces on the floor, and stones filled the hole vacated by the box. A few streams of grit trickled from jagged cracks.

"Damn it," Greer said, scowling at the rubble. "We lost a lot."

"Yes. We need a way to secure it before we lose more." He probed carefully at a piece of mural still attached to the wall. "Be right back."

Adam returned with two-by-fours from his truck and plywood pilfered from the tabletop. He brought the students back down with him and outlined how they were going to build a crude support system in the alcove.

"I want to open the box down here to understand how fragile the contents are. If there are bones, and they are very brittle, we will need to remove and secure them individually for transport."

Adam carefully wound cloth around the angled end of a small crowbar then extended it toward Greer.

"Ms. Dixon, would you like the honor?"

She was happy to take over and quickly applied the wrapped end to an uneven spot between the coffin and its lid. The bar slipped in easily. She slowly pried the slab from its base.

An intense sadness overcame her as a distant sobbing replaced her thoughts. The sound intensified as she gradually lifted the lid higher. She shook her head but couldn't dispel it. Pausing, Greer turned to the group behind her. "What *is* that? Is someone hurt up there?" She jerked her head toward the ladder.

Adam had been watching her progress intently, a hand touching a round stone he wore around his neck. He started at her question, looking as though he'd been caught in the middle of something.

He cleared his throat. "I do not hear anything. Keep going, please."

Greer frowned, assuming the sound to be another side effect of the concussion. She shook her head again, but the weeping swelled into an echoing wail.

Just push through. Focusing on the stone, she carefully lifted until she could slide a hand underneath. Dropping the crowbar, she slipped the other hand under and raised the lid in a puff of dust.

Anguished screams tore through the air. With a crash, Greer dropped the stone as she clamped her hands over her ears and scrambled backward. The screeching continued. The pain in her head exploded in a shower of sparks behind her eyelids. Someone called her name before she passed out.

. . .

Greer awoke in the yard with a circle of anxious faces staring down at her. Adam spoke animatedly into his phone nearby. When he saw her eyes open, he quickly pocketed it and asked the students to clean up for the day.

Squinting tightly, she attempted to breathe past the searing pain in her skull. Greer tried to feel something good, eventually finding the soft tickle of the grass below her and the slight chill as clouds blocked the late afternoon sun.

Adam squatted next to her to feel the pulse in her wrist before laying a broad hand across her forehead.

Her eyes pricked open again.

"Your father is on his way. I wanted to call an ambulance, but he is nearby and wanted to check on you first, considering you woke up so quickly." His forehead crinkled with worry. "Should I call the squad anyway?"

"No. I. No, I'm ok."

She rested a hand on his, hoping to reassure him. Surprisingly she was the one comforted by the touch. He was warm, solid. The swirling in her head eased.

"Greer, I had to carry you out. You said earlier that you were fine." The last he said accusingly, as if she'd deceived him.

She had.

"I was…I will be," she said as he looked at her warily. "It was just so *hot* in there. And I think I forgot to eat lunch." Greer rubbed her temples. "Good lord. What was all that screeching about?"

Adam leaned in close so as not to be overheard. "Greer, you were the one screaming. So, *you* tell me."

Her memory was foggy. She'd been very careful, but the lid had given suddenly. Everything after that was just blind shrieking.

"You were lucky not lose any fingers when the stone fell."

"Oh no! Did I damage it?" While fainting was bad, spoiling an artifact would be the worst thing that could happen in Greer's opinion.

A corner of his mouth turned up in a smirk. "I was a bit preoccupied and failed to check." The smile quickly disappeared. "What did you see? Did something frighten you? Something you cannot explain?"

She rolled her eyes. "Please. This isn't my first rodeo. It was just a lot of ashes and bone fragments."

"That is all?" He looked puzzled.

She heard a car door slam and saw her dad running toward them. Greer sat up and was glad the world stayed horizontal. As he sank to one knee and hugged her fiercely, she realized he was out of breath and immediately felt guilt at putting him through more worry.

"What happened, Kiddo?"

"It was just ... just a combination of things, really. I'll be ok."

He threw Adam a questioning look, but the younger man shook his head, suggesting he was unable to confirm her diagnosis. "She was only unconscious for a few minutes, and continues to tell me that she is fine," Adam said. His look remained doubtful.

Greer shoved to her feet, annoyed they were discussing her over her head.

"Adam, I'm so sorry for the mess. I'll go clean up."

Adam pulled himself upright. "No. You will go home now and stay home tomorrow." His tone invited no reply.

Her dad made a loud noise of agreement.

Gently, Adam said, "Given your concussion, maybe this was all too soon?"

"No!" she said forcefully, surprising them all. She took a deep breath to regain control. "I mean. No. Thank you. That concussion was blown out of proportion."

"I am sure it was not," Adam said.

Her father was watching her closely, clearly tracking her eye movements. "You need rest, ok?"

She sighed. There'd be no arguing with her father on this, and once he told Robert, there'd be three of them against only one of her.

"Fine. I'll take one day off. But I want a full accounting of everything that happens. I don't want to miss a single detail."

Adam flashed a mischievous grin. "Liz will write a report for you. She will be happy to."

Greer laughed and saw spots. Rubbing her temple, she asked, "Dad, would you mind driving me home?"

"Sure thing. I was coming by to check on you anyway."

Adam walked them to her dad's car and closed the door once she was tucked in. Leaning on the open window, he said, "Do not change your mind and show up tomorrow. It is a matter of safety for all of us at this point."

She nodded and tried to stifle a yawn as her father drove them away. Bed was sounding divine right now. Robert would get his own report in the morning.

Our Struggle is Not Against Flesh and Blood

Robert had reacted just as she expected. Before leaving for work, he gave Greer clear instructions to stay home, rest, and drink plenty of fluids. Unfortunately for him, she was feeling irritatingly vigorous. So, when the sunshine beckoned to her long before lunchtime, she struck out on a brisk walk.

Their neighborhood was a tad neglected, yet charming. Unique architecture on each home offered plenty to contemplate. Several runners nodded in passing. Her mind soon drifted to the dig, frustrated at missing anything crucial. She considered casually dropping by, but Adam was right about the safety of the team.

A sudden image of the accident, the broken body in the street, flashed across her mind. Everyone assured her the concussion was responsible for the bloody vision of the reanimated rider. It felt so real at the time. She mentally replayed it over and over as she walked, and, despite the warm day, shivered each time she recalled the way the cyclist shushed her.

Greer was at her best in the field. Unable to dig, she didn't know what to do with herself. In quiet moments, she couldn't shake this unhealthy fixation and doubts about her own mental health. Worse, she felt like she was letting Adam and the students down.

All she needed, after her embarrassing behavior onsite, was Adam or a student hearing about her reaction to the accident. It would mark her odd at best. No one would want to work with her.

...

Adam called her over to the tent as soon as she arrived the next morning. True to his word, Liz had drafted a report. "Room A" was the new official label assigned to the underground area they were exploring. Anyone caught calling it "The Dungeon" would be assigned clean up duty for the rest of the project. The small offshoot from Room A which she had discovered was now called "Alcove A." The dull naming conventions used in archaeology were timeless in their utilitarianism. Despite extensive searching by the entire team, no one had yet located additional cavities or niches within the room.

"Thanks for this," she said as she watched the students work. They were expanding the dig by cutting through turf and creating new grids in the yard. "Do we have money for a DNA analysis on those bone fragments?"

"I may be able to squeeze the extra funding from the dean."

"Once we date them, we'll need to do some serious research into the church leaders from the relevant time period. A cremation burial is atypical."

Adam hummed in agreement. "Yes, it is uncharacteristic for a historic Catholic burial. Usually we find intact bones, certainly no ashes. I feel like their inclusion has a purpose. Research might shed some light."

She tucked the report into her back pocket. "What makes you say they had a particular purpose?"

Adam folded his arms, briefly collecting his thoughts. "There is great attention to detail in the entire burial. The placement was not an afterthought or a rushed internment. And, of course, the fact that it was walled up indicates a desire to keep it secret or protect it."

Adam stopped to examine her face closely, his eyes narrowed in concern. "Sure you are ready to get back to work?" His brow furrowed even as she nodded emphatically. Finally, he nodded and pointed toward the students working in the yard. "Alright, pick a new square in the grid and start digging then."

The day flew by without a single incident or twinge of headache. Maybe the concussion was finally healing, she thought. She was feeling good, almost normal.

When the end of the day arrived too soon, Greer helped Adam load the equipment into his truck.

"Want to grab some grinders and come help me with something back here?" he asked as he closed the tail gate.

"What's up?"

"We took those quick photos of the alcove walls when we first opened it, but the plaster is continuing to deteriorate. We need some close ups to capture as much detail as possible."

"Well, of course," she said, cheerfully.

Adam leaned an elbow on the back of the truck and squinted as if he wanted to ask her a question yet couldn't quite figure out how to say it.

She held her breath; certain he was going to ask after her health again. "What is it? You've been trying to say something all day."

Clearing his throat, Adam scratched behind his ear before beginning hesitantly. "Is there anything you would like to talk about? It has been quite an interesting week, right?"

Greer immediately worried he was going to kick her off the project. "Look, I can't believe I blacked out. I'm telling you it was hot down there. And, ok, the screaming. I just don't know. It's never happened before, and I'm sure it won't happen again." She scrutinized his face, trying to interpret his thoughts so she could stop any argument in its tracks, but all she read there was concern.

"Well, sometimes things are out of our control. I am a good listener if you would like to talk about ... anything that has happened."

She imagined telling her handsome professor all about seeing dead people, hearing disembodied cries, and fighting with Robert. That was all typical stuff any supervisor would love to hear. He would sympathize, say he totally understood, and then give her more responsibility over the class. *Right.*

Keeping all trace of emotion from her face, she said, "Nope. Let's go. I'm starving."

He studied her a moment longer before flashing an inspired smile. "I know just the place."

...

An hour later Greer stood with her hands over her head, lifting the plywood supporting the delicate plaster ceiling. The goal tonight was to temporarily remove the braces one at a time to view the plaster works on each wall. The alcove had been covered in detailed murals depicting multiple biblical scenes. However, it was rapidly deteriorating.

"Turn a little to your left," said Adam. He stretched to reach past her, working to adjust the far end of the support beam.

"No, too far," he said in protest. "This is not working." He stepped back and slowly surveyed the braces.

She felt the plywood slipping. "Could you hurry it up a bit?"

"Sorry."

He stepped close to help, and she detected the spice of his soap under the more recent layers of dirt and sweat. "Alright now? Just let me grab the new camera."

"Wow. That's a nice thirty-five millimeter." He held the camera out to her for a closer look as she made noises of appreciation.

"Wait until you see what it can do."

Adam fired off shots across the first wall, moving support beams as he went while Greer focused on where to find her next hand hold. As he worked his way toward the back wall, she shifted so he could move deeper into the alcove. He moved slowly, photographing the wall inches at a time. He absently reached for her shoulder, nudging her out of his way.

"You know you can *ask* me to move, right?"

He didn't answer, just kept working left to right, top to bottom. He nudged her waist, moving her slightly this way, then that. A self-conscious blush warmed her cheeks. She took a deep breath and had just succeeded in regaining her composure when he slid a hand around her ankle, easing it out of the way for the final shots, and a small sigh betrayed her.

Greer was relieved when Adam stood and set the camera carefully back in his bag.

"You must be exhausted. Let me take over for a minute."

Adam ducked in and raised his arms awkwardly to lift the plywood. Greer gratefully wiggled her completely numb limbs.

"I have this if you can put the central support back in, please," he said, nodding to the long four-by-four on the floor of the main room.

Greer propped the thick beam in place and kicked the bottom edge until it was snuggly supporting the whole structure once more. In the process, one of the back braces loosened and threatened to fall. Greer lunged for it before it could strike the plaster wall, catching herself with one hand on the mural beside her for balance. The moment her skin touched the paint, she felt a stickiness beneath her fingers. She snatched her hand away with a gasp.

"Are you ok?" Adam asked, trying to turn without letting the plywood fall out of place.

Greer looked from the dark red ooze smeared on her palm and fingertips to the wall. The plaster was undisturbed except for where her hand had lifted a layer of dust from the mural. She scanned the wall again for any damage but found none.

Adam had worked his way around to grab the loose brace and prop it into to place one-handed. "You are bleeding. Let me see."

Her first instinct was to hold her hand out to him, so she wasn't sure why she briskly wiped it on her jeans instead. Other than a brief flash of heat when she touched the paint, Greer hadn't felt anything. She flashed the clean palm at him. "No. I'm fine. Um, just some dirt where I accidentally touched the wall," she said with a shaky smile. "But it's all good. That mural should live to see another day." She looked up at him for confirmation; however, instead of inspecting the aging plaster, she found he was inspecting her.

"You actually have some in your hair." He plucked a few pieces from her temple. "Nothing large enough to salvage." He let the flakes fall to the floor as he continued to examine her thoughtfully.

Greer was bewildered when the blush rose back into her cheeks. "Well, let me out of here so I can go wash it off."

He looked slightly abashed and took a few steps back.

"Yes. Of course."

They emerged from Room A with the camera and their bags in tow. It'd been dusk when they descended, now it was fully night. The lonely glow of one last work light illuminated the site.

"The stars have already joined us. I kept you out too late," Adam said.

Greer offered a short laugh. "I never mind suffering for my work."

He reached to touch her hair, stopped, and dropped his hand.

"Oh! Was there more plaster?" The heat returned to her face, and she hid it by hastily pulling her ponytail down, shaking free any remaining dust.

"See you back here bright and early then?"

"Definitely," she said, her face cool once more. "Hey, I can review those pictures tonight, if you like."

Adam handed her the camera before switching off the work light and hoisting it over his shoulder. They walked toward the faint streetlights that indicated the direction of their cars. The neighborhood was silent, everyone having gone to bed for the night. A few dogs howled in the distance.

Greer shivered in the wind sweeping the yard, having no idea she was about to be confronted by a crazed pack of hounds.

Later That Night

Distress and Difficulty

Greer wasn't sure how far Adam carried her after the attack. She floated in and out of consciousness, finally waking as he kicked on a door, shouting to be heard. When it swung open, Greer recognized the long face in front of her. It was the pale, young woman who'd gawked at her during the motorcycle accident. Adam brushed by, carrying Greer beyond a cluttered living room, down the hallway, and into a bedroom. He carefully deposited her on the bed then told her to wait.

She struggled to stay conscious, focusing on other voices in the house, wondering where she was. It could be Adam's house, but he'd never mentioned having family. Then again, she'd never asked.

Adam returned with several washcloths and a first aid kit. As he gently lifted the camera from around her neck, she apologized, "It's pretty banged up. I hope we can salvage the images."

"No worries."

"I'm so sorry. I can't believe I left you alone," she said, shaking her head. "Why are those wild dogs, those *wolves*, loose in the city? Why didn't they attack you?" Confusion and irritation crossed her face. "And, *what* was that light?" she said, accusingly.

Adam sighed, clearly exhausted. "Well, I see your appreciation is long lived. I have been trying to talk to you about something for a while now. Or have you not noticed?"

Greer slowly eased her feet over the edge of the bed, groaning when she put weight on the injured thigh.

"Let me see." He knelt and pulled at the fabric of her jeans where the beast's teeth had left jagged holes. With a quick tug, he ripped the cloth from her knee to her hip. "Oops." The bite was deep and bleeding heavily.

"We need to clean you up. Take these jeans off," he said, reaching for her waistband.

She caught his wrist before he could undo the button. "What do you think you're doing?" she said, shocked.

"Helping. If you are going to be shy, I will turn around, but your pants need to come off. They are full of dirt, blood, and who knows what else." He looked at her a like she was a naughty child who'd been playing in the mud.

"You're right. Of course." However, Greer couldn't countenance a professor, even an assistant one, seeing her undress. "Turn around."

Adam sighed, but obliged.

With most of her weight on the good leg, Greer clumsily removed the ripped jeans. She sucked air through her teeth as the fabric slid over torn flesh. Pulling a blanket over her lap, she sought to retain as much dignity as possible before giving him the all-clear.

Adam pulled up a chair and sat down with the medical supplies. She chewed her lip quietly as he carefully worked the wet cloths over the bite, only letting loose with a sharp curse when he poured rubbing alcohol over the damaged flesh.

"Sorry. It burns, right?" Examining her thigh closer, he said, "This needs a few stitches. Are you going to be upset if this leaves a scar?"

"I'm sure the ER doc can handle it fine."

"No, I am going to do it," he said calmly, as if he did this every day.

Greer stared, uncomprehending. "Excuse me?"

"This only needs a few stitches. If you go to the ER, you will lose more blood while you wait, *and* we will have to explain what happened."

Uncertain, but unable to dispute his logic, she shrugged and waved for him to get on with it.

He pulled a small syringe from the kit, deftly injected an anesthetic, and set to work sewing up the deepest puncture wounds. She watched as he carefully lined up each stitch, keeping them uniform. "Why do you know how to do this?" she asked as he tied another knot and snipped the thread.

He shrugged. "It comes in handy."

A few minutes later he placed a thick piece of gauze over the wound and began to wrap a second roll of gauze around that to secure it in place. "Lift your leg a little?" he said. The pressure of the bandage on tender skin increased as she watched Adam slowly wind the dressing several times around her thigh.

"Here you go!" said a high sing-song voice. A floral peasant skirt appeared inches from Greer's nose. The blonde girl was dangling it from her fingers, effectively separating doctor and patient. "It'll fit," she said, dropping it perfunctorily in Greer's exposed lap.

"Um, thanks," Greer said, turning it over to find the waistband.

Adam stood and tugged on the girl's elbow, pulling her to the door. "Give her time to rest, April."

"Go talk to Mother Rose. She didn't like you banging on the door one bit. And this one ..." April jabbed her thumb in Greer's direction, "she's got a whole rainbow of trouble following her."

He nodded. "Ayuh. I will fill everyone in." He caught the doorknob then stopped to cast an appraising eye over his patient who had successfully tugged on the skirt and was now fighting to keep her eyes open. "I may need some help with this one," he said quietly, pulling the door closed as Greer finally gave up and sank heavily into a pillow.

. . .

"What the *Hell* is going on here?"

Greer shot upright and instantly regretted it as sharp pain in her leg set off a wave of nausea. She eased back down with a groan, closed her eyes and breathed deeply, not even trying to answer the question.

There was no need. Adam bounded in, taking control. "She is hurt, Cahya. Come to the kitchen and let her sleep a while longer."

"She doesn't look hurt. And she's in your bed, so I will stay right here," she said, practically growling.

Greer pried one eye open and glimpsed a very flushed Cahya looming over her.

"I brought her here after she was attacked. There is a serious hound bite under that skirt," Adam explained calmly.

"If a dog bit her, why didn't you just take her to the ER?" Cahya huffed.

"I said a *hound* bite."

In a creak of leather, Cahya sat down hard on the end of the bed. "Well. Shit," she said, placated.

The bed shifted as Adam sat beside her. "Sorry, you need to be brought up to speed. April believes there is more to come," he said. Greer didn't know him well, but she couldn't miss the concern in his voice.

Cahya slumped. "I'd hoped that last time would be the last time."

As the two of them spoke quietly, a confused Greer gradually pulled herself up and limped into the hallway. Her leg burned, but she would not go back. Continuing into the living room, she found it teeming, not only with knick-knacks and mismatched furniture, but a jumble of teens and young adults.

April jumped up to grab Greer's hand. "Sit! You're not ready to be around yet." She parked Greer in a frayed recliner before wandering through a door to a brightly lit kitchen.

A tiny middle-aged woman carried in a tea tray from the same door. The strong scent of mint accompanied her into the room. Setting the tray down unceremoniously, she offered a cup to Greer before taking one herself. "I think it's time you start telling us about what you've been up to, ayuh?" Perched on the edge of a chair with her steely-gray hair pulled into a tight bun, she resembled an owl studying its prey.

The hot tea proved soothing as Greer tried to take in the room and the woman's implication.

The older woman stared over her cup. "Listen, young lady, if we are going to help, you'll need to be honest about the trouble you're in. 'We are from God, and whoever knows God listens to us.' So says John."

Greer's eyes widened, and she almost spit out her tea. She looked around for the exit while trying to decide what explanation this lady expected from her. The other young people in the room watched with varying degrees of interest.

Greer finally said, "Um, we were leaving the dig and this dog, a wolf really, came out of nowhere. And then he and his friends chased me."

"Why?"

"I don't know." Greer felt like she was being accused of something. "It's not like I was waving a steak around, inviting strays."

"No. I'm the one who collects strays," the woman said with a proprietary wave at the people lounging about her living room.

"That's not fair, Mother Rose," said a heavy boy with a large afro. Greer guessed him to be about seventeen years old, but his cartoon T-shirt was more appropriate for a much younger kid, given its message and size.

"Hey, Sam." Adam dropped onto the couch, giving the boy a playful shoulder jab. "Greer, I see you have met my mother, Rosemary Walker." Looking pointedly at Greer's diminutive interrogator, he said, "Mother, Greer is new to her challenges. She seems unaware of her talents as well."

Greer was surprised that this petite, dowdy woman was the aforementioned Mother Rose as the name had conjured the mental of a much cozier maternal figure. She was even more surprised that Mother Rose was Adam's mother. His height obviously came from his father's side; however, she saw the same wiriness and intellect reflected in mother and son as they squared off.

Mother Rose puffed-up. "Well, why have you been coddling her? There's no time to waste if hellhounds are involved."

"The nature of the situation was still rather vague until tonight, so it has been difficult to ... broach the subject."

Greer held up her hands, interrupting. "Hold on, hold on. I didn't mean to disrupt your household. Adam, look, I'm really grateful for your help.

Can someone please just drive me home now?"

Cahya had slipped into the room a moment before, claiming an arm of the couch and draping herself around Adam. "Good idea. Tony, you handle it. Take my car."

She tossed keys toward a man poured into the corner of a high-backed settee. His greasy hair and large, leering eyes made Greer shift further away from him in her seat. Adam deftly caught the keys mid-toss and gave Cahya a disappointed look. She tried to ignore his silent reprimand, tugging sharply down on her jacket.

Adam turned an intense gaze on Greer. "You need to stay and hear us out. This is going to sound a bit crazy, but we can help you. If you will let us."

"Help me with what?"

Looking around the room she noticed the curios they were drowning in were all religious talismans. Catholic saints, crucifixes of various sizes, Stars of David, hamsas, ankhs, trees of life, eyes of Horus, Tibetan knots, and too many fat little Buddhas to count covered every surface. Maybe she'd stumbled into a religious cult.

April breezed back into the room humming out of tune. Without preamble, she began introducing each person in the room, starting with herself. "I can see auras *and* the future. Cahya, who you already seem to have pissed off, finds lost people through her astral projections. Tony there's a very prickly pyro…"

"Oi! Thirty-two days without an accident," he said with a smirk from his corner.

Pointing to a curvy teenage girl with purple hair, April said, "And this here's Francesca…"

"Frankie!" the girl said, correcting April with a roll of her eyes.

"Frankie," April continued, "she's new to telekinesis. If your wallet goes missing, she's already spent the cash. If you come after her for it, watch out, she can read your mind a room away." Frankie's attempt at a benign smile sent a shiver down Greer's spine. "Our couch potato, Sam, suffers from precognition. Cartoons distract him." She mouthed, "Poor thing" behind the back of her hand.

Greer's head swirled at the faces, names, and unbelievable attributes being assigned to their owners. Maybe she was still in the hospital, in a coma, and this was just a bad dream. It certainly wasn't real.

Greer stood, but stopped abruptly and screwed her eyes shut as a surge of pain and nausea threatened to overtake her. With a deep breath, she surveyed the room again, deciding that if she was awake then these people must be playing a horrible joke on her. Either way, it was time to leave.

"It was nice to meet all of you, but I'll be going now." Greer limped heavily toward the front door.

Adam moved to stop her. "Please wait," he said, resting a hand on her shoulder and dipping his head to look her in the eye. He spoke as if he was soothing a spooked animal. "This is a lot to take in. Normally, I would have introduced you to everyone and their talents slowly, but it would seem you do not have that kind of time. Not based on what I witnessed in the last few days."

Warmth radiated from him, and she was confused by the sudden desire to be pulled into the safety of his arms.

Greer had no intention of sharing her own concerns about recent events and what they might indicate about her sanity. She didn't know these people. How well did she even know Adam? She'd taken one class, and they'd worked together for roughly a week so far this summer.

Adopting her most logical tone, the one saved for classroom discussions, she said, "I've had some mishaps lately, but I'm sure I don't know what you're talking about. Please let me go." Brushing his hand away, she headed for the door again.

"You seen a ghost!" said April.

Greer hesitated.

"You've got the sight. You're a medium," the girl said dramatically, as if revealing a secret.

Adam hadn't moved and kept his hands carefully folded in front of him. "You have a unique talent. That is what we call them, talents. We are all psychically gifted here, except for my mother, and support each other like a big happy family." At a snicker from the slouchy Tony, he added, "Mostly," as an ironic smile crept to the corner of his mouth.

"April saw you in the street," Rosemary, or Mother Rose, explained. "She doesn't know exactly what you saw, but she witnessed that boy's aura at the time you fainted." She took a dainty sip of tea. "It doesn't take a big leap to connect the dots between that and what Adam has been noticing."

Greer's attention snapped to Adam. How dare he observe her like some study subject, she silently fumed.

He saw the temper flare and shrugged apologetically. "Like I said, I have been trying to talk to you. And I would have shared all this," he nodded to the room at large, "in my own time. But the hellhounds are a flashing neon sign confirming our suspicions and highlighting the danger you are in."

Greer turned to Mother Rose. "I'm not admitting to anything, but let's say you are right about my ... recent problems."

"We prefer to call them challenges," said Adam's mother.

Greer continued carefully. "Ok. If these recent *challenges* are causing me a lot of trouble, just how can you people help?"

"We likely can't. Not if you don't even know yourself," Cahya said, shaking her head in irritation. She left Adam with a warning glance as she strode from the room.

Greer sighed inwardly. These people were just as mad as she was becoming. If she didn't find a way to leave politely, there was no telling what they might do to her.

The purple-haired girl snickered. "We aren't going to do anything to you. But we might do something for you." Her stare made Greer's skin itch.

"Leave her alone, Frankie," said Adam. "Mother, we should take Greer into the kitchen to explain this further… without the audience. Maybe over some food?" He looked deliberately at Greer at this last part. The rest of the room hurriedly took their leave, except for Sam who was pointing and laughing at something on the television.

Mother Rose led them into the kitchen. It was as dated and completely overtaken by religious paraphernalia as the living room. Adam pulled out a few pans and started making eggs, bacon, and toast while the women sat at the small table.

April had tagged along, and now Greer tried to ignore the brain-probing stare the girl directed her way. She watched Adam's mother carefully light a cigarette and pull a lumpy, homemade ashtray closer to her. Neither of them seemed eager to talk, so Greer took the reins to expedite the evening.

"So, I've had some unique experiences lately, and you say you can explain them?" She tossed back the remainder of the tea and looked at each of them in turn, practically daring them to answer.

Mother Rose dragged deeply then tapped the dangling ash as she blew smoke from the side of her mouth. "It's not that we can explain your particular challenges… yet. Rather we can advise on the larger situation and how to start managing it."

"Everybody's different and going to find their own way," said April. "We can just guide you, is all."

Greer's eyes narrowed as she studied them skeptically. "Like spirit guides? Is that what we are talking about here?" She wondered if they were planning to charge her by the hour for psychic readings.

"No, that's something else altogether," said Mother Rose. "Based on the history of our experiences, we'll offer our best guesses at how to manage your own specific talent."

"Just what experiences have you had?" Greer asked, unconvinced.

The quiet matron sat studying the glowing tip of her cigarette as a look of disappointment softened her features.

April looked to Adam and shrugged a question.

With a nod, he said, "I have it from here, Mother."

The ladies stood and each wished him good night. But before leaving the kitchen, Mother Rose stopped and looked hard at Greer. "'For everything created by God is good, and nothing is to be rejected if it is received with gratitude.' So says Timothy."

Greer leaned back in her chair, relieved the intense woman had left.

Adam slid a warm plate of food under Greer's nose. She was still a bit queasy from the wolf attack but couldn't deny the comforting smell of hot bacon. "Eat up. Psychic encounters take a lot out of you."

Adam sat across from her with his own plate, attacking a few bites before he began. "When I was just a wee boy ..." he said in a bad Irish accent. Greer made to leave. With a smile he started again. "When I was about four, I had an imaginary friend. My parents—my father was still around at the time—did not think much of it. That is until my invisible playmate started teaching me Latin."

Greer pushed her empty plate aside, listening to a story he told so easily that she knew it wasn't the first time it'd been shared.

Apparently, Adam's companion claimed to be a guardian angel sent to train him in the art of prayers and rites to dispel evil spirits. His parents and the family priest were a bit alarmed when Adam began reciting whole Bible passages in the ancient language since the church no longer taught Latin in Sunday school, or used it during masses.

Adam's mother thought this was a sign of her son's divine favor. Already a devout woman, she became even more fanatical in her faith. She encouraged his gift, offering support through extra trips to the library, the church, and the cemetery. At first her own research supplemented Adam's efforts, but she quickly ventured beyond Catholic teachings. She started collecting tools from all faiths, anything with the power to fight evil.

His father was also a religious man; however, he preferred a meat-and-potatoes approach. So, while he did not doubt Adam's unique talents, he wasn't particularly impressed. At first, he started taking extra shifts at the manufacturing plant where he was a senior lathe operator. Then his already hearty drinking habit became excessive as he spent evenings at the local pub trying to escape the new and confusing happenings at his house. Eventually, he just forgot to come home one night shortly before Adam's eighth birthday.

At this point, Greer interrupted with a heartfelt, "I'm so sorry." He looked up from his plate and shrugged. She covered his hand with her own. "No truly. I know what it's like to lose a parent when you're young."

"Oh. Then I am sorry too."

Greer offered a remorseful smile. "I broke your train of thought. Please, go on."

"Well, there is not much more really." He gathered their plates. Greer waited patiently as he rinsed them and dried his hands before leaning against the sink to finish. "After that, my mother started taking in kids who were gifted like me. April was one of the first. She left her family somewhere along the Ohio River, and wandered until she found a place she said felt like home. When Mother bonded with her, April quickly became a little sister to me. There were plenty of others, but not all of them lived with us."

Frankie and Tony wandered in. They each grabbed a beer from the fridge and headed out the back door with little more than a grunt of goodbye.

Adam shrugged. "As you can see, most of them just kind of come and go."

By the time Adam finished sharing his personal paranormal history, it was too late to consider going back for her car and driving home. She doubted she could've managed the drive alone anyway, tired, and injured.

Adam installed her in a spare room that looked to be shared by the transient "family" members. T-shirts, various sized jeans, and a few random under-things spilled out of the small closet. Normally, her curiosity to dig into the workings of such an odd group would've pushed Greer to snoop, but she was too exhausted to investigate. Even as the night's strange events and conversations swirled in her head, Greer quickly succumbed to her body's need for rest.

She slept heavily and dreamt of her mother. The dream progressed as usual until she saw her mother next to the Christmas tree, and Greer again passed into that warm breeze where her mother could gently brush a hand against her cheek. The woman was worried and had a new message. As Greer partially roused from the throbbing in her leg, she recalled her mother's words in the dream—*"It's happening again."*

Adam checked on her early in the morning, pulling the bandage away with a grimace. Seeing her obvious exhaustion combined with the angry looking wound, he declared that she'd be taking another day off from work. Greer wanted to protest, but honestly couldn't summon the strength for a lucid argument. She watched him traipse off to the dig leaving her in April's care for the day.

The pain killers April brought helped Greer catch a few more hours of sleep. When she finally awoke, she rubbed her eyes in confusion. Cahya was in a strange headstand against one of the room's walls. She was sporting a death-metal tank top and yoga pants this morning.

"Um, hello?" Greer said.

Cahya kicked her feet from the wall and gracefully stood. "About time. I'll tell Mother Rose you're awake and you can leave." The quiet, purposeful, way she padded from the room reminded Greer of a large, formidable cat.

Sitting up slowly, Greer took stock of her situation. Her leg throbbed, and she was in a house full of certifiable people who believed in demon dogs, ghosts, telekinesis, and lord knew what else. True, they'd been kind, but she didn't know them and certainly didn't trust them. She'd been away from home all night, so Robert was surely worried to distraction. Worst of all, she was missing another day of fieldwork. But on the plus side, her headache was gone.

April sailed in, a billowing of mismatched fabrics. She handed over a steaming mug of coffee. "Here. Mother Rose needs to talk to you. Then I'll drop you at your car." She floated out again before Greer could protest that she only wanted the ride home.

The coffee was delicious, and she hurried to dress between sips.

The cigarette the older woman held was not long for this world. The smoke tickled Greer's nose so she hung back just inside the kitchen door, holding onto the jamb for support.

Greer spoke first. "Thank you for letting me stay last night, Mrs. Walker. I didn't mean to impose."

"It's Mother Rose, and it wasn't an imposition."

"Well, I still appreciate it. I'll find April and get out of your hair." Greer turned to leave.

"I said it wasn't a burden. 'Hospitality is an expression of Divine worship.' So say the Jews." She tapped fingers impatiently on the table. "You do understand that it's good we found you in time? This isn't something you can handle alone."

Mother Rose worked at the clasp of a chain hanging around her neck. She would've looked like any typical middle-aged woman at breakfast, if not for the open Talmud and assorted religious figurines scattered in front of her.

"I'm still not quite sure what it is that I'm handling. To be honest, our discussions last night left me with more questions than answers."

"Ayuh. You're new," Mother Rose said, a bit testily. "Adam will get you up to speed on the broad strokes quickly. However, it'll be April who really guides you through your gift. Her skills are closer to yours."

"I look forward to it." Greer failed to hide the sarcasm in her voice.

"Take this."

Greer looked at the silver chain being offered from a hand slightly twisted from the first stages of arthritis. "Wow. That's really generous but unnecessary."

"It most certainly is necessary." The woman wiggled the necklace impatiently.

Greer wrapped it around her fingers until she found the pendant at the end. She recognized the small hand with an eye etched into the middle. It was called The Hand of Miriam by Jews and the Hand of Fatima by Muslims. Mother Rose was offering her protection from misfortune and ill wishes.

"I really can't accept this. I don't even wear jewelry," she said, protesting politely as she attempted to hand it back. She was met with a look that made her withdraw with a reluctant word of thanks.

April had entered through the other door, watching silently.

Mother Rose lit another cigarette and waved it toward April. "Now you listen closely to what they tell you, Greer Dixon. If you fail to follow their instructions, you'll put them in grave danger. You'll put us all in danger."

Greer didn't know how to respond. She had no intention of taking direction from April, or Adam for that matter, on supernatural concerns. Yet, a part of her knew that something was off. Things were happening that she didn't understand.

"Put that on right now," Adam's mother ordered, pointing at the charm dangling from Greer's fingers.

It was easier to humor the woman, so Greer fastened the short chain around her neck.

Mother Rose wedged her cigarette between her lips to reach two-handed for the Talmud lying open on the table. She pulled it close and bent to reading. Greer realized she'd been dismissed.

April started toward the back door. "Come on. Car's in the alley."

Greer limped after her as fast as she was able. As she pulled the door closed Adam's mother hollered over shoulder, "Fearing a decision is worse than making the wrong one!"

. . .

Greer was happy to find her car just as she left it. The book bag was on the front seat with her wallet and cell phone still inside. She debated calling Robert then and there but decided it best to just deal with him at home. He was sure to be frantic by now.

She walked through the front door to find Robert was indeed agitated. His clothes were a rumpled mess, and he was talking loudly on the phone. "Check again. She's five-foot-four, reddish-brown hair, brown eyes ... Yes, you checked an hour ago, but look again!" He turned, slamming the phone down on the kitchen counter. He obviously hadn't heard her come in, but he couldn't miss her now, standing in the middle of the living room in a blood-spattered t-shirt and April's silly skirt.

He rushed over to hug her tightly. "My God! Where? Why?" Stepping back to hold her at arm's length, he surveyed her unkempt state. "Is that blood?"

She fell against him, finally letting the fear and pain she'd been keeping in check rush to the surface. It took a minute before she could find her voice.

"I know you were worried. A crazy dog, more like a wolf, bit me. Then Adam and his family said I have to face what's happening to me." She took a deep breath to pull herself together. When she looked up at Robert, his face was red, teeth clenched.

"Let's get this straight. You were at another man's house? All night?"

"Well, I think it's really his mother's house."

Robert looked at her in dismay. "Is that supposed to make it better?"

"I told you a *huge* dog bit me. Adam took me home to patch me up."

"Greer! Dog bites should be seen by a doctor, not a professor!"

She chewed her lip, uncertain how to explain the supposed mythical nature of the animal. "Um, it wasn't a normal dog. Adam thought he could handle it best."

Releasing her abruptly, he snapped at her. "That still doesn't explain why you didn't answer your phone or come home last night."

Greer cracked her knuckles, trying to remember events clearly. "I left my phone in the car. It's all complicated. His mom and sister wanted to help me too."

Robert's face conveyed sheer cynicism. Without a word he stomped into the bedroom where she could hear him slamming dresser drawers.

Robert was one of the most forthright people she knew. It was part of her attraction to him. He always called it like he saw it, even when a little finesse would've spared someone's feelings. She wanted to be completely honest about her recent experiences, but how could she explain the night's events in any terms he might comprehend? She didn't even understand them herself.

He returned a few minutes later in a dark suit and tie. Grabbing his briefcase and keys, he paused after he yanked open the door. "Call your father. He's been out driving all night looking for you."

Greer collapsed onto the couch. Her leg was on fire after the effort of walking in from the car and standing throughout the argument. She was surprised when anger rose instead of tears. It was true she'd caused Robert and Dad unnecessary worry by not calling. But, she reminded herself, they had no idea what she'd been through. Robert treated her like she'd done something wrong just by trying to survive a bizarre situation.

Still, she certainly owed her father an apology. She quickly called him and promised she was safe. They made plans to have dinner that night so she could try to explain.

Too keyed up to rest, she decided to head over to the dig. She didn't care if Adam objected. There were too many questions, both about the project and about herself. Greer wanted answers.

She threw the blood-stained shirt in the trash and April's skirt in the hamper. A long hot shower felt great on her sore muscles and stung fiercely on the inflamed skin of her thigh. Finding some first aid supplies buried in the bathroom cabinet, she redressed the wounds and then carefully pulled on a loose pair of cargo pants. The sun was directly overhead by the time Greer pointed her car toward to the dig.

Darkness

She hobbled painfully to the edge of the site, carefully eased herself down into the dirt grid, and awkwardly hopped down the ladder into Room A.

Liz was the first to see her. "What are you doing here?" The student was clearly irritated. "Professor Walker said you weren't coming in today."

Hearing his name, Adam looked up from where he crouched in front of the alcove. His face betrayed his frustration.

"Greer. I mean, Ms. Dixon. I was told you would be taking the day to rest."

"No, I want to be here. There's too much to do."

Adam took hold of her elbow, trying to steer her back toward the ladder as he whispered crossly. "You had a huge shock last night, both physically and mentally. You need time to heal and adjust to your new circumstances."

Greer resisted his momentum and shook him off. "You were all very kind to me, but I need to be busy right now." She saw several thoughts pass over his features. Curious at her ability to read him, she studied him more closely. He was clearly planning another rebuke and, before he could come up with any reason to send her home, she whispered, "Your Mom said you'd get me up to speed on this hellhound stuff. Wouldn't it be best if I stick close so we can talk about it when the kids aren't listening?"

He gave a huff. "Alright. But ... if you start to feel unwell, promise you will let me know."

"Promise." She said as she grinned and limped behind him to the alcove.

...

While Greer and Adam had been working all day to uncover additional loose stones in Room A, the class had been topside. They'd doubled the size of the original grid and were slowly trying to work their way down to the same depth as the roof of Room A. Good progress had yielded a few interesting artifacts. The most exciting was an old silver crucifix, tarnished and severely distorted, either by its owner or the trials of time.

Greer and Adam didn't manage to find any time to talk about her recent "challenges" or other mystical topics. So once the students left for the day, Adam suggested they get some carry-out and head over to the archaeology library. They could talk privately there in the basement darkroom while developing the pictures of the alcove.

They carried their dinner and satchels down the dim stairs to the basement, and spread the food out on the darkroom worktable, wanting to eat before opening the caustic developing chemicals. Adam took note of her slow, stiff movements. He'd suggested several times throughout the day that she take it easy as he witnessed her struggle to catch up with everyone, and each time Greer had denied being tired. While she knew it'd been the right decision for her mental health to work today, her body was not in full agreement. Easing onto the cold metal stool, Greer applied pressure to the top of her thigh and willed the pain to subside.

His brow furrowed. "Are you alright?"

"Yeah, just really sore." She picked up her sandwich and raised it in a mock toast. "To a good day in the field."

He toasted with his own sandwich back. "Any day in the field is a good day."

They ate quietly for a few minutes before Greer decided, against her better judgment, to take Mother Rose's advice. "Ok, where do we begin my education on these weird talents and challenges? I'm under strict orders from your mother to learn everything from you and April or suffer *dire* consequences."

He sighed. "Mother is always a bit dramatic. However, she is probably right in your case."

Greer's phone rang. She glanced down at the screen. "I forgot; I was supposed to have dinner with my dad tonight." She answered the call while Adam cleaned up their dinner, giving her the illusion of privacy.

"Everything's fine," she said into the phone. "I know, I know. I'm sorry." She turned her back to Adam who'd started pulling out the developing equipment. "Things are just a bit ... crazy right now. Yeah, I plan to explain. Well, as much as I can. I'm actually with someone right now who's trying to help. Adam. Yeah." Adam glanced over at the mention of his name and caught her watching him. They locked eyes. She turned away, continuing to nod into the phone. Greer surprised herself when she finally answered, "Yes, I trust him."

Setting the phone aside with a sigh, she grabbed the camera from Adam's bag, removed the film, and deftly tossed it to him. Most professional archaeologists had long since switched to digital cameras, but many schools still used good old-fashioned film for training purposes. Given Greer's reaction to the alcove and being chased by hellhounds when she carried this roll, Adam had decided they'd preview this particular roll alone. He was convinced there might be a connection between the dig and the paranormal animals.

Adam filled the developing tank as Greer flipped on the red safety lights and hobbled over to the sink to help. She checked the temperature of the chemical. When she nodded it was ready Adam poured it into the tank that held the film.

Greer checked the clock and said, "Go."

She followed his hands as he shook the canister, until she remembered their secondary purpose of the evening. She tried to look serious when she asked, "So, ghosts and hounds and stuff. Let's get this done. What do I need to know?"

Adam shook his head, laughing to himself. "You are asking me to explain all of the mysteries of the universe? In one night?"

"No," she said with a straight face. "Just the facts relevant to me. Please."

He squinted at her. Then, still shaking the developing film, he began at the beginning.

"I am going to get all biblical on you here." Spreading his arms wide, he said, "And God said, 'Let there be light, and there was light. God saw that the light was good, and he separated the light from the darkness'." He returned to agitating the film. "Everyone knows this passage, right?" He paused and Greer nodded in agreement. "Now most people take this at face value. That God created the day, full of sunshine, and a night without it. But there is a deeper, more fundamental meaning."

Greer looked up at the clock. "Time."

Adam paused to trade out the chemical baths for the film then said, "The light and the dark represent the duality of existence. Seeming opposites which are actually complimentary and interconnected. Both are necessary to make the world work. The yin and the yang. Hot and cold. Male and female."

"The seen and the unseen," she said.

"Exactly!" Even in the red light of the darkroom, Greer could see his face light up in encouragement. "Both science and religion agree there is more to this universe than can be seen with the naked eye. Science explores single-celled viruses, subatomic particles, theories of antimatter, and invisible, yet observable, forces such as gravity. Religion teaches us about an afterlife in heaven and the power of faith. Whatever you want to call it, however it works, the *unseen* is real. And it influences the visible world in very tangible ways."

He leaned toward her, gathering her full attention for this next part. "Your talents and challenges come from this unseen world."

Greer gave him a doubtful look. "But the ghosts I saw, and the hellhound that bit me, they were pretty damn visible."

Adam smiled as if she was a small child who'd just worked out a mystery of the grown-up world. "Yes, that is the uniqueness of our talents. We can see the unseen."

"Time," Greer said again.

He dumped the chemicals and started a warm water bath over the film. As she watched, he ran a hand through the stream. "Hot and cold are extreme opposites, but they are still temperatures. Temperature is invisible, yet it can be measured. Even without a thermometer, we can experience temperatures. We know it exists. We see its effects, such as water freezing or evaporating."

She peered up at him, "You're losing me. Why are we talking about water?"

He shrugged. "Just an example." Crossing his arms in thought, he continued, "Alright. If temperature is an unseen but very real part of our cosmos, what other unseen forces are at work?"

"Well, you've already mentioned gravity. There are electrical fields, magnetic ... Wait, I feel like this is a physics lesson."

His eyes were bright. He obviously enjoyed teaching, and this lesson seemed one of his favorites. "It kind of is. It all boils down to this." Cupping his hands as if he held a ball, he slowly rotated them. "The world is made of things we can see and those we cannot. The stuff we cannot see is just as important as the rest. They are equal parts of the same whole." At this he opened his hands as if releasing the imaginary ball of matter into the ether.

"So. Ghosts are real, just invisible. But *I* can see them." She scrunched her nose at him. "How does that work?"

He slowly shook his head. "I have spent years considering that very question, traveling down many different roads. As a child, I simply accepted it. When I grew I obviously began to consider scientific solutions. My mother helped me comb through the writings of many different faiths. In the end, I just do not know. Not yet."

"Oh." Greer tried to look properly thoughtful, but he recognized disappointment on her face.

He patted her shoulder in consolation, and when he left it there, she instinctively relaxed against him. Greer wondered how he could smell so good after a day in the field.

"I am not saying the answer cannot be found, but the universe is complex, ayuh? Even our most consistent physical laws, like gravity, break down at the quantum level. There are rules to this world that we have yet to learn."

"I can go along with that ... for now. But that doesn't help me deal with current problems. Tell me what I am supposed to *do*."

"You use the tools you are given," he said, encouragingly.

Adam gave her shoulder a comforting squeeze. "Time's up," he said. After he pulled the readied film from its tank, Greer helped cut the developed negatives into manageable sections and then clipped them to a wire strung across the room so they could finish drying.

Adam scanned them and his brow wrinkled deeper with concern as he moved down the line of film.

"What's wrong?" Greer brushed up alongside him and peered at the negatives. Almost every cell on the film had a big dark spot in the center of the frame. "What's this? I know we were talking, but I'm sure we didn't overdevelop them."

"No, we did not. If they were overexposed the whole image would be dark. I knew something was going to be odd about these photos given the hounds' interest. I wanted to find a clue tonight but there is nothing to work with here."

"Hold on," she said, determinedly peering one-eyed at the negative only inches from her nose. "We might be able to use the details around the edges. It'll be like a puzzle that's missing pieces. Some of it may be useful though."

For the first time, she witnessed him truly frustrated. He ran a hand roughly through his curls. "No, we should just take new photos."

"Aren't you afraid the same thing will happen if there's something spooky going on?" she asked.

He jammed his hands in his jeans pockets and scanned the negatives again irritably, seeming to consider the options. "You are probably right."

Greer gently elbowed him aside. "Get the photo paper and baths ready. Once these are printed, we'll see what can be salvaged."

They worked silently as they developed the prints. The darkroom became a chemical jungle of dripping photos as they produced both color and black and white copies of each image. When finished, Greer flipped on the regular lights. "Well, what do we have?" she asked as he hung the last pictures at the back of the room.

"Not much. But you may be right about teasing a little information from around the edges."

Greer shuffled over to share his perspective. She gasped when she saw the room full of drying photos. In the center of each white splotch, she could see the faint image of a face contorted in a scream of agony.

Teaching a Shining Light

The tortured photographs were one more piece of evidence that Greer was dealing with something outside of her skill set. They'd scared her enough in the moment that she'd agreed to start training with April immediately. However, by the time she got home, she was regretting the hasty decision.

The energy at the site the next morning was sluggish. Days of rehashing Room A and removing more turf left all the students longing for some excitement.

Greer was unusually content with a day of dull work. Life had been rather too exciting for her lately. Plus, her leg was stiff where scabs were forming over the hound bite. So, she sat, content, steadily removing bucket after bucket of earth from her new grid area while pondering the absurd events of recent weeks.

Nothing had prepared Greer for the problems she was now facing. Her parents weren't religious. They'd dropped by the local Presbyterian Church on major holidays and deposited her into occasional Bible school classes, but they'd said it was only so she could understand the Christian mythology so prevalent in literary and archaeological records. Greer knew the Bible as the highly revised history of one tiny corner of the world. But Adam and his family believed the Bible reflected a reality beyond the human experience.

Her head was spinning from the internal argument.

Greer was sifting another bucket of unremarkable dirt when a shout echoed around the yard. Heads popped up and scanned for the source like a family of prairie dogs zoning in on a potential threat. All eyes came to rest on Rigsby who waved his ball cap over his head as he danced in his grid. Greer's sore leg made her the last to join the gathering crowd.

Squatting on the edge of Rigsby's grid, Adam peered down. "What have you found here?"

"It's wood. I can only see a little, but I think it's the same as Greer's trap door," Rigsby said with a huge smile that almost made him handsome.

"We need to uncover the rest; find the perimeter. Then we will see if you are correct, Mr. Rigsby," Adam said as he hopped down to help.

As they cleared away more soil, it was apparent the planks formed a door identical to the one for Room A. Adam snuck a peek at Greer, worrying how she might physically react to this latest discovery. Meeting his eye, she knelt to carefully place her palm on the iron latch of the door. When nothing happened, no strange heat or disembodied screams, Greer released the breath she'd been holding, and Adam nodded, satisfied.

Once everyone finished congratulating Rigsby, the student asked if he could be the one to help open the door. Greer stepped back, for the first time glad to put a little distance between herself and a new discovery.

Adam strained as he tried to lift the heavy wood. It was initially as stubborn as the other door, then quickly gave way and settled back on its hinges. Rigsby tucked a two-by-four in to support it, just as Greer had.

The musty odor from the opening was not nearly as pungent as it was from Room A. However, Greer detected a distinct dampness to the air as it rose up a set of foot-worn stone stairs. "Well, this certainly looks more typical," she said with a nod.

"Yes. We may have an actual cellar down there," said Adam as the beam of his flashlight skipped down the steps.

The students rushed to crowd in. Adam waved them back, explaining this room would also need to be vented before any exploration. Grumbling, everyone returned to their work for the time being. Since it was Rigsby's find, he got to help set up the generator and fans to draw the fetid air from below.

Liz sat on the edge of the grid, monitoring from under the rim of her hat as the men set up the equipment. Greer pulled herself up next to the fractious student. She'd been trying to find common ground to improve their working relationship. Previous attempts proved futile, so she opted for silent camaraderie, watching the others work.

Their gazes followed Adam. He quickly had the fans up and running then made his way toward the two of them.

"Ms. Bingham, I need to speak with Ms. Dixon. Would you give us a few minutes?"

If ill wishes could be felt, Greer would've been knocked senseless by the look Liz hurled her way. As the student slumped off, Greer sighed at another missed opportunity to smooth the girl's ruffled feathers.

Adam hopped up next to Greer. "You should head out early. Go meet April at the house," he said, careful not to be overheard.

Again, regretting her promise to let them train her, she changed the topic. "Looks like we're going to get rained out soon." Greer stared at the incoming clouds before turning a wry smile on him. "Maybe April can wait and bring Casper around after dinner."

Adam responded with his professorial glare. "You promised to take this seriously."

"I am. I will." Uncomfortable under his gaze, she lowered hers and brushed at the dirt on her jeans. "I don't know what to expect and am not sure what you expect of me. Ok?"

His face softened. Touching a finger to the protective charm she reluctantly wore, he said, "None of us did."

She met his eye and felt compelled to make a new promise. "I'll do my best."

Adam climbed up to the yard, and, as Greer took his offered hand, she caught Liz spying on them from the top of the ladder.

. . .

Adam's street was crowded with cars, so she parked down the block and slowly walked the rest of the way. The faded blue colonial home showed its true age in the light of day. April waited on the front stoop, a slump of fabric, her gaze unfocused.

"I didn't know Adam called you about starting early," Greer said as she approached.

"He didn't," April said, airily. "This way. There's lots to do."

She swept past Greer in a flutter of delicate scarves. Greer hiked up the strap of her bag, painfully jogging to catch up as the eccentric girl hurried down the street and around the corner.

They walked for a few minutes before Greer finally asked, "Where are we going?"

"The church cemetery."

"Why?"

"To see how many ghosts you can talk to." April grinned like a kid heading to a birthday party.

Greer rolled her eyes, wondering again why she'd agreed to this. "If you want me to commune with the dead ... in a cemetery ... shouldn't we do it at night or by a full moon? Not at four o'clock in the afternoon?"

April stopped short. "Why would ghosts care about the time? Not like they have a schedule to keep." She gave a short laugh at her own joke before taking off again at a brisk pace.

They arrived at a small Presbyterian church crowded between rows of houses just like Adam's. Its graveyard was an ancient crumble of lopsided and broken stones poking out of grass long overdue for a trim. April opened the iron gate and let them both inside.

"Leave the bag," said the girl.

Greer dropped her satchel near the gate as instructed and watched April move to the closest stones where she stretched her hands out to lightly touch each grave marker, singing softly as she moved among them. Was Greer supposed to follow?

A few rows into the yard April beckoned Greer to her side. "This one's good. Close your eyes and relax a bit," she said. Greer closed her eyes and felt April take her hand, guiding it forward until it met cool, smooth stone.

She waited a few heartbeats. Sensing nothing, she peeked one eye open. April's own were closed in concentration. "Is something supposed to happen?" Greer finally asked.

"Shh!"

They waited a few more moments, both barely touching the stone. Greer peeked again. "I don't think this is working," she said, feeling foolish and validated at the same time.

"Uhgg!" April threw her hands to her hips. "He's usually so nice!" She roughly grabbed Greer's wrist, dragging her to a grave a few spots to the left. "Here. She's a chatterbox." April slapped Greer's hand on the gravestone. "Fair warning, she's not the brightest bulb."

Greer closed her eyes, wishing to be elsewhere.

"Come on," April said, coaxing either Greer or the uncooperative spirit. Greer thought probably both.

With a sigh, Greer considered the marker beneath her fingers. It was pitted from a century of rain, wind and dust. It was just a stone. She felt ridiculous, but April kept making encouraging noises, so she renewed her focus, concentrating on the stone's age. It suddenly cooled. Greer snatched her hand back with a gasp.

"Don't break the connection," said April, snapping at her student.

Greer tentatively touched the monument again. It was frigid, growing still colder until it felt like a block of ice instead of an ancient grave marker.

"Who are you?" said a thin, squeaky voice.

Greer's eyes sprang open. Her forearm was lost in the abdomen of a tiny woman in a bustle skirt and a high-collared shirtwaist. The style hadn't been worn since the 1890's.

"Eww," Greer said as she carefully extracted her arm from the lady's striped blouse.

April stepped close, invading everyone's personal space, to make introductions. "This here is Minnie. Minnie, meet Greer."

Greer turned big eyes from April back to the old-fashioned woman. Minnie was faded like a photograph that had been left in a sunny window.

"Wow, um, hi," said Greer.

"Hello, miss," Minnie said politely.

April sighed in exasperation. "You got to ask the questions, Greer. I told you she's dim."

Minnie seemed unfazed by the comment, but Greer felt embarrassed for her. "I think she can hear you," she said, whispering to April.

"Oh, she hears me but she don't mind." Twirling a finger in the air, April said, "Minnie, be a dear. Show Greer your fancy hair-do."

Minnie turned slowly in a circle. Greer's hand flew to her mouth in shock. The back of the woman's head was savagely caved in. Blood, and something else, slowly oozed from a gaping, semi-circular wound.

April pointed to the damage. "Horse kicked in her head. Of course, no telling how smart she was before that." Greer stared, stunned. April just shrugged. "Thanks, Minnie."

Minnie turned back to face them, and Greer found it easier to concentrate once she was no longer confronted by the open wound. She'd been hardened to the sight of injuries in her line of work; however, they were liberated from tissue—just damaged bones telling a story.

April tapped her foot. "We don't got all night. Finish up your questions."

Greer cleared her throat, hurriedly evaluating her options. There were so many interesting things a person from Minnie's era could answer. Greer was curious about the working conditions and women's issues that Minnie might have experienced first-hand. Yet, they weren't here for a history lesson, but rather a metaphysical one.

"Ok, well. Um, how'd you get here?" Greer asked. She sounded like a school child and blushed at her own ignorance.

"I arrived in Providence by horse and carriage after I married my husband," said Minnie with a gracious nod.

"Hopefully not the same horse that did her in," said April as she snickered behind her hand.

"That's not what I meant." Greer told Minnie as she popped a few knuckles distractedly. "Let me try again. Um, you're dead, right?" she said, looking Minnie in the eye.

The figure nodded. "That is what Miss April keeps telling me. Although I feel quite well, and I am terribly anxious to return home."

"Well, let's agree that you are, in fact, deceased, ok?" Greer continued. "How did you come here?" She pointed to the ground between their feet. "Just now, when I touched your tombstone, what did you do in order to appear to us?"

She'd managed a coherent question but was dismayed when Minnie just stared at her blankly. April was checking her phone, offering no help whatsoever.

"Maybe you heard us talking?" said Greer, offering a helpful prompt. "Did you have to travel down a tunnel of light to us?"

"I did not travel anywhere, miss. I am always here. It was you who appeared to me."

Greer turned in confusion to April who was still playing with her phone.

"A little help, please? We're getting nowhere."

April looked up and shrugged. "She's gone."

Greer spun back to the tombstone and saw that April was right. She checked for footprints in the spongy grass and drips of blood from the seeping wound, but Minnie had vanished without a trace.

"This way," April said, calling over her shoulder from the next row of headstones.

Greer followed her, throwing a last glance back to Minnie's marker.

"Don't touch stuff. Just walk on the graves. What're you feeling?"

They walked the entire back half of the graveyard with April trailing Greer as she called out her impressions. Most of the graves were 'still' she reported, but some hummed or vibrated. It was more a feeling than a sound. Greer described it like standing close to a large motor. On the graves with this rumbling energy, she called out specific impressions. Some pulsed intermittently like a radio signal fading in and out. Some felt light and happy, while others felt heavy.

Greer wandered, thrilled each time a new energy traveled through her. One twinge left an odd lingering taste on her tongue and she hurried away from it. She drew nearer the largest marker in the cemetery—a five-foot tall obelisk atop a large square base. The whole thing was carved in a severe black marble. It positively thrummed with power and felt heavier than any of the other burials, so heavy that she felt it might sink into the ground at any moment.

The heaviness swirled in an icy storm in her stomach.

She could see the inky marble drawing light into itself and felt compelled to touch it. Reaching a hand toward the stone, it grew suddenly cold just as Minnie's had done.

"No!" April shouted.

The girl lunged and snatched Greer's hand away just before the fingertips made contact. "Never, ever wake him!" She squeezed hard on Greer's hand to drive the point home. Greer recognized genuine panic on the girl's face. After she nodded her understanding, April still eyed her suspiciously, not letting go until she was certain of being taken seriously.

Greer nodded again, this time preoccupied with the blue of April's eyes, so similar to her own mother's.

The girl hurried back to the cemetery entrance without further explanation. Greer caught up, grabbed her bag and followed April out of the gate.

"Ok, what was the point of all that?" Greer asked, perturbed at the ambiguous instructions.

April walked quickly, talking over her shoulder. "Meeting a ghost face-to-face, it's an easy way to test your sensitivity. And your guts."

"Well, how did I do?"

"Not bad, for the first time. You got some natural talent. But I already guessed that." April stopped abruptly and grabbed Greer's wrist. "You need to learn control."

"Ok," Greer said, agreeing with the girl for the first time. While the energy pulses were intriguing, they certainly weren't comfortable. Yet she knew her curiosity had a good chance of pushing her to test the limits.

April leaned in, wagging a finger. "And, for the dear love of God, don't go putting your hands all over graves now."

Greer grimaced, struck by a troubling realization. "That might interfere with my work don't you think?"

"Oh," April said with a little frown. "Adam will figure that out. Just keep your hands to yourself for now."

April promptly turned and led them at a brisk pace back toward the house. Greer hurried after feeling like the warning to keep her hands to herself had been meant in more ways than one.

They lost their race with the steely clouds. Fat, summer raindrops smacked them as they ran the last block. They tumbled through the front door just before the lightening started. Greer's leg burned fiercely, and she realized the rain would've been the lesser evil.

Cartoons blared from the living room. Greer poked her head in, giving a little wave to Sam on his couch as they made their way down the hall to the kitchen. Mother Rose was engaged with her books again at the table. Adam was busy at the stove. The smell of marinara sauce made Greer's stomach growl loudly.

Adam greeted her with a laugh. "I am glad someone is hungry. There is enough pasta here for all of Providence."

April plopped down in a chair. "Good, I'm super hungry too."

"Oh? Did you work hard this afternoon?" he said, teasing.

"Hey! Talking to dead people is harder than it looks."

"I'm famished," Greer said in confirmation.

"See." April waved a hand at Greer. "It takes energy and focus doing what we do."

"Yes, yes. Calm down, Sis."

April jumped up and pecked him on the cheek before moving to the cupboards for plates and silverware, singing under her breath while she worked.

"Is there anything I can help with? Should I call the others?" Greer asked.

"No, thanks," Adam said. "They will all know when it is ready." Tony walked through the door and grabbed a plate from April before he even finished speaking. Frankie and Sam trickled in. They loaded their dishes with food then scattered back to separate corners of the house to eat.

Greer accepted a plate after her stomach growled again. Choosing a seat across the table from Adam's mother, she said, "Hello, Mrs. Walker."

"Mother Rose is fine."

"Can I get a plate for you?"

"I'm not hungry for food, dear," she said with a slow pull on her cigarette. "How did your training go today?"

"It went well, I think. I held a fairly coherent conversation with a real, live ghost."

The older woman looked unimpressed and returned to her book.

Adam pulled up a chair next to Greer and, between bites, quizzed her about the afternoon. He agreed it was a good start, but there was so much more to cover.

By the time they finished, Mother Rose had finally wandered off with her books and a small plate. Greer cleaned up and joined Adam back at the table. He was lost in thought, so she studied the religious symbols around the room while she waited. The storm picked up and surges of rain against the window threatened the quiet.

Adam finally broke the silence. "I have been trying to decide where to start with you. Everyone I have worked with has her own unique abilities and personalities, obviously, so it takes some thought to select the best approach."

She listened attentively, wondering and at the same time dreading what strange secrets he was about to reveal. This afternoon had certainly been eye-opening. She hadn't fully processed it yet.

"You are not religious at all, correct?" he asked with no trace of judgment in his voice.

She gave a small shrug, truly not regretting her lack of faith, but feeling the need to explain. "No. I learned the basic tenants of the major religions, but never believed any of it."

"Even if you do not walk in faith, using prayers and talismans is still helpful. Unfortunately, they are much more effective in the hands of a true believer." She nodded as if she understood, but his brows were raised in sound skepticism at her silent acceptance. "Since prayers, some might call them spells, are kind of my specialty, I am going to teach you a few to aid in calling on the dead as well as sending them away."

She sat up straighter, at once spotting a quick escape. "I really just need the one to send them away, right?"

"We will cover both. With my family on watch, you will be much safer from any evil intent. But you will also practice using your talent by reaching out to friendly spirits. This will strengthen your ability to protect yourself. And sometimes you can use a good spirit to battle an evil one."

She sighed, slumping on the table. "My experience today was incredible, in every sense of the word. This just doesn't feel real."

"I know. You need to trust me now. Please." He touched her elbow on the word trust and inexplicably she knew she would. Her smile sealed the pact.

He clapped and rubbed his hands together as if preparing to dig into a feast. "Alright. An easy one, ayuh?" He reached inside his collar and pulled the large pendant she'd seen the night he rescued her. "Hold your own talisman and repeat after me."

Greer found her Hand of Fatima charm at the end of its chain and held it, feeling silly. But she'd promised to try, so she sucked it up. A sudden pang in her healing thigh reminded her there were worse things than trusting Adam.

He spoke softly, almost reverently. "Follow me. We make the sign of the cross as we say, 'In the name of Jesus, impure spirit, go away.' We can repeat it a few times."

"Easy enough," she said.

"But try to mean it?" He leaned in, making his point. "If you actually need to use it, it is even ok to shout it."

"I won't need much encouragement if I'm being used as a chew toy at the time."

He scrubbed a hand through his curls. "*That* is a motivation which I hope will not be repeated."

Leaning back in the chair, she fidgeted with the charm. "So, that covers the bad ghosts easy enough. What about the good ones?"

"Well, these prayers are not just for ghosts, but any spirit. Keep that in mind." He rose from the table. "Hold on. We need more nourishment." He pulled the freezer open. "Want some ice cream?"

"Sure. Chocolate, if you have it."

He held up a carton of double chocolate fudge. "Why would I have any other flavor?" Greer helped him pull out bowls and spoons and then sat back down at the old table to enjoy a few bites before he started in again.

"So, April will cover specific circumstances, but my advice is to call on an angel when in true need of a positive spirit. There are an unlimited number of prayers to do so. Many are quite long; however, here is a condensed version that should work. Ok, hold your charm again. It never hurts to make the sign of the cross too." He urged her to do the same as he said, "O Angel of God, make me worthy of thy tender love, thy celestial companionship and thy never-failing protection!"

Greer burst out laughing.

Adam scowled, supremely annoyed.

She tried to apologize but ended up simply holding her side in hysterics.

He slowly crossed his arms over his chest and leaned back in the chair, waiting.

A minute later Greer finally stopped giggling yet failed to hide a lingering smile. "I'm trying so hard to believe you. Truly."

"I asked you to take this seriously. We are doing our best to offer you protection. Cahya has been watching the astral plane and hunting all over town in search of the hellhounds."

She giggled again. "Oh. Well. That's very nice of her."

His voice dropped an octave. "I *thought* you had experienced enough by now to understand the danger you are in and the need to prepare yourself for what may come."

She tried to tamp down her scientific derision for the supernatural and open her mind to what he was saying. "You're right. I appreciate the help. It's just ... seriously? I still can't wrap my head around everything that's happened in the last few weeks. I'm a scientist." Waving her arms, flailing for the point that eluded her, she continued, "I understand real things. Things I can *feel, hold* ... objects and experiences that can be classified." She ended with her hand palm up between them on the table, focused on the imaginary object she held.

His chair slid roughly across the tiles as Adam stood abruptly. "Let me show you something."

He was interrupted by the kitchen door slamming open. Sheets of rain blew through the doorway as Tony and Frankie hurried inside and began pillaging the refrigerator.

Adam took hold of her hand and pulled her from the kitchen. "Come," he said as he led her down the short hall and into his bedroom where he closed the door. He tugged up the hem of his shirt. Greer made an odd squeaking noise and grabbed for the door handle. "No, wait." His tone was gentle. She watched, uncertain, as he raised the shirt up several inches exposing his stomach. "If you need to experience something real, feel this."

Four parallel scars ran from under his shirt and continued below the waist of his jeans. Her nervousness vanished, replaced by curiosity. Reaching for the shirt, she carefully pushed it up out of the way following the wide, red tracks across his tight belly and over his chest until she found their jagged source just under his left nipple.

"This looks like a claw mark," she said, intrigued.

"Yes." He tensed when she reached up to examine the marks with her fingertips. "More specifically, a hound's claw," he said, clarifying.

"As in hellhounds? Is that what you're telling me?" She ran her fingers back down over the trail of scars wondering if her own leg would heal similarly.

He cleared his throat. She stepped back, suddenly self-conscious at their proximity. He let the shirt fall back into place.

"These scars are why I know you must take this seriously."

Greer stared down at her hands as she cracked her knuckles and contemplated everything he'd told her, shown her. "Will you tell me what happened?"

He took a deep breath before diving in. About five years before, Adam had been dating a fellow college student named Sarah. She was an empath from Oklahoma who'd become well entrenched in his family and their unique lifestyle. She was a history major at Brown, focusing on religious studies. They'd talk for hours about his extraordinary experiences. All of this served to bolster Sarah's own belief system.

That spring Sarah had been working late nights at the main university library on a special project. The problems started there. She would fall asleep over her books only to wake up sobbing or screaming. She couldn't shake a growing sense of terror, becoming paranoid about unusual noises and being alone. Adam took to walking her to and from all her classes as well as the library.

However, one night he was working late across campus, and, for some unknown reason, she decided not to call when she was ready to go home. From what he later pieced together; Sarah was walking back to her dorm alone when the hounds set upon her. She lost them temporarily and called Adam on her phone, begging for help.

By the time he arrived at the location she'd given him, she was gone. He heard ferocious barking in the distance and ran toward the clamor. He caught up to Sarah in time to see her still being chased by the hounds. He shouted at the animals thinking they were just a stray pack of dogs, but they were undeterred and quickly overtook Sarah, pulling her to the ground. Adam tried to wade into the pack as they tore into her. He roared yet could barely hear himself over her screams. He pulled a few of the creatures off by brute force before one of them took a swipe at him. The pain brought him to his knees. That's when he noticed the unusual smell and eyes of the attacking beasts. He began reciting a protection prayer and the hounds left. Sarah was motionless on the ground in front of him.

"I was too late. There was no chance to say goodbye," he said, finishing quietly. He ran his hands roughly across his face then fell back on the bed with a heavy sigh.

"That's heartbreaking, Adam."

"It was a long time ago, but I still regret that I could not do more."

"What more could you have possibly done?"

He stared at the ceiling while an unshed tear remained trapped at the corner of his eye. "Maybe I should have realized the real danger sooner. It was my first encounter with such truly wicked spirits, and I was not ready. Since then, I have been more vigilant about training our new family members."

"Have you had many evil run-ins? Since then?"

"A few. Although nothing quite as serious. A random ghost or minor demon here and there. It is usually easy to handle them once we understand what we are dealing with."

"Yeah, the hellhounds that attacked me have already proven deadly. Point made."

He patted for her to take a seat beside him. "I realize this is a lot to accept. Especially since you have no religious leaning. I think Sarah absorbed the implications of her talent quickly because of her preexisting beliefs. But. In the end. It was not enough to save her." His sorrow felt fresh.

Greer was taken aback by how open he was being with her and at her own instinct to comfort him.

"You're still taking her loss pretty hard. You must've loved her very much."

"Yes, and yes. But I would take your loss hard too. I refuse to lose anyone else. Since I was a child, I knew I was destined to protect others from the dark forces troubling this world."

"That's a lot for a little boy to take on." She found the whole idea absurd and unfair. Greer felt the need to challenge him. "How could you be so sure this is what you're meant to do? And did you even *want* to do it?"

"My wanting had nothing to do with it. It is my fate."

"You think you have no choice?"

"No."

"There is always a choice, Adam."

She watched his face carefully, searching for any doubt but found only unyielding conviction.

The Flood

Greer drove home that night in the pouring rain, contemplating Adam's dedication to his supernatural calling. Despite what she'd witnessed, she struggled with how any intelligent person could believe in such things. The thought still consumed her as she parked in front of St Agatha's the next morning. Adam pulled up in his truck up a moment later. Her leg was feeling better, so she offered to help carry equipment across the soggy yard to the small tent.

Scrutinizing the flat, gray sky, she said, "More rain is coming. I hope we get something accomplished before it does."

"Good thing I had the students cover the exposed areas with tarps yesterday."

"I'll start pulling them up."

Greer yelped as a man silently stepped out from the tent behind her.

Adam startled as well. "Father Doyle," he said rigidly. "We were not expecting you. Certainly not this early."

Doyle clasped his hands behind his back and nodded curtly. "I want to stay on top of things here."

"Again, I do provide weekly reports. However, I will make certain the church is notified immediately if anything important comes to light. If you will excuse us now."

Adam didn't wait for the priest to respond, instead motioning for Greer to follow him as he bent and tugged the corner of the large tarp covering the new work area around the second door. It was a slow process so Doyle soon lost interest and tramped away.

As they continued folding and dumping water from the tarp, the students arrived and picked their way over to help. The last section to be uncovered was the sheeting draped directly over Room A's door and tripod. Rigsby pulled it away and hollered, "Holy crap! Professor!"

Everyone scurried over, finding Rigsby staring down at the wide-open door.

Adam had always kept his cool in class, even when a student made a particularly bone-headed move with a tool or artifact. Now Greer saw his body taught with stress and heard steel in his voice.

"Who was in charge of closing Room A, yesterday?" he asked, carefully delivering each word.

Jones responded, his face challenging and confident. "Professor, I closed the door myself. It was covered before the first raindrops fell yesterday."

Adam scanned the young faces around him. "Does anyone have something to say?" All eyes answered by looking down, away or frantically around the circle. "No?" Apparently, he believed in their innocence because his muscles slowly uncoiled. "Then we will have to assume a passerby has disturbed our dig." With a frown, he nodded to Jones. "Grab the ladder and some flashlights. Hopefully, nothing has been disturbed down there."

Jones and Malcolm hurried over with the equipment. Adam lowered the ladder in carefully. Everyone cringed when they heard it splash at the bottom.

Greer followed Adam down the ladder, stepping into ankle-deep water. When they flipped the flashlights on Greer let out her own curse.

"The door must've been open all night for this much water to run in," she said. "Who the hell would've been messing around in here?"

"Look what it did to the mural," Adam said, grumbling as he crouched in the alcove.

Greer followed his light as it played around the base of the alcove. The plaster had been saturated causing the bottom few inches to literally dissolve into the murky water. Moisture wicked further up the wall where it was causing discoloration and crumbling.

"I need to run over to the school and find a pump. What a disaster." His earlier anger was creeping back in.

Greer stepped carefully, trying to survey the damage, feet sinking into the mud of a once hard-packed floor. "At least there was nothing else valuable down here." Her light stopped short on something pale in the water. "Some debris washed in though." She bent to pick it up.

Searing pain shot up her arm. Blood and fire raged in her mind. The gleam of sharp metal filled her vision as she witnessed rows and rows of knives hanging on a wall. Agony consumed her. It burned her arms and chest as she fell hard to her knees. Cloudy water splashed all over her, but it did nothing to extinguish the growing heat. She held her head and tried to cry out.

Adam dropped to his knees in front of her. Snatching the amulet from beneath his shirt, he grasped it tightly in one hand as he placed the other hand on Greer's chest, over her own charm. He began chanting.

Breathing hurt, yet she tried to focus on Adam's words. She only made out a little of the Latin through the haze of pain. It was a struggle to remember the prayers he'd taught her just the night before.

Finally recalling one, she began haltingly, "In the name of Jesus ... In the name of Jesus, impure spirit, go away! Go Away! In the name of Jesus, impure spirit, go away! In the name of Jesus, impure spirit, go away!"

Greer redoubled her effort when Adam's talisman started to glow. As the silver light grew, the heat and pain receded. After minutes, which felt like hours, the last of the bloody visions and pain faded away.

Exhausted, she slumped forward. Adam caught her against his chest, holding tightly as the amulet continued to glimmer between them.

A shudder ran through her as remnants of the vile images flashed through her mind. "It was ... unspeakable," she said, barely able to form words.

"Shh, it is over," he said, soothing her with long strokes of her hair.

Greer sought his gaze, tears trailing down her cheeks. "It ... I," she stammered, wanting to make him understand, but not comprehending herself.

He pressed his forehead gently to hers and she let him hold her close. As the tears subsided and she was able to draw a few deep breaths, she felt whole again.

With a final wipe at her eyes, she looked down at the protrusion in the water.

"That's not a piece of wood."

He smoothed a piece of hair behind her ear. "No. It is a bone."

Malcolm poked his head down the ladder and called, "Do you want us down there, Professor?"

"No!" Adam said as they hastily separated. "We will be up in a minute."

She pushed further away. "Great. I'm sure he saw us hugging," Greer said crossly. "The whole class will think there's something going on. I'll get no respect now." She stood and scrubbed at her tear-stained face with a dry corner of her shirt.

"Don't move," he said as he retrieved her submerged flashlight. Shaking the water off, he looked about. "Malcolm did not witness anything," he said absently as he sloshed toward the ladder and looked back in her direction, seeming to evaluate the distance.

"Can we just get the hell out of here?" She felt overheated and dizzy. The last thing she wanted to do was pass out into the muddy water where more bones could be lurking just under the surface.

"That is what I am working on." With that, he abruptly tossed her over his shoulder, carrying her to the ladder for the second time in a matter of days. He lowered her onto the first dry rung. "You can make your own way up this time, right?"

Greer nodded, blushing as she climbed. Ignoring the questions that bombarded her at the top, she bee-lined to the tent where she kicked over a bucket and sat down. Scrounging in her bag for a water bottle, she let the first gulp soothe her raw throat. *Did I scream again?*

Adam could be heard calling out assignments, keeping the students occupied. He joined her a few minutes later. Pulling up his own bucket, he said, "We have to drain the room to see what we are dealing with. I am rather certain that bone did not wash in last night."

She followed his train of thought. "You think we'll find a connection to the burial in the alcove."

"Do you?" He took a swig when she offered him a drink. "I will go find that pump if you are alright watching the kids."

Her hand trembled as she took the bottle back. "I'll keep an eye on them, but I'm not ... touching ... anything."

"Good. Please do not go near the room until we know more. And even then, not unless I am with you."

"Agreed. We can't have anyone witnessing the effect this place is having on me. I'm not sure I can even go back down there." She looked at him in alarm. "Oh my God, my career is over!"

"Keep it down," he said in a loud whisper as he placed a steadying hand over hers. "We are going to get it figured out." He added a reassuring squeeze.

"That's what I'll do," Greer said. She jumped up and abruptly began sorting through the files on the trestle table, unsure of what she was looking for. "I'll find the answer. We need to know more about these rooms and who built them. I'll have to dig deep into the history of St. Agatha's and the people important to her." Her voice had been rising in panic the longer she searched.

Adam slowly reached for the scuffed-up laptop on the table. "Slow down. Start with the files on here. I went over them all before starting the project, but maybe I missed something that will jump out at you now ... in light of recent events."

"And if we don't find anything helpful?" she asked, still gripping a stack of papers anxiously.

"Well, then we will rely on some local talents for help." He winked at her.

She watched as he squelched through the spongy yard to his truck. The students seemed to have everything in hand, so she fired up the laptop.

It took Adam some time to return with the pump. The students helped set it up quickly, but the floor needed time to dry before anyone went back down. Going down too soon, working in mud, would destroy the identification of strata and risk damage to any artifacts close to the surface. With the threat of rain still hanging overhead, they'd be lucky to get back in before the next afternoon.

Adam put off telling the students about the bone Greer found. He thought they'd be tempted into unauthorized exploring. Instead, he pointed them into the newly discovered space, which was being called Room B. Their working theory was this new room was a typical root cellar. The students were probing nooks and crannies for seeds or other evidence of food storage to confirm that was indeed its purpose.

In the meantime, Greer poured through various files the city and church had provided as part of the salvage excavation request. No one had anticipated significant finds; this was a quiet, local cathedral. The church leaders were already upset by the discovery of the cremated remains from the alcove. They weren't going to be at all happy at the news of more human bones. Greer was convinced the bone she'd touched was not alone down there.

Adam ducked under the tent cradling a few small artifacts. "Can I borrow the computer for a few minutes?" he asked.

"Sure. I could use the break." She set the laptop on the table and called up the artifact database for him. Resting her elbows on the plywood, she watched as he tagged and recorded a handful of objects.

He nudged her with an elbow. "Are you doing alright?"

"Oh," she said, rousing out of a daze. "I'm tired."

"Head home. Get some rest."

"I believe I'll take you up on that offer today. Can I take the laptop with me? I have a few more files to get through."

"Almost done and then it is all yours."

A few minutes later she tucked it into her bag and moved to leave. Adam stopped her with a quick word.

"You have been through the wringer today. No training tonight."

"Really? I'd like to wrap up all this crazy stuff so I can get back to work."

"It is more important that you rest. But I want to give you something to think about." He paused, appearing to debate his next words carefully. "The road ahead will be difficult. Even more so without support from the people you love." Regret fell over his face, briefly aging him. "You should talk to your fiancé and your father. Tell them about your special talent."

"I don't imagine they'd believe me since I have obvious misgivings myself."

"Alright, maybe not tonight, but at some point, soon, you'll need to tell them."

With an inward sigh, she granted him the response he wanted. "Ok. I'll give it some thought. See you in the morning."

. . .

At home Greer decided to make Robert's favorite meal. Between his hours at the firm, hers at the site, and her mystical evenings, they'd seen little of each other recently. Dinner was almost ready when he walked in the door.

"Surprise!" she said, calling cheerfully from the stove.

He placed his briefcase on the edge of the counter and surveyed the mess she'd made of the kitchen. "Your cooking is a bit of an event." He hung his suit jacket over the back of a bar stool.

Her face fell as she turned back to stir the thickening sauce.

Robert stepped in, hugging her from behind. "Smells good."

"Well, it's ready. Grab some plates."

While they ate, Greer quizzed Robert about his work. He liked the firm and was learning something new every day. She debated this as an opening to bring up her own new experiences.

After dinner they snuggled on the couch, enjoying a movie together. Between the comfortable evening and her second glass of wine, Greer finally felt ready to test the waters. She traced random circles on the back of Robert's hand, pondering exactly where to start. "So ... do you think ghosts are real?"

His focus never left the TV. "Don't know. Probably not."

She watched another scene of the movie before attempting again. "What about angels then?"

"Not really."

She turned to face him, suddenly curious. "Why not? You went to church all the time as a kid."

Robert hit the remote to pause the movie. "What are you talking about?"

She shrugged. "I just wondered what you thought. I realized we've never discussed our beliefs about God or about an after-life. You know? It's probably something two engaged people should talk about. At least once."

His face wrinkled up like he smelled something rotten. "Really? Most intelligent people believe in science, not religion. What's there to discuss?"

"Never mind. Just turn the movie back on." She gave him a quick peck on the cheek.

He stared at her for a moment, puzzled. "What's up with your eyes anyway?" he said.

Greer dodged scrutiny by snuggling back in against him. So many concerns stacked themselves, one on top of the other, in her mind. Why did her eyes look brighter? Would Robert ever believe in her ghost-vision? Would he ever consider such a talent favorably? Never mind. She told herself the mumbo-jumbo stuff would go away once the current challenge was managed. Shouldn't take long.

Her thoughts drifted to Adam, his family, and their many gifts. She'd have to avoid them when this was all over or run the risk of Robert finding out too much.

Former Things Long Past

Fortunately, there'd been no new rainfall overnight, although the morning was heavily overcast. High humidity meant the floor of Room A was drying slower than hoped. The fan did little to accelerate the process.

Adam had carefully secured the trap door and all tarps personally the evening before, clearly agitated when the school declined to fund a security guard. Everything was found in place this morning though. Whoever had opened the door before hadn't returned.

The students finished excavating the area above Room B and began staking out new grids adjacent to the existing excavation field. They were excited about the expanded search, hoping to discover more buried rooms.

Greer returned the laptop sans any new insight. The history of St. Agatha's Cathedral and her people was disappointingly conventional. However, she had been mulling over a new idea.

"Can I run something by you?" she asked lightly as she slid the laptop across the table to where Adam shuffled more paperwork. "Since I struck out with the official documents, I'd like to try a few alternate avenues. There must be more we can learn. Can you spare me for the day?"

Adam struck several red lines across his documents and tossed them aside with a disgruntled look before giving her a perfunctory smile. "Of course. Since we are waiting on the floor to dry, it will be business as usual around here."

"Do you think the students will be upset if I leave? I feel like I've missed a lot of time onsite."

He gave a small snort. "Liz is the only one bound to take notice, and I think she is not likely to mind."

"Ohhhh?" She flashed a knowing grin. "So, you've finally caught on to that particular crush, have you?"

With a melodramatic sigh, he said, "It is a cross we professors often have to bear."

"You do have it rough." She laughed, happy at their rapport and his approval of her plan. "I'll check in with you before the end of the day."

Distracted, he called out to Rigsby who was currently in danger of falling down the open stairs to Room B.

"There's something else," Greer said, moving into his sightline to recapture his attention. "I want to step up my training tonight. In fact, I want you guys to teach me everything I need to know as fast as possible. Ok?"

He leaned against the table, taking a minute to mull it over. "While I agree we need to continue your training in all urgency, this is not like cramming for an exam. Training often requires a great deal of physical energy and can be dangerous if you attempt too much at once."

Huffing in exasperation, Greer threw her hands to her hips and watched as the students worked, longing to get her hands dirty with them, finding answers through familiar techniques. There was a touch of desperation in her eyes when she turned back to him.

"I really need this to be done, and fast. I'm going to push as hard as you'll let me."

He recognized her drive and quickly conceded. "Good luck!" he called after her as she hurried to the car.

. . .

Her first stop was the city archives. Adam's research included a few architectural plans that the church had filed when the bell tower was repaired decades ago. It was a long shot, but she hoped there may be some additional drawings related to the land or the building, or other church elders to investigate.

Archaeology was far more about hunting and researching documents, than it was about digging. Thousands of hours of research go into any endeavor before field work is ever approved. This project was unique in that the archaeological team didn't have to prove why they wanted to dig; the purpose and cost were already justified.

"Hey there, George," Greer said.

The heavy-set clerk at the city records desk was not impressed by her peppy greeting. However, he did brighten at the bag of bagels she'd brought along to grease his slow wheels. After offering no more than an eye roll as she described the search she was planning, he granted her the usual free run of the records room. "Just don't make a mess," he said as he unlocked the fire door and pointed her toward the familiar rickety table in the middle of row upon row of file cabinets and bookshelves.

Facing a room full of paper records was a blessing and a curse. Handling old documents appealed to all of Greer's senses. The smell and feel of the slowly deteriorating paper, the delicate handwriting that threatened to fade out of existence right before her eyes—it was all as exhilarating as it was frustrating. She popped in some ear buds, cranked up some gritty, bayou blues and set to work.

The file on the bell tower was a bust. So, armed with a complete list of St. Agatha's leaders, both clergy and lay people, Greer decided to pull other deeds owned by each person. After that she could find the associated building plans and land surveys. She considered reviewing powers of attorney as well. If these people were leaders in the church, they were likely leaders in the larger community, tasked with the management of other businesses and properties.

This would likely take days; however, wishful thinking had her hoping to find a few clues today that might begin to shed light on the secrets beside the cathedral's walls.

Hours later her stomach was growling, but Greer refused to break for lunch, only taking time for water and a few stretches. She had just settled back to work when the ringing phone interrupted her.

"Hey, Kiddo. Are you busy?" her dad asked from the other end of the line.

"Yes, actually. But I always have time for you. What's up?" She popped the other ear bud out and stood to stretch again.

"Two things really. First, I'm checking in since I haven't heard from you in a few days. Second, I wanted to confirm our plans for the Fourth."

She'd been pacing around the table, anxious to get back to work, but that brought her up short. "Wow, I really lost track of time."

"Do you still want to get together for the holiday?" he asked tentatively.

"Yes, of course!" she said as she ran her palm back and forth across her forehead. "I've just been preoccupied."

"I hope you're not working too hard. I've been extremely concerned since the accident."

"No need to worry, Dad." She was met with silence on the other end. "Really."

"Ok, but you still shouldn't be working so hard."

Greer had been rearranging and scanning the land deeds spread across the table as she paced. They belonged to one of the older families in town, the Bartletts who were moderately well-to-do, but like many other founding families, were forced to sell off properties during the last century. She stopped as her eyes fell on a remarkably familiar address.

"Are you still there?" Apparently, her father had been talking for some time.

"I'm ... here."

He heard her hesitation. "Greer, what's the matter?"

"Um ..." She wavered between full disclosure and sparing his feelings. "It's just that I'm doing this research and came across an old deed for Serenity House." Her throat constricted.

When he finally responded, she heard the grief bubbling to the surface. "The same place they found your mother?"

"Yes. It used to be owned by an old family named the Bartletts."

"Well, that's not too surprising." He was working hard to keep his tone even. "Many of those old houses were too big for later generations to maintain as private homes. They split them into apartments or sold them to the city. Right?"

Greer dropped into the chair. "I know. It's just hard seeing it in black and white. I like to pretend it doesn't exist."

"I drove by all the time. Right after. Then I just couldn't stand it anymore and vowed not to go back."

"Sorry, Dad. I shouldn't have mentioned it."

"It's ok. We should probably talk about her more often than we do."

She paused to steady her voice before responding. "We should. That'd be good." Hurriedly flipping the deed into her read pile, she said, "Dad, I'm going to try and finish up here. There's still a lot to get through."

"Sure. I'll see you soon. Chin up!"

"Love you too, Dad."

She tossed the phone aside and tried to literally shake off the anxiety the deed had brought on. A minute later she jumped back into the waiting pile of records.

They Will Watch Over You

Greer raised her hand to knock on Adam's front door early that evening, only to be almost crushed by Tony and Frankie rushing out, seemingly in the middle of a deep conversation about the best strip club buffet. Frankie mumbled her apologies. As Tony drove them off on an old, very noisy bike, a shock of red hair flashed in Greer's memory.

Entering unannounced through the wide-open door, she found Sam watching his cartoons. He returned her wave enthusiastically. Adam was in the kitchen loading the oven for dinner.

"You're a great cook, aren't you?"

"Not great, but I am persistent. We would die of food poisoning or starvation if anyone else in this house was left in charge of dinner." He handed her a cutting board and vegetables. "Would you mind helping with salad?"

"I think I can just about manage that."

As they worked, Greer filled him in on the day's findings. There had been no smoking guns pointing to nefarious or occult dealings. Still, she hadn't shaken the dread she felt at discovering the deed for Serenity House. Adam said he wasn't familiar with the building, so she explained its history as a half-way home, housing recently released felons during their transition back into society.

She had planned to omit the detail that her mother's broken body was found there when she had a sudden change of heart, believing he would understand her gut reaction to stumbling on it.

"Can I tell you something?" she asked even as she remained uncertain she'd be able to say the words out loud.

"Of course."

"We should sit."

Adam waited, hands folded on the table, giving her time to gather courage. Over the comforting smell of dinner roasting, Greer chose to tell Adam about the worst night of her life—the night she lost her mother. She told him everything; more than she'd ever shared with Robert.

It had been an unspoken agreement between Greer and her father that the details of her mother's death never be discussed. They were too heinous to be voiced more than once. Even the experienced officers who visited them that snowy evening had difficulty getting through their report. The officers told the story in low voices. But, as she feigned inattention, staring through the frosty window, they revealed more than a pre-teen girl should hear. In the end she handled it better than her father.

Greer's mother had been a history professor. She loved all things ancient and mysterious that gave her insight into how people lived, organized, and worshiped. Trinkets and stories from various cultures made their way to the dinner table almost nightly. Greer was fascinated by her mother's passion for these dead and distant peoples.

Her mom had volunteered at the homeless shelter downtown, feeling they were a people already forgotten by the world around them. Her dad frequently voiced his worry about a woman's safety in that part of town. Her mother always brushed him off and pushed on with her work.

Serenity House was in the same neighborhood, and a few of the men who lived there worked at the shelter as part of their parole. They were rough around the edges to be sure, but the historian appreciated them and catalogued their experiences as part of her larger view of the story of man.

The night Greer's mom didn't come home was an ordinary winter evening until the moment a fellow volunteer heard screams coming from behind Serenity House. By the time police arrived and forced their way past a crumbling gate into the back alley, her mother was dead. Her breasts had been sliced from her chest, animal bites had torn flesh and broken bones, and, ultimately, she'd been set on fire. The police were able to douse the last of the flames, but not before she lost her hair and clothes. Greer still shuddered to think of how many people witnessed her beautiful mother lying naked and mangled on the cold, dirty ground.

Each word tore at her heart as she wrenched the horrific details from the darkest corner of her memories. Her tears kept a slow and steady pace even when her voice faltered. She let the tears flow. They felt right, telling Adam felt right.

When she finished, she wiped her eyes and nose on a napkin he'd silently pressed into her hand. Feeling exposed, she looked to the door, estimating how many steps it would take her to escape the weight of the story she'd just delivered. Glancing at Adam, she expected to see horror and revulsion on his face. Instead, his gaze was composed, tender. He took her hand, rubbing his thumb firmly across the back. "Thank you for sharing this with me. I know how difficult it was."

She wiped her eyes again and released a shaky breath, easing into the feeling that he truly did understand the shock and despair she'd experienced. "Are you sure it's ok that I told you? It's completely sickening. And here I'm spilling it all over your supper."

"I am fine, having seen as bad and heard worse. In fact, Sarah... remember the empath I told you about?" Greer nodded that she remembered. "The hounds had pretty well savaged her chest and throat before it was all done. I can still smell the fur and oily smoke they left behind."

"Oh God. I didn't mean to dredge up all of that for you."

"It is important to remember." He crossed himself just as the oven beeped. Moving to rescue the roast, he paused and, turning back with a sad smile, he added, "Sometimes."

Adam reviewed rudimentary protection spells over dinner before turning Greer over to April for some hands-on experience. The girl led the way to her small room on the second floor. Colorful fabrics draped the walls and most surfaces so that it looked like the room had been decorated by a pot-smoking hippie.

A lumpy beanbag suddenly bounced off Greer's chest. "Grab a seat," April said. "Let's start at the top."

Beanbag chairs were designed for a certain kind of conversation. This was not going to be that kind of chat. Greer did her best to look attentive as she reclined at a steep angle in the squishy chair, but she was practically staring at the ceiling.

April began the lecture. "There's seven kinds of spirits. Human and non-human. There's intelligent ghosts, like good ol' Minnie. And residuals. They're people, but they're like a song or movie on repeat. Can't talk to them." April rustled deeper into her seat and pulled a shawl from underneath her, only to wrap it loosely around her hair. "Non-humans are poltergeists, demons and elementals. Some people say poltergeists are the wild energy of teenage girls. But I never seen that."

"That makes only five," Greer said after April had been quietly fiddling with her shawl. Greer noticed distraction and discomfort on the long face when April began again.

"Six is shadow people, who're probably never human to begin with. Lots of people think they're ghosts of *aliens*. Ha! Or from other dimensions. Can't prove it, right? Don't get Cahya started on them though," she said as a warning. "And last, but not least, is my favorite—

animal spirits." April smiled to herself.

"I have to say the animal spirits that bit me would not be my favorite so far."

"Well of course. But hellhounds ain't really animal spirits, silly. They were never real, live dogs. They're lesser demons."

"Oh," Greer's eyes got big at the mention of demons. The beans under her crunched loudly as she squirmed and pondered the implications of getting bitten by a demon. Would it damage her soul? She'd probably be more concerned if she actually believed in souls, Heaven, Hell, and such. If hellhounds existed that implied the Bible was actually right about the existence of Hell. *Could it be wrong about the rest?*

April lit a candle on the table beside her, absently waving a hand over the flame. "When someone tells you there's dozens of types of spirits, they're really saying a spirit's form. Not what they're made of."

"So, for instance a partial apparition and a whole apparition are both a human ghost?" Greer asked.

"Yay!" April smiled, glad that Greer was finally following along. "Now, a spirit's form is important if you're trying to work with it. And it's *super* important when you're trying to get rid of one."

"Should I be writing all of this down?" Greer asked. Her fingers itched for pen and a notepad.

April lazily waved her off the idea. "Nah, you'll get the hang of it."

This was a new concept. Greer wanted to attack this like a course at school if she was going to take it seriously. April seemed sure, so they'd try it her way.

"Ok, I'll just take mental notes then. What are the forms, and what do I need to do about them?"

April sighed. "Well, that's the thing, ain't it? Spirits have endless shapes. Orbs are little lights that fly about and disappear. People claim to catch them all the time in photos, but that's just dust. Real orbs last a long time, move in every direction and speed, and flash in and out in a wink." Snapping her fingers to illustrate the point, the girl was leaning in now, engaged in her lesson.

"Yes, I've heard of them. A lot of our old family photos had orbs. Dad always said it was that dusty old house." Greer chuckled. April narrowed her eyes, weighing the flip comment. Greer stopped. "What? What did I say?"

"Nothing ... nothing. Partial and full apparitions, they're what everybody thinks of as real ghosts." She used air quotes to punctuate her meaning. "Now a vortex is sure rare, but you'll find one or two in old towns like this. Most common are spirits only making sounds, nothing visible at all. Those aren't much fun."

Greer kept her thoughts to herself.

"I could keep going, but this is boring."

April crawled out of her chair and began collecting various objects from around the room. Placing them in the center of the floor, she motioned Greer to join her.

They sat cross-legged across from each other on the hard wood with April placing four candles in a rough circle around them. "Here, put this behind you," she said as she handed over the last candle. Next, she placed four small objects—a shell, stone, feather and match—in a smaller circle between them.

Greer surveyed the items. "Shouldn't the candles all be the same color or something?"

April smirked. "You watch too many movies." She began lighting the candles. "Color don't matter. It's just the flame and your intent."

"You're losing me."

"Flame is energy, right? A candle burns. Adam says it's matter turning to heat. Anyway, energy comes out, and ghosts draw on energy. Same as when they pull energy from a battery. Or from you. Ever wonder why flashlights die and it gets all cold in every ghost story?"

"You can't be serious." A tension headache was starting behind Greer's eyes.

"It's true," April said, eyes wide on an open face. "That part of the stories is anyways. Spirits don't hardly have any energy of their own. Adam thinks they might even be negative energy."

"Like anti-matter?" Greer asked.

"Yeah, like that. So, they barely got any energy or sometimes negative energy. Especially demons, we think. They go pull it from the world so as they can be seen and heard." April gave a final adjustment to the candles and items between them.

Greer guessed that everything was being aligned precisely with the four compass points, if the bad movies were true at all.

"Ok. I'll buy it. But you said intent is important. How?"

"Well, there's no fancy explanation for that. Not yet anyway. But Adam really wants a neuroscientist in the family."

"I'm sure," Greer said, heavy on the sarcasm.

April flashed a look of irritation before continuing. "It could be something to do with brain waves, or something science hasn't discovered yet, but all I know is concentrating on a particular spirit always seems to work. It's called channeling." She held her hands straight out, palms up, motioning for Greer to join her over the inner circle of objects. Greer obliged with a light grasp. "Now, this here is a spirit circle. The stuff inside stands for the four elements—the shell for water, stone for earth ..."

"Yes, feather for air, match for fire. Got it," Greer said impatiently.

"Exactly, smarty-pants. Now I talk with my guide just about any time I want, even without this circle, because of my own talent. But, if we're wanting to help him stay visible for a while, he needs an energy boost from this ritual." April closed her eyes. "Let's go."

True to her word, April began chanting without further instruction. Greer's fingers tingled as if a low electrical current was running between them. She shifted her focus to April's face. Too long to be considered classically pretty, there was a serenity and grace in the girl's features even now as she squeezed her eyes tightly shut in concentration. Greer listened to the prayer and hesitantly joined in.

At first, she felt nothing apart from the electricity tickling between their hands, but as April's chant became more intense, the air around them cooled.

Greer opened her eyes when April stopped chanting.

"Hey, Sonny," April said to the hazy image now sitting with them in the circle. Her wispy hair floated in waves of static as if she'd rubbed a rubber balloon over it.

Greer let out a squeak. As apparitions go, Greer would say this one was not fully formed; however, he was complete enough that she could make out bell-bottomed jeans, a loose shirt, and a scraggly beard on his skeletal face.

April withdrew her hands and waved an introduction to the spirit between them. "Sonny, this is Greer." Sonny's gaze seemed a little unfocused as he nodded in Greer's general direction.

"Hello," said Greer, trying to sound confident.

"Hey, Sonny, we need to hook her up with her own guide. Anybody free?"

Greer's jaw dropped. "Is that really how it works?" April hid the lower half of her face behind her skirt, having a good laugh at Greer's inexperience. Irritated, Greer turned to address Sonny, only to find his wavering form laughing at her as well. "Ok, you've both had your fun. Can we move on, please?"

"Aw, come on. Sonny never gets to have any fun." At this April high-fived the apparition and Greer became convinced the evening could only get stranger from here.

Tucking her arms and legs back into place, April settled down. "Ok, fine. Sonny's my spirit guide. Been with me a long time. Since before I came to live here even. But I didn't always know it was him. Not until I learned how to call him in this form." April smiled at her personal ghost in the manner of a child smiling at a favorite uncle, ready to be led through some new game.

Sonny's voice was surprisingly robust when he finally spoke. "You know, you already got some guidance?"

Although his manner was entirely casual, a shudder rippled down Greer's spine at the reality of speaking with another ghost. She quickly rallied and said, "April and Adam have been a lot of help, yes."

He shook his head in a strange bobbing motion. "Nah. Several spirits are near you. They've been helping you."

Greer tried to process what he said, turning her head in each direction searching for these spirits Sonny could see. "Are any of them my guide then?" she asked.

"Probably not. They're choosing not to come forward. But stay chill, they're with you."

"Why can't I see them?" Greer whispered to April.

"Not all spirits are going to want to be seen, even by a person with talents. I can see Sonny anytime, and the spirit circle helps you see him too. But he could hide from me ... if he wanted." She winked at her spirit friend. "When your guide wants you to know him, you'll have a good connection."

"Ok. How do I connect then?"

Sonny closed his eyes and extended his hands into the center of the circle. April and then Greer placed their hands over his. This was awkward since his hands didn't have any actual mass. The girls just tried to keep their own hands hovering above, and not in the middle of, the cold spot that was him.

"Clear your mind," he said.

Greer closed her eyes, knowing that clearing her mind would be impossible. She'd tried meditation and even hypnosis at a party with some psych majors. It never worked for her. Losing control of anything, especially her thoughts, was a terrifying idea.

April and Sonny started a low tuneless humming. She made an effort to follow along. Immediately thoughts of the dig, Serenity House, Robert, her father, and the strange family she was putting so much trust in, all intruded.

"You're humming way off-key," April said testily.

Greer let out a deep sigh and tried again.

"Much better," said Sonny.

Greer nodded at the spirit's encouragement and experimented with a few notes until she hit on the sound they were making. She closed her eyes and focused on their droning tune. The smell of warm wax from the candles was comforting. Oddly, the absurdity of the situation melted away, and she began to relax. Soon she could feel a vibration running through the room.

April spoke in a bold voice, sounding years older, "All gentle spirits who hear us now. Help our friend, Greer. Who will come forward to show her the way?"

Greer peeked her eyes open to find only Sonny and April still sitting, quietly humming.

Next, Sonny softly called, "Fellow spirits. Who will help this child?" before returning to his hum.

The vibration in the room continued to grow—a low electric current running through every part of her body. As the vibration intensified it became a buzzing in her ears. The buzz was in a peculiar harmony to the droning of the three inside the circle. Greer listened intently. She thought she could hear many voices talking over one another inside the noise.

April suddenly called out. "Purest of spirits! We call upon your aid for our sister!"

The buzzing stopped, and they all popped opened their eyes. Greer expected to see another wavering form, or at least an outline similar to Sonny's mildly luminous figure. Instead, a tiny, very bright ball of light hovered in the center of the spirit circle. Greer looked at April and Sonny for guidance, but she only read confusion on their faces. She opened her mouth to ask a question when the light abruptly winked out.

April blew out a huge whoosh of air. "What on earth was that?"

Sonny's form wavered wildly even as he began fading. "Not sure. Looks like your friend isn't getting a guide." His silhouette disappeared completely.

"Sonny?" said Greer.

"Come on, Sonny," April said, whining.

"Later kid," came his faint answer.

Greer wasn't sure which of the two girls he was apologizing to. She dropped her hands into her lap where she started cracking her knuckles.

"Was this typical?"

April snuffed out the candles and started cleaning up. "I don't do this lots, calling a spirit guide that is. But no. I don't think it's normal." She walked to a bookshelf where she stashed her elemental objects in a carved wooden box.

"Huh. What do we do now?"

April put a hand to her hip, cocking her head at a steep angle, and gave Greer a whole lot of attitude. "*We* aren't going to do anything. *You're* going home and try again on your own."

Greer stood up, unexpectedly angry. "You promised to help. I need this to be over." She followed April around the room as the girl swept up clothes, still somehow managing not to clean the room at all. "I can't possibly do this by myself!" she protested when the girl continued to ignore her.

"Yeah, you can. Maybe that's the problem. Maybe your guide don't want to be seen by anyone else."

April grabbed another scarf off the floor and, instead of putting it away, draped it over the others already dressing an over-burdened lamp. "I need to rest," she said dismissively. She fell across the bed and pulled her shawl over her face.

Greer picked her way through the mess on the floor. Soft snoring from the bed stopped her at the door. Looking back, she could hardly separate the girl from the mounds of fabric. Despite her poor manners, April did seem confident in herself and her student's abilities. Greer wished she was as convinced.

Downstairs, Greer collected her bag from the kitchen table then hurried back through the swinging door. She stopped abruptly when it only opened halfway, and a low curse issued from the other side. Adam entered the kitchen rubbing his forehead with one hand while holding a stack of books in the other.

"Oh, Adam! I wasn't paying attention." She touched the red spot blooming above his temple. "Nothing's going right tonight," she said, testy at herself and the whole situation she found herself in. *Were séances going to be a regular thing now?*

"No worry, my head is unusually hard. Just ask anyone who lives with me." He dropped the books on the table. "Take a seat and tell me what is going on."

She slumped into the chair next to him and explained her failure to acquire a spirit guide. "Ugh. I just feel so lost in all of this voodoo." Greer pulled her ponytail down and shook her hair trying to ease a slight headache.

"Well, it is definitely not voodoo," he said, correcting gently "That is something else entirely."

"I know, I know," she said with a sigh. "Ghost stories are true. God is real. I'm still getting used to it all, ok?" She accepted his nod as approval. "It's just that I don't seem to be very good at this, and I very much dislike things I'm not good at."

Adam broke into a big belly laugh, causing Greer to give him a dirty look when she felt like he'd gone on a bit too long. He wrapped an arm around her shoulders and gave her a squeeze. "I should not laugh," he smiled, still chuckling. "However, your statement is painfully obvious to anyone who has ever met you. Fortunately, you seem to be good at a great many things."

She blushed at the compliment. "Dad says I'm like Mom that way."

He squinted, briefly studying her closely. "I would imagine you resemble her in many ways. Anyway, I am not casting stones. I also avoid difficult things, until forced.

"And my current situation is certainly forcing the issue."

Adam pushed the pile of books toward her. "Which is why I pulled together some mandatory reading for you."

Greer snorted. "Ghost homework?"

"Something like that," he said, serious. "Greer, we do not understand the specific challenge you are facing, so we need to prepare you for anything and everything right now."

She sorted through the stack, reading the titles out loud. "*Hexes and Their Countermeasures, Demons, Devils and Evil Spirits, Channeling for Beginners,* and *A Biblical Guide to Spirits*. Well, it won't be weird at all when Robert sees me reading these around the house."

"Come on. You can slap another book cover over them. You never did that in school?"

She arched an eyebrow, giving him her own look of reproach. "No. I. Did. Not."

"Well, work it out. You need to get through these as soon as possible. At least get the gist, then we can talk the rest out."

Greer shoved the books into her bag. "You don't need me for more training until tomorrow night?"

"Right. Get some rest and hit the books in the morning."

"Ok. I'll work on these. And I'll try seeking my spirit guide again to make April happy."

She was rewarded with his boyish grin and a wink from his sapphire eyes.

Have I Need of Mad Men

The sun was already high in the sky when Greer awoke. She blindly patted the other side of the bed to locate Robert but found only cool sheets. He'd probably gone into the office hours ago. Legal interns put in ungodly hours, and Robert was determined to be one of the best, so he'd likely be gone all day.

She lazily rolled out of bed and aimed herself toward the bathroom where she talked herself out of a shower. Choosing to curl up on the couch in the oversized T-shirt she'd slept in, she sipped a fresh coffee with one hand and opened *Channeling for Beginners* in the other.

Page after page carried on about the importance of opening your mind to the higher realms, having faith in your inner voice, and being prepared to ignore unhelpful spirits. There didn't seem to be a lot of practical advice, just generalizations on how to be receptive to new perspectives and energies.

By lunch time, Greer had read or skimmed the entire book and felt rather less informed than when she began. Still, having promised to be a good student, she decided to do a little channeling on her own.

She worked on a turkey sandwich as she walked around the apartment collecting the items she needed. Finding the objects to represent the elements took a little creativity.

There were a few candles and an old matchbook stashed under the bathroom sink from the last time Robert treated her to a romantic candle-lit bath. Scrounging around the living room bookshelves, she came across a geode from a school field trip. Water was simple enough—a glass filled from the tap. Air posed a challenge. Wandering around the small apartment, considering the mementos she'd collected over the years, Greer realized the only personal items Robert kept were his clothes. His well-worn lacrosse cap was the only thing she could say held sentimental value for him. Eventually she settled on a photograph of beautiful clouds pulled from their slim photo album.

Pushing the coffee table aside, she placed the four objects in the middle of the floor and sat cross-legged in front of them. Then she lit the candles in a circle around herself. Greer closed her eyes and tried to recall all the tips from the book, wondering how she could improve upon the experience with April and Sonny.

She experimented with the meditative hum and soon struck a reasonable tone, only to stop abruptly at a noise outside the door. She imagined Robert finding her in the middle of a séance. It wouldn't go well. As the sound faded down the hall, she slowly blew out the breath she'd been holding.

Starting again, sensing the hum was right, she attempted to clear her mind. Thoughts of the dig and Adam were pushed aside. Hum, focus, hum, focus. When the strange vibration began, she couldn't believe she was doing this all on her own. Sudden nerves threatened her concentration.

"Friendly spirits, hear me," she tried hesitantly. "I call upon you for help and guidance."

Hum. Focus. The vibration in the room grew until it became an audible hum of its own. Greer felt the electric tingle pulsing through every cell, much stronger than before. She scanned around the room for apparitions or the little ball of light. Nothing materialized.

As the vibration intensified, Greer recalled one of the phrases she'd read that morning. It seemed fitting, so she said aloud, "Spirits of the dead, come to me now. Aid me on my journey."

The air trembled. The hum changed in frequency. Greer again heard the multitude of voices in the buzz, all talking over one another. The sound and pulsations swelled becoming painful to her ears, making her dizzy and nauseous.

Something was terribly wrong.

Rushing to blow out the first candle, Greer came face to face with ... another face. With wild eyes, a snarl of a mouth, and a sharply hooked nose, the visage in front of her was anger personified. The rest of the figure was a no more than a hazy contour suggesting a short, stocky man with large arms and an even larger belly.

She fell back as the room stopped vibrating and the buzzing voices ceased. "Oh God," she whispered.

The cruel face cackled silently.

Greer scuttled back on all fours out of the candle circle. When the form followed, she shot up and ran out the front door, finally stopping on the sidewalk. The sunlight weaving its way through the trees overhead offered meager comfort. Greer glanced around cracking her knuckles, hastily trying to collect her thoughts. *Damn.* She wasn't wearing pants. Darting back into the building, she lingered in the lobby, preferring embarrassment in front of the neighbors to what likely waited inside her apartment.

Obviously, she'd connected with what the book had called an "unhelpful" spirit. Just how unhelpful remained to be seen, but surely she could undo the summoning or convince the ghost to go away of his own accord.

When a door down the hall opened, Greer realized how much she didn't want to be seen half-naked. Without a plan whatsoever, she pushed open the door to her apartment. Finding it silent and empty, she crept over the threshold and pressed the door closed behind her. She heaved a sigh of relief and started cleaning up, considering herself lucky no damage had been done—Robert hadn't discovered her secret, and she'd successfully returned a nasty spirit to the ether.

Pulling her shirt off as she headed toward the shower, Greer jumped when something cold touched her exposed shoulder. It wasn't a draft, but rather felt like a solid mass of ice touching her bare skin. Slowly glancing down, she saw the indistinct outline of a hand there.

Whirling around, she clutched her shirt to her chest and screamed at the hideous face just inches away. She backed slowly down the hall to the bedroom and slammed the door. The shirt fell, forgotten, as she fumbled with items on top of the dresser. She always took her jewelry off before bed so the Hand of Fatima pendant had to be there.

She clutched it and spun just in time to see the figure emerge through the closed door. Holding the pendant at arm's length, she struggled to remember the prayer of protection Adam taught her. The ghost advanced quickly as she finally found the words:

O Angel of God,

Make me worthy of thy tender love,

Thy celestial companionship,

And thy never-failing protection!"

The apparition vanished.

Greer fell across the bed with a sigh of relief, wondering how April and Adam had ever believed she was ready to do this alone. She was terrified and obviously unprepared.

Sitting to put the necklace on, clasping it tightly, she sat shivering, waiting for the apparition to return. As the shadows in the room lengthened, she decided enough time had passed that it was safe to assume the terrifying ghost-man would not return.

Robert was due home any minute, so she jumped in the shower to warm up and relax her tense muscles.

He walked in a short time later to find her reading on the couch. "Long day," he said plaintively as he dropped his briefcase on the counter. "What's for dinner?"

"I hadn't thought about it. What're you in the mood for?"

She glanced up as he crunched into an apple from the fruit bowl, instantly paling when a blurry profile began to materialize right behind him. Greer gripped her pendant, mouthing the prayer of protection as quickly as she could. The figure faded away.

Robert stopped mid-bite. "You ok?"

"Um, let's go out to eat tonight," she said brightly as she grabbed her purse and Robert's hand, rushing him out the door.

She needed to get rid of him and call April for help.

Robert pulled open the driver's side door.

"Where're we going?"

Inspiration struck. "Um, instead of watching that game from home tonight, why don't you call the guys and meet down at the pub? It's been a while since you had a night out."

"Yeah, it's been a while." He hesitated in the street, undecided. "Yeah. Ok, good idea." Climbing into the car, he zipped off without a backward glance.

Greer frowned. *That wasn't hard.*

Greer waited out front impatiently for April. When the girl pulled up, Greer hustled her through the lobby, then slowly cracked the apartment door open, peering around the edge. April heaved a sigh and pushed it open with a bang.

"It ain't going to be sitting here all alone watching the TV." She made herself at home, plopping on the couch. "Spirits need energy to draw on or they can't appear. They ain't hardly ever visible unless they're drawing energy off something big nearby, like someone talented or a sacred place."

"Oh."

Greer watched from the middle of the room; her arms crossed tightly in a stubborn refusal to accept the predicament she was in. It wasn't long before a chill caused goosebumps puckered her skin.

"Here we go," April said knowingly.

"Here we go, what?"

"You're getting cold. He's drawing energy from you." She pointed to the goose bumps on Greer's arms. "He'll be here any second."

April was right. The horrible apparition materialized in front of Greer, legs in the middle of the coffee table. Not on it, but in it, through it. His mouth moved in rapid fire speech, but no sound escaped. Whatever he was saying wasn't very nice. He pointed at Greer accusingly then headed her way. She backed up, bumping into the kitchen counter with a squeak.

"Make it stop!" she yelled at April.

April rolled off the couch as the ghost charged closer to Greer. "What'd you do to piss him off?"

"I didn't do anything! I just tried to call a spirit guide." Greer edged sideways along the counter, side-stepping the ghost to hide behind April. "Please make him go away!"

"What did you say? Tell me the words *exactly.*"

"When?"

"When you called on a spirit guide," April said, throwing her hands in the air, exasperated.

Greer wracked her brain. "I said the same thing you did. Um, I called on all spirits for help and guidance. Or something like that." She side-stepped again to keep the experienced girl between her and the unwanted house guest.

April raised both hands and chanted:
The light of God surrounds me,
The love of God enfolds me,
The power of God protects me,
The presence of God watches over me.
Wherever I am, God is ...
All is well.

As the figure dissipated, Greer heaved a sigh of relief. "Thank you! I didn't know it'd be that easy."

"It isn't."

"But he's gone?" Greer waved her arms around the now empty space, feeling for any lingering cold spots.

"He'll be back," April replied bluntly as she grabbed an orange from the fruit bowl.

Greer watched in disbelief as the girl calmly pulled at the peel, sucking at the dripping juice. Greer was unimpressed with the level of support she was receiving. "But you're going to get rid of him for good."

"Well sure. But it'll take some work to get it done."

"Ok. What's first?" Greer asked as she cracked each knuckle one by one. "April, be serious. Maybe you should snack later?"

"Here's the problem. You called on a lost soul." April leaned on the counter and took another juicy bite of orange.

Crossing her arms defensively, Greer asked, "How? And why does it matter?"

"If I heard right, you called on *all* spirits. You can't do that," she said with a shake of her head. "When channeling the spirit world, you only want to call on positive energies. There's a big difference between talking to spirits of the happily-departed and ghosts of someone who's unaware or unhappy about their current after-life situation."

Greer perched on the edge of the couch, holding her head in hands. "How am I supposed to tell?"

April tossed the peel in the trash. "It's a whole different vibration. You know. When you meditate." She said, licking her fingers as she sauntered over to sit with Greer. "Positive spirits who're living in the light are way up on a higher plane. They've got *God's* power. They only need a boost when you're asking them to help you. Negative spirits are dwelling in darkness and skulking about on a low plane. They got hardly any energy of their own, so they got to suck it from the life around them."

A feeling of disgust washed over Greer. "You're saying I summoned a leech?"

April shrugged. "Basically."

"Well. It needs to be gone before Robert gets home."

"Got any sage?"

"No, definitely not. So that's real? Incense and all helps?"

"Nah, not really. It just don't hurt neither." April started dragging the coffee table out of the way. Greer jumped up to help.

"You got salt though, right?" At Greer's affirmative nod, April said, "Good. Grab it all."

Greer rummaged in the cabinet, locating the salt. April poured it out in a circle on the living room floor. Recognizing the start of a spirit circle, Greer retrieved the candles and elemental items she'd used earlier. She spaced the candles evenly around the circle while April poured more salt to create a smaller circle inside. Then she plucked the stone, match, cloud picture, and glass of water from the center where Greer had placed them, instead positioning them at four evenly spaced points between the candles around the salt perimeter.

"Why are you doing that?" Greer asked.

"We're going to catch your mazikim inside this bitty circle, and we don't want to give him nothing to draw energy from." April pointed to the small circle. "Hop in."

"What?" Greer asked, incredulous. "You said we're trapping the spirit in there."

April sighed. "We *are*. You're bait."

Greer timidly stepped inside the circle, most definitely feeling like a worm on a giant, ghost hook.

"Now what?"

"We wait," April answered in her sing-song voice.

. . .

Greer shifted from foot to foot inside the salt circle which was not much larger than she. "What's a mazikim?" she asked.

"Hebrew for a harmful being like your grumpy visitor."

"So, you think my evil ghost is Jewish?"

"Nah. It doesn't matter what you call them. They're the same in any language."

How much longer? Robert could come home any minute."

April didn't answer but sat in prayer on the floor just outside of the candle circle.

Greer cracked her knuckles and switched to the other foot again. A stray thought troubled her. "Hey, why can't we hear this ghost? He seems to have a lot to say, but I haven't heard a word of it."

"Who knows. They're all different." April put a finger to her lips. "Now shush."

The candles flickered, and the temperature dropped rapidly. Without further warning, the hazy figure materialized in a corner of the room. He immediately zoomed toward Greer, silently snarling unpleasant things.

"Don't move." said April.

Clenching her fists at her side, Greer held her ground. Her heart was racing so that it surely missed a few beats.

The spirit unknowingly entered the circle as he wrapped icy hands around Greer's throat.

"Stay there!" April yelled.

Scrabbling at his hands to pull them away, Greer's fingers felt trapped in a cold ooze—like trying to grasp pudding. Every breath arrived with frozen daggers. She tried to scream, but her throat felt cut to ribbons by the ice. She looked desperately to April for help.

Eyes squinted shut, April raised her hands and hurriedly prayed. At the end of the prayer she shouted, "Get out, now!"

Greer took a big step backward, being careful not to bump the salt line. The spirit squeezed tighter. Remembering a self-defense class she'd taken in high school, in one quick movement she ducked down, spun to her left, and lunged away from the ghost. He lost his hold on her as he came against the salt barrier.

The ghost screamed silently; his face contorted in an unbridled fury.

Rubbing her throat Greer moved behind April and asked, "Now what?"

"Now we finish the prayer." April sorted through the many chains around her neck until she produced a golden cross. She nudged Greer so she could take her hand. Holding the cross in front of her, she called out a new prayer:

In the name of Jesus Christ,

I command all human spirits to be bound to
The confines of the cemetery.
I command all inhuman spirits to go
where Jesus Christ tells you to go,
for it is He who commands you.
AMEN

"AMEN!" Greer echoed. She followed up with an elated shout as the raging phantom rapidly faded to nothing.

April clapped her hands together. "Alrighty, bye."

Greer touched her forearm to stall her. "Hold on, April! That was incredible. Incredibly horrifying, but amazing! You can't just leave."

"It's late. He's gone. What more is there to do?" the girl said, whining.

"Well, for starters you can explain what just happened. Why did he leave?"

April pulled a face that indicated her estimation of Greer's IQ had just dropped a few points. "Because we asked him to."

Greer waved her hands for April to stop. "Whoa. Hold up." She rubbed her throat again. It felt raw inside and out. "God, I need a drink."

April set her hands on her hips, cocking her head she spoke as if to a child, "We snagged him then asked him to get out with St. Michael's prayer. It's standard stuff. Even *you'll* learn it."

"Gee, thanks."

They heard a key at the door. The candles and salt were still all over the floor. Greer panicked. "Hurry!" she whispered loudly.

When Robert walked in he found April clutching candles to her chest while Greer deposited an odd assortment of objects onto the counter. With big eyes, Greer took a swig of water from the glass in her hand before setting it down beside the other elementals.

"Hi, honey," Greer said casually before choking on the half-swallowed water.

Robert looked past her to the salt on the floor. "What, the hell?" he stammered. He was always a man of few words.

"Um, we were just doing some research," said Greer.

"Later," April called as she slipped out the door.

Robert stood staring as Greer grabbed the broom and began sweeping. She sorted through possible explanations as she attacked the salt.

He narrowed his eyes at her. "Ready to tell me what's going on?"

"I don't know what you mean. I told you we were doing some research."

"You've always thought of me as a jock, but you know I'm not stupid."

"Of course, you're not stupid, Robert." She fell into the nearest chair. "It was just ... just girl stuff. A lark. I was humoring April." Her hands were busy with her hair, twirling and tying it into a loose knot. "So, how was your night out with the guys?"

Robert shook his head. "No. Don't redirect. Tell me. What's going on with you?

Her stomach dropped. This was it. Taking a deep breath, she hoped for the best and began.

Ministering Spirits

Greer dressed just after dawn and slipped out of the apartment before Robert could wake. When the car failed to start, she decided to walk all the way to Adam's house, providing lots of time to think.

A sleepy-eyed, half-dressed Adam answered her knock. "Come on," he said through a cavernous yawn.

She offered him the extra latte she'd picked up at a nearby cafe, anticipating the need for a peace offering to whoever she roused this early on a Sunday morning. He accepted it with a mumble before leading her into the kitchen where she made herself at home, dropping her bag and hopping up to sit on the table. Lifting the coffee to her nose, allowing the aroma to fill her senses, Greer breathed in, and contentedly relaxed her shoulders. She studied the man in front of her and realized she had imagined correctly; his unruly curls looked the same fresh out of bed as they did after a day of digging.

"Really, I shouldn't have come this early." She caught herself staring as Adam sleepily scratched his bare chest, but she was reluctant to avert her gaze. "I just couldn't face Robert this morning."

Adam took a slow slurp of coffee. "April filled me in last night. I take it you finally told your fiancé, and he was not very understanding?"

"Ha! That's an understatement." She began pacing the kitchen, her emotions bubbling over. "He looked at me like I had two heads when I told him about my new talent, as you call it. When I tried to explain the danger I've been facing, the hounds and visions, he acted like I was purposefully trying to ruin his life! He didn't listen at all."

Adam leaned against the kitchen counter in his cotton pajama pants, waiting out her tantrum.

"I don't know what to say to him. He thinks I'm crazy or that I've joined some cult. He certainly doesn't like you or the fact that I'm working with you," she said waving a hand at Adam. "He told me to quit the dig! Can you believe it?" Her hands flew to her hips, face flushed with anger.

Adam took a bigger swig of coffee. "Unfortunately, these are fairly common responses from family members."

This did nothing to calm her mood. "I don't know what to do. He said he doesn't want to hear another word and that I'd better not see you or April again." She grew even more frustrated as she realized she had to fight back tears.

"It will take time. Remember your own resistance to these truths? And you were experiencing them first-hand."

Greer stopped pacing and considered Adam who was being calm and understanding, even though she'd just interrupted his sleep and bellowed at him in his own house. Losing a little steam, her anger was displaced by an ache.

"Robert doesn't understand that I can't handle this myself. He doesn't even believe there's something to be handled. But look at the mess I made yesterday." The tension of the past few weeks and last night's fight with Robert boiled over and tears filled the corners of her eyes. She hugged herself tightly trying to regain control.

Adam set his cup down to place a hand on each of her arms, rubbing gently, steadying her. Greer stiffened and balled her hands into fists. "Damn it!" she said fiercely. "I need to pull it together. This isn't your problem."

Adam pulled her close, enfolding her. "But it *is* my problem." Greer's arms were still crossed between them, but she let herself be embraced. "I am responsible for you now," he said with a quiet sense of resolution.

She pressed her cheek to his chest, focusing on the touch as she slowed her breathing and banished the tears before they could fall. He smelled like warm, growing things. Curious, she tipped her head back to meet his gaze. When a soft hiccup escaped her, she felt the chuckle as it began its slow rumble up from his belly.

"Thank you," she whispered.

"You are more than welcome." He worked to stifle a yawn even as he smiled down at her. "It has been a tough morning, ayuh? Let me cook you some breakfast."

Greer put a hand up, stopping him. "Wait. I woke you up early and basically cried on your shoulder. I'm not a good cook, but, please, let me apologize with some scrambled eggs." She realized her hand was resting on his very exposed skin and began to extricate herself from his hold.

He let go slowly. "I will never say no to someone who wants to feed me."

Greer was beginning to learn her way around his kitchen, so, as he sipped coffee, she prepared a quick breakfast of eggs and toast. After refilling their cups, she slid into the seat across from him and they ate in companionable silence.

Adam was scooping the last of the eggs from his plate, and Greer was brewing a second pot of coffee at the counter, when the back door opened. Cahya stood in the doorway. She was wearing torn jeans, dark circles under her eyes, and a look that could kill.

"Why am I always finding you two in compromising positions?" she asked sharply, staring pointedly at Adam's bare torso.

"Morning." Adam called over his shoulder before turning back to finish his plate.

While he'd failed to notice anything amiss, Greer had a front row seat to Cahya's indignation. "I just made some fresh coffee," Greer said, quickly grabbing the steaming pot before the machine finished dripping. "Can I pour you a cup?"

Greer cringed as Cahya stomped through the room and slammed her way through the hall door.

Adam looked up sharply. "What is her problem?"

Greer silently refreshed his cup, knowing he'd find out on his own soon enough.

. . .

Once April was awake, the three of them sat down to draw up a plan. Obviously, Greer still needed a spirit guide so they would try summoning again with Cahya's help. That meant April had to spend the afternoon honing Greer's meditation and channeling skills. Adam would take over in the evening, teaching her how to defend against evil spirits. He also wanted a family meeting to see what information everyone had gathered during their own investigations around the city.

The incense was overpowering in April's room. When Greer complained, April told her to quit being a baby and focus already. Unfortunately, Greer had an exceedingly difficult time calming her mind.

The first soul they spoke with was an old woman who'd died peacefully in her sleep. She slowly, but coherently, answered Greer's questions about the afterlife. Yes, there was a white light and yes, she felt surrounded by love after she passed into it. They asked her about any negative spirits or even demons that might be attached to Greer. The lady said she could sense darkness nearby but couldn't provide any helpful details. Turns out she'd just been passing by when the girls called and thought it'd be nice to chat. Her sweet, toothless smile was the last thing to fade when she departed.

"Too bad she couldn't say no more about the darkness she was feeling," said April.

Excited, Greer leaned forward. "Did you hear what she said about walking through a meadow to a beautiful white light? It's so cliché, I know. But a real ghost just told me it's true! It's incredible!" She glanced thoughtfully at the middle of their spirit circle. "We should properly document all of this."

A middle-aged man who died of cancer materialized next. He had little to say about his own life. April claimed that spirits often generalize their life experiences during these discussions, acting rather detached, as if the events happened to someone else.

The man did have a name. He was known as Curtis Moore during his earth-bound days; however, he couldn't recall if there were any more Moores around who might be missing him. He seemed free of worry for the people he'd left behind.

Curtis had a similar story of approaching a light through a beautiful valley with a crystal-clear river. After a few probing questions, they found he was rather in-tune with other spiritual activities in the area. He could see an actual black void hovering on the edge of his vision whenever he looked at Greer, but said the darkness stayed just outside of his own light. Curtis warned the girls it seemed powerful and he urged them to seek God's intercession right away. They thanked him as he hurried away.

April huffed in frustration. "Let me think awhile," she said dismissing Greer with a wave of her shawl. Closing her eyes, she settled into her usual meditative pose.

Welcoming the break, Greer stood and stretched, her back cracking and popping. They'd been sitting still on the floor for hours. Pulling back the assorted layers of fabric that stood in for curtains around the grimy window, she looked down on the street. It was a sunny afternoon, and everyone was out running errands after church.

As a scientist, Greer was struck by the similarities she'd heard in the death experiences this afternoon. As someone who'd considered herself an atheist, or at least a healthy agnostic prior to meeting Adam and his family, she was trying to process the implications of a true afterlife. Did it mean she'd see her mother again? Many well-intentioned mourners had assured her that she would. The spirits today were disappointing in their lack of concern for their living friends and family. They hardly even remembered them. Would her mother recognize her if they met now? Could she call upon her in the sacred circle? She imagined her mother happy and free from regret, living in the loving light which the elderly woman and Curtis had described. It didn't seem fair to impose upon whatever peace her mother may have found in her death.

The door opened. Greer turned away from the window to see Cahya stalk into the room. Her chest was emblazoned with a skull and roses. Without a word she sat down by April in the circle and motioned sharply to Greer to join them.

With a sigh, Greer parked her tired rear end on the hard floor once more. She clasped the offered hands and worked to match their melodic hums. It was easier to slip into the meditation now after so many hours of practice. She was rather bored actually. Her mind was like a tranquil pond—a few thoughts lazily swam in the depths, but the surface was unbroken.

Deep in thought, Greer was not prepared for the strength of the new vibrations that hit her. Perhaps having a third person in the circle amplified it? Or maybe Cahya herself held a stronger power than April? Every hair seemed to stand on end as electric shock waves rippled through her, building and building until it became a real effort to breathe deeply. She barely managed to whisper along with the other women as they began the prayer for guidance. Every cell prickled with energy on the edge of being painful. The pain sharpened then abruptly stopped.

Greer heard a solitary, enchanting tone.

Her eyes flew open. A brilliant pinpoint of light, like the one that had appeared the other night hovered in the circle. Cahya and April still each held her hands, and their eyes remained closed as they continued the prayer. April's guide, Sonny, had joined them at some point, hovering behind her inside the circle. His eyes were closed too.

They carried on, oblivious to the lovely sound that emanated from the light. It was unlike anything Greer had ever heard—a single exquisite musical tone with all the complexity and beauty of a symphony condensed into one perfect note. It intensified, filling her heart and mind, pushing everything else aside.

She heard no words but felt a presence. Thoughts of love, comfort, and support flooded through her.

"Thank you," Greer said to the light just before it blinked out again.

The others halted mid-prayer and opened their eyes.

"What did you see?" Cahya asked intently. Greer realized it was the first time the woman had spoken to her civilly.

"It was beautiful," said Greer, feeling as if maybe it'd been a dream.

"I didn't see nothing," said April, complaining.

"It was like the light we saw before, April. Only it stayed longer this time. And it ... sang."

"Sang?" April's long face pulled into a frown. "Did you know you're grinning like an idiot?" April pulled her shawl tightly around her shoulders, hunching over in a funk.

"Am I?" Greer looked around the circle feeling completely and genuinely happy for the first time since, well, probably since her mother's death.

Cahya folded her arms. A look of concern replaced her usual one of annoyance whenever Greer was around. "Your guide has shown itself after all."

"But we didn't see nothing!" April whined again.

Cahya said, "This guide isn't an ordinary soul; you've bagged an angel. And you're lucky to have such a powerful ally. You're going to need it."

April pouted. "I don't know about angels as spirit guides. Sonny, how's it work?"

Sonny shook his head, stumped. He flashed a peace sign as he faded out.

Cahya spoke in a clipped tone, "Unfortunately, you can't summon this angel like any normal spirit guide. It's only going to show up when you're in the greatest need." Cahya gracefully unfolded her legs and stood. She flashed a skeptical look on her way out. "April, she has to learn to rely on herself as much as possible."

The girl looked to Greer, sizing her up with a dramatic squint of her eyes. "Oh, would you stop smiling!" April said as she threw a pillow at Greer's head.

Catching it before it landed, Greer couldn't help but laugh in disbelief. "Sorry, but it was an *angel*."

April huffed in exasperation as she started cleaning up the circle. "What a pain. Now you won't have no day-to-day help, only in emergencies." She stopped and pointed an accusing finger at Greer. "You're going to have to work lots harder."

"It's ok, I can handle it." Greer beamed. "I think."

. . .

The family sat together in the crowded living room. Sam, with his perpetual cartoons, was greeted and then forgotten as they caught up with each other. Everyone had answered Adam's summons except for the pyro guy. Greer couldn't remember his name again, but imagined he was playing with matches at some strip club, uninterested in her personal problems.

"Thank you all for coming," Adam said rather formally. "Each of you has been keeping a close eye around town for unusual activity. I had time to chat with Frankie and Tony; however, we have all been so busy I thought it best for everyone to hear a full report."

He filled them in on the afternoon's angel surprise. His mother agreed this was a great honor even if it didn't help with Greer's everyday challenges. In a show of support, Mother Rose planned to add additional prayers for Greer to her daily devotions.

Frankie, the mind reader, reported no uptick in murderous or psychotic thoughts in town. Frankie had nothing relevant to share but had successfully rearranged benches in a nearby skate park.

Cahya had been openly agitated, tapping her boot heel on the hard floor in a staccato beat, while the others talked. At the end of Frankie's glib description of her day, Cahya interjected in a full roar.

"While you've all been out playing, I've been busting my *ass* every night!" Angrily stabbing her finger in the air at each point, she continued her rebuke. "I've searched every back alley and abandoned building for demons, hounds, and God knows what! But it's great that you're all having fun."

"Cahya, we all know how hard you are working," Adam said raising a hand to calm her. "Please. Tell everyone what you found." He gave an apologetic yet encouraging smile.

She ignored him, addressing the rest of the room in a patronizing tone. "You all might like to know I found several homeless guys who saw the hellhounds during Greer and Adam's little chase the other week. One this afternoon swears he smelled them several times near the church dig since then."

Adam said, "Great work ..."

Cahya cut him off, shooting him a dark look as she carried on. "*And*, I found two cases of potential demonic possession in the West End." At this she strutted back to lean against the door frame once more, arms crossed. A scowl marred her striking features.

Adam was taken aback. He sat quietly thinking for a moment, running a hand through his dark hair.

Mother Rose assumed control. "This is important news. Unfortunate, but not surprising. We need to learn more about the demonic possessions. Frankie and April should go meet these people, discover the truth behind their stories. Then we'll make a plan to help them."

"And we need to know how they might be connected to Greer," Adam said after regaining his composure.

Cahya turned sharply on her heels and slammed the front door on her way out.

A Light on My Path

After the family went their separate ways for the evening, Adam crooked a finger at Greer, inviting her across the hall to his room. One corner of the room held a large antique desk overflowing with books, papers, and still more religious paraphernalia. He took a seat in the matching swivel chair in front of it, shuffled through the mess then pulled some items from the drawers.

"Take a look at these," he said. "We need to beef up your everyday protection."

Surveying the religious charms scattered on the desk, Greer poked at a few, uncertain.

"Are these magic or something? We really need something for the work site. If I can't dig, I'm useless to you there. Not to mention I'll have to choose another career." Worry fell over her. She refused to consider a new life path.

He hummed in agreement as he rubbed his chin in thought, hand rasping against the growing stubble. He squinted then swept all the objects back into a corner of the desk.

"It is time for something a lot stronger than that little pendant around your neck."

"How many charms do you expect me to wear? I noticed April sporting at least a dozen on any given day."

He leaned back, laughing loudly. "She does like to be prepared." Cocking his head, he studied Greer intently. "And, in your case, her method may be wise. However, there are a few alternatives to consider first." Pulling a book from the mess before him, he flipped it open and pointed to a page which held over a dozen diagrams of amulets and religious symbols.

There were a few icons she'd never encountered. "What's this one?" she asked pointing to a drawing that looked like a snowflake.

"That is the Helm of Awe. It was used for protection in the Nordics well before Viking times. It was also said to cause delusion and fear in one's enemies."

"Sounds like fun," she said with a slight grimace. "It actually looks rather innocuous."

"Also ineffective."

Greer's raised eyebrows encouraged him to elaborate. He easily fell into the role of professor. "This charm is incredibly old. While that usually bolsters the strength of an icon, this one fell out of use long ago. So, the Vikings, or their descendants, must have considered it useless or found something that worked better. They were a results-driven people."

"Good point." Greer tapped a finger to her lips, considering the other images. "So, if I'm following your thinking correctly, we want to look for symbols that are ancient and, most importantly, still in use. They'll have stood the test of time." She reached over his shoulder to point to several of the drawings. "We can rule out these Celtic and alchemy icons as well as all Nordic runes. No one uses them anymore except for small cults. And, let's be honest, no one employs the Ankh or Eye of Horus for scared purposes these days."

"True. They are only used today by bored teens as tattoo designs."

Greer bent closer, studying the page. "Aren't we only left with icons from contemporary, mainstream religions?" Pointing, she identified each as she named them, "The Christian cross, the Jewish Star of David, etcetera?"

"Basically, yes."

"Then how does that help us?" Exasperated, she rubbed at her temples. None of this was easy.

"Hold on. Have a seat." He guided her to the bed. Greer perched on the edge, watching as he arranged several rows of papers across the blanket. He fastidiously straightened the last row before continuing the lecture. "The basic history of every major religion is roughly outlined here, one religion in each column. Some are older than others, and some are more geographically widespread. But all of them are over 1,000 years old and considered a legitimate shared belief system.

"Now each system has an origin story, a revered prophet, and a penultimate goal of happiness and enlightenment. That happy place looks a little different for each of them, and they all have varied ways of getting there. However, I think you will agree these are all simply different paths leading to the same destination."

"Yes. I've read this theory many times. The similarities of each religion are truly striking. But it's still considered an extremely controversial idea."

"But why is it controversial?" Adam's eyes lit up.

With a smirk, she answered. "Well, no one wants to admit they're wrong. Especially for fear they won't achieve their happy ending." Greer was enjoying playing student to his teacher.

"Exactly! So, it is up to academics such as us to point out the obvious. Still, we get no thanks for it," he said with a sigh.

Greer laughed. "No, we absolutely don't. I'm sure there are a few priests down the street who'd prefer you convert to another religion before you shared such ideas at mass."

With a hand to his heart, Adam said, "I am a good Catholic boy. I truly am." He pointed again to the collection of documents. "But I cannot deny the truth I see in front of me."

"Adam, if each religion has a unique path to the same truth, which path will best help me?"

He ran a hand through his hair and scrubbed at the back of his head roughly. "Good question. And one I've been struggling with all day."

She raised her palms in question. "And?"

"I have no idea," he said with a shake of his head. "However, I believe the most powerful answer will come from whichever path you select for yourself. I decided I cannot choose for you."

"You're a big help."

He shrugged, somehow looking lost and excited at the same time as he studied her and the decision before them.

She surveyed the names in front of her: Taoism, Islam, Judaism, Buddhism, Christianity and Hinduism. They were familiar to her in the way that the world's empires were familiar. Each had been studied extensively in school in terms of important facts, dates, and theories which impacted people and places.

"I'm not on any of these paths," she said, her chest tight with a growing sense of anxiety.

"I understand that it feels overwhelming that I am asking you to choose one now."

"You could say that." Her tone was sarcastic, but then she softened into a gentle smile. "My parents were officially Christian. They even baptized me when I was a baby. We went to church on Christmas and Easter. Sometimes. I learned the stories, but they were just that, stories. I didn't believe any of them."

"Well, we could consider those your first steps on the road to Christianity. A tepid start." He sighed. "I hope it is enough to keep you going." He scooped the documents into a tidy stack to drop on the desk then scooped up a book before sitting down beside her again.

"Christianity is full of rich symbolism. With its long history and numerous sects, it has more icons than any other modern religion." He flipped the book open and thumbed to a section with dozens of diagrams. "Just the variation in crosses alone is enough to base a whole doctorate on." He flipped by a few more pages. "There are symbols for each of the hundred or so well-known saints." He raised one brow, putting on a slightly skeptical look," Did you know the Catholics now count over 10,000 official saints?" With a small shake of disbelief, he turned a few more pages before he continued. "Then you have the fish, the Chi Rho, the anchor ..."

She touched his hand, stopping him. "Hold on. They're too many. How can I possibly pick one?"

"Here is my thought." He brushed a stray lock of hair from her cheek. Reflexively, Greer turned to meet his hand. "Yet it must be your decision," he said, catching and holding her gaze. "Since your guide is an angel, I believe you would be wise to reinforce that connection."

Instinct told her he was right. It made perfect sense. Just rolling the idea around in her mind felt reassuring.

"Yeah." She straightened. "How do we do that, exactly?"

"Alright. We need another book." He rummaged around the voluminous desk, bringing back another aging volume. "Each major religion includes angel folklore. There are plenty of ancient stories and drawings that date prior to Christianity. However, since you want to focus on a Christian path, we will review the specific lore outlined there." Adam found a page beautifully illustrated with toga-clad angels stacked in literal tiers, one upon the other. "There are three primary hierarchies: Counselors, Governors, and Messengers. Each of those has three ranks for a total of nine orders. The Counselors are dedicated to God and do not seem to intervene in human affairs. Now, in the Governors category, we find the Powers rank. The Powers can be very helpful as they are protectors—fighters of demons and other evils. However, it is said they also avoid interacting with humans. What you really want is the last hierarchy which includes the Archangels. They have swords and armor which they use to protect the innocent and the just."

"That sounds promising. Do you think one of them is my guide?"

"Possibly. But I must be honest, this is rather new territory for me. For all of us."

Greer lifted the book from his lap. "Michael is one of the archangels, right?" She began reading through the descriptions. "There are four, or seven archangels, depending on the teaching. Should I select one angel in particular? That seems rather presumptuous."

"If your guide is any indication, it would not be easy to call on a specific angel. Although praying to Michael is quite popular. Instead of trying to focus on one angel, maybe we can find a way for you to call on their collective power."

He retrieved a small, antique box from a desk drawer, its lid decorated with a delicate, filigree cross. Adam placed it carefully between them and murmured a quiet prayer as he opened the lid. Inside was a jumble of tokens and amulets. Unique fertility symbols, crosses, and more tumbled around the box as Adam used a finger to stir through the contents.

He drew something out and held it up for Greer to see. "This one I think," he said approvingly.

Greer cupped her hand under the small pendant, and he dropped it into her waiting palm. It was a petite pair of angel wings, so meticulously worked in gold that each feather looked silky soft, ready to fly away.

"It's incredible," she said breathlessly.

"I knew it was special when I discovered it and have been holding onto it for some time."

"Where did you get all of these?" She nudged through the box's contents.

"Here and there. Some were gifts. Some I found. Some were left behind."

She saw his eyes slide out of focus and knew he was reliving memories too painful to forget. Like the image of his poor Sarah, ravaged by hounds. Trying to recall him back to the present, she said, "So, I just put this on, and we're done?"

Adam roused at her question. "Now, you know it is not that easy." Reaching under his collar, he withdrew his own amulet. "You witnessed some of the power I can channel with this."

"You're not kidding." Greer reached for the blue stone, hesitated. "May I?" He nodded and she pulled it closer. He'd used it twice to help her, yet she'd really only seen it when it was a glowing ball of light.

The talisman was a heavy, perfectly round stone about two inches in diameter and less than a half-inch thick at its center, tapering to half of that again at the edge. The incising was primal—a large circle with a small circle in the middle.

"An ancient symbol for the sun," she said knowingly. "This cast a silver light when you used it but it's actually blue now." A thought bloomed. She asked excitedly, "Is this bluestone? As in the same bluestone found at Stonehenge?"

"I believe so, but I have never met a geologist I trusted enough to take a look at it for me."

"Wow! This is fantastic!" She flipped it around, finding the back of the stone blank. "So how does it glow?" she asked, perplexed.

Adam wrapped his hand around hers. "The light comes when I pray for help such as saying the Lord's Prayer. I choose to say it in Latin because I believe the language's age is beneficial. I should probably recite it in Aramaic, come to think of it. But English may do just as well." He paused. "I just realized I should do a test to compare the efficacy of the three."

"According to April, the object's potency all depends on your intent, right?" She looked from the charm to his blue eyes, comparing them to the stone.

"Ayuh. Intent is critical."

He returned her gaze. Greer noticed a faint glow starting to peek from between their fingers. They both instantly let go. Adam turned the amulet over and over. It was a dull bluestone again. "That was odd," he said, a look of mild concern crossed his face.

She removed her necklace and slid the angel wing pendant on next to the little Hand of Fatima. Fastening the chain at the nape of her neck, she asked tentatively, "How do we turn mine on?"

Adam glanced at the clock and sighed. "It is late."

Greer was feeling bold as well as curious. "Come on, let's get it done now. I don't want to get home until after Robert is asleep anyway. I have no idea what to say to him right now."

"Alright." He considered the room around them. "This should actually be done in a church if we were doing it properly, but we will have to make do. Go borrow some candles from April."

Greer returned to find Adam placing a small gold cross, a Phi Rho pendant, a porcelain angel figurine, and a beautifully carved wooden dove inside a small circle on the floor.

"Place and light the candles, please."

Once they were seated inside the light of the circle, he pointed to Greer's new angel wings. "Hold the pendant between both hands, as in prayer." She complied, and he placed his hands on either side of hers. "Begin with quiet focus on your goal. Clear your mind of all thoughts except your desire to connect to the angels. You can think about the nine orders we talked about or just angels in general. Then I will lead you in a special prayer. Just follow along until you internalize it."

Greer took a deep breath then nodded for him to begin.

Whether it was the hours of meditation she'd done that morning or the reassurance of Adam holding her, she found it easy to focus now. At first, she systematically reviewed the orders of angels, the number of wings each type possessed, the roles they played. However, she was soon thinking a singular thought—wishing to witness an angel's protective light.

This was when Adam began to chant:
Eee Nu Rah
Eee Nu Rah
Eee Nu Rah
Zay

He repeated this slowly as she tried to follow along. She picked it up quickly, maintaining concentration on the gold wings they clasped together. They continued the mantra, over and over. Greer didn't tire; she felt relaxed and peaceful.

There was a tug and their tempo increased. Greer felt the power they held. It swelled, drawing them to their knees, still chanting.

Suddenly, Greer heard the same exquisite sound as when her guardian angel appeared. Her eyes flew open and she found Adam staring intensely back. A muted golden glow emanated from their clasped hands. They sped up the cadence of the prayer again until they were unable to go any faster, all the while watching the light shimmer between them.

They continued the prayer unbroken, speaking and breathing in perfect rhythm. As the glow brightened under their fingertips, Greer leaned in; seeking what lived in the light. Adam, mesmerized, bent nearer until they were face to face, bathed in the illumination of the other-world. Their lips touched in a soft kiss, their breaths flowing between them. The unearthly music filled her ears as the radiance of the light filled her vision. Her perceptions were heightened until she was acutely aware of Adam's calm heart, his strength, and his own amazement. It was sensory overload, yet she wanted more. She hungrily deepened the kiss. The music soared for a brief moment before the golden light flared and went out.

They slowly parted and locked eyes. Greer opened their hands to look at the pendant. It held their warmth, but it now only offered an ordinary, earthly gleam.

The bedroom door banged open to reveal Sam, standing in his Superman pajamas with a look of sheer terror plastered across his face. "He's coming!"

Sam immediately returned to his worn couch cushion. Greer and Adam followed him out begging him to elaborate but he refused to respond. They watched him sit stone-faced, a brightly colored gargoyle.

Adam ran a hand through his curls with a shrug. Greer relaxed once she realized he wasn't alarmed. Still, she had a nagging feeling that Sam's outburst meant more than Adam was letting on.

She hesitated to ask for a favor but had little choice. "Um, do you think you could give me a ride home?"

"Of course!" He looked glad of something to do. "I certainly cannot let you walk home alone."

They were quiet in the car, even as Greer's mind buzzed. So much had happened in a single day, and none of it could be shared with Robert. She felt ready to burst with the need to talk about it with someone. "What did that strange prayer mean, anyway?" she finally asked in a rush.

"Huh?" She'd obviously interrupted Adam's own train of thought. "Oh. Eee Nu Rah ..."

"Yes, that. It isn't Latin."

"No, it is much, much older. Its origin is unknown, but many claim it is a proven invocation to the angels. It basically means I bring all of myself, body and soul, into the company of Angels."

"Well, it certainly seemed to make a connection. Do you think it kind of linked my tiny wings with them? Like a dedicated phone line to the angels?"

"Ayuh. Hopefully. We will test it in the morning, at the dig."

She noticed his accent always became thicker when he was tired. Exhaustion was likely to hit her soon too, but at the moment her thoughts were still tripping over each other, keeping her wide awake.

"Is it always that intense when you use your talisman?"

Adam glanced over out of the corner of his eye.

She went on, "I mean, it was rather overwhelming. The music, the light. I really felt pulled into something incredible."

"Music?" He asked puzzled. When she didn't clarify, he went on, "You will get used to the experience; however, I admit that was unusually ...intense." He was quiet for a second while he flipped the signal and turned the corner. "I did not mean to kiss you," he said, clearly troubled.

Averting her eyes, she tried to project indifference. "No problem. I'm sure we were influenced by the magic of the moment." Greer groaned inwardly at her poor choice of words.

"Not magic. This is real, Greer."

"Yeah. I meant, the chanting, glowing, and ... stuff."

Adam looked sideways at her again, smiling a little sadly. "Well, it should not have happened, ayuh?"

She shut up and watched the streets roll by knowing the ease between them had been strained. The kiss was certainly a problem since they were both otherwise committed. So why did she feel disappointed at his apology?

When he dropped her in front of her building, she promised to be early to the dig the next morning. After a perfunctory wave he pulled away.

Greer snuck into the apartment as quietly as possible then crept down the hall and into bed. Robert didn't budge.

For in Truth

The next morning Greer's car still wouldn't start. She begged a quart of oil from the building's superintendent who was rather irritable until she promised to bring him cookies in return for this favor. Persuaded, he topped off the oil himself and tipped his cap as she got under way bright and early as planned. Robert's alarm, she realized thankfully, was just going off as she left.

Her mind was a jumble of concerns—Adam, their kiss, and, most importantly, how effective her new wings would be at the dig. She arrived first, eager to give it a try. Since it was dangerous to go it alone, she counted the minutes until Adam's arrival.

"Good morning!" She met him halfway, talking excitedly. "Are you ready to try out my charm?" Thoughts of the kiss had faded, replaced by anticipation and the worry of experiencing bad reactions to the dig.

"Yes, of course," he said, uninspired. "Let me just finish this coffee?"

She felt selfish when she noticed the dark smudges under his eyes.

"I kept you up too late," she said.

"No, you were fine. Cahya and I had an argument after I dropped you off."

"Oh." She bit at her lip, waiting, but he didn't say more.

She stared at his coffee longingly. "I was in such a hurry this morning that I forgot to get my latte."

"Here," he said handing her his cup. "Finish this one. I am not sure any of us can handle you decaffeinated."

"Hey!" she said with an air of indignation then stopped. "Actually, that's fair." She gulped the remaining coffee greedily. "Thank you."

Adam tossed a crowbar over his shoulder and led the way to the trap door. She moved the pulley system off the door so he could lift it.

"What did I miss around here on Friday? Fill me in on all the details."

"Well ..." He paused to carefully lower the ladder down. "Well, we found four individual burials."

"Four?" She was shocked and did nothing to hide her aggravation. "And you didn't think to mention this all weekend long?"

He halted part way down the ladder and addressed her bluntly. "You had more important things to worry about."

She sighed heavily because she knew he was right. Again. She would've pestered him with a million questions all weekend instead of learning. Those questions were forming now as she made her way to the dirt floor below. It was cool, sending a shiver through her.

The four shallow graves were randomly located but oriented in the same direction. Adam explained that each skeleton was somewhat incomplete. Greer gave a cursory inspection of each.

"This one's missing a femur. Several ribs over here. That one's misplaced her right foot, and that one is very obviously missing its skull," she said, pointing at the grave furthest away.

"It is rather curious, right? Before you do a thorough examination, we need to test the protection of your pendant." When he saw her bend close to the bones, lost in thought, he added, "Before the kids get here, right?"

"Yeah, let's do it." She cracked her knuckles. "You told me I should start each day with a new prayer, right?" At his nod she grasped the winged pendant and said, "All you holy angels and archangels, praise the Lord forever. Amen."

"Good. Give it a try," he said, pointing to the nearest body.

Greer knelt, her knees making depressions in the damp earth. She started to reach for the skull in front of her then quickly recoiled. "I'm being an idiot. I'm nervous," she said, staring at the bones before her. By the size and shape of the eye ridges she guessed it once belonged to a young Caucasian woman. Like herself, she thought. She should be bolder, but memories of the pain and bloody images she saw before slowed her hand.

"I am here with you," said Adam as he stood on the other side of the grave, hands clasped.

Reassured, Greer took a deep breath and brushed her fingers across the exposed skull. She glanced up at Adam who was tensed, ready to spring forward and pull her away. That gave her courage. She rested both open palms on the bone and felt nothing. Not even a twinge of pain. Her mind was blissfully free of horrific images of death.

She beamed up at Adam. "It works!"

His shoulders relaxed, and she heard him say 'Amen'.

"Thank God, truly. This is a good start. However, you do understand that you require more training, right?"

"Hello, down there!" Rigsby called from the top of the ladder. "Are you ready to give us our assignments for the day, professor?"

"Yes, I will be right up," Adam called back. He scanned the graves. "I know you want to review each of these in detail. Liz will be down with my notes so you can add your findings."

She didn't hear him as she was already leaning over the first skeleton with a small brush and magnifying glass, completely absorbed in this new find.

Greer spent the entire day in Room A, skipping lunch. With painstaking scrutiny, she'd been able to add a few notes about each skeleton. Previous wounds that had healed, the possible methods with which the missing bones may have been extracted, and the manner in which each body had been posed in the grave were all details that could help them decipher what had happened here.

She was able to touch every single bone without suffering any negative reactions. In fact, she experienced nothing. The connection she usually felt, her intuition about the life of the long-gone, was absent. The implication nagged at her.

Liz worked with her throughout the day. The girl was fascinated by the new bodies, positing multiple theories about the missing pieces. Greer was excited to have the student finally engaged as she taught her how to read the bones.

Alone at the end of the day, Greer sat against the rough stone wall surveying the room, trying to let all the puzzle pieces it presented resolve themselves into a coherent image. She played a variety of scenarios out in her mind. So far, the facts of this dig didn't match any historical pattern.

Adam came down the ladder and folded himself into a seat alongside her.

"It just isn't making sense," she said, arguing with herself. "There never should've been one grave under a rectory, much less five. The unusual state of each body is not normal for Catholic burials. What the heck happened down here?"

"Your previous visions are likely clues to what happened. I am afraid this room was used for some very unchristian purposes."

She grimaced. "Do you really believe that my vision was true? That would make this some kind of torture chamber."

"It is hard to imagine what else would explain both what you saw and the bodies before us. We need to figure out the who and why before we give our final report to the powers that be." Tilting his head back against the wall, he surveyed the room with lidded eyes. "The church is not going to be happy about any of this."

Greer studied the room again, hands on her hips. "Maybe I should go back to the city archives then," she said.

"Might not be a bad idea." He pushed away from the wall. "Time to go. The kids already left for the night."

She gathered her tools into a bucket and carried it over. He took the handle from her. "Here, let me. That leg is still healing, right?"

"It's feeling pretty good actually. Hey, did you give the kids the day off tomorrow?"

Adam started up the ladder. "Of course. Only a monster would make them work on Independence Day. You are not going to be here, are you?"

"No," she said as she arrived top side. "We have plans with my dad. Well, I guess I have plans with him now. I'm fairly certain Robert won't be joining us."

"Sorry to hear it." He pointed to the pulley. "Will you get that, please?"

She moved the tripod into place after he carefully lowered the trap door. Then they both pulled tarps over the area and weighted them down with sandbags.

"You should come over tonight to do some training." He hastily added, "With April."

She shouldered her bag and gazed down at her boot as she scuffed at the grass, hoping he couldn't read her disappointment. "Sure. It's not like I'm rushing home tonight."

He stared at a point somewhere behind her. "I will let April know you are coming." She saw him tense before he said, "Hello, Father Doyle."

"Good evening. I came to observe your progress." The priest projected eagerness, rocking on his toes, hands clasped behind his back. However, Greer felt he was anxious to be somewhere else.

Adam scooped up the tools and headed for his truck, addressing Doyle offhandedly, "Actually we are done for the night. You will have to come back later."

Greer understood why they couldn't reveal the bones but was still surprised at Adam's dismissal. He'd didn't strike her as one to buck authority; rather his distaste for the priest seemed personal.

"I'll just have a peek around myself then," Father Doyle said in a clipped tone, refusing to be put off from his task.

Adam's tone dropped an octave, "Absolutely not. That would be hazardous. I must insist you wait." He glared at Doyle until the priest returned a scowl and strode off without so much as a goodbye.

Greer was relieved to be rid of the man.

She didn't start her car right away, wanting to give Adam a head start back to the house. It was obvious his fight with Cahya was about Greer, so she'd give him time to warn his girlfriend she was coming over. Better yet, he'd clear the angry woman out of the house entirely. Did she know about their kiss? Adam was such an honest guy that he'd probably told her about it the moment he got home.

Greer couldn't claim to be as forthright. She hadn't shared a single word with Robert last night, let alone confessed to a kiss that may, or may not, have been supernaturally influenced. Touching the wings at her neck, she wondered if she was worthy of their protection.

. . .

Greer had worked with April late enough to avoid Robert again when she got home. Exhausted, she'd slept in the next morning. She could hear her fiancé rummaging in the kitchen now. To avoid the inevitable for just a few more minutes, she took a shower and dressed before venturing out for breakfast.

"Good morning," she said, greeting him as warmly as possible.

He continued to sip his coffee and read the news on his open laptop. Greer poured herself a double cup and stood across the counter from him.

"Did you work late last night too?" She tried to sound sympathetic.

"Of course," he said without looking up.

Encouraged that he'd actually responded, Greer circled the counter and slid onto the stool next to him.

"So, Dad is expecting us for dinner. Are you ready for his famous coleslaw?" She grinned, hoping he would take the bait.

He closed the laptop and twisted to face her. "Depends. Are you done with the dig and those weird people who have you believing in voodoo?"

She inhaled and slowly counted to three. "It isn't voodoo. They're helping me with the ghosts I've been seeing."

"Ghosts. Yeah, that's completely different."

She struggled not to raise her voice. "It is entirely different, and I need you to understand." She reached for his hand. "I know it's not easy to believe. But please ... try to trust me."

Robert withdrew. "Go alone today. We'll talk again tomorrow if your father helps you see some sense."

Suddenly anxious to be gone, Greer shoved a package of toaster pastries into her bag and left. As the car sputtered to life, she punched the radio on and broke open the pastries, trying to enjoy the ride out to her family home on the outskirts of a state park. Her father was currently living in Vermont full time, popping back into Providence for consulting work. They always met back at the house on holidays.

She found the house still brimming with memories—the happy and the heartbreaking. The refreshing waft of pine in the yard and familiar creak of the front porch were an immense comfort today.

"Well, hey Kiddo! You're early." He gave her a huge bear hug. "How're you feeling? I wish you'd called more often. Your eyes still look different, lighter." He continued to jabber as he led her into the kitchen. "No Robert today?"

"No."

"Oh." He hesitated, hearing more in her voice than she'd intended to reveal. "Want to talk about it?"

"No."

"Want some wine?"

"Oh my God, please!" She dramatically fell across the table feigning thirst.

Her father shook his head, laughing as he poured them each a large glass of white wine. Joining her at the table, he pushed one toward her. "We won't tell anyone we're drinking before noon, ok? I have a reputation to uphold."

She wrinkled her nose at him over her glass and drank heavily. They sat and talked about the dig and his book. He asked after her health several times, and each time she assured him there had been no more fainting spells.

They killed the first bottle of wine and were into the second when she declared, "I'm starving! Can we please cook now?"

"I thought you'd never ask."

They bumped about the kitchen in amiable silence. He whipped up his semi-famous coleslaw while she managed to warm up some beans. Then they talked quietly of trivial matters on the back patio while he grilled the burgers. As they ate a leisurely meal in the dappled shade of the patio, they watched birds flit from tree to tree and squirrels dart across the small lawn back into the safety of the surrounding forest.

With a full belly and a warm heart, Greer felt more like herself than she had in weeks, probably since before the accident. It would be nice to hold onto this feeling. Carry it home with her. Maybe she could, but she had a difficult discussion to tackle first.

After one more sip of wine she finally broke the silence. "Dad, I need to tell you something."

"Sure." He watched her from the corner of his eye, knowing too much scrutiny would spook her.

"This is going to sound crazy. You'll think I've hit my head." She held out a hand to stop the comment she knew was coming. "Which I did. I know. But I'm not nuts. You have to believe me."

"I believe you," he said as he carefully set his glass on the table, preparing for what came next.

"Ok. So. Well." She wiggled in her chair. "Oh hell! I can see ghosts, Dad!" He watched her calmly, still listening, so she plowed on. "Admittedly this began after the accident. However, I know I'm not losing my mind because other people have seen them too."

"Who are these people?" he said before tossing back a big gulp of wine.

"Adam, my assistant professor, and his family. They all have talents. That's what they call such supernatural abilities, my ability. Their talents are a little different, but they've faced similar challenges in the past, and now they are helping me."

"And this has been going on since the accident?"

"Yes. Remember my dream about Mom at the hospital? How it felt different? More real? Well, I've seen real ghosts since then. I've talked to them, and I've been chased by them. That part was horrible."

He shifted forward in his chair, leaning in, suddenly tense. "Do you believe you are in danger?"

"A little bit, yeah. Adam and April are training me to protect myself." She paused for a quick swig of wine. "Dad, I honestly couldn't accept any of it at first, but too much has happened. I know I'm not imagining it. And I know I need their help."

He sat back and whistled out a long breath, just staring at the trees until she couldn't stand the silence any longer.

"Well, do you believe me?" she asked anxiously.

"I not only believe you, but I might be able to help explain some of this. Forgive me for not telling you sooner, but I'd hoped you'd never have to know."

Over the course of the next few hours, her father described her mother's secret life. He remembered many of the visions and odd things that happened around her. He shared what he could about how she'd worked to hide them from everyone, everyone except her husband. He couldn't say when or how he came to believe in her abilities, but he couldn't remember a time when he wasn't aware of them. They were simply part of who her mother was, and he loved her unreservedly.

Greer sat back stunned. "Really? Mom experienced all of this too?"

"Well, I know she saw ghosts. Occasionally she'd get a premonition of the future. Sometimes I wonder if she foresaw her death. But that's a lonely line of thinking." He pulled off his glasses and scrubbed the lenses with his shirt tail.

"Did she ever deal with evil spirits or demons?"

"Yes, sometimes. She'd tell me a bad apple had popped up and then she'd leave for a few days. I don't know what she did while she was gone. She just said it was safer for me, and later you too, if she didn't come home until they were gone. You were too young to notice at first. Eventually we started telling you she was taking trips for work."

Greer frowned, searching her memory for those so-called trips. Had she seen anything as a child? Felt anything? Had they all truly been in danger?

When he saw her apprehension, he switched gears. "Most of the ghosts were harmless. There was one; she called him Shakespeare, an actor who appeared to her in full makeup. He was so distraught at dying during the highlight of his career that he pestered her to watch his penultimate performance over and over. It went on for a year. Your mother was so tired of his one-man show of King Lear that she started drinking heavily in the evening to pass out and avoid him."

Greer barked a short laugh. Her mother had always been a creative problem solver.

Pushing his glasses up on his nose, her dad said, "You laugh, but I was getting truly worried about the situation."

Her face fell and she leaned forward, elbows on her knees. "So, you really have no idea about how she managed the bad apples? Did she use prayers? Talismans?"

"Sorry. I really don't know. She said if you started showing signs of similar encounters at puberty then she'd start teaching you. Until then, she wanted you blissfully unaware. I can't tell you how relieved I was when you hit eighteen without any phantom issues."

Uncertain of what else to say, they reverted to staring at the wildlife, each sorting through a private swirl of thoughts.

Would it have been possible for her mother to change her fate? Maybe she saw the place but didn't know the time. Did she even try?

He abruptly leaned forward, started to say something, stopped then finally took her hands in his own. "Do you forgive me?" he asked as tears glinted behind his glasses.

"How can you even ask, Dad? Time passed. If nothing happened, you had nothing to tell me." She surprised them both with a laugh. "Anyway, I'm not sure I would've believed you."

"There's that." He chuckled before growing serious again, "So you say this guy, Adam, is helping you? Do you trust him?"

"Yes," she said without hesitation.

In Smoke, a Fire Sacrifice

Greer wished her mother would visit her dreams that night. She had so many questions. Instead, she slept soundly and awoke disappointed.
Either the alarm never went off or she slept through it, so there wasn't time for a shower if she wanted to arrive before the students. She pulled on her usual jeans and T-shirt, adding a ball cap over her ponytail. The car had difficulty starting again, and she made a mental note to get it into the shop this weekend.

As the streets passed, she found herself zoning out, utterly preoccupied with thoughts of her mother. She'd left her childhood home with a big hug from her dad and a lot to think about.

Pulling up in front of the church, she quickly hopped out to help Adam as he pulled supplies from the back of his truck. "Guess what," she said flatly, still undecided about her feelings on the topic. "My mom had gifts too. Dad just told me yesterday after I got up the nerve to tell him what's been going on."

"I am not surprised," said Adam as he slung some equipment onto his shoulder and headed off toward the trestle table. She hoisted the big fan but almost dropped it as she hurried to catch up.

"You're not?"

He plucked the fan from her grasp. "Not at all. Talents are often hereditary. Were your mother's the same?"

"Dad couldn't remember all of the details, but they sounded similar."

"Well, I am glad you spoke with him. It is really helpful to have an understanding family when dealing with any challenges."

"His support means a lot to me," she said, silently brooding over her unresolved issues with Robert.

"Here come the students. I half expected them to be hung over this morning."

"Who says they aren't?"

Greer started removing the tarps. She could see the one over Room A was already pulled halfway out of position. She cursed under her breath and stomped over. "Adam, someone was messing with the site again!" she shouted.

The door was shut, but the tripod lay broken next to it. She cursed the culprit.

"Damn," he said, agreeing as he strode up next to her and surveyed the damage. "I hope whoever this was did not lose any fingers in the process."

"It would serve them right, but I wouldn't want them to contaminate the site any further."

"Jones and Malcolm," he called as he waved the students over. "Come help clear this up."

Jones. That was the name Greer could never remember. Jones.

"We need to rebuild the tripod. Let me grab some wood from the truck. Please get the rest of the team started on Room B and any cataloging not finished on Monday."

She assigned tasks to the other students while she tossed the splintered wood onto the refuse pile.

They'd all been working diligently for about an hour when the new tripod and pulley system were ready. Greer was prepared to take notes on any damage caused by the vandals.

Adam grasped the iron ring of the door and prepared to pull. "Are you set? Is everyone in order?" Adam asked.

"All except Liz. She hasn't shown up yet," said Greer.

"She is the last one I would have expected to miss a day."

He began lifting the door. Rancid smoke rolled out. Malcolm and Greer stepped back, but Jones and Adam were choking on it by the time the door was fully open. Jones slid the new two-by-four into place to prop the door open.

"Go get the fan and duct work," Greer said to Malcolm as Adam moved away to clear his lungs. Pulling her shirt up over her mouth, she squatted on her heels, risking a peek. Nothing was visible through the thick smoke, so whatever had burned was probably no longer on fire. "I don't see anything. The flames must have smothered when the door closed."

Adam wiped smoke from his face as he knelt beside her, trying to see through the darkness. "It is no use until we get the fan running," he said as he pulled her back from the edge.

Greer checked on the students who had a dozen questions which she was unable to answer, but she promised an update as soon as possible. In the meantime, they needed to keep at their tasks given the dig's approaching deadline.

When she returned, Adam had stationed himself at the open door, wearing a deep scowl. With his arms crossed angrily over his chest, he brooded over the rising smoke. "There was nothing down there that could burn, except the bracing in the alcove. What the hell are we going to find down there?"

Greer didn't have an answer and refrained from guessing. She was anxious to see what damage had been done. "Maybe the university or church will finally hire night security now?"

"The smoke is clearing," said Adam as he knelt to peer inside.

Greer peeked over his shoulder. "Where's the ladder?"

"I think it was inside."

She rummaged around in Adam's truck until she found rope thick enough to support a person's weight. Slinging it over her shoulder, she hurried back to find Adam still staring into the hole. He hadn't moved an inch. Tying one end of the rope to the tripod, she motioned for Jones to help move the whole thing over the opening. Then she handed the loose end to Adam. He took it without looking and dropped it in.

"Give me a flashlight," he said.

"There's still a fair amount of smoke. Are you sure it's safe?" She cast a dubious look at the stinking hole.

"I am going down," Adam said, concern and determination hardening his features.

Greer monitored his descent with her own flashlight while Jones kept an eye on the tripod. "He's down," she said to a nervous Malcolm. He'd stayed to watch as well.

They heard Adam cough a few times and could see the dim beam his flashlight cast through the residual smoke.

She called down. "How bad is it? What can you see?"

"Pro nobis, ut Deus!" Adam yelled from below.

His ash-smudged face appeared in the circle of light cast from above. "Greer, call 911."

"Oh my God. Why? What do I tell them?" she asked frantically.

"Tell them we discovered a body."

After she called the emergency number, Greer asked the students to help lower her down into the room. On her way down, she warned them to stay clear of the door.

The room was hazy with fine particles of dust and ash drifting through the air. The acrid smoke felt oily in her lungs, reminding her of the hellhounds. Adam was an obscure form on the other side of the room, but she could easily make out the burnt remains of the ladder at her feet. The flashlight only cut a few feet ahead, causing her to pick her way carefully around the open graves to where Adam knelt in front of the alcove.

She gasped at the sight of badly charred remains. The skin was blackened wherever it was not burned completely away, exposing bone. Wisps of clothing and hair remained, but the style and color were not recognizable.

Adam was on his knees deep in prayer. Not wanting to disturb him, she circled the body looking for clues as to who this was and what they'd been doing here. She couldn't imagine why a curious teen or even a looter would have started a fire. The nights were plenty warm, so a homeless person wouldn't have needed one either.

Shining her light into the alcove she was furious to see that not only had the supporting scaffolding burned, but the flames had obliterated the last remnants of the delicate mural. The few inches of plaster that had not crumbled to the floor were covered in thick, greasy soot.

A small pile of debris caught her eye. Squatting low, she scrutinized it without disturbing anything, knowing the police would already be unhappy that she and Adam were down here. The small mound held a piece of shiny, curled wire, part of a pen, and a t-shaped rod that Greer immediately recognized as a soil probe.

She whirled to face Adam. "This was a probe and a notebook. They were hunting for something. Someone was messing with our dig."

"I know," he said, answering softly.

She threw her hands to her hips. "What do you mean, you know?"

Adam stared down at the body, tears in his eyes. That's when she noticed the burnt thing clutched between his hands. Reaching down to gently remove it, she confirmed it was Liz's ridiculous fishing hat.

It didn't take long for the police to set up a perimeter and order everyone except Adam and Greer to leave. Adam had told the students of Liz's death, sparing them the details. Although they clearly hadn't been close to her, the boys looked dumbfounded. They were sent home with instructions to wait for Adam's call once police released the site back to the school.

After the paramedics unnecessarily checked them for injuries, Greer and Adam were questioned separately by the responding officers. They answered the same questions all over again when the homicide detective arrived. Once he initially cleared them, they were allowed to sit together under the tent, waiting in case police had additional questions. A considerate deputy even brought them coffee.

Despite the heat of the afternoon and the warm drink in her hand, Greer couldn't shake the icy feeling in her bones. This fire felt wrong in so many ways.

"What was she possibly thinking?" Adam wondered as he watched the officers poke all around the dig, continuously climbing up and down from the room like ants.

"I'll tell you exactly what she was thinking. She thought there were more bodies down there and wanted to impress you by finding them." She felt a lump form in her throat as they watched Liz's body being hauled up—an anonymous black body bag strapped tightly down to a stretcher. "I had been thinking the same thing myself."

He looked at her sideways. "You wanted to impress me?"

"No! God no." She stood and crossed her arms, watching the last of the officers climb out of Room A. "I've been thinking there are more bodies down there. The graves uncovered when the room flooded were oddly spaced around the room, yet directionally aligned. It just makes sense there might be more buried a little deeper. I bet when they're uncovered, they will demonstrate a consistent burial pattern."

They watched again as Liz was placed into the coroner's van and driven away.

"Someone should contact her parents," said Greer.

"I already called the emergency number the school gave me, but I got voice mail. I asked the Dean to keep trying. I also asked him to inform the board of St. Agatha's before they hear it on the news."

She cracked her knuckles and searched for something to keep busy. "I'm going to see if the police still need us."

The detective cleared them to leave the site and ordered them not to skip town. Greer had assured him that would not be a problem at all.

"Since we're done here, I thought we'd do some training tonight," she said, hopeful.

Adam didn't answer, only continued to watch the police work.

She looked to the activity in the yard and back again, debating. "Hey. Do you want to grab some grinders and go work our other job?"

"You go," he said, ducking his head and turning from her. "I need to stay a little longer."

She placed a hand on his shoulder in an attempt to comfort him, but he jumped like he'd been shocked.

"Adam. There's nothing more we can do for her."

He turned back to her but wouldn't meet her eye. He looked utterly miserable. "I know." He put a hand up to pat hers. "But I need to be here. You should go home tonight. We can train tomorrow."

Reluctantly, she let go and left, looking back over her shoulder several times. It felt like a mistake to leave him alone.

An Exile's Baggage

She'd showered and started dinner by the time Robert got home from work. He sat at the counter, eating with her but not speaking until she cleared away their plates.

"So. Did you talk to your father? Are you done with the dig?"

Greer let the pan she was washing slip back into the sink.

"Yes, I talked to him. No, I'm not quitting the dig."

"That's a problem."

She stared at her soapy hands, hands that would rather be combing through dirt right this very minute. Picking the pan up again she took her frustration out on it as she rigidly replied, "It's my job. I can't just quit. This is my career we're talking about."

"Don't care," he said. "Something has been wrong about this from the beginning. You have to walk away."

Deflated, Greer sighed and leaned against the sink.

"Can we not do this today, please? Someone died today."

Robert came to the sink and pulled her around to face him. His hard look had softened; he now wore genuine concern.

"Greer, someone died there, and you want to stay?"

"Well. It's not like that's normal."

"Exactly!" The derision was back in his voice. "Mother and Father have been terribly upset since things went all strange. You need to make all this nonsense stop now."

"I'm sure it won't happen again."

He stepped back sharply. "This can't go on."

She studied him, calmly considering their many years together and their most recent arguments. "You're right, this can't go on. We seem to need different things. Maybe I should leave." Dropping the sponge in the sink, she crossed her arms, waiting for his response.

He stared at her open-mouthed in utter disbelief. "Are you saying you don't want to marry me?"

"Maybe. I don't know. I'm saying not right now."

He grabbed his keys from the counter and left.

Greer finished cleaning up and collapsed on the couch, contemplating what came next. She could picture exactly how her career would be impacted if she walked off the dig like Robert asked. If she claimed to have ongoing health issues from the accident, she could probably get away with it. She'd have to redo the fieldwork requirement next summer, delaying completion of her degree. Plus, if word got out, she was too ill to complete a dig, it'd be very difficult finding a job after graduation. The archeology world was a small and underfunded club, so no one could afford to hire an unreliable employee.

She tried to imagine handling her new challenges and talents without any support. Sure, her dad believed in her; however, he admitted to knowing little about mom's daily management of that side of her life. Without Adam and his family, Greer would be ignorant and alone in dealing with any future spirits that tried to harass her.

Would giving up this dig alleviate the worst of the current supernatural problems? Some of her most frightening experiences seemed to be tied directly to the site. Maybe her talent would even go dormant if she avoided it entirely?

Greer didn't turn on a lamp when the room grew dark. Instead, she gazed at the moon through the window. When Robert came home and went to bed without a word, she began remembering how many wonderful nights she'd spent with him. Nights when they'd shared so much. Were they beyond all hope?

Greer's head and heart ached. She wished she could talk to her mom.

Walking quietly to the bedroom, she slipped under the covers and watched the steady rise and fall of Robert's chest as he slept. He was kindhearted, if a little selfish at times. He'd always been a source of comfort, even though he'd never realized the true toll of her endless grief for her mother. Robert had proven an unvarying fixture in her life, until recently.

Greer snuggled up against him to place a gentle kiss on his cheek. He stirred a little and moved to wrap his arm around her. She wiggled closer. He responded half-heartedly, so she renewed her efforts. They shouldn't go down without a fight, she thought.

"Robert," she whispered.

Her hands lightly played down his neck to run appreciatively over his chest. Kisses followed their path.

He roughly pulled her up to his mouth. As she pressed against the length of him, she matched his kiss. Tugging her shirt off, he rolled her onto her back and bent to her neck and breasts. She pressed her nose into his short blond hair to smell the sunshine that perpetually clung to him.

"Look at me," she said and raised his chin with her hand.

Greer looked into Robert's beautiful green eyes and suddenly realized she no longer saw her future there. A lump formed in her throat, yet she also felt relief. The strain of hiding her other life from him, of hiding herself, had weighed heavily on her conscience. Worse, was the recent realization that he didn't trust her. He didn't understand the other-worldly challenges she now faced because he'd never truly believed in her.

. . .

The battered car objected to the heavy load of clothes, books, and miscellaneous items Greer shoved into it the next morning. Her neck hurt from sleeping on the couch. It had been hours before she'd finally quit packing and tried to sleep. When she did, her dreams were a jumble of dark rooms, cold stones, ghosts, and burnt body parts... and her mother. She'd been wishing for the familiar dream to return, and, when it came this time, it was far more vivid than before.

In the dream, Greer crept down the hallway and found her mother by the Christmas tree as always. She passed into the warm breeze where her mom held her cheek to cheek.

But the dream was not entirely a happy reunion. Her mother brought a dire warning. She'd said, 'He is coming.' When Greer's twelve-year-old self asked who "he" is, her mother was vague. 'He cuts; he burns," was all she could remember. Greer was warned to prepare herself against the darkness.

Sitting in her car this morning, struggling once again to get it turn over, Greer felt a long way from darkness. However, she was worried and needed to talk to Adam urgently. He'd called an hour ago to say the church had convinced the police to release the site so everyone was expected back at the dig. At this point she was going to be late even if the car did start.

As the students worked that morning, no one spoke, only threw each other uneasy looks. They remained somber throughout the day and seemed to be taking the dig and Liz's fate seriously. Greer was pleased to see them present and focused when they might have gone running scared.

The project's timetable had suffered another hit due to the police investigation, so there was no time to spare. The students volunteered to stay until dusk, while Greer and Adam worked well past dark to finish the cleanup below ground. Adam wouldn't think of asking any of the kids to go in so soon after Liz's death, but the room needed to be cleaned and restored as soon as possible.

The fan and duct work were left running all day to continue clearing out the smoke particles. Adam used a soft brush to remove soot from the stone walls while Greer followed along with a HEPA vacuum to lift it all from the floor.

The alcove presented a bigger challenge. They gently sifted through the debris on the floor looking for any pieces large enough to salvage, finding none. So, with a collective sigh, they moved on to the walls. Any part of the mural that might have remained intact would need to be painstakingly cleaned.

"We really should call a paint restoration specialist in for this," said Adam, worried.

"Why bother? There's no more than a few inches left. And will the church really pay to have it moved?"

"No. But to be thorough, I want to clean it all."

"Yes, of course."

Greer mixed a small amount of mild detergent paste in a bucket, dipped a small paint brush in it, and handed it to him. Then she took up her own brush and started on the opposite wall. With little room in the alcove, they were pressed back-to-back as they worked. Greer found his solid warmth reassuring as images of Liz's body occasionally found their way to the front of her mind. Recalling the eerie grin left behind after the facial skin had burned away made Greer shudder.

"You ok?" Adam asked over his shoulder after he felt her tremble.

"Yeah. Just got a chill. You ok?"

"Yes, thank you."

He hadn't been exactly chatty today, but Greer felt like their rapport was returning to normal. Between their kiss and finding dead students, they had traversed some thorny territory in their new friendship.

She dipped the brush again and started on the side wall. "You know what I don't understand is how the fire even got started. Surely Liz knew better than to light one. And I didn't see evidence of what she used to start it. No lighter or candles."

"That has been bothering me too." He finished his wall and moved to help her. "I asked the detective about it before he left. He refused to tell me anything about the investigation but asked me for my theory. I would say that indicates he had no idea either."

"Well, however it began, the fire obviously went out after the door was closed and all the oxygen in the room burned."

"Yes, but that trap door is heavy, and the two-by-four had to be removed for it to close. I cannot imagine why Liz would have destroyed the tripod, removed the two-by-four, and then closed herself in here. It makes no sense."

She looked up at him, horrified. "Someone locked her in here!"

He didn't have to answer; she read his thoughts in the slump of his shoulders and the dip of his chin.

Righteous anger flared in her gut. She wet the brush again and pressed it to the plaster. When the oily soot didn't dissolve, she pressed harder and harder until she was slapping the wall, knocking dirty plaster from it with the handle and her fists.

With a curse, Adam caught her hands. She froze, staring down at the mess she'd made when she noticed wood lathing peeking out from the missing plaster. A small hole in the lathing revealed a dark cavity beyond.

"What the hell?" she said, rolling back on her heels momentarily stunned. As Adam leaned in she came back to her senses and beat him to the punch to peer inside. "I can't see anything. It feels big though. There may even be a slight draft." She was flushed with excitement. "This mural is toast anyway. I'm going to grab some tools so we can open this up."

"Hold on a minute," he ordered gently as he took her place to inspect the opening. He stepped back and thoughtfully inspected the remaining mural around them. "There really is very little left." He paused then seemed to make up his mind. "Alright. Let's do it."

They carefully scraped at the plaster, feeling only a little bit sorry for destroying the last few inches of mural. As the plaster slowly flaked off, exposing the thin boards of lathing underneath, damp air seeped through the cracks between. Using the claw of a small hammer, they pried each lath away and stacked them in piles outside of the alcove. Adam stopped occasionally to capture photographs of their progress as Greer single-mindedly attacked each obstacle between her and what was hidden beyond.

She handed Adam her hammer and he handed back a flashlight. The flick of a switch revealed a narrow tunnel made of rough field stone matching the rest of Room A. At the end of the tunnel was an old, darkly stained, oak door.

Greer slowly walked toward the door and reached out her hand for the thick iron ring set as a handle.

"Stop," Adam said just behind her.

Greer whipped her head around and spoke to him over her shoulder. "I need to see whatever is in there, Adam."

"I know you do, but we cannot forget that we are professionals here. We will open it in the morning with masks and the fan at the ready."

Ignoring him, she reached for the handle again. "I need to see," she said.

"Greer! Control yourself," he snapped.

Greer sought her talisman and rubbed the warm wings gently between her fingers while she drew in a deep breath. She knew he was right, of course. The strange desire to open the door was fading, and she brushed past him, leaving the tunnel before it could return.

They hurried to tidy up and scrambled topside. "Tomorrow," she said as they finally closed the trap door.

After loading equipment into his truck, Greer propped her arms on the side to rest her head.

"Lunch was a long time ago," she said with a groan.

"It was. Come over to the house for a quick dinner before working with April."

She shook her head and yawned. "Sounds fantastic, but I can't. I need to find a hotel."

"Why exactly?"

"I kind of moved out of my place this morning." She nodded toward her overstuffed car. "I packed everything that would fit for now. I'll need to make one more trip back."

He laughed loudly, stopping short when he saw her frown. "Sorry, sorry," he said, patting a soft apology on her back. "I am not laughing at you. It is very unfortunate that you left Robert."

"Then why the hell are you laughing?" she asked, propping hands on her hips.

"Because Mother would have my head if I let you stay at a hotel." Slipping an arm around her shoulders, he said, "You are family now, whether you realize it or not. Come stay with us."

Greer pondered her options for a minute. If she accepted his hospitality, there'd be no going back to Robert, ever. He'd never forgive her living with the very people he believed had warped her mind and ruined their life together. Then she remembered she didn't want to go back. The decision had been made last night, and it was the right one. The acceptance and understanding which Adam's crazy family offered her was more than Robert had ever provided.

"Ok, thanks. Don't worry though. I'll start looking for my own place as soon as possible."

"It is so amusing that you think it will be that easy to escape my mother." He chuckled as she raised an eyebrow in doubt. "See you at home."

. . .

Mother Rose was indeed thrilled to add a new member to the

household. The rest of the family displayed various levels of enthusiasm. Sam surprised them all by breaking away from his cartoons long enough to give her a quick hug.

They found April had already started clearing the spare room before they arrived. The girl now sang various hymns as she helped unload Greer's car.

"Where do you want this last box?" Adam asked.

"Anywhere. Thank you!" Greer said as she and April shoved miscellaneous items into an old trunk. Finished, April dropped the lid and pushed the box to the back of the closet. "Thanks, April. I couldn't have done it so quickly without you."

"Well, I can keep a better eye on you now I guess," said April.

Greer blinked, unsure how to take the comment. Since the girl left humming another song, Greer decided to take it as an encouraging remark.

"I promised you dinner, so hurry down once you settle in," said Adam.

She smiled to herself as she hung a few things in the closet and stored more clothing in the old dresser. Her books would have to stay packed until she could buy a bookshelf. The important ones that April and Adam had loaned her were on top in the meantime.

She turned when she heard someone at the door. Her smile faded as Frankie and Tony entered the room. Frankie leaned on the dresser while Tony lounged on the end of the bed.

"Oh, so you're sleepin' 'ere now," Tony said, running a hand slowly across the quilt.

Greer tried not to reveal revulsion on her face, but her effort was wasted as Frankie announced in her rapid manner, "Give it up, Tony boy. This one has no interest in you whatsoever." She snuck a peek into the dresser before Greer shooed her away and closed the drawer.

Tony flashed a smarmy grin. "Never say never, luv."

"You should go away, Tony." Frankie said as she poked out a finger, tracing a strand of hair that had fallen from Greer's ponytail to frame her face. "She's not going to change her mind."

Greer resisted the temptation to smack her hand away, choosing to stand her ground. "What a warm welcome. I'm sure I'll see you two at dinner." She stared Frankie directly in the eye and actively imagined her walking out of the room. If she was reading Greer's mind right now, she wanted Frankie to have a crystal-clear picture of her wishes.

"Come on. Let's get out of here," Frankie said abruptly.

Tony slowly slid off the bed and gave her a wink. "Oi, I could use a drink."

Greer took a few more minutes to tidy the room, making sure she heard them leave the house before she ventured downstairs. Raised voices as she approached the kitchen sent her on a detour into the living room to give the quarrelers privacy.

She waved hello to Sam and nodded at Mother Rose who was reading in her petite armchair. Greer selected a Koran from the coffee table to occupy herself and hoped the argument would wrap up soon. Her stomach growled loud enough that Adam's mother was giving her odd looks.

The voices continued to rise until she recognized Cahya. "I don't care! ... day and night. You always go overboard! ... help without moving her in!"

Adam's deeper voice interrupted, indistinct through the door.

"... if she stays, don't expect me to! I've seen the way you look at each other!"

"Cahya!" she finally heard Adam say. "Enough!" His words returned to an unintelligible rumble.

Greer renewed her interest in the verse she'd flipped open. She could feel Adam's mom watching her and avoided making eye contact. They all jumped when the back door slammed and then startled again when something banged in the kitchen.

While her guilt urged her to stay put, her stomach wouldn't let her wait any longer. Greer tentatively opened the kitchen door to peer inside. She expected to find a mess, but everything was as it should be. Clearing her throat, she pushed all the way into the kitchen. Adam looked up from the short glass in his hand then to the stove where something was burning.

She felt like the elephant in the room. "I've caused you trouble in more ways than one." She hesitated. "Should I leave now?"

"No. I should apologize." He tossed back the amber liquid in his glass before setting it down hard on the counter. "You should not have heard that." He stood in front of the stove watching the pan crackle and hiss for a minute before he pulled it from the burner and scrapped the scorched remains of what appeared to be an omelet into the trash. He nodded toward the table. "Have a seat and let me take another stab at dinner."

"I can help."

"That would be nice."

Days of Discovery

The Secret Things of the Dark

Adam wanted Greer to ride along with him to the site in the morning; however, she worried someone might get the wrong impression seeing them arrive together. Even after he pointed out they were always the first to arrive and the last to leave, she was adamant about driving separately.

The students pestered Adam for updates on the murder investigation, but there hadn't been any news from the police. They seemed to take this in stride and were soon completely overtaken with enthusiasm over the new tunnel.

Adam and Greer had other plans for them. Liz had been an excellent student, and Greer believed she'd been on the right track in searching for additional burials in the dirt floor. They couldn't get their hands on any ground penetrating radar machines on such short notice, so they planned to work the theory the old-fashioned way.

Jones, Rigsby, and Malcolm, all armed with a thin soil-probing rod, stood together on the wall closest to the ladder. Working their way meticulously across the new grid strung across the floor, they pushed the rods down as far into the dirt as they could in search of anomalies. If the rod hit something hard or seemed to push through far too easily, a small flag was left to mark the hole. They color coded the flags—red for stopping on something hard and green for the softer spots.

When they arrived at the opposite wall, they turned to survey the little sea of flags in search of a pattern. Rigsby's face lit up at the tell-tale configuration of rough green rectangles with red flags scattered in their centers. "Our theory was that we'd find more graves, right? I'd bet that areas of soft dirt with hard stuff in the middle are bone-filled graves. I think we friggin' found them!"

Greer looked up from her diagram of their work and encouraged the other two boys to share their observations. "Do you notice anything else that might support this theory?"

"Well, they are fairly regularly spaced and all aligned in the same direction. Like you would see in a cemetery." said Jones.

Adam collected everyone's soil probes. "Yes, your logic is sound, now there is a lot of work to be done. Jones, please take these topside and bring back shovels and buckets. Malcolm, go with him." He called after them, "Get brushes and trowels too."

"Where do we start?" Rigsby asked bouncing excitedly.

Greer held up a hand to still his fidgety feet. "Hang on a sec."

She walked over to observe each of the four exposed graves then moved to the middle of the room. "All four of these bodies were adult Caucasian women around the age of sixteen to thirty. None of them show signs of experiencing childbirth. All have strong arm bones and worn tooth enamel. I believe they were all young, working-class women who did manual labor such as laundry," she noted, pointing to each. "But there are differences. I know it's not much to go on, but I think we should focus on the bones missing from each. The body closest to the wall is missing the skull, while the one near to the entrance is missing much of her foot. What happened in the middle?"

Adam nodded, confirming her assessment. "We will start at the foot of the woman missing her skull with the expectation that the next body will be missing a jaw or cervical vertebrae. Good plan."

The students began slowly and carefully. While they dug, Greer and Adam finished their measurements of the tunnel, pulled open the oak door and set up the tube and fan to pull any fetid air from behind. Greer had argued the fan was completely unnecessary as the cracks around the door had already allowed a good amount of air to transfer into the tunnel without any negative effects. Still, Adam insisted on following protocol.

Checking on the students, Greer found they'd already dug a few inches down. Greer began to feel flushed and dizzy. When she sat down for a break, Adam noticed her pallor.

"Ms. Dixon, can I speak to you for a moment?"

She nodded weakly and tried to get up. With his back to the students, he caught her around the waist, helping her stand. He kept a steadying hand at her back as she slowly made her way over to lean on the wall. Greer pressed her forehead against the cool stones for relief.

"You look awful. Tell me."

"I don't know." She tugged her angel wings from under her dusty shirt. "I did my usual prayer this morning, but I'm feeling like I did when we opened the stone casket. Hot. Nauseous."

"Go take a break topside."

"No. I won't be left out of this. It's too important." She gripped her wings tighter. "We have to find out what happened to these poor people." In a coarse whisper, she added, "And what's happening to me."

He gave her a hard look. "Well, you cannot do any of that given your current state."

"Can't you do an extra prayer for protection? Or show me how to repel whatever is causing this feeling?"

"Hey, guys," he called over to the students. "Take five and bring back some waters for us, please."

Once the students were outside, Adam eased Greer into a seat on the floor. He sat cross-legged across from her. "Please oblige me and say your angel prayer again." When she was done, he took her hands in his. "Don't mind the dirt," he said when he noticed the thin layer of grime covering his palms.

She smiled since she was just as filthy after a day spent playing in the earth.

"We only have a few minutes. If this does not work, please promise you will leave for the day."

Greer didn't want to make such a promise, but he gave her that professor look until she sighed and nodded in agreement.

"Say it with me if you remember this one. If not, then make sure to practice it."

When they finished, Greer opened her eyes, already feeling her head start to clear.

"Any better?" he asked, eyeing her curiously.

"Yes, actually. Thanks."

Hearing the student approach above, they abruptly released each other's hands.

"I am going to hold you to your promise," he said.

"I'm sure you won't need to. Now let's get back to work."

Adam went first down the short tunnel to the oak door. He turned off the fan then helped Greer pull it and the tubing out of the way. With a nod, he eased the door open so Greer could shine her flashlight beyond. The scent of mold rolled past them.

Her beam bounced around a small, dark chamber with long shelves built into the stone walls. As soon as she stepped inside, Greer felt goosebumps rise on her arms and the cool, damp air weighed on her lungs. She scanned the ledges up close. They seemed to be part of the original construction, precisely hewn of the same granite creating the foundation above Room A and the adjoining cellar.

A hot breath on her neck made her jump.

"Sorry," Adam said, "Just trying to get a better look." He flipped his own flashlight on and quickly scanned the rest of the room. "Looks like we have a very empty crypt here. The church records say nothing of this."

"Is this a crypt… or a catacomb?" Greer said. "Look."

She was standing in a small corridor leading out of the far end of the room. Adam had to duck to poke his head into the narrow passage where Greer was letting her light play off of several more archways leading away into the darkness. She confidently set off for the nearest one, only to stop short of the opening, suddenly feeling the electric prickle of energy she'd experienced in the graveyard exercise with April.

"What is it?" he whispered.

"I don't know yet." Greer grasped her golden wings and said a quick prayer of protection.

"Let's take it slowly," he said as he motioned for her to let him take the lead. Ducking into the room, he did a quick scan and then waved for her to follow.

This room was not empty. All but one of the six shelves were occupied by a dusty set of bones.

"Don't touch any of them."

Greer rolled her eyes at him. Her head was so abuzz with psychic energy that she had no intention of touching the remains; however, she still didn't like to be told what to do. The vibrations increased rather unpleasantly as she moved in to inspect the nearest skeleton. Moldy robes draped the still figure and served to identify him as a church official but not a priest. The burial lacked a name plate or any other identifying marker.

"How are you feeling?" Adam asked after inspecting each corpse.

"I'm ok, but I'm feeling them without even trying. A jumble of angry words is churning just beyond my hearing. I feel like they're all trying to talk to me at once." She closed her eyes and gripped the wings tighter. "No, it's not that they want to talk so much as they're trying to get into my head."

"Should we leave?"

"Absolutely not. We have a job to do. Let's see the next room."

The next room was full of bodies in older, disintegrating robes, all neatly lined up on their granite graves. Greer was becoming numb to the stinging energy emanating from each body, but she had to constantly focus to keep the voices from intruding on her own thoughts.

The corridor took a sharp turn to the left and revealed more doorways spawning from the blackness.

After investigating two more rooms, Greer asked for a break. "They really don't like me," she said of the bodies. "I have to say the feeling is mutual." Battling the constant barrage of negative energy was draining. She started shivering from the damp and the exertion.

"You should probably eat." He shined his flashlight down the passage. "Look, steps, so we are close to the end. We are headed north now, toward the apse of the cathedral. There is nowhere else to go."

She pushed away from the wall. "Ok, let's finish."

By the last room, the skeletons were completely bare; their robes having fallen away to dust long ago. Greer hung by the archway, conserving strength by staying as far away as possible from the remains. But Adam was still doing a thorough survey and taking notes in a small notepad he pulled from his pocket. He gently prodded a rib cage with his pencil and made a small hum of interest. "You should really take a look at this."

Greer's curiosity won out over her hesitation to draw near. On any other dig she would've been reviewing each of these bodies with a magnifying glass, but she didn't have the luxury of time or protection at present.

She clenched her teeth as the vibrations increased with each step closer to the grave Adam was examining. Kneeling to look at where his pencil hovered above the sternum, she saw a dark gray cross on the bone, or rather in the bone. She leaned closer. The cross had been burned into the bone.

"What does it mean?" she asked.

"Well, it's a bit hard to tell in this light, but it looks like it was done posthumously. I've never encountered anything like it. From my reading, I would guess it was an extreme form of purification performed on the body." Sitting back on his heels, Adam hummed a small question before popping up, almost hitting his head on the low ceiling. "Be right back," he said excitedly.

When he returned a few minutes later, his eyes were bright with the thrill of discovery. "I carefully moved the robes on some of these other fellows. Several of them have the same mark."

"We'll add that to the list of oddities about the burials around here." A shudder ran through Greer, and an icy chill swept through her veins. "I've got to get out of here now, Adam."

He saw her shivering and helped her into the hall, leading them toward the stone stairs only a few feet away. When she put a hand against the wall to support herself on the way up, he bent to wrap an arm around her waist. "Here, lean on me."

The steps, carved from the hard quartzite bedrock, showed a surprising amount of wear on their treads. Greer wouldn't have expected a catacomb to be highly trafficked.

They quickly reached the top where a marble slab, about half the height of a standard door, held two small holes filled with grime. The holes were a hand's span apart and had scratch marks around each. Greer could imagine a handle had once been affixed through them.

Adam tried pushing but it didn't budge.

"Do you think there's a doorbell?" she joked through chattering teeth.

Adam looked at her askance. He helped her sit down and tried pushing again, this time with both hands.

"Let's just go back the way we came," she said.

"No. I want to see where this comes out." He tried again, grunting with effort. When his hands started to sweat and slip across the marble, he tried using his shoulder.

"Adam."

"Hold on. I know I can get it."

"Adam!"

He stopped at her shout and turned to look where she was pointing. At the bottom of the stairs, a shadow, darker than the rest of the surrounding gloom, hovered below. The temperature plummeted.

Greer gasped and her hands flew to her temples. "No! It's in my mind. I can't stop it!"

Adam turned back to the marble hatch and threw his shoulder against it, then again, harder. Greer groaned and slumped against it even as he tried one more drive.

When the small exit gave way, it swung all the way open with a bang. Adam dived to catch Greer's head before it could hit the floor.

The cold grip the shadow had on Greer's mind released, and she felt a flood of warmth course through her. She opened her eyes to see the cathedral ceiling soaring above. The light from the stained-glass windows danced down the walls. Her head was balanced on Adam's chest bouncing along until his breathing began to slow.

"Huh. We're behind the altar, aren't we?" she asked.

"Ayuh."

. . .

After a quick stop for some water, they hurried down the ladder to check on the kids who were confused by their arrival from topside versus the tunnel. Adam brushed them off with a promise to share details later, and it was quickly forgotten as the students began excitedly recounting their own morning's findings. Rigsby was thrilled to report he'd uncovered the cranium. When the skeleton was fully exposed, they'd realized, as suspected, it was missing a bone. The mandible, the lower half of the jaw, had been completely removed.

Adam sat back on his heels, grimly studying this newest skeleton. "This is not what I expected," he told Greer. "It will certainly provide a lot of experience, but this is obviously not what I would call an ideal school project."

"Do we need to get the police involved since there are so many burials?"

"No. The graves are too old for them to have jurisdiction. Given the strata we dug through to find the trap door, we already estimated this room was sealed off from the world in the early 1800's."

"What about access from the... you know," she said with a darting glance toward the alcove and its hidden tunnel.

Adam shook his head. "I really don't think so. This tragedy belongs in archaeological hands—our hands. Of course, we need to keep the college and the church up to date on our findings."

"Do you think the church will still want to erect the new office building here?" Jones asked; his dark eyebrows rose in morbid curiosity.

"Knowing that they are building over a charnel house?" asked Greer.

"Yes, they will still build. However, I suspect both organizations will want to keep this room's existence hidden."

"There are so many graves," Greer said sadly as she assessed the macabre mosaic the little red and green flags created across the floor.

"Can we start digging on the next one?" Malcolm asked, adrenaline pumping.

Adam said, "Of course. Go grab some lunch first. There is a lot to do. Tomorrow, I want the three of you to probe the floor in Room B next door."

"Let's hope you don't find anything." Greer called after them as they were scurrying outside.

"I bet that's the first time an archaeologist ever said that!" Rigsby called back as he continued climbing the ladder in search of his supper.

Adam and Greer purchased grinders from the nearest deli and ate as they walked back, trying to talk through plans for Liz's funeral around mouthfuls. Word was the family wanted a small, private service. Adam was still trying to convince them the class wanted to attend.

When they descended the ladder, a dark figure was crouched over the most recently opened grave.

"Father Doyle! What are you doing!" Adam said, alarmed. He rushed over, grabbing the man's shoulder to pull him away from the remains.

The priest almost lost his balance, barely recovering as he stood and spun to face the taller man. "I could ask you the same, Mr. Walker." His voice was hoarse with fury. "First a student dies on church property. Now I see you've discovered more bodies." His face was rapidly turning a deeper shade of red as he spoke. "Just when were you going to inform us?"

Adam crossed his arms and locked his stance before answering tersely. "We have only just discovered the new bodies. It will all be in my report at the end of the week."

"A weekly report is not adequate to such a serious situation. The church will not be pleased with how you've managed this. Not at all!" said Doyle, trembling with anger.

Greer perceived Adam's shift in weight. He was literally digging his heals into the dirt. She sought a way to diffuse the situation but was coming up blank. The priest had a point.

"Father Doyle, I have fulfilled every duty to the school and the church in this matter. I understand this is upsetting to you. We will provide a full report after sufficient time to investigate. Those are the terms, and I will abide by them."

"This will not stand. This is holy ground!" he finished, shaking his fist at Adam.

Despite the tension running through him, Adam's expression had remained entirely quiescent, finally breaking into a sardonic twitch as he smoothly replied, "I did not place the bodies here; I only found them, Father."

The men stared at each other, neither prepared to back down. Finally, the priest's shoulders slumped in partial defeat. "I'll stay and watch then," he said, conceding ground.

Adam uncrossed his arms but held firm. "No. That is not safe for you or my students. I must ask you to leave."

Doyle fumed, puffing his chest enough to strain against his cassock. "If you think I ..." he began just as the students made their way down the ladder. He stopped abruptly, seeming to think better of throwing a tantrum in front of the boys.

Recognizing his temporary victory, Adam adopted a gracious tone and waved a hand toward the exit. "Thank you for stopping by, Father Doyle. I am sure you will be the first to see our report."

Crimson faced; Doyle hastily made his way out.

The students hardly noticed his exit as they jumped back into their work. By dusk, the team had made a lot of progress. The third grave, running parallel along the first wall, held another woman, missing more bones, this time the top few vertebrae. Adam did a final review of the room and then told them to knock off for the evening.

"Are we ever going to get night security here?" Greer asked as they closed the trap door and pulled the tarp into place.

"Apparently not. The dean said odds are slim to none. He promised to try, but I have not heard a word since."

Greer shook her head with a discouraged sigh. "Well, it's late. I'm going to pass on training tonight."

"Ayuh. I am meeting a friend. See you in the morning."

"Oh. Ok. See you."

Greer sank into the driver's seat, exhausted but happy with the day's work. Adam's taillights rolled down the block to the local bar where they'd shared drinks after finding the first trap door. She vaguely wondered what friend he was meeting as he never talked about anyone outside of school or his family.

Greer listened as the engine tried and failed to turn over. After a few more attempts, she gave up with a bang on the steering wheel. It was her fault for not getting the ancient thing into a repair shop.

Should she walk to the bar and ask Adam for a ride? No, he'd invested all of his free time lately to her protection and training and was obviously in need of down time. Her dad was back in Vermont. She didn't have April's number.

Slinging her bag across her chest, she set off down the street under an overcast sky. There were too many lights in the city to see stars anyway. Longing for the family home and her old telescope washed over her. Maybe she'd drive out there to spend a quiet weekend alone once the car was fixed. So, without the stars to guide her, she walked, entertaining herself by reciting the mythical Gods tied to the heavens, sun, and moon.

She was mentally ticking through the various Greek and Roman Gods, the roles they shared in the creation and maintenance of the skies, when she noticed a shadow lurking in a doorway. It might be a harmless vagrant, but she crossed to the other side of the street out of an abundance of caution. Glancing out of the corner of her eye upon passing, she saw the doorway was empty, and she chastised herself again for being afraid of the dark.

Turning a corner, she resumed her mental exercise. Yet not a half block away, she was sure someone moved in the gloom on a front stoop. She cursed under her breath, crossing the street again. Surreptitiously peeking at the porch as she went by, her heart skipped a beat when there was indeed a shadowy form occupying the landing.

Greer turned right at the next corner even though it led her away from the most direct route to Adam's house. Walking swiftly, she planned to turn left at the next corner, returning to her original course.

Just as she was hanging a left, another figure appeared ahead. This one did not skulk in the shelter of a building but rather stood in the middle of the sidewalk. A chill ran through her. It was no living man. It was just an inky outline of one. The legs and arms were only suggestions in the dim light from the streetlamps which seemed to be absorbed into its darkness.

Greer spun on her heel, running down the block and around the corner. The shadow man was there, waiting.

She bolted across the street. When she looked over her shoulder, he was gone so she slowed to a fast walk, continuing to glance back. It appeared she'd shaken it. The street signs ahead helped Greer get her bearings. She was only a few blocks off track. Grasping her little wings, she began a prayer of protection.

As she hit the intersection, she checked over her shoulder once more. Three sinister figures were moving rapidly toward her. Shocked, she sprinted ahead without another look back. Yet, even as she ran, she could sense them nearby. They felt cold and desperate. Icy fingers clawed at her mind. They're closer!

Greer stumbled over an uneven patch of sidewalk, falling hard on her left knee and elbow. Scrambling to her feet, her body flared with fear while her mind began to feel heavy with loathing. She knew they were closing in. Greer had never been a good runner, and soon the physical fatigue and the strange spiritual weight of these creatures bore down on her.

Breathing heavily, she tried to pick up the pace, catching glimpses of the shadows darting at the edge of her vision. Across the street, another corner, a small park ahead. Her lungs were burning. Running beneath the trees she skidded to a stop, rested her back against rough bark, and gasped for air.

The echo of hounds barking broke her momentary reprieve. Frantically, she reviewed her options. Her phone was in the book bag slung across her chest, but she couldn't tell a 911 operator what was happening. Even if she could make something up, it'd take police too long to arrive. Double back and outsmart the phantoms? Doubtful. If she sensed them, they surely had a supernatural bead on her.

The cold and dread grew again, and she knew she had to move but lacked a strategy. Taking hold of her pendant, she panted an angelic protection prayer as she took off again.

Greer had only traveled a few yards before the first shadow appeared before her. She veered only to be confronted by another. Switching direction to leave the park, yet another specter blocked her way.

Her legs trembled with exhaustion, and her lungs were on fire from the long chase. This was the end. Slowly backing away, she held her wings out and called out the most powerful prayer she could remember:

The light of God surrounds me,
The love of God enfolds me,
The power of God protects me,
The presence of God watches over me.
Wherever I am, God is ...

All is well.

Instead of scattering in fear, the phantoms slithered together and melded into one large, obscure blob. It undulated and pulsed erratically as anger, fear, and malevolence emanated from its depths.

Frozen in terror and morbid fascination, she watched, unsure how or where to flee.

The blob surged and heaved, slowly developing a distinct shape. Light from the quaint park lampposts glinted off oily scales growing to cover a thick body. Six legs and six arms alternately flexed as the torso began to fill out. The rough form of a head slowly separated from the chest, chin lifting to reveal a mouth full of daggers and eyes that glittered like obsidian.

Greer screamed!

Finding her feet again, she ran toward the brightest lights nearby. She heard the creature behind her—the scratch of claws on pavement and a low bubbling hiss. Its breath was so foul she smelled it a dozen yards away. The stench was unlike anything she'd encountered, even after years of digging dead things out of the ground.

This area of town was not well kept. Old houses, like Adam's, were interspersed with struggling family business. All were closed for the night, failing to offer refuge in this moment of need.

She screamed again in frustration and despair.

Then she saw lights ahead. Her heart leapt with joy until she had a thought. What if the monster didn't mind witnesses? She couldn't put someone else in danger in her search for safety.

The stomach-churning smell and her feeling of terror swelled as the creature came into sight again. Despite her best efforts, it was gaining. So were the barks and howls. The beast was close enough that she saw slime dripping from its mouth, heard the hiss as it hit the pavement.

Greer was exhausted. Even her adrenaline was failing. She let out an involuntary cry when the creature leapt, gaining another few yards on her. She was sure the claws would tear open her back in a second.

A door suddenly opened ahead, and a plump young woman hollered to her. "Greer! Over here!" As the woman beckoned, the light above cast a warm glow on her golden hair.

Greer jumped from the sidewalk, tripped down the short flight of stairs, and practically fell into the Good Samaritan's outstretched arms. The woman quickly pulled her over the threshold into a small hallway before slamming the door shut. Greer raised a hand in warning, worried that the monster would throw itself against the heavy wood or even materialize through it. After all, she had no idea what she'd been fleeing from. But there was no bang. Nothing appeared through the door.

Calmly collecting a mop and pail, the lady offered a smile that immediately reminded Greer of her mother. "You should come in and stay for the night," she said.

Greer was doubled over against the wall trying to catch her breath. Her head throbbed and her gut was a sick tangle, whether from too much running or proximity to such overwhelming evil, she couldn't be sure. She tried to say thank you but only managed a rasp and nod.

The woman smiled again and pointed with the mop. "This way."

We are Only of Yesterday and Know Nothing

Greer awoke on a small cot next to a cold, timeworn furnace. The homey scent of wood smoke wafted from its long dormant belly. She blinked a few times then bolted upright, recognizing she had no memory of entering this room or falling asleep. The last thing she recalled was the soothing voice of the young woman who had seemed somehow familiar. Surely their paths had crossed before. Greer decided it didn't matter as the situation couldn't have gotten any worse. In shock from the chase, she'd been ready to accept any shelter.

Cleaning supplies were stacked tidily against the opposite wall. An antique radio occupied the small table beside the cot. The blanket she'd slept under was musty, but free of vermin. Grateful for the modest hideaway, she also felt a strong impulse to leave.

Weak light peeked around the half-open door. Beyond it was a narrow hall lit by a few bare bulbs unceremoniously tacked along the ceiling. At one end was the large wooden door she'd entered by last night. The other direction held a narrow stairway which led up to a brighter light. Heading for the light, she was surprised by a song floating down the stairwell.

At the top, she was perplexed to find herself in the wing of a small stage. People in street clothes were clustered under dim stage lights with open hymnals, singing. When the director saw Greer, he waved the choir to a stop.

"Can we help you?" he asked.

Greer approached, nodding her apologies to the choir. "Um, I was looking for a young woman who helped me. I think she may be on your cleaning crew?"

A few chuckles rose from the choir before the director said, "Our cleaning crew consists of two ladies who're old enough to have known Jesus personally."

Her brow furrowed in confusion. "Maybe the theater owner just hired someone new?"

More chuckles prickled at her nerves as the director quieted them with his hands. "This hasn't been a theater in years. Our little church took over the building when it went into foreclosure. And I assure you, we can't afford to hire anyone new. We all volunteer our time."

Disconcerted, Greer offered an apology and exited the steps from the stage into the house seats.

"Ok, let's start at the beginning of the second verse, folks." The director said as he tapped his baton.

"Excuse me?" she yelled from half-way up the aisle. She felt their stares of mingled curiosity and annoyance. "Sorry, but can you please tell me where I am?"

The director looked at her with concern. "Why you are at the Second Chance Fellowship on Pleasant Street."

"Oh. Ok, thank you," she said with a brief wave goodbye, still having no idea where she was.

Pushing on the old brass handles of the theater's double doors, she stepped out into the warm summer morning. Searching up and the down the street, trying to get her bearings, she found nothing familiar. Fortunately, her phone was still safely tucked in her book bag. She opened the map application and found that she was many, many blocks from the dig and Adam's house.

Without money for a bus or taxi, she decided to call for help.

"Adam?" she asked tentatively when it stopped ringing.

"Thank God! Where are you?" was his strained answer. "Yes, yes, it is her," she heard him say in response to a muffled voice. "Are you hurt?" he asked, back on the line.

"No, I'm ok. Can someone come get me, please?"

She gave him the address, and he promised to be there in a few minutes.

When Adam pulled up in front of Second Chance, Greer was leaning next to the old box office window. Her grateful smile at seeing him vanished when she read his tense expression. He jumped out of the truck and stomped over.

"Where the *hell* were you all night?" His face was flushed, drawn tight in aggravation.

Taken aback by his accusing tone, Greer went on defense. "Actually,

I've been trying to avoid becoming a snack for some six-armed, evil monster thing! Did I call too early and wake you?"

"You think I slept at all since we realized you were missing?" he shouted.

She threw her hands to her hips and glared up at Adam. "Well. That is unfortunate. Being chased by vile creatures tends to be inconvenient for me as well."

"You were chased?" He pointed a finger in her face. "You seem to be making a damned habit of that!"

Greer grabbed his hand, yanking it down to her side. "Don't you dare point a finger at me! My life was perfectly normal before you."

Still in her grip, he wrapped the hand she held around her lower back and pulled her roughly against him. Greer's anger dissolved; her voice wavered. "Before you, and damn ghosts, and ..." she said haltingly as his silvery-blue eyes bore into her.

Her protest was cut off by his forceful kiss. Without thinking, Greer wrapped her free hand around his neck, pulling him tightly against her mouth. His day-old beard chafed. Realizing why the stubble was there made her kiss him harder. Tugging her other arm free, she slipped her fingers into his dark curls. Greer paused for a ragged breath before he caught her bottom lip between his teeth and pulled her back in for more.

A small shudder ran through Adam. He slowly broke the kiss but didn't relax his hold. With her hands still twisted through his hair, Greer gazed up at him. She felt lightheaded, happy, confused, and safe all at once.

Resting his chin on the top of her head, he whispered, "Sorry."

Greer looked up, not sure she'd heard him correctly. "What?"

"I said I am sorry."

Leaning her head against his chest, she realized he was exhausted. Greer dropped her hands reluctantly. "Please don't be."

Moving his hands to her hips, he gently pushed her away.

Greer twisted, pretending to look down the street so he wouldn't see the tears that sprang to her eyes. "You've done so much to help me, and I've repaid that with nothing but trouble," she said as she stared into the blurry distance. Quickly wiping her eyes, she turned back to face him. "I didn't mean to cause more by kissing you. Forget it ever happened."

"You know I am with Cahya," he said flatly.

"I know, I know." Greer scooped up her bag and walked swiftly to the truck. "I said forget it." She yanked the truck door open, threw her bag in, and climbed up before he could say more.

Adam stood on the sidewalk watching her. Greer ignored him, determined to press on despite another terrifying night and mortifying morning. She didn't know why he was just standing there staring, but she caught him shaking his head before rounding the front of the truck.

. . .

A livid Mother Rose gave them a ten-minute tongue lashing. Greer couldn't tell who she was angrier with—Greer for walking alone at night or Adam for letting it happen. She decided it was definitely Adam since Mother Rose had given her a tight hug when they walked through the kitchen door.

When the older woman finally ran out of steam, she shakily lit a cigarette and sat down hard at the old table. One hand covering her heart, she puffed away while they made their final apologies to her and retreated to their separate rooms.

Greer took a quick shower and changed into a fresh set of work clothes as she worried over whether the students were working carefully without them. Adam was pouring them each a cup of coffee by the time she returned to the kitchen. She was glad to see his mother and her cigarettes had vacated the room. Greer wasn't in the mood for any more reprimands.

Grabbing the hot mug, she murmured her thanks. "Are you ready? I'm worried about what the kids have been up to while we're away."

He only offered a small grunt of agreement before he took a huge gulp of the steaming coffee. She watched him over the rim of her cup. It would seem she needed to find that new apartment sooner rather than later.

He took two more swigs from his mug. "Hurry up so we can drive over. We will discuss your latest paranormal encounter this evening," he said without looking at her. Grabbing keys from a hook by the door, he walked out.

Her throat burned as she threw back the last of her drink, but she wasn't going to keep him waiting. Taking her bag from the back of a kitchen chair, Greer stopped short at the sight of Cahya standing in the open doorway with an undecipherable expression. Greer pulled the back door closed and wondered just how long she'd been there.

Revelations

They were pleased to find the students proceeding well on their own. Jones had taken the lead and was directing the team.

Over the course of the day, they uncovered five more skeletons. Each one advanced the pattern of missing bones. The church and college were anxious for a status report, so Adam called in the day's findings to each and promised a full written report after the last grave was uncovered. However, he declined to mention the graves under the cathedral as he was sure it would bring the whole diocese down for a look.

Adam had taken the students on a quick tour of the catacomb. The boys loved the door hidden in the church altar but were otherwise unimpressed with the remains when compared to the secret ones they were uncovering in Room A. Greer was glad they weren't clamoring to spend more time in there as she was putting off her official investigation another day, wary of encountering the strong physic energies and that cold thing again.

Greer was exhausted by the time she climbed into the truck early that evening. They'd let the kids go to their dinners, closing up shop alone. Adam had hardly spoken to anyone all day, except to issue curt instructions. He was silent on the ride home as well.

They parked in the alley behind the house where Adam turned the engine off and sat staring at the wheel.

Greer cracked her knuckles and gazed through the windshield. She knew what she had to do. Why did this hurt? "I'll pack my things and be out tonight," she said.

"What?" he asked, turning to her with a confused look. Apparently, he hadn't been listening, but now she had his full attention.

"I said I'll move out tonight. It's not a problem." Greer picked up her bag and reached for the door handle, wondering if she'd be welcomed back to train with April.

Adam shot out a hand to stop her. "No!" She looked at him, alarmed. Pausing for a moment to collect himself, he continued earnestly. "You are not safe alone."

"I'm sure I'll be ok. Either way I can't take advantage of you or your family any longer."

He squeezed her hand tightly. "You are not going anywhere. Promise me."

She quietly considered their entwined hands.

"It is settled," he said authoritatively before she could respond.

Inside, April was haphazardly preparing dinner. As she stirred, she apologized profusely for not being able to psychically locate Greer the night before, even with Sonny's help. The girl said it was like Greer had dropped off the city's supernatural grid.

Over the meal, Greer relayed the details she could recall from the night before. Adam and April listened quietly and only asked a few questions. When she finished, Adam leaned back in his chair, linking his hands behind his head. "I have never heard of this kind of creature. Maybe it is some kind of demon or several demons working together?"

"But what kind, and who's controlling it?" asked April.

"And the hounds. I heard barking again. Why are they targeting me?" said Greer, wondering aloud.

Adam slapped his hands on the table. "We are missing something. Something big," he said frustrated.

April cocked her head at Greer. "You knew that lady? That saved you?"

"Well, she knew my name and looked vaguely familiar. Maybe we went to school together? I can't remember for sure."

April snickered. "I'm pretty sure she was your guardian angel, silly."

Greer raised her eyebrows in amazement. "Really?" A few short weeks ago she would've outright dismissed, even privately ridiculed, anyone making such a claim, but now she paused to give it some serious consideration.

Adam drummed fingers impatiently on the table. "Yes, yes. That is nice, but even a guardian angel is not going to save her every time. We need to figure this out once and for all." He headed for the hall door. "I need to do more research. Come on, Greer, we need to get into the attic."

As Greer hopped up to follow him, April complained about doing the dishes all by herself.

On the second floor, Adam led her into his mother's room. The number of religious items and paintings decorating every surface would put a museum to shame. Stacks of religious books lined walls in the space between furniture. She was impressed by the sheer volume of work that Mother Rose had consumed. Adam had certainly inherited his scholarly habits from her.

Yanking open a small door in one corner, he led her up narrow, dusty stairs. He switched on a bare bulb at the top and grabbed an ancient camp lantern resting on a battered bureau.

"Watch your head," he said as he ducked under a series of beams.

Greer followed, carefully brushing away a few spider webs and their owners as she picked her way to the far end of the room. Adam stopped by the solitary window at the front of the house and bent to open several trunks deposited there. When she caught up, Greer noticed the leather wrapping each trunk was cracked and worn at the corners. The hemp handles on one wooden box had completely disintegrated.

"Family heirlooms?" she asked.

"You could say that." He was carefully pulling books from the first trunk, setting them aside. "They are from a priest who mentored me. He was like a father in many ways." He grinned up at her. "A God father, if you will."

She rolled her eyes at his bad pun as he handed her the lantern. "Hold this please. It will go faster."

"What exactly are we looking for?"

"This priest of mine studied some of the ... less traditional ... aspects of the spirit world. He sought something beyond the common visions of Heaven and Hell. And everything in between. The rare mention of ghosts, angels, and demons in the Bible sparked his imagination. Of course, he had to study it quietly since the church did not fully approve."

"The church approves of so little. It's not hard to believe he'd be ostracized for studying the occult."

"When he passed, he left his library to me." Adam had moved onto the second trunk. "I keep some of the books down in my own little library."

"Ha! You call that mess of papers and books in your room a library?"

Adam scowled briefly, trying and failing to look exasperated.

"Yeah, I said it. You know it completely lacks organization."

"I will not disagree with you," he said, chuckling. "As I was saying, I keep the books I find most useful downstairs. The stuff up here is a little more off-the-beaten-path, so to speak. It has been some time since these were used, but I hope to find something here that will help."

She trained the light into the wooden box as he made his way through its contents. When the two stacks he'd created on the floor teetered, he started a third one. Finally satisfied, Adam stood, brushing his hands on his jeans. "That should do it."

Greer was still peering into the trunk when a small book caught her eye. It was bound in smooth, blood-red leather. Despite its plain appearance, something about it called to her. She gently pulled it from the pile and placed it on top of the other books Adam had selected.

He gave her a quizzical look and then scooped two of the piles up with a shrug. Greer closed the trunks and wrestled the last pile into her arms, almost dropping the light in the process.

The living room was noisy with Sam's cartoons, so they sat at the kitchen table to comb through the books. As they read, they occasionally recited a passage out loud or debated a point. Greer couldn't stop herself from taking copious notes.

A few hours later, Tony and Frankie came stumbling through the back door, the heady scent of beer wafting from them. "Hello, luv," Tony sneered as he shuffled by. Frankie giggled viciously as she opened the refrigerator to pull beer and half of the food out while Tony clumsily sang an ode to his drunkenness. Greer tried to ignore their banging around until Tony dropped to an elbow on the table, knocking her book away. At a small flick of his wrist, a thin flame sparked from his fingertips. "Looking a bit frigid over here. Do you need a real man to warm you up?" he said with a coarse laugh.

"Do you work at being this rude, or does it just come naturally?" asked Greer.

Tony slid in close to whisper loudly in Greer's ear, "I've got somethin' natural to ..."

"That is enough." Adam's tone was an order, not a suggestion. He rose, gathering his pile of unread books and gestured for Greer to follow. Surprising, the smaller man stood his ground so that Adam had to shoulder him out of the way as they left the kitchen.

"Where did you find that guy?" Greer asked as she followed Adam to his room.

"A cultural exchange program for gifted assholes," he said with a sigh. "Really, he just found us. They all seem to find us."

"Or do they find you?"

He shrugged.

They dropped the remaining books in the middle of his bed and, each picking a side to lie on, they went back to their reading.

Greer had lost all tack of time when she finally paused, her eyes watering. "Are we on the right track? I've read about a bunch of demons but haven't found anything matching my monster."

Adam yawned and stretched his arms wide. "No idea. We are only halfway through, and these are just the ones I thought might be most useful. You saw how many more are upstairs."

"I'm going to fall asleep soon, but I really want to find something tonight. Not knowing is awful."

"Ayuh. I would really like to understand the challenge you are facing. Once we identify the spirit and its goal, we can deal with it more effectively."

He picked up the largest tome and carried it to his desk. "Keep going. We are bound to find something soon."

"Ok," she said in agreement. She poked through the untouched books until she found the red one she'd rescued from the trunk. Its leather was unexpectedly supple compared to the many other volumes. Opening the cover, she found a handwritten title on page one. It read "Journal of Father Alo, Societas Jesu Christi" in a spidery scrawl. Society of Jesus, Greer translated. So, Father Alo was a Jesuit.

She turned the page to find a journal entry dated April 14, 1832 in the same hand. Curling up against the headboard, she began reading.

The Jesuit had made his way to Rhode Island at the request of a local bishop. His official mission was to teach at a local parish school. However, as she made her way through the entries, a secondary mission slowly came to light. Father Alo was on the hunt for a demon.

. . .

She ran down the hall barefoot and rounded the corner to see the tree once more, its clean fragrance stronger than ever. The woman next to it, staring out the window, was solid, yet glowed as if made from the very moonlight streaming through the glass.

"Mom!" young Greer shouted as she impulsively rushed to her mother, arms flung wide. She stopped abruptly when her mother turned from the window to face her. Greer screamed.

Blood oozed from her mother's chest, flames licked at her nightgown, bloodied hands reached for Greer as her mother struggled to speak. "He is coming, my darling. You must prepare. He is coming!"

"Who's coming, Mom? Who?" Greer cried and fell to her knees.

"The Prefect," her mother fought to say through tears. Then she screamed as the small flames flared brightly, consuming her.

. . .

Greer awoke screaming with Adam bent over her, calling her name. She barely registered his face and the fact that she'd been sleeping before she broke down sobbing. He sat and tenderly lifted her to him, holding her as she wept. Greer pressed her face into his crumpled shirt, taking comfort in the warmth and, now familiar, scent of him. It reminded her of an ancient, wild forest; complex and soothing, entirely distinct from the strong, freshly cut pine tree in her nightmares. The fear and heartache began to ebb.

He was shushing her softly when she heard someone cough close by. Greer pulled away and was embarrassed to find Mother Rose, April, and Sam all standing around watching her.

"I'll be ok" she said to the room. No one moved. "I ... I had a dream about my mother. It was awful."

Sam walked over and patted her on the top of the head. "She's always with you." Then he left, presumably to return to his cartoon viewing.

Mother Rose sat at the end of the bed. "Tell us."

"All the particulars, if you please," said April.

Greer began tentatively, noting the vividness of the dream. She'd felt the flames her mother suffered. Mother Rose clucked sadly while April looked fascinated. When she finished, Adam assured the other two that he could manage alone, and, to her relief, they quickly left. She threw herself back onto the bed covering her face with her hands.

"Are you alright?"

Greer felt the tears near at hand but willed herself to keep it together. "I think so. It was just ... terrible."

"Yes, it was."

"Thank you for not treating me like I'm crazy."

He was taken aback. "Why would I do that?"

"Well, most adults don't cry over their bad dreams," she said uncomfortably.

He shook his head. "That was not a bad dream, Greer, and you know it."

"I know," she said, gazing intently at his sky-blue eyes until she noticed strange marks all over the left side of his face. "What happened to your cheek?" she asked, reaching up to lightly touch the random creases and smudges.

He looked sheepish and raised his hand to cover hers. "I fell asleep on my desk."

They both laughed as he helped her up and steered her toward the kitchen.

Greer was relieved when she realized it was a Saturday morning. There was no need to rush anywhere, and they had all day to do more research. After breakfast, she took the red journal up to her room. She explained there was no hard evidence; however, she felt on the cusp of making a connection between Father Alo and recent events. Adam promised he'd work on the puzzle of this prefect her mother had mentioned.

It was getting close to lunch time, and Greer was almost done with the journal. The father's references to his demon hunt were sparse and couched in cryptic terms. If she'd never experienced her recent paranormal challenges, she would've missed the references entirely, dismissing them as a bored priest's mystic musings.

Cahya materialized in her doorway. Her face was flushed, and her hands were tight fists at her side.

Startled, Greer set the journal down and asked, "What's wrong?"

Cahya slowly stalked into the room, one boot in front of the other. "You. You're what's wrong," she said, grinding each word through clenched teeth. "Nothing's been right since you showed up."

Greer raised her hands in front of her, trying to placate the woman. "Now, I've apologized for all of the trouble. And I'm incredibly grateful for the help."

Cahya prowled around the end of the bed. "Oh, you're grateful, alright. A little too grateful I'd say."

Adam had apparently told his girlfriend about one or both shared kisses. Even so she resented the insinuation. "I didn't ask for these challenges or talents. I'm handling them as best I can. Everyone in this family is just being supportive."

Cahya glared down at her. "You're taking advantage of them. Especially, Adam's kind heart."

"I most certainly am not. I've offered to leave several times."

"Then why didn't you?" Cahya said in a growl.

Greer looked the woman looming over her directly in the eye. "Adam asked me not to."

All the color drained from Cahya's face, but she quickly rallied. "You don't know what you're doing. You're weak. Incapable of fighting anything more dangerous than your great-grandmother's ghost. You've got no idea what you're getting Adam into."

Greer pulled herself straighter, done being intimidated. "You're right. I don't know what the hell I'm doing. But I might just figure it out with help from this family."

"You mean help from Adam!"

"Yes." Greer glared, holding her ground, even though Cahya looked like she wanted to punch her.

Cahya's shoulders fell. "You're going to get him killed."

"From what I've seen, Adam can take care of himself." He'd certainly proven capable so far, but a small worry had just been born in the back of Greer's mind.

Cahya's leathers creaked as she shifted from foot to foot. Her hands flexed. She started to say something, but clamped her mouth shut again and stormed out.

Sitting down hard on the bed, Greer replayed the conversation in her mind. She wondered at Cahya's motives. Did she just want Greer to leave Adam alone or did she truly believe he was in danger? Whatever the answer, Greer thought it best to skip lunch and hide in her room awhile. She was anxious to finish the journal anyway.

. . .

A while later Adam rapped on the frame of the open door. "Anybody home?"

She glanced up from the journal and couldn't help but smile at the sight of him lounging in her doorway, sandwich in hand. He smiled warmly in return.

"You missed lunch." He handed her a turkey on rye.

"Thanks," she said between bites. "You're my hero." She meant it as a joke, but instantly regretted it when his grin faded.

"How is the reading coming?"

"Um," she flipped to the end and back again. "Two entries to go. Father Alo left rather obscure references to his supernatural work. Much of what he recorded was about his concerns for the children he taught. Not all of them came from easy backgrounds. I was able to tease out a few things that I'd like to run by you though. There is one obvious link to us. Guess where he was preaching?" She paused for dramatic effect. "From April, 1832 to June of 1833 Father Alo ministered at our very own St. Agatha's!" She took a big bite of the sandwich and waited for his reaction.

Adam mulled this over for a moment. "Interesting. It could help narrow my short list of prefects even further. Finish that up and come compare notes at my desk."

Greer bit at her lower lip, thinking. "Hey, we should probably work at the kitchen table. So we won't be in Cahya's way."

His gaze flicked to the open door and back again. "No need. Cahya left."

"Still, I don't want to be in her way when she gets back," Greer said casually. She gathered the journal, a few other books, and a notepad.

"Did she talk to you?" he asked warily.

"Yes, we had a little ... chat," she said as she fidgeted with the scraps of paper bookmarking her morning's work.

He stuffed his hands in his pockets and lowered his gaze. "I imagine it was unpleasant."

She hugged her research to her chest. "Well, it could've been worse. She's just really worried about you."

"Greer, Cahya is gone." When he looked up, she saw regret in his eyes. However, he also looked resolute. He didn't have the look of a man with a broken heart. He ran a hand roughly over his face. "We broke things off."

Greer felt a little lightheaded as memories of Adam's bare chest and warm lips paraded through her mind. "I really hope I wasn't the cause."

"You were. There were other reasons too."

"Oh." Greer stood, clutching her papers, feeling like an idiot without a clue what to say.

He closed the small gap between them then bent down to brush a light kiss across her lips.

"Oh," was all she could say again.

He swept a strand of hair behind her ear. "Come downstairs with me." She nodded, and he rewarded her with a big smile. "We have a lot to talk about."

Adam spun in his desk chair, talking as Greer sat on the end of his bed, the bed he'd shared with Cahya until just a few hours ago. Greer kept reminding herself as she battled to keep her thoughts on the research. Adam's confession about her causing the breakup was exciting as well as nerve-wracking. If she was being honest, her feelings for him had started prior to splitting from Robert.

She focused long enough to give a synopsis of the priest's time at St. Agatha's, even reading aloud some of the more interesting phrases that seemed to refer to chasing demons.

"If anyone was going to be sent by the church to fight a demon, a Jesuit certainly makes the most sense," said Adam. "After all, they do consider themselves to be God's soldiers."

"I agree. No one would've considered these references to be actual events. I believe he kept them vague intentionally; however, I can certainly identify with the realities behind some of these entries. He mentions searching the shadows for great evil, hearing the howl of wild hounds, and seeking truth in the fires and darkness of Hell on Earth."

"If we assume that he was demon hunting near St. Agatha's, we find many common factors." He ticked them off on each finger. "There is the dig location, the hounds that bit you, the fire that killed Liz, and the shadow-men-turned-monster that chased you."

"Seems like a lot of coincidences, doesn't it?"

"Too many to call coincidences." He leaned back in the chair, locking his hands behind his head. "We still need to determine how this all ties to you. It might just be that you are a talented person with the right sensitivities to trigger a reoccurrence of this particular spirit."

"That wouldn't explain my experiences outside of the dig."

"Good point. However, those are not directly related to the shadows and fire, correct?"

"Right." She reflected on the dead motorcyclist and the angry ghost in her living room. "Wait. Except for my mother! She's been warning me about a prefect who's coming. She didn't talk about him when I was a child. My dreams of her definitely changed after the accident. Could she know about whatever Father Alo was following?"

"Seems unlikely, but there might be a connection." He spun around to the desk. "Take a look at this." She placed a hand lightly on his shoulder, self-conscious of such a casual touch, but desiring the connection. She leaned over to peer at the list on his notepad. There were several names and titles, all prefects at local churches for the last twenty years. He started crossing many of them off. "If we remove all those who did not serve when Alo was at St. Agatha's the list is pretty short."

"Only three names. Thomas Walton, Jeremiah Bartlett, and Charles Easton. Hmm. Bartlett sounds familiar."

"Well, they are an old, well-known family in Providence, ayuh?"

"Yes, but the name just came up recently. Where was it? I know! The Bartletts have a history with St. Agatha's. The name came up in the old land deeds at the city archives."

"Makes sense, but it is hardly a smoking gun."

"But that wasn't all. The Bartletts also owned the half-way house where my mother was killed."

Greer saw the understanding dawn on his face.

"How could I have been so blind?" He jumped up and rummaged for a book in one of the stacks against the wall. "Here it is," he said, excitedly brandishing a book titled Catholic Saints over the Centuries. "It was staring us in the face this whole time," he shook his head in disbelief as he quickly flipped past whole chapters.

"What? Tell me." Anxiety and curiosity bubbled in her veins.

He thumbed a few more pages before turning the book so Greer could see a full illumination depicting Saint Agatha. "Here she is. One of the oldest and most popular saints. What do you notice?"

Greer scanned the picture and immediately made the same connection Adam had. St. Agatha was famously missing her breasts. She groaned.

"The Prefect Quintianus cut off Agatha's breasts when she refused him."

"Yes. And then he tried to have her burned at the stake."

Greer paced the crowded room.

"So, what do we really know? Some moldy biblical prefect killed an ancient saint in the same way my mother and your Sarah were killed. How does that help us find the prefect who is alive and killing today? And how could he commit the murders and burials we found in Room A? That was over a hundred years ago."

Propping his elbows on the desk, he studied the book before him. "I do not know yet. But, it is the best lead we have."

Greer broke off her pacing. "Oh God. Liz was burned too. There was so much damage that I'm sure even the coroner couldn't tell, but what if she was tortured in the same way?"

Adam buried his head in his hands, unable to speak. Greer saw the responsibility immediately weigh on him. His broad shoulders slumped; his head bent even lower. She ran both hands across his shoulders and down his arms, encircling him, holding him while he silently wept for another soul he couldn't save. She murmured words of comfort and gently floated kisses throughout the waves of his hair until he was able to lift his head again. He pulled her closer for a firm kiss then turned back to his book, drying his eyes with the heel of his hand.

Pacing again, Greer speculated aloud. "But why attack Liz in the first place? She wasn't like me, or my mom. She didn't have any special talents, right?"

Adam shook his head. "Not that I noticed."

"So, maybe she was just alone at the dig, and he saw an opportunity. Are we looking for someone who has talents of his own? Is that how he can summon the hounds to help him?"

"Possibly." He threw his hands in the air in frustration. "Or we could be looking for a ghost!"

"You think the ghost of Quintianus is doing this?" she asked, surprised.

Adam leapt out of his chair and took her place pacing the floor. "It is possible his spirit is materializing for these murders. Or he may be possessing someone in order to carry out his plans. You did mention that the Bartlett family has popped up in connection with the church and your mother. So, right now, I am leaning toward possession."

"Possession is a real thing?" Greer said in a squeak.

"Absolutely. And a very disagreeable thing at that."

She slid into the chair, pulling the prefect list close. "Ok. I assume we need to figure out what he is before we can do anything about him. Let's put April and her spirit guide on the case."

"We will need a few more people."

Casting a Net Into the Sea

Greer studied Adam's expert possession team gathered around the kitchen table. Mother Rose was stubbing out her latest cigarette. April sat humming quietly to herself. Frankie had refused a chair, choosing instead to sulk by the sink.

Adam pushed through the door with several books tucked under his arm. Pulling out a chair, he placed the books on the table and nodded to his mother.

She took this as her cue and started right in. "You must understand how extremely difficult it is to determine whether someone is possessed. It's not like in the movies where heads spin wildly while they spew evil wishes in foul languages. Oh, sure there is record of levitation and talking in tongues when people have been exorcised, but those are rare cases."

"Rare in what way?" asked Greer, completely nonplused about the idea of encountering a levitating demon. She was also struggling to silence the inner voice screaming at her that this was all a terrible farce, and she should run far, far away from these people.

"Well, they are rare in that the entity made itself known at all. Most spirits want to hide inside their host so they can do the most damage without getting caught. A spirit showing itself is called manifesting. Someone can be possessed, but until the spirit manifests you might hardly guess something is amiss."

Greer sighed. "Great. So, we can't just look around town for a crazy person. It could be anyone?"

Mother Rose hummed in agreement and tapped a new cigarette from its pack. "First, you'll need to decide how likely it is that this spirit has already manifested."

"It seems pretty dang powerful to be summoning hellhounds and this multi-headed thingy," said April.

"Which, to my mind, means you are dealing with a very severe possession which hasn't yet manifested," Mother Rose said.

Adam said, "So, it is an intelligent entity if it is manipulating its victim without any physical signs?"

Blowing smoke delicately from the side of her mouth, Mother Rose paused before answering. "Ayuh, I think it's smart and extremely old to maintain such control. Now you'll need to decide whether you're dealing with a demon or a ghost."

"A ghost can actually possess people?" Greer asked, incredulous.

April giggled. "Of course, silly. I let Sonny do it all the time. He says it's nice to taste food and ..." She stopped mid-sentence as Mother Rose caught her eye.

The older woman leaned over the table. "April! What've I told you? Possession is not a game. It doesn't matter how benevolent you believe a ghost is. You will not let one, even Sonny, take control of your own body! Watch out for false prophets. They come to you in sheep's clothing, but inwardly they are ferocious wolves. So says Matthew."

The girl mumbled an apology and chose to pick at a loose thread on her skirt.

Frankie sighed loudly. "Why exactly am I here for all this?"

"You are here ..." Adam said as he shot Frankie his own hard look, "because you are going to use your telepath abilities to help us identify who is possessed. We also hope you are sensitive enough to tell us something about the entity involved. Is that alright with you?"

With a conspicuous eye roll, Frankie grabbed a soda out of the fridge before returning to her perch at the sink. Greer was glad to see her stay. While she didn't trust the girl farther than she could throw her, she knew Frankie's skills were needed if Adam had invited her here tonight.

Confused, Greer said, "I really appreciate everyone's help, but, Adam, where do we even begin? Do we send Frankie wandering around the city until she bumps into our bad guy?"

Frankie tried to laugh but only succeeded in choking on her drink. While she sputtered over the sink, Adam pulled out a map of the city and unfolded it on the kitchen table. With a red marker, he drew several Xs. Pointing to each in turn, he said, "Here is the dig; here is Serenity House; there is the school library where my old friend, Sarah, may have first encountered the hellhounds. These are all locations where Greer and others seem to have experienced major activity related to this Prefect spirit."

"What about the fountain where the dogs bit me? Or the church the monster chased me to?" Greer asked.

"We are more interested in where those encounters originated," said Adam. "Something at those locations allowed the spirit to manifest in the first place, so they are key. April will use Sonny at each of these locations to see if they can cause the evil spirit to show itself or find another spirit who can shed light on its identity."

"We'd better have some back up," April said matter-of-factly.

"Of course, you will, dear," said Mother Rose. "We won't send anyone alone into these locations. And, Adam, make sure that neither you nor Greer are at the dig by yourselves. Not even for a moment."

Adam looked at Greer knowingly until she blushed. "I've got it. I've got it," she said. "Apparently I'll need a babysitter at all times."

"Only if you want to stay alive, or at least sane," Frankie said with a smirk.

"What about those two demonic possessions Cahya found the other night?" Greer felt uncomfortable saying the woman's name.

Frankie responded, seeming interested in this conversation for the first time. "April and I checked them out. They were just junkies. If something other than heroin had been possessing them, it was gone by the time we got there. One of them had even OD'd before we found them."

Mother Rose and Adam made the sign of the cross and moved on with the meeting.

An hour later, they had a plan for the next day. Each site would be investigated as a team. Greer would work with April and Sonny trying to contact the local spirits. Adam and Frankie would walk the nearby streets to get a read on anyone under possession. Mother Rose's role was to say prayers at home as she didn't possess any supernatural talents; she was more like the family librarian. Greer couldn't imagine Adam ever allowing his mother to put herself in danger anyway.

The first location they planned to try was the school's liberal arts library. Frankie argued it was a waste of time since they weren't certain it was where Sarah first encountered the hounds. However, Adam assured everyone it would be good practice for Greer even if nothing panned out.

Adam sent Greer off with April while he made further preparations. After a few hours, he poked his head around April's doorway to check on them.

"Hey, you two should knock off for the night."

April and her guide, who was floating serenely inside the active spirit circle, both yawned.

"Seriously, Sonny?" Greer asked, skeptical.

"What?" the ghost replied lethargically. "It's just a habit, man." He winked out, and April began cleaning up the circle's elements.

"Greer," Adam said shyly. "Can I walk you home?"

Grinning, Greer hopped up and linked her arm in his. They walked the few feet down the hall to her room, stopping just outside the door. Adam took her hand, rubbing the back of it gently with his thumb.

"I am afraid we did not find time to talk about ... this." He glanced down at their joined hands. "About us."

"It's ok. There's plenty of time." Greer leaned against him, wrapping her arms around his waist. He did the same and rested his chin on top of her head. They stood together just enjoying the closeness of the other.

He placed a kiss in her hair before releasing her from the hug. "You really do need to get some sleep," he said huskily.

She sighed and let go as well. Frankly, she was glad to put off any serious discussion about the status of their relationship until she was more certain of her own feelings. "Night," she said, giving him a quick peck.

He watched as she softly closed her door. It was another moment before she heard his footsteps retreat down the stairs.

. . .

The following morning, the possession team shared a quick breakfast and group prayer led by Mother Rose before heading over to the John D. Rockefeller, Jr. Library, which was just across the street from the archaeology library.

As it was a Sunday during summer break, they didn't see another soul as they mounted the short flight of steps to the front doors. Adam had to swipe his staff ID card to unlock the door since the library was not officially open until noon. He wished April and Greer good luck before they disappeared inside.

Glancing around the lobby, Greer asked, "Ok, where do we do this?" She felt well prepared and eager to get started.

April nodded toward a set of stairs, and they walked down a level. There they found a hall of private carrels that could be signed out by the day. All the doors currently stood open, and April led them to the one at the end of the hall.

With the door closed and locked, the women quickly set up their spirit circle and began to chant quietly. They hoped anyone else who might be using the carrels today would pick the first one they came to.

Sonny quickly appeared and began his call to nearby spirits. April and Greer maintained a low chant as they held hands over the center circle. Their job was to power Sonny while he searched the other realm.

After an hour of work, they'd only made contact with a bitter professor who wanted updates on the stock market and a flamboyant librarian who was sure someone had pushed him down the library stairs to his doom.

Worn out, April wished Sonny good-bye and let go of Greer's hands.

"Thank you. I'm not sure how much more I could've taken," Greer said as she rubbed the feeling back into her hands and arms. The constant tingling of the circle's energy made her entire body feel slightly numb.

April began cleaning up. "Well, we knew it'd be a long shot. Call Adam and tell him we're done."

Greer walked out into the hall and dialed Adam's number. He answered quickly and anxiously asked whether she was ok. She assured him that all was fine, but the summoning was a bust. He and Frankie had also been unsuccessful. They agreed to meet out front in five minutes.

The women stood in the shade of the building, chatting while they waited on the others to return. Sunshine drew Adam's face into sharp relief as he came around the corner. Greer admired his strong features and the tan he was developing from their weeks of field work. Maybe she was looking forward to that personal discussion with him after all.

"Are we done now?" Frankie whined.

"No, it is early. We have time to investigate at least one more location today," Adam said, exasperated with Frankie's lackluster attitude.

"I really want to do this, but I'm kind of wiped out," said Greer. "Can we have lunch first?" April and Frankie agreed and started rattling off their preferred diners. Greer looked to Adam hopefully.

"Of course," he said with a chuckle. "I am not going to risk your lives on empty stomachs."

Greer took his arm as they headed down the block. "I didn't know you were risking our lives today," she said, teasing.

Adam stopped abruptly. "I would never put you in harm's way unless it was the only way to protect you."

Greer was taken aback by his grave tone as she'd only been joking. She wrinkled her nose up at him. "You know that doesn't make sense, don't you?"

He lifted her hands and brought them together on his chest. "When you have special talents, like you and I do, there may be times where you have to do something risky to solve a more dangerous problem. However, I would never want you to do so without great forethought and help at hand."

"No worries," she said lightly, tugging him toward lunch.

"But I do worry," he said, tugging her back to him. The furrow in his brow supported his statement.

The only thing Greer was currently concerned about was her rumbling belly. Grabbing his hand, she playfully pulled him down the sidewalk after the others who were just disappearing into a deli.

"Come on. I'm starving!"

Over lunch, they decided to tackle Serenity House next. April argued there'd been so much activity, and so many bodies, at the dig site that they should expect some serious trouble when stirring the supernatural pot there. Serenity House was the safer bet.

It was a warm, clear day, but they opted to squeeze into a taxi together for the ride over to Serenity House. No one said it aloud, but Greer was certain the others were as uneasy about the neighborhood as she was.

The taxi dropped them off a block away as Adam wanted to approach on foot, get the lay of the land. Frankie agreed a slow approach would allow her time to sense whatever waited ahead.

The dread in Greer's stomach iced over as they drew near the house. It may have been a reaction to the entity they were stalking, or simply knowing they were approaching the place of her mother's murder. It didn't matter. The place felt all kinds of wrong. She couldn't wait to get the hell out of there.

Stopping short of Serenity, they watched two rough looking men in work shirts share a cigarette as they exited the front door. They gave Adam's group a once over as they rolled by. Frankie gave an involuntary shudder. She shook her head with a look that said no one wanted to know what her brain had just overheard.

Greer's sense of unease tied her in knots. She wanted nothing more than to walk away from this horrible place. Her mother had been tortured, killed, and set on fire mere feet away from where she now stood. She couldn't back out now. Not when all these people were here to help her. She pressed a fist tightly into her stomach and took a steadying breath.

"This place is chock-full of dark energy," April whispered.

"I think we can all feel it," said Adam, agreeing. "Our plan to split into teams again might not be wise. We should go together."

He led them into the narrow alley beside Serenity House. It dumped them into a small back yard bordered by a detached garage. Beyond the garage was another, larger alley behind the row of houses. This was the place where Greer's mother died, at least where her body had been found.

Greer reached out to snatch Adam's hand before he could step from the shadow of the garage. "Don't! I can't get any closer ... and ... and stand where it happened." Her face was ashen, her eyes begged for any alternative.

He hugged her close and motioned for April and Frankie to go ahead. Once they were alone, he spoke gently. "This will be terribly difficult, but I know you are strong enough to handle it."

Greer closed her eyes, willing herself to be brave, to honor her mother by searching for the truth. If Adam had faith, then she would find it in herself to face what awaited in that alley. She took his hand, giving it a squeeze—more to reassure herself than him—and let him lead.

It looked like a hundred other alleys throughout the city. Over time, the homeowners' cars had pressed wide ruts into the crumbling brick pavement. Greer looked at the overflowing waste bins, discarded furniture, and tools littering the backstreet. Her mother's last view of this world was a dark, oily landscape of refuse.

What a horrible place to die.

"Come on, get inside before we're seen," April said, pointing to the garage. "We can't do no summoning out here."

Both doors on the outbuilding were badly weathered, but one sagged a little more than the other. Adam grabbed the rusty handle of the better one and lifted it with a loud screech of wheels in unused tracks. They darted glances in each direction, but the lane remained quiet. They were glad to find it rather empty inside. Light straining through the grimy window on the far wall showed an old lawnmower, a few rakes, and some bags of rock salt. On the far side some, old furniture and boxes were perilously stacked against the wall. Adam waved everyone inside and pulled the door closed again.

Greer helped April hurriedly set up a spirit circle. April motioned for everyone to take hands then led a low chant. Greer tried to follow along but had trouble focusing past the horrible churning in her stomach and a grinding buzz between her ears. She shook her head, trying to clear it.

"Sonny says there's a dark entity near you, Greer," April said breathlessly.

Greer looked over both shoulders expecting to see a shadowy form hovering there. The only thing floating nearby was the dust they'd kicked up.

"Close your eyes. Focus!" April snapped.

Adam squeezed Greer's hand tighter, and she felt a warm surge pass from his fingers to hers. Doing her best to ignore the buzzing, she renewed her efforts on the chant.

It was already hot and stuffy, but Greer felt the heat climb. Sweat broke out on her temple; wisps of hair tied to stand on end before falling limply around her face. She was finding it difficult to breathe and realized her friend's chants had become ragged. Adam's hand grew slick with perspiration.

A low cackle echoed around the room. Everyone's eyes flew open to find a man standing in the center of the circle. Greer was shocked by how extraordinarily real he seemed. He was short, with a jagged scar running from his jaw down to his collar bone. He wore ripped jeans and a dirty work shirt, not unlike the ones they'd seen earlier on the Serenity residents.

It leered at Greer. "Oh, he's got plans for you, little girl."

"What plans?" asked Adam firmly, the voice of a leader.

The figure whipped his head around to stare at Adam. "Not here to talk to you, choir boy."

"What are you here for then?" Greer asked, more irritated than scared.

"Here to keep my eye on you, little peach." Its smirk made Greer's stomach do another flip.

"Why would you be watching?" April asked.

Sonny's outline was barely visible behind the girl. Greer thought a spirit guide should be proactive, step up to protect its human, but Sonny looked like he wanted to be somewhere else.

The figure tossed a look of disdain at the girl. "Oh, yeah, he has plans." He breathed into Greer's face, and she pulled back sharply from the foul odor. The figure made a sucking sound. "Course, maybe I got some plans of my own."

He lunged from the circle, darkly stained hands reaching for Greer. Instinctively, she dropped Adam and April's hands, breaking the circle. The man kept coming. She grabbed her angel wings and extended the other hand, palm-out, to the entity. In a steady voice, she prayed St. Michael's prayer; the same one April had used to banish the lost soul from her apartment weeks before.

Her necklace shone brightly as she prayed. Then everyone else's talismans began to glow as well. Adam's sun pendant threw its silver light while April's several charms illuminated a rainbow around her.

The entity cowered from the light. It shriveled smaller and smaller until it seemed to disappear right into the dirt of the garage floor.

When it was gone, Greer lowered her hand and hooted a short laugh of victorious relief. Glancing around the circle, she was annoyed to find the others staring at her, mouths agape.

"What?" she asked. "Did you think I wasn't paying attention during my lessons?"

"What the actual hell did you do to me?" Frankie's eyes were squinted shut as she rubbed her temples roughly with the heels of each hand.

"Whoa! What did you do?" April asked uneasily as she examined the many charms hanging around her neck.

Greer shrugged. "What're you talking about? I did exactly what you taught me to do."

"We didn't teach you that," April said.

"What's the big deal? That horrible man is gone. I'd think you'd all be happy," Greer said, feeling keyed up and ready for a fight.

"That was so not cool," Frankie said, groaning. She rubbed her temples as she slowly circled the room.

Confused, Greer looked to Adam for an explanation. He rested a hand on her shoulder and gave her a weak smile. "You did a great job. No one is questioning that. Your method though, was a bit ... unorthodox." When shrugged in continued bewilderment, he said, "You seem to have drawn on our powers as well as your own. Did you see our talismans glowing along with yours? You did that."

"It felt like you were trying to pull my brain out through my eyeballs," said Frankie.

"Um, not really. I guess I thought you were just doing your own thing," Greer said, taken aback. "I didn't mean to do anything wrong."

"Of course not," said Adam. "But you took us by surprise."

April said, "Time to go. That evil's gone for now, but I feel lots of trouble brewing here."

Without waiting, Frankie yanked the door open. They all cringed again at the squeal of metal, but quickly ducked out and were halfway down the alley before Frankie could finish pulling it shut again.

. . .

Greer jumped in a hot shower when they returned home. She stood under the stream wondering how she'd pooled everyone's talents to bolster her own. The only explanation she found rational was that she'd discovered an effect of the spirit circle which they'd never tapped into. Despite everyone's shock, she was rather proud of how she'd handled herself.

Wandering down to the kitchen in sweats and a tank top to help with dinner, she hummed a happy little tune. Adam already had two big pots steaming on the stove.

"Let me help?" she said as she boldly slid a hand into the back pocket of his jeans.

He pulled her in for a quick kiss. "Thank you. We are keeping it simple tonight. Just pasta."

"It's been a long day. I don't care what we eat as long as we do it soon."

He handed her some lettuce and carrots then stopped short. "Are you feeling alright?"

"Yeah, yeah. I'm not tired or sick like when I touched that bone. The necklace is really working." She started chopping up a salad. "Why?"

He lifted her chin between his thumb and forefinger, turning her lightly from side to side. "I do not want to alarm you; however, your eyes look very different."

"What are you talking about?" she said, blowing it off.

"Greer, there were some light flecks in there before. Now they are lighter all over."

"I did notice some changes and just figured it's some kind of ocular damage from the concussion."

"Maybe," he said followed by a hum of doubt.

"Well, I don't know. People's eyes don't just change color. Come on," she elbowed him away from his sauce. "I'm hungry." She peered into the large pot of marinara and her stomach growled loudly as she gave it a stir. "It smells delicious. What's your secret?"

Adam moved in close behind her, bending to leave a soft kiss behind her ear. "My secret is," he whispered as he kissed her neck, "I open two jars of store-bought sauce and turn the stove on."

She giggled at the next kiss. "Stop tickling."

"Hmm," he said as he parted his lips to run the tip of his tongue down her neck.

She sighed, dropping the spoon and splattering sauce. He kissed his way back up until she lifted her chin, pulling his lips to hers. She reveled in the taste of him. Forgetting all about food for the moment, she turned into his embrace.

"Careful," he said, drawing her away from the hot stove. They swept across the room in a blind embrace until he collided against the table. Greer pressed him against it as she ran her hands down his chest and then lower to feel the growing hardness through his jeans. Adam ran his hands through her hair and deepened the kiss.

Sharing his breath, sharing his heat, Greer forgot everything around them. She popped the button on his pants, tugged at the zipper, and slipped a hand inside to feel the fevered skin hidden there. Adam shuddered and broke away for a moment, searching her face.

She stared back at him daring him to stop her.

He groped for a chair, fell into it, and pulled her to stand in front of him. Taking hold of her shirt, he slowly raised the fabric, kissing a narrow trail up her stomach. She inhaled in anticipation as air hit the bare skin of her breasts. He cupped one in each hand and slowly traced circles around each nipple.

Greer moaned and melted down into his lap. Sitting astride, burying her hands in his damp curls, she pressed herself against every inch of him, capturing his mouth once more. He slid a hand down the back of her waistband to clutch the round fullness there.

They heard April's sudden yell from upstairs. "They're screwing in the kitchen, Mother Rose! They're doing it!"

"Not in my kitchen," Mother Rose trilled from the living room.

Greer reluctantly broke the kiss and pressed her forehead to his. They both laughed quietly. Adam snuck in another quick lick to her chest, sending a shiver through her.

"We will finish this later," he said in a husky promise.

She wrapped her arms around his neck and pressed her nose to his hair. He still smelled of soap from his own hurried shower.

"I wouldn't miss it."

Let Your Light Shine

Disappointingly, they'd fallen asleep over another pile of dusty books, only to wake early and drive over to the dig the next morning. It was a rather ordinary day by recent standards. Adam and Greer debated over whether they should bring April and Frankie in for a spirit circle that evening. While Adam was very anxious to learn more about the Prefect and his possible human vessel, he preferred to have a better understanding of Greer's ability to channel powers before summoning spirits in such a charged environment.

Adam decided to see how another quick trip in the catacombs went before committing further. Greer didn't last more than a few minutes inside the first body-filled room before she was cold and weak from the surrounding energy. So, Adam sent her out to continue digging up the remains in Room A while he worked up a formal report on the areas discovered under the cathedral.

They were still disputing the best course of action at home that evening when Cahya surprised them with a call. She'd been meditating and offered to come over later if they cared to hear what she had to think.

April also surprised them by volunteering to help prepare dinner. However, Adam and Greer soon realized she just wanted to keep an eye on them, making some new demand or excuse anytime they came within a few feet of each other. Teasing her, they stole a kiss over the silverware drawer. The girl gagged, sending them into hysterics. They only promised to behave after she threatened to leave without eating.

The couple locked eyes suggestively across the table while April chatted away. She'd decided Greer's new talent was pretty impressive.

While Greer still had reservations, she hoped they'd find a way to control it.

Cahya arrived as they were cleaning up, looking bitter and heavyhearted. "Come on," she said and made her way upstairs without waiting to see if they were following.

April plopped onto a beanbag chair in a billow of skirts. "What've you got?" she asked breezily.

Adam and Greer hung back, waited hesitantly as Cahya methodically settled into a lotus position on the floor. Greer thought she still looked agitated, if someone in a Kenny G T-shirt and yoga pants could looked agitated.

"Mother Rose called me about what happened in the garage. I didn't want to call back... but all of my meditations keep pulling me back to this unique power of Greer's. All people can channel to some degree, some much easier than others," she said with a glance toward April. "But it sounds like Greer not only channeled each of you, but more specifically your talents. It seems she is accessing much higher frequencies than a newbie should be able to. I can't even do it. I tried," she said, finishing with a slight blush at her failure.

"Sounds possible in theory, but I have never seen it happen before," Adam said, eyebrows arched in uncertainty.

Cahya blinked at him. "There is much in this world that we never see."

Confused, Greer sat down across from Cahya and asked, "So how do I control this channeling? It seemed to be painful for Frankie. I don't want to hurt anyone."

"I'm not sure you can control it," Cahya said directly. "At least not for quite some time."

"You're a big help," said April.

Cahya pursed her lips and stood. "Do what you want with this. I just needed to tell you so I could clear my head." She brushed past Adam on her way out without a look back.

"Now what? Do I practice trying to channel someone's talents?" Greer glanced at each of her friends for guidance. Adam was lost in his own thoughts, and April stared blankly at the ceiling, twirling a scarf.

Greer was growing tired of waiting, tired of asking for directions all the time, so she decided to take the bull by the horns, as it were. Settling into a lotus position, she relaxed her hands on her knees, closed her eyes, and began to chant. Softly at first, building to a higher pitch and frequency as she persisted. The familiar tingling began at her fingertips and toes, soon finding its way to her center. Her whole body hummed with energy.

Eyes closed, she tried to visualize Adam and April. In her mind's eye, Adam was standing tall near the door, surrounded by hazy waves of orange and blue light. A small silver spark hung at the center of his chest. April was a lump on the beanbag with a dappled rainbow hovering overhead.

Greer focused on Adam's spark and April's rainbow. She imagined pulling those lights to herself. The silver ember at Adam's chest burned stronger, flickering into a bright flame, while April's multitude of colors became more defined and brightened to the point of obscuring the girl's elongated features. As these auras intensified, so did the sense of power inside Greer. The thrum of energy became a strong vibration pulsing within her. Each pulse was a golden wave of light that brought a feeling of joy, power, or love. It was exhilarating and she never wanted it to end, until it suddenly became a bit overwhelming. She tried to focus on the waves of energy as they crested. They threatened to spill over, out of her. They needed release. How? Where?

She heard someone calling her name. In her mind's eye, she saw Adam next to her, his features obscured by the brilliant, silver light of his talisman. She searched for April and found her rainbows filling one whole corner of the room. She could see Adam shouted her name, but she barely heard him over the pounding energy. Reaching out mentally, trying to find some place for it to go, she found nothing, just more light. She quaked with each surge.

"Stop! Greer, stop!" Adam finally yelled loud enough that she heard. He was kneeling in front of her and shaking her by the arms.

She didn't know how to stop! Drawing a deep, ragged breath, she tried to push the energy down, into her core, but the waves kept crashing. Adam continued yelling. April was mute and motionless in her corner.

"Stand back!" Greer heard another voice command.

A small figure with a muddy yellow aura was moving toward her. She felt a large round object being pressed into her hands; at the same time, she recognized the smell of cigarettes and rasp of Mother Rose's voice.

"Put it in here!" Adam's mother was shouting. "Focus it all into here!"

Greer held the object at arm's length in front of her and tried to focus. It was a dark lump amid all the glowing colors of the room.

"Do it now!" yelled Adam.

Greer imagined all the golden light traveling from her into the dim object. What she'd initially mistaken for a vase took on a recognizable outline as the object began to glow. It was one of Mother Rose's many big-bellied Buddhas. It now shone like a bright camp lantern. Her shaking eased as the waves of energy radiated from her core, down her arms and through her hands into the statue. She felt relief as the energy ebbed from her into the Buddha ablaze with golden light. The last of the light left her in a snapping release. The statue flared then exploded.

Shielding her face with her arms, Greer realized everything had abruptly gone dark. Taking a slow peek, Greer was not at all surprised to see small shards of ceramic scattered in a dusty circle around her.

April and Adam were staring with their mouths hanging open. Mother Rose stood, rigid and scowling at all three of them in turn. "I hope you plan to clean this up, Adam," she said tersely as she tried to tuck a few stray hairs back into her tight bun. It was the first time Greer had seen the woman with a hair out of place.

"Ayuh," he said, answering vaguely. She cleared her throat loudly and he pulled his shoulders back, standing at attention. "Yes, of course, Mother."

"You shouldn't have let her do that," Mother Rose said in a sharp reprimand. "She obviously wasn't ready, and, from the looks of it, neither were you."

"He didn't know I was going to do it," Greer said in his defense. "I didn't even know. Well, I knew what I wanted to try, but not what would happen." She offered an apologetic shrug.

"Well, what happened is you channeled too much energy with nowhere to put it! What'd you think you were going to do with all that power?"

Greer cast her eyes down, embarrassed that she'd failed to think her plan through.

"I can take it from here, Mother," said Adam.

Mother Rose cast a disapproving look around the room, turned, and left. April followed her, looking at Greer with a trace of fear, and grumbling about the vacuum cleaner.

Greer buried her face in Adam's shoulder. "I ... I didn't think."

He stroked her hair. "You scared me."

"Really?"

"You were convulsing. I thought it was a seizure, and that maybe your power, combined with the concussion, was causing you permanent harm."

"I was ok. I think." Greer said with a degree of doubt. "You and April have taught me so much, but I'm really sick of waiting on this demon to kill me. I wanted to try something on my own."

"But I could not help you," he said, clearly troubled.

Placing a hand to his cheek, she smiled a little sadly. "I didn't expect you to."

She pulled him to the door and led him down the hall into her room. "Stay with me tonight?" He tipped her face up and kissed her tenderly before carefully closing her door behind them.

"Guess I'll just do the all the cleaning up then!" they heard April holler down the hall.

But Greer wasn't laughing as she slid her jeans off and kicked them away. Sitting down on the bed, her arms felt heavy as she tugged the now dusty shirt over her head. Tossing it into the far corner, she looked up to find Adam watching her.

Pulling at the hem of his shirt, she slowly worked it up over his stomach. Impatient, he grabbed the fabric, yanking it over his head in one swift motion. Her fingers fumbled at his waist trying to work the button. Adam stepped in again to finish the task and let the denim fall to the floor.

"Why do you always have dust in your hair?" He chuckled as he brushed ceramic flakes from her hair.

"You know why." She stood on tip toe, playfully nipping his ear until she suddenly felt lightheaded and lost her balance.

He caught her against his chest. "Are you alright?" he asked, concern evident despite the rasp in his voice. "Your eyes seem a little too bright."

"Of course." She tipped her head back to give him a reassuring smile, but that only brought a fresh wave of dizziness. "Oh! Maybe I should lie down."

He helped her onto the bed and studied her apprehensively. "Are you going to pass out? Should we elevate your feet?"

"No. Please." She patted the bed beside her. "I'm just tired."

He eased down beside her and tucked the blanket around her.

"No wonder. You basically just ran a physic marathon."

"Yeah, I guess." She was frustrated by how difficult it was to keep her eyes open. Reaching up she traced the stubble along his jaw line. "Will you still stay?"

He kissed her firmly and then again affectionately on the forehead before scooping her into the crook of his arm.

"Rest, Greer."

She snuggled against his shoulder and fell asleep with the scent of the forest filling her dreams.

Make Known to Me the Path of Life

They were uncovering the last two skeletons in Room A. In total, eighteen bodies were laid out in three rows of six across the floor. While they were all missing various bones, none of them showed signs of being burned like the nineteenth body from the alcove.

Greer rose from the body she'd been working on with Rigsby and Jones. They were using dental picks and small brushes to carefully clear away the last of the dirt around the bones. Crossing her arms over her chest, dust trickled from her brush down the front of her shirt as she scanned the room.

"What are you thinking?" Adam asked as he knelt nearby, working on the very last skeleton to be revealed. It appeared to be yet another female.

"What if there are more?" she asked.

"More bodies?"

"Yes. What if there are more people buried under these remains? Could we be looking at multiple layers of burials?"

Adam stood and stretched broadly. They'd been working at a frenzied pace all morning to finish. The church and university were very anxious for answers.

"It is possible," he said. "Churches often layered burials in the crypts and under the church floors, right? Even ancient cultures often layered burials in places of worship. Sometimes it seems the purpose was to provide a connection to their ancestors. At other times, it seems to have been sheer convenience."

"I know there's a lot of pressure to finish this thing fast, but we have to make sure we've accounted for everything."

He nodded and grabbed two shovels. Handing one to Greer, he motioned her toward the first grave along the far wall. "It is unlikely that the layering would have been precise, so we can dig a small test trench around this body. If we do not find anything, then we will not have to move this skeleton yet."

"Why? We're going to remove all of the bones before excavation on the new building is complete. Let's just move it now," she said, arguing.

"Just trust me, alright?"

The two of them carefully dug until they had made a trench about one foot wide and three feet deep. The afternoon had grown hot and muggy even in the subterranean room. They finally stopped, exhausted.

Greer wiped her forehead against her shoulder and pulled her ponytail down to shake dirt out of her hair. "Ugh," she said, running a hand through the sweaty mess.

"You are a dirty girl," Adam said in a low voice, teasing.

"You're filthy," she retorted, playing along. "Have you seen those pit stains?"

Adam pulled the fabric away from his skin, grimacing when he caught a whiff of himself. "I would love to take this off."

"Why don't you?" she said with a shrug.

"I would prefer not to answer any questions about my scars."

Greer decided to change the subject. "Well, it looks like my theory is a bust," she said as she pointed to the new, empty trench. "I still want to probe the rest of this area once we remove the bones. Just to be sure."

"That would be reasonable on any other dig, but our time here is almost up." He took her shovel and started for the ladder. "I have been told we need to complete our work by the end of this week."

"But that's two weeks ahead of schedule." Greer continued to argue as she climbed up after him. "How can they expect us to finish by then?"

He answered her topside. "The church and school want as little publicity about this as possible. The sooner it is done the better. I have already tiptoed through two press interviews, and the board members are being pestered daily by local media for updates."

"Well, it would help if we had some answers of our own. Are we ever going to get the DNA results on the bone fragments?"

"The lab said any day now."

"I've been thinking I should try touching the bones without my wings on. You know, get a real feel for them."

He stopped and looked at her horrified. "After what happened before? How could you consider such a thing?"

She shrugged, feeling bad for upsetting him, but feeling worse for not being able to help the victims in the ground below. "I used to hear the bones, you know? Even before the accident, they told me their secrets. I think it's worth risking taking the pendant off long enough to learn more about these women." Fingering the little wings at her collar bone, she wondered just how horrific the visions would be. Could she really handle it?

"Absolutely not," Adam said sternly. "There is no telling what that might do to you. Wait for the family to help. And keep that charm on at all times. Promise me."

She gave him a quick nod, yet she was greatly troubled that she wasn't doing more to reveal the victim's stories. Greer didn't feel true to herself or them by forgoing her usual sensing techniques.

Adam called out to the students to wrap up for the day. Everyone began packing equipment and pulling tarps over the open foundation.

Rigsby popped out of Room A and shared his sketch of the latest skeleton, noting the missing feet. "They're just gone, man. So weird," he said, shaking his head. His wild hair had grown long enough in the last few weeks that it almost obscured his eyes. Greer decided their student hedgehog now resembled an alpaca.

"Good work, Rigsby." Adam said as he added the sketch to the folders in his bag and sent the kid home.

Greer almost called Rigsby back when she noticed the hatch to Room A had been left wide open. She sighed. "Help me close up, will you?" she asked, waving toward the open door.

She struggled a bit to pull the ladder up on her own and gladly let Adam take over. Bending to remove the two-by-four block that held the door open, Greer noticed movement in the room below. She whipped a hand up to stop Adam as he was about to heave the door into place. She silently pointed below. Adam ran over to his bag and returned with a flashlight. He motioned for her to hang back. She ignored him and peered over the edge as he trained the light into the room below.

"Who's there?" he yelled down. "There is no other way out. Show yourself!"

Slowly a figure stepped into view. It was Jones, looking rather sheepish.

"Jones! What the hell?" Greer said tersely. Her heart was still racing despite the relief of seeing a familiar face.

"Rigsby left me down here," the student answered as he kicked at the dirt, avoiding their gazes.

Adam looked to Greer who lifted an eyebrow in doubt. He lowered the ladder. "No. Stay there," he said when Jones started to reach for the bottom rungs.

Greer followed Adam back down into Room A. She looked Jones over with a skeptical eye while Adam scanned the area with his flashlight. While he had been an exemplary student so far, Greer knew people could fall prey to the desire to loot an archaeological site. Whether to sell artifacts on the black market or keep them for personal collections, even someone like Jones was suspect. However, his clothing was snug on his wiry frame with no obvious bulges in his pockets, and he carried no bag, so she had to admit he looked clean.

Adam completed his circuit of the room and walked down the tunnel to ensure the oak door was secure. He shook his head at Greer, not finding anything amiss. Shining the light up and down Jones, doing his own inspection, Adam asked, "How did you get left behind?"

The boy shrugged, hands in his pockets. "I was busy. And you know Rigsby."

Adam stared hard at the student's plain, square face. On any other dig, he would've immediately taken the student at his word, but this was not a normal site. Too much had happened for him to brush off any unusual activity. He threw another questioning glance at Greer.

She said, "Go home. No one works alone from now on, got it?"

"Ok," Jones said before he bee-lined up the ladder.

He was out of sight before they made it to the top themselves. Closing the trap door and pulling the tarp over it, they swapped stories about losing track of time on projects.

. . .

They discussed the dig over dinner, but April and Mother Rose only half-listened. Mother Rose wanted them to go check the site psychically. Adam argued that, after Greer's latest trick, they needed another night or two to prepare before stepping into such a hot bed of paranormal activity. In the end, his mother agreed.

Frankie banged through the door as they started dishes. They hadn't seen her in a few days. Adam suspected she was staying with any number of girlfriends.

"Hello, Francesca," he said as she moodily spooned dinner from the pots left on the stove.

"Hellooo?" Her attitude indicated she wasn't interested in a conversation.

He took a deep breath and continued, "Frankie, would you please make time tonight to discuss your telekinesis with Greer? Learning how you manage your talent might prove useful to her. She seems to have developed the ability to siphon powers."

The teen froze and cast Greer a suspicious look. "Give me an hour." Plate in hand, she hurried into the living room. They heard her greet Sam over the blare of his cartoons before the door finally flapped shut.

"Charming as always," Adam said with a sigh. "I hope you can glean something from her experience though." He reached across the table to take Greer's hand. He turned it palm up and traced the lines with his thumb.

"Are you going to read my fortune?" Greer asked, teasing.

"I wish I could."

An hour later, Frankie, without a knock or greeting, walked into Adam's room and fell across the end of the bed. Greer set aside the book she was reading, turned her attention to the taciturn girl and waited. After watching Frankie tap out texts for five minutes, she lost her patience.

"Can we get started?" Greer asked, doubtful she was going to get much practical information out of this encounter.

Adam glanced up from his desk where he was studying a book on demonic possession. He gave Greer a look that said better-you-than-me and went back to reading. After another minute of texting, Frankie sighed and turned the phone off. She looked sideways at Greer.

"What is it you want to know?"

"Well, I'm not sure. Why don't you tell me more about your gift and how you use it?"

The girl looked sideways at Adam.

Greer thought she understood Frankie's meaning. "Why don't we talk upstairs in my room? Just us girls." Greer tried to offer a reassuring smile.

Frankie threw her a look of teenage annoyance; however, she stood and motioned for Greer to follow. In her room, Greer cleared away books covering the quilt to make a seat as Frankie checked her phone again. When the girl finally decided to share how she'd first discovered her telekinetic powers, it all came out in a mumbled rush.

When she was about fourteen, her mom let a new boyfriend, Ricky, move in. He and Frankie didn't get along. He mostly ignored her, but when he did pay attention, it was never good. He yelled all the time and threw things. Eventually he moved on to smacking her across the face when she mouthed-off, which she did all the time.

One time when her mom was at work and Ricky was home alone with Frankie, he demanded she make him lunch. When Frankie flat out told him no, he grabbed her by the throat and shoved her into the coat closet, knocking her head hard on the door jamb on the way in. She heard a thump against the door as he propped a chair under it. She rattled the knob, pounded on the door, even threw her shoulder against it, but she couldn't escape. Frankie screamed horrible things at Ricky and yelled that her mom would kick him out of the house for this. She heard him laugh before he turned up the TV to drown her out.

When she was tired of screaming, Frankie sat down to think. She refused to cry. Her mom would be gone for hours. So, she sat and stared at the knob in the little bit of light that leaked in from under the door. She locked her eyes on it and imagined all the ways she would get even with Ricky when it opened. Her butt went numb, and she felt dizzy from the bump on her head, but Frankie kept eye-balling that door, trying to think of a way out.

She fell asleep for a while and woke up to hear her mom talking with Ricky on the other side of the door. Frankie waited for the shouting and for the bang of the front door as he left for good. Instead, she heard her mom snorting and snickering, already too drunk to take the situation seriously. Then Frankie heard nothing, the lights went out, and the apartment was quiet. Her mom had left her.

Frankie screamed in a white-hot fury. In the complete darkness, she saw a blinding light that seemed to start from right between her eyes. This time instead of imagining the doorknob turning to set her free, she pictured the whole door blowing off its hinges. A second later, it had done exactly that.

She grabbed whatever would fit into a pillowcase and her backpack. That first night after leaving home was the hardest; it was freezing, and she had to sleep on a park bench. Eventually she found her way to a group shelter where Cahya sometimes caught her eye. One day Mother Rose showed up working in the soup kitchen. Mother Rose kept asking nosy questions until Frankie got mad and made the soup ladle Mother Rose held fly across the room. Certain that everyone had seen what she'd done, Frankie ran. But Mother Rose had followed her out and hollered down the sidewalk after her. She said she knew what Frankie was and that it was ok. Frankie had no idea what she was so how could this old lady know anything about her? So, she just kept running.

Greer leaned back and shook her head in amazement. "Wow, Frankie. That's awful."

"Eh. It's nothing," the girl said with shrug.

"How did Mother Rose find you then? If you left?"

"Oh, I came back a few weeks later. This loser at the other shelter kept stealing my food and bullying me around. I got so mad that my power made her cot flip over. She was still on it, so she got hurt pretty bad." Frankie was turning her phone over and over in her hands. "I didn't mean to hurt her, but she really had it coming. Anyway, I decided to come back to see if this crazy old lady really did know what I am."

She stopped and stared at the blank screen of her phone.

Greer found Adam still bent over his desk. Wrapping her arms around him from behind, she buried her face in the crook his neck and breathed him in deeply. Adam's hum of approval emboldened her to add a few soft kisses. Spinning his chair to face her, he pulled her down into his lap and returned the favor. He nuzzled her neck, gently chaffing the delicate skin with his five o'clock shadow.

"Stop," she whispered.

"Why?"

"Because we have work to do," Greer said even as she pulled his chin up to capture his mouth.

He drew away playfully. "Very true. Tell me what you learned from our little Frankie."

Greer sighed and slumped against him. "Not much honestly. That's why we need to get back to work."

Adam sounded surprised. "She really could not help at all?"

"Well, her power seems tied to strong emotions, specifically anger. After that, it's just a matter of focusing that anger. I don't really get angry, so I don't see how her method will work for me."

"I beg to differ," he said, squinting at her cynically.

"Not really. I mean, ok, I get worked up when things go wrong at a dig. But I was more upset than mad about Liz's death and breaking up with Robert."

He asked gently, "What about losing your mother?"

Greer gazed inward, searching her memory. Finally, she shook her head. "I've never been angry about her death, only sad. There was no one to be mad at since we didn't know who did it."

"You could have been angry with God."

Greer shrugged. "I never really gave Him a second thought."

"Most people rant and rave at God about the unfairness of losing a parent. I may have blamed him myself a few times after my father left."

"I guess since I never believed in God, I never considered blaming Him." She absently rubbed the golden angel wings between her fingers.

"But now we know who is responsible."

"You're right. This Prefect seems to be to blame. But we don't even know if he's a real person. How can I be angry with a ghost?"

Adam frowned. "It may be a great deal easier than you think when we meet this Prefect face to face. I believe that, whether a ghost or demon, he is inhabiting someone corporeally. In my experience, the activity around you has been too strong to be guided by a spirit who has no solid footing in the physical realm. So, there will be a very real person for you to deal with when the Prefect finally manifests and makes himself known to us."

She stood and slowly paced. "Should I confront him about my mom?

Will he even know who she was?"

"Hard to say. This spirit seems highly intelligent and purposeful. Look at the cycles of his attacks. There was your mother, then five years later it was Sarah, and now five years later it is you."

"What about Liz? Don't you think he got her too?"

"Yes. However, she was not his target, just a convenience for him."

Greer clutched her stomach and sat down on the edge of the bed with a groan. "That's so awful. I don't even have the words."

He crouched in front of her, resting a hand on her knee. "It is unfathomable. But I am determined to end it before anyone else is hurt."

"I'm with you. You know I am. But why us? Even as a reluctant believer, I can't imagine why God is letting all of this happen."

Adam sat and rested his elbows on his knees then blew out a slow breath. It was a moment before he spoke. "That is the big question. Everyone's question. One I have asked many times. I have no answer other than it seems to be His will."

Greer shook her head. "His will? If He is even really a he," she said making finger quotes. "I understand that as God, he gets to make the decisions. But isn't Divine Providence supposed to mean that God has this wonderful plan for us? I thought the deal was that if we behave, like good little children, and do what we're told then we'll get into Heaven."

"That was the happy, childhood version you heard somewhere along the way. Providence is just as likely to be disastrous on a personal level. God's plan for us can be very joyful. Yet, even the most blissful life invariably includes pain, suffering, and struggle. Each person hopes the scales will tip more toward good than bad. I have witnessed people who grappled with so much horror in their life that it seems the scales can never be balanced ... and still they believe."

"Why does He do it?" she asked quietly.

"To allow us to grow."

"Ugh!" She threw her hands up. "Suffering seems rather unnecessary for growth. If we were all at peace, then people would spend their days sharing and learning. The human race could invent amazing new technologies, travel to distant stars, and discover the secrets of the universe. We could evolve!"

"Ayuh. And maybe we will get there one day but, in my heart, I feel that He needs us to fight for that peace and knowledge. They are not things that can just be handed to us."

"You're saying we'll value it more because we worked for it?"

"Not just value it, but we cannot even attain it unless we put forth great effort. Your mind, body, and soul must be willing to follow His path. No matter how difficult."

Greer rubbed the angel wings again. "You've obviously thought a lot about this. And you've been living on this path for a long time, haven't you?"

"As best I can." He watched her worry and smiled. "Your faith will help you as we face the challenges ahead. I am preparing you as best I can, and I will be with you."

"I know. Thanks." She leaned in to kiss him perfunctorily on the cheek. "So. Frankie." Greer said trying to change the subject.

"Yes, Frankie. She is young and rather new to her talent. I am sure there is more to her skill, but she is simply unable to articulate it at this point. You are on your own for now with how to manage the siphoning. We will keep searching for another resource though."

"That's ok," she said cheerily. "I'll just try not to do it anymore."

Adam cast her a doubtful look.

Gird Yourselves, Yet be Shattered

There was a flurry of activity at the site the next morning. They needed to carefully remove each set of bones, tag them, and catalog them over the next two days. This would give them only two days to probe and dig under the current burials to make sure there were no more remains or artifacts, as well as do another search of the catacomb before they would have to formally close the project down. Friday afternoon was the hard deadline as the church's construction crew wanted to start bulldozing over the weekend.

Adam gave the students a warning. "Make sure you note the name of each bone, the position it was found, and any major anomalies or damage before placing it in the box. We will study them in greater detail back at the lab."

Greer added her own stern message. "Remember, these were real people. They are not just your study projects. We will treat their remains with the utmost respect."

Greer kept a close eye on the students as she worked as she didn't like seeing this process being rushed, yet they were at the mercy of the church. She tried to remind herself that many archaeological excavations were cut short by the needs of governments or businesses who valued the new over the old.

"Careful. Those phalanges are easy to lose track of," she called over to one of the boys who seemed to be practically tossing bones into his box. She shook her head and went back to work with one eye trained on the offender.

When she was done with her third body, she took a break topside. Adam found her drinking water in the shade of the tent.

"We are making good progress," he said, content.

"I guess." Was her unenthusiastic reply. "Nothing better get lost. These kids aren't very careful in their work."

"From what I have seen, very few people are as meticulous as you."

She watched him from the corner of her eye as she took another swig of water, unsure if his comment was meant to be praise for her work or a complaint about her hesitation to jump into his supernatural world.

Greer was growing a little tired of inaction on that front herself. She pushed to her feet. "I've been thinking."

"Alright?"

"Yes. It's time to bring the team here to the dig. We need to make contact with the Prefect. We've put it off too long."

"I am not sure you are ready, Greer."

She shook her head, frowning her disagreement. "April worked a little more with me last night, and she agrees I'm as ready as I'm going to be. We need to try. Tonight. I think once we have all of these bones cleared out it may not be quite as intense when we make contact."

"Really? Based on what experience?"

"No experience, obviously," she said, showing her irritation. "However, I'd imagine that if the victims' remains are gone then I won't be psychically bombarded by their pain. The only ghost we will have to deal with is the Prefect."

Adam sipped slowly and scrutinized the excavation area. Most of the students were still working down in Room A. Someone had just disappeared into Room B, and Jones was currently carrying a box from Room A over toward them.

"You may be right," he said. "But the bones in the catacomb will remain. They may be a factor given that shade that came after you."

"I don't care. I'll deal with it. Or April can put a spell on the door or something."

He frowned when she said the word spell. "You still seem to confuse prayers with magic." When she shrugged him off, he took another moment then shook his head as if questioning his sanity. "Alright, we will go down tomorrow night."

"Good." She was happy with her assertiveness.

"Good," he said, agreeing quietly as she caught his slight grimace. It persisted as he nodded at Jones who'd just stepped under the tent.

"What's good, Professor Walker?" Jones asked as he very gently placed his box of bones on the worktable.

"Nothing," Adam said before he reconsidered, "I mean, you are doing a fine job, Jones."

The boy didn't seem to hear the praise. Without looking up from the remains he'd just delivered, he delicately traced a finger along the skull before turning and heading back across the yard.

"It's nice to see at least one of them taking this seriously," Greer said as she gave the bones a once over.

"I should hope you've all been taking this seriously," said Father Doyle as he stepped in front of the tent. His cassock flapped in the breeze, giving the impression that he was about to take flight.

"You know we are, Father," Adam said, hardly trying to disguise his dislike for the man. "Our work here is almost done."

The priest entered the tent and walked around peeking under the lids of random boxes as if he owned the contents of each. Greer started to snap at him when he almost knocked one over but bit her tongue in time. However, she was sure her face had betrayed her irritation when she lunged to prevent the fall. Doyle brushed her off with a flick of his wrist.

"The Church will be glad to be rid of this wretched business. We have big plans for the future of this place. I am personally relieved to see you all leaving soon."

Greer thought Doyle's smirk was very unbecoming for a man of the cloth. *We all have our weaknesses.*

Adam placed himself between the priest and Greer. "Our time is short and there is much to finish so, we are sure you need to be on your way," he said in a tone that invited no response.

Doyle's mouth twitched. "I wouldn't do anything to slow your departure." His smug look as he backed away and strode across the yard for one more look suggested he thought he'd won this little war of his own making.

. . .

Since there were still two bodies left at the end of the next day, they agreed to put off any spiritual confrontations one more night. Greer practiced her prayers and some summoning with April. She'd hardly slept since Adam agreed to call the Prefect front and center.

The entire class worked swiftly on Thursday to clear the final remains. They'd been using metal probes and exploratory trenches to check the floor for more bones as each grave was cleared. Nothing was found.

Greer entered the catacomb again to assist with the final review. She had performed a few extra prayers of protection before entering and was able to make it to the second room before the shivering cold and energy overload forced her to turn back. She left feeling frustrated as Adam and the students finished without her.

The mood was subdued, almost glum as they all began the process of closing the site. Final photos and measurements were taken. Shovels, buckets, brushes, dental picks, and dustpans were cleaned and packed up. Not everything would fit in Adam's truck, so a few students offered to transport them back to the lab at the archaeology library.

The remaining boxes of bones were to ride over in Greer's car. Adam confessed he was a little uneasy about her being alone with them, but she flashed him a look that made him back down. She knew if she couldn't handle a few dusty bones then life as she knew it was over.

Some excitement broke out just before they left. Adam received a call from the biology lab. The long-awaited results were in on the ashes and bone fragments found in the alcove. Everyone waited intently while Adam nodded into the phone a few times.

"Well, there is not much to tell," he said after hanging up, admitting his disappointment to the eager faces surrounding him. "The bones fragments were very small and obviously badly burned." He glanced at Rigsby who was practically coming out of his skin in anticipation. "There seems to be some contamination as multiple partial DNAs were found. However, the lab was able to determine that the remains are female. They were also determined to be more than 100 years old as they contained no fluoride or other elements that became standard in a city-dweller's diet as of the early 1900s."

"Yes!" Rigsby exclaimed with a little fist pump in the air. Everyone stopped to stare at him. "What? That means the ashes match the other bones by date and gender. That's gotta mean something, right?"

Adam's face remained neutral. "The gender is clear. But, as you should know, carbon dating is just not perfectly accurate within such short time frames."

"So, the dating is wrong?" Rigsby asked, deflated.

"No, not necessarily," said Adam. "We will officially say it is indicative, yet inconclusive. We really cannot draw any hard conclusions with such little data."

At this, all the students' hopeful expressions wilted.

Feeling a bit let down by the power of modern science to solve this particular puzzle, Greer still tried to rally the kids. "Look. Don't be discouraged. Any data is better than none. And more tests can be run later... if we get the funding."

"Well, that is unlikely," Adam said with shake of his head.

Greer ignored him and pressed on with not quite a smile, but what she imagined was a look of optimism. "You've helped to uncover some forgotten history. These women were lost. Now they're found. That's because of you. Don't forget that."

Murmurs of assent trickled through the group, and they all went back to their earlier tasks with a little more pep in their step. Greer did so as well, avoiding Adam's gaze.

The trap door was the last artifact to be recovered. Adam still needed to decide on the best way to remove it for transport and storage. There was nothing special about it, except that it led to a crypt of horrors. However, he decided it unwise to discard it at this point.

He'd finally decided to use the pulley system to lift the door and its frame out of the ground. "Grab the other end of this rope, Rigsby." Adam tossed the thick rope over the short span of the door. "You other two will lever the front of the door up when I say." With everyone in place, he called go. The rope slipped easily under one end of the frame.

Greer watched from the tent. Normally she would've insisted on helping, but today she was satisfied to watch from a distance, her mind churning over the coming battle that evening.

"Alright, we will do the same thing with the other side," Adam said. Malcolm and Jones slid long crow bars under the frame and began lifting. This side didn't rise as easily. Adam called a halt so Jones could work his crowbar further underneath.

When the frame finally broke free, Rigsby hurriedly slid the rope under and passed it to Adam who tied it around the length of six-by-six that hung from the pulley. Rigsby rushed to the back of the pulley and grabbed the rope running through it. He yanked, and the weight of the trapdoor lifted from the supporting crowbars.

Greer saw what happened next as if in slow motion. Rigsby let go of the rope with one hand to pump the air in a hoot of triumph. Adam shouted as he leapt toward the slackening rope. The other boys rushed to scramble out of the way, except Jones, who'd moved in closer for leverage. He went sliding in the loose dirt as the door fell. When his lower leg disappeared underneath it, his howl of pain echoed off the cathedral walls.

"Call 911!" she yelled, running toward Jones. Sliding to a stop next to him, she clawed at the dirt around his leg while Adam heaved frantically at the pulley to raise the door again. The other boys rushed to help, giving Adam a hand as he swung the door out of the way before securing the mechanism.

Blood soaked the ground. It ran freely from Jones' leg where the tibia and fibula poked out at odd angles through the skin. Greer applied pressure above the wound. Adam ripped his shirt off and handed it to her. She tied it tightly around the leg and was glad to see the river of blood slow to a mere stream.

Their wait for the ambulance was silent until the sirens drew near. The medics sprinted across the yard, hardly slowing as they navigated the descent into the excavated area crowded with students. Adam cleared the kids back onto higher ground, and Greer let go of Jones' leg so his pulse could be taken and an IV started.

Slowly climbing from the mess in the grid, Greer made her way back to the tent. Someone tried to hand her a rag. She stared at it uncomprehendingly. "For your hands," the thoughtful student said. Greer realized she was covered in blood and accepted the dusty cloth, proceeding to clean up with little success. Adam appeared with a bottle of water. She held her hands out, and he washed them clean.

Greer watched, troubled, as the medics placed Jones on a backboard, securing him to it for transport. It was practically the same process they'd planned for the trap door she thought. Furious, she turned to Adam. "I refuse to believe this was an accident."

He didn't answer, running a hand through his hair repeatedly as he watched another student being carried away.

She grabbed his arm and forced him to look at her. She tried to keep her voice down, but had difficulty containing her anger. "I said, this wasn't an accident. Somehow that damned Prefect caused this."

Adam glanced at the last two remaining students huddled, wide-eyed and talking in hushed tones. Greer couldn't tell if they were curious about the exposed scars on Adam's chest and stomach, now that his shirt was wrapped tightly around Jones's leg, or if they simply wondered how their teacher was going to handle the latest situation.

Greer didn't want to wait to find out. She told Rigsby and Malcolm to immediately finish packing the tools and then meet her at the lab to unload.

In a low voice she told Adam, "We're going to end this tonight."

Adam had observed sullenly while Greer directed the student's efforts to pack away tools at the library. He still hadn't spoken when he pulled the truck up in front of the house an hour later, and Greer didn't try pushing him.

They wandered in separate directions for showers and met up again in the kitchen where April was pulling a bubbling casserole from the oven.

"I'm just going to leave this set here while you two talk," the girl said before leaving in a swirl of skirts.

Greer slumped in her chair, grateful that April hadn't asked about their day. "Do you think that will take long to cool?" she said with a nod to the steaming dish.

Adam poked at the casserole with a spoon then took a small glass from the cabinet and drained an amber bottle into it.

"Are you upset with me?" Greer finally asked.

"No," he said, his back to her. "I am worried about you."

"You don't want to do the summoning tonight, do you?" she said reproachfully. "But you wanted me to learn all of this supernatural stuff. To be able to fight for myself."

Adam set his glass aside and heaped casserole onto two plates. Pushing one in front of Greer, he folded his arms on the table then he leaned in, waiting until she finally made eye contact. "I do want you to be strong and prepared for the fight to come. However, you seem to be picking a fight right now instead of preparing for one. That is a dangerous frame of mind to be in."

"I'm not being reckless, I'm being confident."

He reached for her hand, but she pulled back.

"Confidence is great, Greer, but I need you to be careful. I need you to let me help."

"You have helped me. Now I have to do a little for myself." She picked up her fork and motioned for him to do the same. "I want to get back over there soon, ok?"

They ate in silence until the rest of the family started wandering in. Then they began to work out a rough plan for the evening. No one could be sure of what they'd be walking into.

. . .

Adam decided it best to wait for the cover of darkness. Greer had argued, but, in the end, relented. Tony, Frankie, and April accompanied them.

"Knock it off," said April, snapping at Greer when she cracked her knuckles for the third time since they'd left the house.

Greer helped Adam move the plywood that'd been left over the entrance to Room A after the trap door was removed. Since the demolition was to begin in the morning, there was no reason for anything more secure. Lowering the ladder into the hole, Adam led the group down. The room was cool and smelled of overturned earth. The archaeology class hadn't refilled any of the graves or test trenches since heavy equipment would soon be churning up the ground.

"Watch your step," Greer said, cautioning the team as they picked their way around the room in the dim light cast by camp lanterns she and Adam carried.

April ran her hands along the stone walls, apparently trying to get a sense of the energy. Frankie was drawn to the alcove where she struggled to study the fading murals in the weak light. Tony took a position in the center of the room with his hands shoved into his pockets, waiting impatiently.

"Come on, April," Greer said. "Help me set up the sacred circle."

It was difficult to get the element totems equidistant on the uneven floor. April thought it'd be ok as long as they all held hands to close the circle. When they came together, Adam and Tony offered to stand in the open graves since they were taller. The effect was almost comical in Greer's mind, but she resisted the urge to giggle and took a deep breath to calm her nerves.

"Is everyone ready?" Adam asked with a wary eye on Greer.

"We've been over the plan several times. We're good," she said bluntly.

April reprimanded Greer with a hard squeeze to her hand. Then, taking charge, the girl said, "Let's start with good protection before we open this circle." She led the group in the familiar prayer. "Now focus. And don't let go of hands, or you'll be breaking the circle."

As the low chant began, Greer felt the familiar tingle begin in her hands. Sonny, the laid-back spirit guide, hovered near April. Greer thought he looked rather reluctant as he placed a hand over his charge's. "Join me," April said. Everyone except Tony began a low humming chant along with the girl. The electricity in the room grew.

As Greer focused on April's voice, her body vibrated with power. Behind her eyelids, she could see everyone outlined in various colors of energy. April was a swirling rainbow, while Frankie was a dull tan, and Tony shone a brilliant orange. Adam's outline was a clear blue while the stone talisman glowed silver at his chest.

Greer returned her attention to the sounds and feelings in the room. She was afraid to focus too intently on her friends lest she accidentally siphon them.

As the power reached an almost unbearable level of fire in Greer's veins, April began the call to the spirit they were here to confront. "We summon the one who calls himself Prefect. We demand you show yourself to us here in your pit of horror and death." The air cooled and the energy in the room subtlety changed. April cried out again. "We summon you, wicked Prefect. Come before us now!"

A dark form unhurriedly materialized in the center of the circle. It resembled one of the no-faced men who'd chased Greer through town. A shiver coursed through her at the memory.

"Who are you to summon me?" said the figure in a deep rasp.

"We are the ones who will end you," Greer said, full of hubris.

A loud cackle bounced off the stone walls as the dark figure expanded within the circle. "You pathetic creatures enter my sanctuary and desecrate my treasure. And you think it is you who will destroy me?"

Adam began the Pater Noster. The others joined, and the dark figure shrank back down in size.

April began another prayer. It was the same one used to banish the irritable soul Greer accidentally summoned in the apartment she shared with Robert all those weeks ago. Greer knew it by heart now. Yet, before she could finish, the dark form shouted angrily, "Leave! You trespass here!"

The group started April's prayer from the beginning again, "Saint Michael the Archangel, Defend us in battle. Be our protection against the wickedness ..."

"Leave!" the figure screamed as frigid air blast from the center of the circle.

Little white clouds of breath developed around the circle as everyone continued praying:

... and snares of the Devil
May God rebuke him, we humbly pray.
And do thou, O Prince of the heavenly host,
By the power of God, thrust into hell Satan and all evil spirits
Who wander through the world for the ruin of souls.

They recited the prayer three times, yet the dark spirit remained. His small form hadn't faded or flickered once. A low chuckle somehow escaped a face with no mouth. "You are all weak. You have no power here."

The Prefect raised its arms and said something unintelligible. Greer felt a cloying weight creep across her skin. An icy web of energy weaved itself around her body. It drew her arms against her torso, trying to pull her hands from their hold on April and Frankie. She tightened her grip, but the web crept around her throat and ribs, squeezing. Her breath became shallow.

April began to chant, "Oṃ Amideva Hrīḥ." Greer had done her best to learn this during a few meditation sessions. It meant "to overcome all obstacles and hindrances." While it didn't have any visible effect on the spirit, it did help Greer focus.

As April maintained her mantra, Greer tried to concentrate on her angel wings, urgently whispering a plea to her own spirit guide.

Adam loudly began another prayer of banishment as the others joined in.

The dark form sneered and twisted its body into an unnatural angle. Greer felt the heavy web loosen around her and fall away. The inky form howled and writhed in the center of their circle.

Triumphant, Greer shouted, "You've killed so many. The women you buried here, Liz, my mother! We're sending you back to Hell!"

The Prefect turned. She knew it was facing her even though there were no features to tell her so. "Your mother," he said in a hiss. "Yes, I am so pleased you reminded me of her!"

Suddenly the figure burst into flames. It stunk of burnt oil and the intense heat threatened to blister their skin, but Greer didn't flinch. Finally faced with her mother's killer, she found the rage that'd been hiding all of these years. Before her stood the one responsible for that horrific night and every heart-breaking night since. This monster was the fount of her deepest despair.

She concentrated on her internal energy, trying to summon the intense power she felt when the little Buddha exploded. When she found it, she eagerly fed it the pain of a broken child. Exhilaration turned to alarm when she realized she'd started siphoning her friends. Even with her eyes open, she could see a thin line of energy flowing to her from each person in the circle.

"Greer, what're you doing?" April asked frantically.

"Stop!" Frankie yelled.

Greer recoiled from their energies, shifting her focus inward. There, down deep, she unlocked her fury for the Prefect and drew on it. She imagined it flowing from the inferno in her gut like molten lava through every vein until the tips of her fingers seemed to burn with their own fire.

Greer released April and Frankie's hands as she stepped inside the circle.

Tony was practically shrieking in terror as he watched the sinuous orange flames of his power flow from his fingertips to join the other's energies as they streamed into Greer.

Adam struggled against Greer's pull on his energy and yelled, "No! Together! We have to do it together!"

The others were shouting at her too, but she blocked them out, focusing solely on the power she was summoning and the target for which it was intended.

The air crackled with energy as she raised her hands toward the Prefect. To her dismay, the spirit didn't cower from her, but laughed instead. Greer's rage surged. Screaming, she tried to force her energy out toward him. The power failed to strike a blow. It bounced wildly around the room, blowing chips off the stone walls, scorching the wooden beams overhead until; finally, it exploded and knocked her team down.

With the circle ruined, the Prefect burst into a dark mist which swelled until it filled the entire room. The heat in Greer's core was quenched. Feeling empty and cold, she shivered as the darkness pressed in on her and said, "I'll be back for you, my Agatha. Very soon." The mist flew into the alcove and down the tunnel to the catacomb.

Greer followed.

She ran headlong down the tunnel and through the first empty room. Stopping just inside the pitch-black corridor, without a lantern, she waited for the cold energy to lead her on her chase. The hum of energy in the space drew her forward. Her quarry waited in the darkness ahead.

Reaching out to touch the damp stone wall, she slowly edged forward, trying to get her bearings and recall where the first archway opened into the passage. Which of the rooms would it hide in? Or would it wait in the corridor simply waiting for her to walk into its arms? A light would've been helpful.

She held her breath as she approached the first doorway. When nothing attacked her, she continued. The shivering began almost immediately, and the energy spiked. With one hand tracing the wall she stretched the other in front of her and began Saint Michael's prayer.

Laughter bounced off the walls.

Greer took a deep breath and dug deep into her core again, tapping the anger and heat that had driven her only moments ago. She felt the energy rise within her then imagined it focused into her outstretched hand. Her fingers took on a golden glow. Encouraged she picked up her pace, following what felt like a trail of emotional ooze around the corner and down the dark passage until she reached the final room.

Here she stopped and turned to face the room. The Prefect was difficult to make out in the dim light from her fingertips. She was pleased to see that he seemed to be cowering against the far wall.

Bringing both hands together in front of her she thought of her mother and unleashed the pent-up anger, a decade of heartache. Light streamed from her hands toward the shadowy figure holding it in place.

"Greer! Greer!"

She heard Adam's voice bouncing down the hallway. She didn't want him here. Distracted, her light faltered.

The shadow took advantage and rushed forward, passing through her like a thousand needles of ice. A dark whisper penetrated her thoughts. She cried out and crumpled as her own heat was overcome.

As the lantern light hurried ahead of him, Adam could make out Greer kneeling on the floor where she'd fallen, overcome. He dropped to his knees next to her, searching for injuries. She batted his hands away.

"I failed," she said, rocking back and forth in defeat.

"It will be alright." Adam tried to pull her to him.

"No! It will never be ok. I failed." Greer tore away, furious tears burning against the cold of her skin as the trembling had returned.

Adam nodded at the others who'd arrived in time to witness her breakdown. When they'd gone, he wrapped his arms around Greer's hunched and weeping form. "I am here. We will do it together next time, and we will succeed."

Pressing her face to his chest, she let the grief overtake her.

My Heart has Failed Me

Greer awoke the next morning with the worst headache of her life. She'd refused to accept any further offers of comfort the night before. Adam had tried many times to sit with her or hold her while she slept. He'd finally retreated after she threatened to throw a book at him.

When she sat up, her head alternated between throbbing and spinning. It would've been smart to lie back down until it passed, but she'd made a decision in the night and wouldn't put it off. She was leaving.

With a large duffel bag and her purse slung over one shoulder, she banged an overstuffed suitcase down the narrow stairs. Sam briefly poked his head out from the living room before ducking back in. Adam swung through the kitchen door with a coffee mug in hand. He stopped midstride.

"What are you doing?" he asked wearily.

"I should think it's obvious. I'll send for the rest of my stuff."

"Why, Greer?"

"You know why. Between the Prefect and my own incompetence, I'm putting you all in danger."

"We will be fine."

"No," she said firmly. "You'll all be better off when this maniac and I are out of your lives. The dig is complete, so you don't even need me at work." She wheeled the suitcase to the door.

Adam rushed to block her way. Coffee spilled down the side of the mug and onto his hand. He winced and licked the splatter off. "You are frustrated and scared. Perfectly normal given how incredibly new you are at all of this. I never told you it would be easy."

Greer lashed out at him. "You're right. You didn't say it'd be easy, but you said it'd be possible." Her eyes sparked as she challenged him to deny it.

He set the mug on the floor and slid the bags off her shoulder to take her hands. Bending to meet her eye, he said, "Greer, it is not safe for you to confront the Prefect on your own. I am begging you to let me help."

She knew he truly believed he could protect her, but she had no faith in herself. Putting this family, or anyone else, at risk was unthinkable.

"Don't worry, I'm not going after him. I'm leaving town. I'll stay with Dad for a while. Once I'm gone, the Prefect will leave you all alone."

"It rarely works that way. You will still be in danger no matter where you go."

She squeezed her eyes shut, trying to manage the headache pulsing at her temples. "Move. Please," she said, imploring Adam with her eyes.

"I cannot." He wrapped his arms around her and hugged her close. "Stay." He pressed a kiss to her lips.

She turned her head away, afraid to get lost in the depths of his intoxicating eyes. "I can't," she said, even as she wished for nothing more than to be held by him as her problems all melted away under the warmth of his gaze.

"Greer, I ... love you." He caught her chin and kissed her deeply.

She gave in to him for only a moment before breaking away. Afraid to lose her nerve, she pulled back and stared at the floor. "I have nothing for you," she said, feeling hollow inside.

He watched, stunned, as she opened the door and banged her suitcase down the front step to the sidewalk. She heaved her bags into the trunk of her beat up car.

"Greer!" Adam called hoarsely behind her.

She paused briefly as she pulled the door open but refused to look at him. Dropping into her seat, she cranked up a heavy blues riff in an effort to stave off tears. Winding her way through town, she was about to get on the highway when her phone rang.

"Hello? Ms. Dixon?" an unfamiliar voice said.

"Yes, this is she."

"Oh, wonderful! Darling, I called to schedule your dress appointment."

"What? Who is this?"

"Why Stefan, your bridal coordinator, dear. The one and only. Now when can you get in to pick out your dream gown?" he asked in a twitter.

Greer held the phone between her shoulder and ear while she turned onto the highway and merged with traffic. "Stefan, I assumed Carol would've told you."

"Told me what, sweetheart?"

"I apologize that no one's contacted you, but Robert and I are no longer engaged. So, I won't need a dress or that outdoor wedding Carol wanted. Can you please cancel all plans and refund any money Carol Cole may have deposited?"

"I am afraid I cannot possibly do a refund without someone signing off in person."

"Well, I'm heading out of town so maybe Carol can do it?"

"Oh, it really should be you, dear," he said.

Greer rolled her eyes. As she found herself searching for the next exit, she realized that it was her mess to clean up. "Ok, I can be there soon."

She hung up and started working her way back into town. Carol was always so organized and on top of social plans; it was surprising that she'd forgotten something this big. Greer wondered if Robert told his parents there was a chance the wedding might happen after all.

Robert hadn't crossed her mind in weeks. Between the dig, ghostly woes, and Adam, she'd been completely occupied. She allowed herself to think of Robert now. Did she miss him? Did he miss her? He hadn't called or texted once since she moved out. Maybe Adam expected her to run back to Robert now.

She shook her head. Of course, she'd never go back to Robert. And she didn't care what Adam thought. Yes, Adam had bent over backward to help her. Yes, he'd shown her infinite kindness and understanding... well, that didn't mean he was right. He may know the supernatural world, but she knew the real one well enough. Removing herself as a variable in the equation would change the equation. It was simple science, or math. Whatever.

She thought of her mother and wondered if Mom would've approved of Robert. No, now that Greer knew her mother had a secret supernatural life of her own, she guessed Mom would've leaned toward Adam. Adam always smelled good too. Mom had loved it when Dad wore cologne. She claimed he smelled like the Sahara before pinching his rear. Greer smiled at the memory and couldn't wait to mention it to her father.

When she'd called him earlier that morning, her dad insisted on meeting her at the house. He was already settled in by the time she'd finished with the dressmaker and arrived at the family home. Without a word her father offered her a drink and led her to a seat on the back porch. She tried to pretend nothing was wrong, speaking of innocuous events. He rewarded her with a belly laugh when she reminded him about the cologne then refused to clarify the inside joke behind it.

After they'd been quietly watching the birds and trees for some time, he asked, "How long do you think you're going to be here, Kiddo?"

"Is it ok if I don't know?"

"Of course. But it's not like you to run away from a problem."

"You don't know what this problem is."

He studied her intently. "Lay it on me."

Greer took a big gulp of her wine and did her best over the next hour to fill him in on the multitude of crazy and dangerous events since their last visit. He asked a few questions and listened intently. When she was done, he simply nodded as if the conversation hadn't involved evil ghosts and the death of her student.

"You told me not long ago that you trusted Adam. What's changed?" he asked.

"It's not a matter of trust. I just don't want anyone to get hurt."

He refilled her glass with a thoughtful hum. "If I understand correctly, he wants to help you, and it sounds like he's the best one for the job."

"Mom left us for those fake work trips, right? If I'm not there, then this Prefect monster will leave everyone alone. There's no need for any help."

"Are you sure? It doesn't sound like you were its only target." He continued as if listing points in a lecture. "You believe the Prefect has been attacking in a cycle. That implies more than one victim. If you remove yourself from the cycle, which I can certainly support, what happens? Does this evil thing just pack his bags and go? Or will he move on to someone else? Maybe someone who isn't ready for the fight?"

She sat, astonished, wondering how she could've been so dense. Of course, the Prefect would find a new target. Her heart and mind immediately battled. The mind was winning. Shrinking back in the chair, she made herself small. "I can't go back, Dad."

"I never said you should."

They watched the sun sink behind the treetops. Greer rubbed her arms as the air cooled.

He picked the conversation back up. "But if you didn't go back ... what would you do?"

Greer considered her options. Leaving town meant giving up Brown. She'd need to apply to another archaeology program to finish her masters. The wait could be an entire year, delaying her degree and the start of her career. That would've been unthinkable a short time ago; however, so much had changed. Her new spiritual powers spooked her. She was terrified to confront her mother's killer again. All paths looked difficult. At least this road, the one away from Providence, kept her alive and sane. Most importantly, she wouldn't be responsible for anyone else coming to harm. It seemed an easy choice, and she told him so.

"Ok." He pulled his glasses down, peering at her over the frames. "Is it easy to walk away from Adam too? He told you he loves you."

"It's not really love, Dad. He just feels responsible for me. He lost his old girlfriend, Sarah, to the Prefect. He couldn't protect her and wants a second chance by protecting me now. He's confusing his feelings for her with me."

"You sound like your mother."

. . .

In the deepest part of the night, she heard a whisper. She followed the sounds into the hallway. The hem of a white nightgown disappeared around the corner. Her bare feet padded on the cold wood.

The pale figure turned and smiled at her. "My darling! Why are you here?"

A young Greer rushed into the warmth of her mother's embrace. "I missed you, Mom."

"I missed you too, but that was no reason to leave your friends." Her mother's hand stroked her hair.

"Don't make me go back. I can't do it," the girl said, pleading.

"Yes, you can. You must." Her mother bent until they were face to face. "It's time, Greer. You must do this for me and for yourself. For the many who've come before. You must!"

A small sob escaped from the girl. "But... how?"

Days of Decision

Awake, O Sleeper

Greer drove back to town after breakfast the next morning with her father's words echoing in her mind. He'd reminded her that she'd always have a home with him; however, he was very proud of her for leaving to confront what waited. He only wished he could help.

The car sputtered to a stop as she pulled up in front of Adam's house. She sat for a few minutes, unsure of what to say to him. Adam might not even let her back in. He'd looked pretty torn up when she left.

Gathering her courage, but not her luggage, Greer went to the front door and knocked hesitantly. There was no answer. She heard Sam's cartoons playing inside so she knocked a little harder.

When the door opened, she was met by Tony, beer in hand.

"It's a little early," Greer said, nodding to the bottle.

"Nah, luv. It's not early if you've never stopped. Besides, I were just keeping up with your boy." He leaned against the door jam and took a swig. "You're wanting to see him, I imagine?"

Greer debated coming back later. She hadn't expected an audience for this conversation.

"It's alright, luv. He'll be glad to see you." Without turning his head, Tony called Adam's name then flashed a lurid smile. When Adam didn't answer, Tony hollered again.

She heard a grumpy reply from the kitchen.

"You're wanted, mate," Tony called back as he continued to hold up the door frame.

Greer felt completely foolish and was about to leave when Adam finally emerged through the kitchen door. She was disturbed by the state of his clothes and dark circles under his eyes, but the real shock was seeing him weave down the hall as he sipped on his own beer.

He stopped cold when he saw her.

"I'll just come back later," she said and turned to go.

Tony laughed. "Your white knight ain't so spotless, is he?" The phone in his pocket rang. He pushed past her with a wink as he answered.

Adam swayed in the middle of the hall as Greer addressed him awkwardly from the doorway. "I'd hoped to talk. Maybe you can call me when you're, um, ready?"

He raked a hand roughly through his mop of hair then rasped it across his unshaven cheek. "Ayuh," he muttered.

She glanced down at her feet. "Um, ok. Just call me later then." She turned again to leave.

"Wait! Stay. Talk."

Uncertain, yet relieved, she stepped inside and closed the door behind her. "I never should've left. I hope nothing happened with the Prefect last night?"

"No, nothing happened." Adam glanced at the bottle in his hand. "Give me a minute to, uh ... clean up."

"Oh sure, sure!" she said a little too brightly. "I'll wait in the kitchen." The smell of beer and cigarettes wafted from him as she brushed by. The kitchen was a disaster with various empty bottles spilling from the trash can and dishes littering the sink. One of Adam's shirts was on the floor. She picked it up, wrinkling her nose at the strong whiff of sweat and whiskey.

When he finally joined her, he'd showered and dressed in clean clothes but hadn't shaved.

She'd been occupying herself with a demonology book that'd been left open on the table. "Are you sure the Prefect is a demon?" she asked as she finished the page.

"Yes."

He stood, watching her.

"What made you decide?"

"Seeing his power. It is far too strong and unique to be a ghost."

"Because a ghost can cause trouble, but it can't do things it wasn't able to do during life. Did I get that right?"

"Yes."

Adam was still standing, and she squinted up at him. "Are you going to sit down? You're making me nervous."

"It depends."

"On what?" she asked surprised.

"On why you are here." He crossed his arms and frowned down at her.

"I'm here to get rid of the Prefect once and for all. I shouldn't have left, but I was scared. I'm still scared."

"You are serious about seeing this through then?" He was still watching her like he anticipated her to bolt at any second.

"Yes," she said, rising to face him.

"I can actually help you?"

Greer reached out to touch his arm, withdrawing when he flinched. "I'm serious, and I need you. But, only for this," she said, placing a hand on the open book. "Only for the Prefect. The rest ... us being together ... it's obviously not a good idea."

He swallowed hard. "I am incredibly sorry to hear you say that."

"Can we just focus on getting rid of this demon? Please?"

"Ayuh." He cleared his throat. "Of course."

She heard the strain in his voice and saw the hurt written clearly on his face. Guilt ate at her for being the cause of it.

He sat and pulled the book she'd been reading in front of him, flipping to a bookmarked page. "So. I was reading ... I was reading this ..." He rubbed his eyes with the heels of his hands. "Oh, hell. I need some coffee."

"I'll get it." She was happy to do any small thing to ease his discomfort.

"Thank you," he said, wrung out.

"Sure. I could use some myself." She quietly filled two cups to the very brim. "Hey, I was thinking about something. The cyclical nature of these attacks. They've happened about every five years, at least in the recent cases we're aware of."

"I noticed the same thing and considered searching old newspaper articles for similar attacks."

"Here." She handed him the steaming mug of coffee. "It's worth researching. More importantly, it may help us figure out how he got here and why."

"How so?"

She was encouraged to see some of his focus returning, so she pressed on. "Ok. I've been thinking about the cycle. If it was truly every five years, wouldn't the police and media have warned the town of a serial killer? I don't think his attacks can always be so frequent."

"Well, a few years is like a century in the news cycle. The public forgets." Adam shrugged and drank more coffee.

"True. However, the Prefect is a spirit. He doesn't belong on this plane of existence. Maybe time works differently for him?" Greer tapped a finger on her lips thinking. "Maybe think of it this way ... If you take a globe, a three-dimensional map, cut it up and flatten it into only two-dimensions so it will fit on the pages of this book ... What happens?"

"It has gaps," he said. "And you have to stretch and distort it to make it flat. An age-old dilemma of map makers."

"Right! So, imagine a four-dimensional being ..."

"Some scientists have theorized there are up to eleven dimensions," he said, interrupting.

She blinked at him. "Yes. So whichever dimension demons originate from, when they come here maybe they have to kind of compress themselves, like a globe being flattened into a paper map. The Prefect may be moving directly from one attack to another from his own perspective, but there are gaps in our own time where he just doesn't overlap with us."

Adam nodded appreciatively. "I never thought of the spirit world that way. I have imagined it as very pervasive, everywhere at once. However, your theory could certainly explain the looping we see with a lot of typical ghosts." He leaned in, hurt feelings temporarily forgotten, absorbed in speculation. "You are familiar with the typical haunting where a spirit repeats the same words and actions over and over? Often a traumatic event that led to their end?"

"April covered the different types of ghosts long ago. My theory would definitely seem to apply. Hmm. Do you think human spirits and demons occupy the same dimension?"

"I would like to think not," Adam said as his expression wrinkled in distaste. "Although most ghosts I have encountered seem rather unhappy about their current state."

Greer laughed and was happy to see a small grin peek from Adam's scruffy face. It was a long way from normal between them, but she was glad to find they could still work together.

Her stomach let out a loud growl, and this time Adam laughed out loud. "Mind if I make us some lunch while we talk?" she asked.

"None for me, but you go ahead." At his queasy look, Greer realized he really had been drinking all night and was bewildered to find him that upset by her leaving. His sense of duty apparently ran deeper than she thought.

He poured himself another coffee and leaned against the counter, watching as she made a sandwich. "If we visit the library and find record of the Prefect's other attacks, what do you expect that to tell us about his methods and motives?" he asked, quizzing her.

"We already know his motive, don't we?" Greer took a big bite of turkey and talked around it. "He is obsessed with Saint Agatha. Everything has been about her. Room A is right next to a church dedicated to her, the mural in the Alcove is her story, the manner in which he tortures his victims ... Liz, Sarah, my ... Mom. He has recreated Agatha's death over and over and ..."

She paused when Adam wiped his thumb at the corner of her mouth.

"You had a bit of mayo there," he said.

Greer couldn't decipher the look on his face. She brushed his hand away with her own, wiping at her lips indelicately. "Sorry, I'm a mess. I'm just excited that we might finally be figuring this out."

"I agree that Saint Agatha is the ultimate target. With the real Agatha dead and gone for a very long time, the Prefect is choosing surrogates to play her part." He placed his mug in the sink and stared out the window, thinking. "We know you are the surrogate in this cycle. I still think Liz's death was an anomaly, by the way. He sent the hellhounds after you long before she was killed. We already know what he is planning, and we know that he is planning it now. We still need to figure out how he plans to do it."

"How does he move between dimensions? How can we close that door? Can we stop him from coming back or send him back as soon as he arrives?" She leaned back in the chair. After the rush of figuring out the bad guy's motive, Greer now felt the crush of questions as to what to do about him.

Unfazed, Adam was ready with a suggestion. "Typically, you would want to do an exorcism, but I do not know any local priests well enough to talk them into one. The Church very rarely performs them and then only after months of investigation."

"Can't you do it?"

"No." He rubbed a hand across his face, clearly exhausted. "I have never tried and doubt I would be capable."

"But you're strong. Both spiritually ... and physically," she said, a small blush creeping up her cheeks.

He looked at her askance. "Thank you, but an exorcism is not something to enter into lightly."

"Then we'll need to find another way. A less traditional way, maybe?"

He rubbed his eyes again and yawned broadly. "I am going to take a nap while you do some research at the library. First, I will ask Mother to call everyone for a family meeting tonight."

. . .

That evening Greer sat on the edge of the chair, uncomfortable with the looks April and Mother Rose were throwing her way. They plainly disapproved of her behavior over the last forty-eight hours, upset by her lack of commitment to Adam and to the spiritual fight.

Adam, still unshaven, looked better for having had the nap. Greer was glad he seemed improved as she'd had trouble keeping her mind off of him while at the library, worried he might change his mind about helping her after he had more time to think things over.

He filled the family in on the details of the failed confrontation at the dig. Greer followed with an overview of her new theory and the results of her afternoon's work.

Providence had boasted dozens of newspapers and chronicles since its founding in 1636; however, she'd concentrated on the three with the largest circulation and longest publication history. There were records of quite a few deaths that seemed attributable to the Prefect. The most interesting was a young woman in 1832 who survived the attack for a short time. That was the same year Father Alo began investigating murders on behalf of the Jesuits. The poor girl lived just long enough to describe her attacker to the doctors who'd valiantly tried to save her. The girl reported the killer as a faceless man who smelled of fire. Of course, everyone dismissed the description as the ravings of a dying woman.

"In the end though," Greer said to the unusually rapt audience," I could find no clear pattern. The Prefect would appear every five years for a while, and then it would be decades before I could find mention of him again. One cycle saw him arriving every two years. I likely missed cases reported in other papers. If there is a larger pattern, I'm just not seeing it."

"It was a long shot," said Adam. He addressed the entire family, worry shadowing his face. "Alright, now you know what we know. We need everyone's help. Please review your resources, talk to your contacts, and meditate; whatever you can do to help us discover a way to put an end to this demon. Father Alo tried to do so two hundred years ago. Clearly, he failed. But he was on his own. I believe we can succeed if we all work as a team."

There were several nods around the room while a few other family members seemed unconvinced of the need to tackle this particular challenge. Mother Rose watched everyone carefully from her perch near the kitchen as they talked through ideas for the next hour. "That's enough," she finally said, calling a halt with a hand raised. "I expect you all to do your best as this is a grave matter. Meet back here in twenty-four hours to share what you've learned."

Frankie tagged along after Tony who was talking about visiting a biker bar. Greer hoped they were meeting a relevant contact there. She also hoped that Frankie would wait outside but had her doubts about both. Sam was watching his cartoons again. April announced she was heading upstairs to contact Sonny.

"Thank you, Mother." Adam bent to give her a quick kiss on the forehead.

"No need. This is vitally important, and something our family was destined for. I'll go back through my books and pray about this." As she left the room, she let a hand dangle next to her, brushing it across any religious items in her path—a Buddha here and a crucifix there. "'If you don't tend to one another, who then will tend to you?' So says Buddha." She picked up a tiny statue of the Madonna and Child and carried it with her on the way upstairs.

Adam motioned for Greer to follow him. "Come with me. I think I know where we need to be."

There is No Fear in Love

Greer held a flannel blanket and thermos filled with coffee in her lap. As they pulled up in front of St. Agatha's church, she threw Adam a questioning look.

"Um, didn't they start the heavy excavation today? We can't go back into Room A."

"Right, the room is gone."

"Good," Greer said with a shudder.

"We are going inside the church itself. I have a hunch it was the Prefect's preferred location." He grabbed the stuff from her lap and climbed out of the truck.

She hopped out after him, walking quickly to keep up with his long strides and peppering him with questions. "I thought demons couldn't enter a church. You think the burials in Room A were as close as the Prefect could get to the church itself?"

"This way," he said as he led her around the corner to a small heavy oak door set into the stone wall on the side of the church. He wiggled the handle then gave the door a little shove.

"Are we breaking in?" Greer asked, grabbing his free hand.

"No. I know one of the priests here. He said he would leave this door unlocked for me." Adam grunted as he tugged harder. "But he warned it likes to stick."

They entered a side chapel on the south end of the church. Moving through the side aisle and into the nave, they took a few minutes to appreciate the layout. The cathedral was a typical cross shape with the long nave intersected by the shorter transept about two thirds of the way down its East End. Greer could see a small chapel punctuating each end of the transept. The short end of the nave held a chancel, with benches for the choir. This one had a rather ornate rood screen—a lattice work enclosing the chancel. The altar resided separately against the curve of the north wall.

The walls and pillars were formed from white limestone. The high arched windows showcased beautiful stained-glass windows. Greer had often appreciated them from the outside during the dig. Now they were glassy dark against the night. Adam's priest friend had left a light on at the altar and one in the vestibule at the main entrance, down at the far west front of the cathedral.

"Watch your step," Adam said as he led Greer by the hand over the slightly uneven stone floor to the chancel. The ornate railing in front of the choir matched the rood loft above. The loft boasted an elegant angel, wings spread wide as if in flight. The wrought iron of the screen had been worked into a tight scroll pattern that allowed someone just behind it to see through while hiding them from the congregation's view. Pulling the heavy door to the choir open, Adam led her to a wooden bench inside. "It may get a little chilly. Do you want the blanket yet?"

"How long are you planning to sit here?"

"It could be a while. We are on a stakeout for the Prefect. He could be visiting regularly if he has such a strong tie to the building."

"Because of his fixation on Saint Agatha? And because he probably used to work here?"

"Ayuh. That is the general idea. We are the only ones who have permission to be in here tonight. If anyone else shows up, we might find out who the Prefect has been possessing."

He poured some coffee into the lid of the thermos, offering her the first sip. She accepted it gratefully, preparing for a long night of sitting on a hard bench. It couldn't be much worse than working all day on your hands and knees in a hole in the ground she decided.

They sat quietly, taking in the details of the church. The usual statues, tapestries, and religious symbols didn't seem likely to draw the interest of a demon such as the Prefect.

Greer blurted out what she'd just been thinking. "Why here? Aren't there other cathedrals dedicated to her in the world?"

He thought for a moment before answering. "Undoubtedly, although I have not researched them. Agatha was born in Sicily, and much of her story took place there. So, we cannot be sure why the demon has chosen to harass our little Rhode Island church. My guess would be that the conditions were right for his purposes. If I consider your theory on how his astral dimension is interacting with ours ... it could imply his physical location varies just as his timing does. It is possible the same attacks have been happening elsewhere at different times."

"Yes!" she said, answering too loudly. Clapping a hand over her mouth, she glanced around before continuing in a hushed tone. "But how does he pick which women to attack? In this whole city, why would he pick me?"

"Well, in the many years my family and I have been facing challenges, we have found spirits are often drawn to talented people. That is people like you, someone sensitive to the supernatural side of the universe."

"And my mom, and Sarah, had similar gifts. It's like our special ability paints a target on us?"

He nodded. "Something like that."

She slumped in her seat exhausted by the idea. "Ugh. Can I have more coffee, please?"

The benches grew harder the longer they sat. Greer walked around occasionally and did some squats to loosen up while Adam tried stretching out on the bench for a while. After three hours, Greer had had enough.

"I don't think he's coming, and my butt can't handle this stakeout any longer. Let's call it."

"Not just yet. Alright?" Adam folded the blanket over a few times and patted it with his hand. "Here. Some cushion. I have the feeling we should wait a little longer." She sat down and admitted the blanket helped. But, too soon, she was up and pacing again.

"I don't like it. If anyone comes walking in, we have nowhere to go." She scanned the endless space of the nave through the screen. "Maybe we can go sit up in the gallery. We'll have the advantage of being able to see him from above."

He scooped up the blanket and coffee. "I have a better idea." Leading her cautiously from the choir, around the side and through the shadows, he located a small spiral staircase. They ascended slowly, feeling carefully for each step. Greer knew they had reached the top when she heard a thud followed by a hissed "Ouch."

She felt Adam's warm hand slip into hers, and he slowly led her forward. Gradually she could see a soft light filtering from below. They were in the rood loft above the chancel. The wrought iron railing up here hid the altar boys from view as they lit the candles along the top of the screen. A few low support beams crisscrossed the area as Adam had discovered with the top of his head. Releasing her hand, he shook the blanket out over the wood floor. They sat, and Greer immediately felt more at ease now that they were up high and shielded from view of anyone entering the church.

"It's rather beautiful up here," she said. Greer laid down on the blanket and studied the ceiling along the nave. "I've always loved Gothic architecture. The rafters look so impossibly delicate that you'd never suspect their true strength."

"Kind of like some people I know," he said.

Greer ignored the comment. "If we're going to stay awhile, tell me more about your childhood. Was this your church?"

He scooted closer to her so his voice wouldn't carry. "No. We attended one closer to the house. But I got to know the priest here when the dig was being planned. Not Father Doyle," he said, quickly clarifying. "I'm not sure where he works."

"Oh. So, your childhood church. Did you like it? Did you go often?"

"I was like any other kid attending Bible school at first. When the family priest became a bit scared of me, a younger brother at the church took me under his wing. He is the one who I inherited all of those dusty books from, ayuh?" She nodded to show she remembered. "I still went to church with Mother, but this young priest, Father Harper, tutored me on his own. Our lessons would have frightened the pants off the other kids."

Greer giggled. "Oh my. I just pictured you conjuring spells and slaying demons all while in a pair of little, school-boy shorts."

"You think you are very funny, but you are not far from the truth."

They counted the minutes together in silence until Greer complained of feeling chilled.

Adam stretched out next to her and propped his head on an elbow. "I should have brought along another blanket."

"That's ok," Greer said in the middle of a wide yawn.

"Hey, none of that now. We need to wait a little while longer. Besides, it is your turn to tell me about your childhood."

"Well, it was rather exciting. Dad indulged me in every whim as long as it was educational. We built crazy things, explored lots of local places, and tried to find the answer to every silly question that I could come up with. There was always a new adventure waiting around the corner. I learned so much from him."

"Your father sounds wonderful," he said a little wistfully. "Of course, I only met him for a few moments when you collapsed at the dig, but he seemed very caring."

"He's amazing. He's always been there for me, even when I knew he was heartsick." She paused in reflection. "He was never selfish with his time or love." Greer let out a slow breath. "Losing my Mom changed us forever. I think we became closer than we would've otherwise, yet there was still a distance between us. The space where we refused to talk about her. Because it hurt too much."

"I am sorry." He swept a strand of hair from her forehead.

She shivered and snuggled closer. "Yeah, Dad has always been really great, but there were things he didn't notice. Mom saw everything. Every tear. Every giggle. My childish dreams and little victories. She was experiencing them with me."

When she fell quiet, he slid an arm under her, held her, and waited patiently.

"I really can't think of a single moment she missed. Not a single disappointment," she said through a tight throat. She swallowed the lump stuck there and rallied. "But I'm probably remembering her through rose-colored glasses. She must've had some faults, right?"

He simply stroked her hair in response.

"But I guess that's how a mother's love works. It never fails." She tilted her chin up, looking to him for agreement.

He smiled. "It shaped your heart."

She felt tears start but, before they could fall, he kissed them away.

"What are you doing?" she whispered.

"Loving you," he said as he skimmed over her face, delivering airy kisses.

"Well, stop."

"Why?"

His lips found hers, and she instinctively returned the pressure.

"No," she pulled back. "You don't love me. You're confusing the need to protect me with love."

"You think I cannot recognize the difference?" he asked, his voice growing husky and urgent. Cupping one breast firmly, he kissed the hollow at her throat then worked his way down to take the breast in his mouth, working the nipple through her thin cotton shirt.

She gasped. "Well, I don't know if I can tell the difference right now." Placing a hand between them, she gently pushed against his chest.

He paused but she recognized the determination in his eyes.

"Greer, as you have seen, words have power. I learned this at a young age. Therefore, I am always very careful. With. My. Words." He punctuated each word with a soft kiss. "I am telling you right now: I love you."

He didn't wait for her to reply, but instead caught her mouth firmly, taking her fully into his arms, pulling her closer. She pressed against him, seeking the strength and warmth he offered. Encouraged, he hugged her tightly, deepening the kiss. Her hip ground sharply against the floorboards. She ignored the pain, yet he must have sensed her discomfort and, rolling onto his back, brought her on top of him.

Greer slid her hands under the hem of his shirt, gliding over the scars on his belly then moving higher to spread across the expanse of his chest. She hovered above him and slowly rocked her hips back and forth, rubbing the fabric roughly between them.

Adam plunged his hands into her loose hair and drew her down to his mouth. He traced her lips with his tongue before he sent it exploring her mouth again. A shared moan escaped them.

She unbuttoned her shirt as he reached behind to deftly unfasten her bra. Tugging at the button and zipper on his pants, she worked to free him from the tight denim.

"I will always love you, Greer," he said as she returned to his mouth for another kiss.

She froze. "Oh my God. What am I doing?" She straightened. "I can't do this." Greer slipped from him and groped in the half-light for her shirt.

Adam sat up and reached for her. "Why? I love you, and I know you are in love with me too." He was wide-eyed and tense, dismay clear on his face. "Why do you keep running from me? Help me understand."

She clutched her crumpled shirt to her chest in an unsuccessful attempt to cover her bare breasts. "I can't do what we were about to do. Especially not in a church," she added in a loud whisper. "Oh God." One hand covered her face in confusion and embarrassment.

Adam was suddenly amused. "What better place?" He dropped the wry tone when she threw him a mortified look. He shifted closer and held out a hand. "Come to me." He spoke as if coaxing a wild animal to him. "Please," he beckoned but she simply stared at his open palm. "God has given us to each other. I fought His plan for us at first. You saw how I fought it. But I know that you and I are destined for each other."

Greer started to tear up. "I'm sorry, your God told you wrong. You need a love that I can't give."

He knelt in front of her. "Why not?" he said, demanding an answer.

She had to tell him the truth but couldn't look him in the eye. "When my mother died, my heart went with her. I tried to love Robert ... in my own way. Honestly, he'd really just become a habit. He deserved more and so do you. You want too much from me."

He caught her chin, forcing her to meet his gaze. "Yes, I want all of you, and I am giving you all of myself in return."

"Adam, you're asking for my soul, but it's numb, broken. I can't share it with you. With anyone. There won't be anything left for me." She straightened, steeling herself against his coming denial.

"I understand the depth of your sorrow, but your soul, your spirit, isn't shattered in the way you think. It is beautiful. I feel it. I know it. And your heart will only grow stronger if you make me a part of it," he said as he cradled her face in his hands. "Close your eyes." He cut her off when she protested. "Greer, please. Close them."

She complied even as she was wishing herself a world away, far from his inevitable disappointment.

His thumb stroked her cheek and he spoke gently. "Now search your heart. Do not listen to your brain. I know it is running with a million thoughts and excuses. Listen to your heart."

Greer took an uneven breath and tried to settle her thoughts. She wanted to show Adam she'd really tried. She owed him that much.

"Yes, Greer," he murmured as she stilled under his touch.

After having practiced so many times during training with April, she found that now, in a moment, it was easy to sweep away all the clutter in her mind. She focused on one thing, Adam. The warmth of his strong hands on her. His earthy scent. She suddenly realized it took no effort to focus on him because he'd never left her thoughts. Not since the day he smiled at her in the churchyard.

"I love you, Greer. I love you," he said in soft encouragement.

A warmth began to radiate deep inside of her, and it rapidly built, taking on a life of its own. It wrapped itself around a frightened, forgotten spot in her heart, buttressing it, offering it sanctuary. A feeling she'd lost so long ago, peace, washed over her, displacing all doubt and fear. She recognized it for it was—love.

"Greer, open your eyes," he whispered.

When she did, she found golden light from her angel wings shining between them.

"Oh, Adam," she said breathlessly. "Adam, I guess I knew ... but I didn't truly believe."

Joy filled her at the realization her heart was open to real love: joy at discovering this love was right in front of her. She showered him in urgent kisses only to stop suddenly and throw her arms around his neck. "I'm scared," she whispered. "Don't let me break again."

"Never," he answered as he gathered her to himself.

He lowered her carefully to the blanket then ripped off his shirt and shoes, tossing them in random directions. She laughed lightly, holding his gaze as he slipped off her shoes and jeans. "Slow down. I'm not going anywhere."

"I am not taking any chances." He winked as he slid his own jeans down to the floor.

Greer lay back and beckoned him to her, then slowly melted on the inside as he kissed a slow trail down her neck and back to her mouth. She caressed his cheek and studied the brilliant eyes locked on hers, noting the silver flecks in them. She felt truly seen and understood by their owner.

"I love you," she said as a confession, still astonished at how full her heart felt. "I love you."

A loud bang echoed in the church below, freezing them in place. Adam put a finger to his lips, carefully extricated himself from her grasp, then crawled over to peer through the screen.

Greer held her breath, waiting. When he didn't move, she hastily pulled on her shirt and joined him. They held their breath, scanned the darkness and waited. When all stayed quiet, Adam rolled over onto his back and let out a small sigh of relief.

Greer sat next to him, leaning against the screen. She played with the curls around his ear while he ran a finger lightly over the fresh scars of the hound bite on her thigh.

"It looks awful, doesn't it?"

"Barely a scratch and healing well. I was just remembering when it happened. I would have done anything to take away your pain."

"Really?" she asked surprised, cocking her head to get a better look at his face and finding his brow furrowed. "Way back then?"

"Ayuh," he said, propping on an elbow to plant a kiss on her forehead. "I told you that I have known for a long time."

Once they dressed, Adam silently motioned that it was time to head down. Greer scooped up the blanket and thermos, leaving his hands free to guide her on the stairs and be ready to confront anyone who might be waiting for them below. When they stepped down into the nave, there was no sign of a disturbance.

"Must have been a mouse," he whispered.

"A really big mouse," she said doubtfully, "but sure." Greer shooed him in the direction of the side chapel where they'd entered. She was anxious to get safely home and into Adam's bed.

Take up the Whole Armor

She shook Adam awake the next morning. "Get up. We've made a mistake."

He rolled over and pried open one eye to squint at her in the morning light. "What?" he asked exhausted after two sleepless nights.

"We were wrong," she said.

He threw an arm over his face and sighed. "If you regret last night, can I please be allowed a coffee before we talk about it?"

"Oh!" she said, taken aback. "No, not that. I don't regret a single moment of last night." She leaned over to kiss him playfully. "In fact, I can't wait to repeat it."

He uncovered his face. "I am confused then. What are you going on about?" he asked through a yawn.

She sat up and talked excitedly with her hands. "We believed the Prefect has been recreating Saint Agatha's death, right? But, according to the Bible, he only tried to have her burned at the stake. In the story, an earthquake granted her a reprieve." She paused and with a puzzled look said, "I never understood why he didn't just reschedule." She continued with another wave of her hand, "Anyway, she was sent to prison and apparently died peacefully there years later."

"Huh. You are right." He scratched the stubble on his jaw. "I have read the story many times but did not catch the disparity."

"How well do you remember the paintings in the alcove?"

He rolled over and propped an elbow under his head. "Not much left to remember, now was there? They were so degraded, and our pictures were practically useless. At most, I would claim they were reminiscent of several biblical events. I could not pin it down to a single story. You think they depicted the story of Saint Agatha?"

"I think that's exactly what they were. The Prefect's preferred version that is. In the alcove there was definitely someone burning at the end." She watched him expectantly.

He followed the logic of her thought to its end. "The Prefect did not get what he wanted with the real Agatha, so he is changing the story—writing his own ending with his new victims."

"Exactly!"

He sat up and ran a hand through his hair. "That is great reasoning, but how will it help us?"

"We need to let him think he's winning. Lure him in and make him think he's getting exactly what he wants, and then, Bam!" She smacked her fist into her palm. "Another earthquake foils his plans."

"An earthquake?" He looked at her with concern. "Are you feeling alright?"

She wrinkled her nose at him. "Not a real earthquake, of course. We can have Frankie just shake stuff around a bit."

"And then?"

"And then ... I'm hoping he'll be thrown off guard enough for us to get past his defenses and finish him."

He laid back and propped his hands behind his head, thinking. She snuggled in next to him resting her head on his shoulder. He brought an arm down to stroke her back.

When he'd been quiet too long, she anxiously asked, "So? Will it work?"

"It might. It just might"

. . .

They had a plan. Mother Rose declared that everyone in the house had a role to play if they were going to defeat this evil.

Frankie was happy at the opportunity to smash things in a self-inflicted earthquake. Since they certainly couldn't damage actual church property, Mother Rose donated a few of her less-cherished items to the cause. Frankie thought the props were too sparse to really sell a natural disaster, and demanded Adam give her cash to buy a few more statues to shatter dramatically.

April's concern was how to quickly establish the sacred circle which could contain the Prefect. They would need to hold him while reciting the prayers of exorcism. Adam decided to build a ring from spare wood to which they could tack the necessary candles and elemental objects. By suspending it high overhead in the church and dropping it around the

Prefect when he stood in the right spot, he'd never see it coming. With Frankie's kinetic talent, she could easily raise the ring into the rafters. However, they quickly realized she'd be too busy with her little earthquake to hold it there and release it at the right time.

Tony came through with a brilliant idea. If Frankie could raise the ring, and Adam could tie it off in the rafters with rope, then Tony could use his talent for fire to burn through the ropes and drop it at the right moment. It'd be the work of a heartbeat for him.

Greer was a little concerned that he might burn something important, so she asked about his accuracy. Rather put out, he gave her a concentrated look until she gave a little yelp. Rubbing her forearms, she found the fine hairs all singed on the ends. They were a bit prickly to the touch now. She looked at Tony apprehensively, and Adam practically growled in warning at his dodgy family member.

Frankie's telepathy didn't seem to lend anything to the plan. However, Mother Rose insisted she might be able to read the Prefect's thoughts and help predict his next move. At the very least, she and Tony could be human batteries if Greer needed to draw power once the Prefect was trapped. Greer insisted she didn't want to tap into anyone else's power. It felt very unsafe since she wasn't able to control the ability. Mother Rose gave a little "humpf" and a nod of her head as if to say time would tell.

Adam had called Cahya, asking her to lend her special skills and connection with the spirit world to the exorcism itself. She had declined.

Mother Rose also wouldn't come with them to the church, seeing as she lacked talents. In fact, she'd be more of a hindrance since Adam would worry about protecting her instead of focusing on banishing the Prefect. He whole-heartedly agreed with her assessment to stay behind. However, she did promise to pray continuously from home for success and everyone's safe return.

As they wrapped up, Adam asked everyone to take a little time to rest and review their roles in the coming confrontation. They were to be back later for dinner then head over to the church to prepare. The exorcism would begin at midnight.

After everyone dispersed, Greer told Adam she wanted some time alone. He kissed her cheek and promised he'd be in his room studying the prayers for tonight if she needed him.

. . .

Greer sat crossed legged on her bed and tried to settle into a low chant. When the bed proved too soft, she moved to the floor and tried again. Twenty minutes had passed, and she'd failed to slow the thoughts racing through her mind, much less reach a state of meditation. Frustrated, she jumped up, grabbed her purse, and hurried down the stairs.

Pulling the front door shut, she leaned against it and took a deep breath. It was a humid summer evening, and she felt worse for the stickiness that now clung to her lungs. Pushing away from the door, she hopped into her car and took off, barely registering the buildings and streets rolling by.

Greer drove aimlessly until she finally realized where she'd been heading all along. Two blocks later she turned right into Swan Point Cemetery. It was easily the most beautiful cemetery in the city, probably in the whole state. Her mother was buried here because they could find no lovelier place for her to rest. Greer visited infrequently.

She drove past cherry trees that had long ago lost their blossoms yet still offered comfort in their shade. The winding roads sloped gently down the hill to the shore of the river. Greer parked at the water's edge. Stepping out near the tall grasses lining the bank, Greer looked out across the river. It was so wide here that the other side was considered a cove. She could just make out a few small boats moving in and out on the far shore. The water was tranquil and smelled of fresh living things.

Although the cemetery was only a few short miles from College Hill where she'd been attending graduate school for an entire year, Greer had only driven over once. She'd told herself that life was always too busy, but, today, she finally admitted that she'd just been avoiding the pain.

Leaving the car, she walked up the hill. Passing the little gazebo they called Stranger's Rest, she veered to the left and counted off the rows of headstones. She was careful not to brush against the markers or walk directly on top of the graves as she held a newfound respect for the spirits which might still linger there.

She stopped. Evangeline Marianna Dixon read the name on the tombstone. Her mother's name. A tightness clamped down on her chest. It was still so brutal to see her mother's beautiful name carved into the cold granite.

"I know I haven't been here, Mom," she said, beginning hesitantly. "There's been a lot going on. For real this time."

She crossed her arms. "Why didn't you tell me about your strange powers? I might've believed you." She gave a little snort. "Ok, it might've taken a bit of convincing. I am my father's daughter after all. But ... I would've believed you."

She paced at the foot of the grave. "I have so many questions for you. You could've taught me all about your gifts. What exactly were you able to see? To do? Dad doesn't seem to know. Whatever. I'm sure you would've helped me control my talents. They scare me, Mom."

Moving closer to pluck a weed, she tossed it aside. "Talents, ha! I'm not sure why Adam calls them that. If you'd said something, at least I would've been a little more prepared for all of this." Lost, she threw her hands in the air.

Greer walked carefully over to the headstone and rested her hand on top. She was curious as to what may happen while being careful not to actively call upon her mother. The granite was cool and slightly gritty to the touch. When nothing otherworldly happened, she grew bolder and brushed the dust away from the stone.

"Mom," she said as she knelt beside the grave. "Has that really been you in my dreams? I can't tell. How are you doing it? Maybe it's not you. Maybe it's all in my head. Adam would argue that it's not. I trust him, Mom. I know you would too. I wish you could meet him."

She tensed, balling her hands into fists. "You've missed so much! But, Mom, I found him! The one who took you from us. He may be an actual demon, but I'm going to finish him. Adam has promised to help. I know we can do it!"

She felt anger burning in her heart. "All these years without you. I've needed you. I need you now. Maybe if you'd told me about your challenges, your powers, I could've helped protect you. Why didn't you tell me?" Hot tears streamed down her face.

Greer sat down hard. Curling up against the stone, she let herself wail and sob, blubbering nothing more than, "why" whenever she could form words. It was the first time she'd cried for her mother in years. The hurt had always been kept tucked away in a quiet corner where it couldn't upset anyone, couldn't upset her. She didn't want to feel it now, yet knew that if she lost the battle tonight, she wouldn't have the chance to feel it again.

Giving into the pain was oddly comforting. Once the tears had run their course, she leaned on the front of the headstone, feeling her mother's name at her back.

Greer lost time as she picked at the blades of grass and watched the clouds drift by. Through the trees she caught a glimpse of several small boats floating down the river.

Pulling her knees up to her chin she gave a shaky sigh. "I don't know if I can do this, Mom."

. . .

No one spoke during dinner. The whole family ate together for once, but each was lost in private notions of the coming battle.

Greer stole glances around the kitchen as she ate. Tony and Frankie stood at the counter while they indelicately scooped dinner from their plates. April, and Mother Rose sat with Greer at the table. Only Sam was missing, eating in the other room in front of his cartoons. He had at least given Greer a good luck hug before he left the kitchen. Adam wasn't eating. Instead, he paced the linoleum floor, one hand on the amulet at his neck, silently mouthing the prayers he'd been working on for the Prefect.

A sense of gratitude overwhelmed her. All these people had been complete strangers to her such a short time ago. A few of them were irksome, but she couldn't fault them for their support.

Greer was so used to going it alone. After her mother's death, Greer worried about her father trying to do it all on his own. He often seemed tired and sad. She'd believed if she needed too much from him, he'd get sick or resent her, so she did as much for herself as she could.

The only other steady person in her life had been Robert. Their relationship had been low-key and comfortable. Yet, in all their years together, Robert had never been the center of her world like love songs claimed he should be. He never required much from her and was more like a side project to her real passion—her studies.

This odd family had started to mean more to her than they should. She'd grown to care for the people in this room and couldn't believe they were now ready to fight for her. Ready to go to war against something they still didn't completely understand.

And then there was Adam. Adam who was leading them into this fray. Adam who had been there and believed in her from the first moment she'd faced danger. He'd confessed his love to her, and last night she'd confessed it back. Her feelings for him were so different than those for Robert. Of course, she'd been attracted to both of them physically, but she always felt somewhat indifferent toward Robert. Their diverging career paths and the pressure to prove herself to his family had become like a job, and it left her a little empty inside. In contrast, Adam shared a passion for archaeology which was often difficult to explain to someone outside of the field. Their conversations were easy and thoughtful. He'd always treated her with respect. Adam felt like home.

Looking again at all the quiet faces, she realized she ought to tell them how grateful she was. The words suddenly stuck in her throat. She was terrified they were going to get hurt on her account, so she kept her mouth shut. There would be time for thanks when this was all over.

Adam finally stopped pacing and addressed the family. "Alright, I want to be sure that you are all absolutely clear on the plan for tonight. Each of you must complete your tasks as we have laid them out. Our success depends on it. No one can get distracted."

"Yeah, yeah, we got it, mate," said Tony.

"To be certain, we will go over the plan one more time," Adam said. He led them through each step in their strategy and was happy with everyone's replies. There were nods all around. It was a good plan.

Mother Rose asked everyone to grasp hands and asked Adam to lead them in The Lord's Prayer. "It is time," he said when they finished. "Continue to prepare yourselves as we get the church set up." Adam finished with a heartfelt plea. "Above all, you must have faith tonight."

They collected the gear stashed in the hall and headed out.

Greer stopped Adam and wrapped her arms around his waist. "Thank you," she said past a little lump in her throat.

He held her close and kissed the top of her head. "There is no need to thank me."

"Yes, there is. You're risking a lot to help me."

"Well, I love you."

She stretched up to give him a quick kiss. "You too." She placed a hand on his cheek, pulling his gaze to hers. "I'm really worried someone could get hurt tonight."

"It is possible' however, I will do my best to keep us all safe."

Satisfied, Greer hugged him tightly. "I know you will."

Greer was confused by an urgent tap on her shoulder. She turned to find Sam standing behind her. He said, "Love will save you from the darkness inside." Then he went back to the couch and hooted at something on the television.

April was fidgeting in the middle of the bench seat when they climbed into the truck. "Save all the kissy-face stuff for after. There's lots to do."

Adam started the engine and smiled at Greer. "You must always make time for the most important person in your life."

"Damn, you're right!" Greer reached across April to grasp Adam's hand on the wheel. "We need to go to the library now!"

April glared at her. "Are you high?"

Greer ignored the girl and squeezed Adam's hand tighter. "Think about the bodies in Room A. While so many were buried in shallow graves, one set of remains was burned and given a place of honor at the altar. Why the difference in the way the Prefect treated his victims? The body under the altar was obviously the most important to him."

Adam leaned in. "I agree. And so, you want to take the ashes from the library? They are official school property, and we are not authorized to remove them."

"Too bad. We need them." Greer couldn't believe she was advocating stealing archaeological artifacts. It went against everything she'd ever believed about her work. "We're just borrowing them really."

April said, "You don't need those old ashes. You're the lure tonight."

Greer took a moment to think. "I have this gut feeling those ashes might be even bigger bait. I've been trying to figure out what happened to all of those missing bones. Why did he take them in the first place, right? When the ashes were tested, we got back a jumble of results—multiple DNAs, unspecific ages.

"You think he took a bone from each victim and cobbled together his ultimate Agatha," Adam said, following her train of thought.

"Exactly. And when he burned this new, rearticulated Agatha, he was burning his supreme Agatha and all who came before her, all at once."

April let out a little whistle, "That would've created lots of psychic energy."

Greer continued, "If that's the case, and we know he treasured the ashes because of their preferential treatment, what do you think he'd do if we threaten to destroy them?"

Adam had already pulled out onto the street and was racing toward the church. "April, we are dropping you off. Tell the others we will join you as soon as we have the ashes."

Love Never Ends

While the ashes from the alcove had been cataloged and properly stored in the archaeology library basement, they weren't held under lock and key, making it quick work to swipe the lock at the back door and sneak the remains out of a very empty library.

Greer clutched the catalog box as the truck raced through town. Her stomach was in knots at the knowledge of what they'd just done at the library and what they were about to do at the church. She cracked her knuckles loudly.

Adam squeezed her hand. "Steady, Greer."

She squeezed his fingers back but couldn't muster a reassuring smile. Distant screams were echoing on the edge of her hearing.

By the time they pulled up in front the church, Greer was having trouble breathing. She swiped at the door handle, unable to pull it open. Adam was halfway down the path to the front entrance before he realized she wasn't following. He hurried back and found her struggling, a death grip on the box of ashes.

"I can hear them," she said with a gasp.

Adam looked down at the box crumpling in her hands. "Oh, God! Let me take that." He snatched the box from her and set it on the curb. "I forgot how they affected you before." He stroked her arms slowly and whispered gentle encouragement as she regained her composure.

After a moment she batted his hands away and said, "I'll be ok now."

"Alright, but I am going to carry these. Do not touch them again."

"You'll get no argument from me."

He followed her into the cathedral, carried the box through the chancel, and deposited it on the altar at the far East End while Greer looked for the others.

She found them up on the gallery level inspecting the wooden sacred circle suspended high above the transept just in front of the chancel. April was concerned that the candles and elemental items would break free when the circle dropped over the Prefect. Tony was certain he'd fastened them securely, and the rest of the family members were, surprisingly, agreeing with him.

Greer rested her hand gently on April's shoulder. "I'm sure it'll work." However, her own confidence was shaken when she realized just how uneasy April was with the preparations. She'd never seen the girl tense for a single moment until now.

Adam called up, "We need to get everyone into their places now."

Greer was surprised when April spun to give her a quick hug before disappearing down the stairs. The others were finding hiding places behind the thick stone columns along the gallery. She hurried down after April.

Greer stood near the altar, but not close enough to be distracted by the agony emanating from the box of bone and ash. Focusing on the stained-glass window high above, she held her angel wing pendant. She repeated Saint Michael's prayer while they waited.

Her feet were tired of standing on the stone floor and her voice was slightly hoarse from repeating the prayer for what she imagined was the 200th time. Just as she began again, the front door banged open at the other end of the cathedral. She jumped reflexively at the sound, only to quickly admonish herself and tighten the grip on her wings. Greer continued to pray as she turned to face her tormentor, "... all evil spirits, Who wander through the world for the ruin of souls ..."

A lean figure limped down the nave toward her, stopping just outside the light from the candles April had strategically placed in the transept and chancel.

"You have something that belongs to me," it said.

"Your days of tormenting those poor women are over." Greer tried to keep her voice steady despite the cold fear griping her belly. "I'm releasing their souls back to God so they can finally rest in peace."

"That will not be happening. In fact, my intention is that you will join them in a private hell of my own making."

The Prefect sounded different than before, when she'd made the mistake of trying to fight him inside his room of horrors. He sounded more human now, yet dark and familiar in the way a nightmare will always feel like it is repeating.

Still clutching her wings, she took a few steps forward to lure the Prefect closer. At the same time, she gave the signal everyone was waiting for, "If you want me, then you'll have to come and get me!"

His cackle echoed off the walls of the cathedral as he moved toward her. "Don't mind if I do."

"Oh my God," Greer said, in shock as the figure emerged into the candlelight. Jones, the student she'd helped mentor all summer, was hobbling toward her. His filthy hair and clothes were barely worth noticing compared to his gaunt cheeks and sunken eyes. He resembled nothing of the tidy, healthy student the ambulance had wheeled away barely a week ago.

She recognized the feeling of an icy web wrapping itself around her body, constricting her arms and breathing, caused her body to tense in fear. Yet all she could focus on was the sickly young man drawing nearer. "Jones ..." she said and instinctively reached out to help him as he moved closer. Greer felt responsible for bringing the Prefect into this poor boy's life.

Jones' gait faltered for a second when she called his name, and the tightness around her body released. She dared to hope that she'd reached the human part of him for, at that very moment, the portable sacred circle was falling around him in the transept. The tail-ends of the support ropes were still smoldering as the wooden frame bounced hard and came to rest in a small cloud of dust. Jones, or the Prefect as she had to remind herself now, stopped in his tracks. However, a sneer quickly spoiled his face, as he continued forward.

April and Adam stepped from the shadows. Greer rushed to join them around the circle, and they all began to chant. Tony appeared and hurried through the chancel to the altar. Picking up a small vial, he opened the box of ashes, poured the holy water from within over the remains, and said a quick prayer:

Eternal rest grant unto them, O Lord
And let perpetual light shine upon them.
May they rest in peace.
Amen.

"No!" wailed Jones.

As Tony was finishing the benediction over the jumbled remains from the alcove, Adam looked up at the gallery and gave a nod to Frankie. Immediately, small statues and wooden figures which the family had stashed around the sanctuary began to rock on their pedestals.

The four gathered around the power circle and increased the fervor with which they prayed for the exorcism of the demon Prefect from Jones' body. Adam's amulet was flashing bright silver, and Greer's wings shone a brilliant gold, increasing the light in the transept until it touched the rafters high above.

One by one the statues crashed to the floor. The figure inside the circle shrieked, and a foul odor emanated from him. He sank to his knees and let out another inhuman howl.

"It's working!" Frankie yelled from the safety of the gallery.

While the others continued their chant, Adam began the Pater Noster. Greer was trying to focus all her energy on the Prefect, but she spared Adam a glance as she could see him straining. Every muscle strained and the veins were popping out in his neck and temples as he raised his arms high and called out louder and louder.

Suddenly Jones' body wrenched at an impossible angle, arms stretched wide and head thrown back. His mouth opened in a strangled scream as a black mist erupted from him. Jones collapsed on the floor, apparently unconscious while the mist writhed in the center of the circle.

The statues stopped falling. Frankie had run out of ammunition. Worried the spirit might catch on if he lingered any longer, Greer tried one last threat, as she shouted, "Agatha is safe from you forever! You'll never have her, so leave this world!"

It was a mistake. The mist rapidly coalesced into a roughly human form directly in front of her and cried out, "No! Then I will at least have you!"

The figure retreated into itself until it was a small, shadowy sphere in the center of the sacred circle. It chanted in an unknown language, until it finally exploded outward hitting the wall of the circle. With a loud crack, the wooden frame split, and the shadow rushed beyond the confines of the barrier knocking everyone over backward.

With the wind knocked out of her and a quickly developing bump where her head had met the stone floor, Greer was slow in getting up. Her eyes darted around the dim space, looking for Adam and the others. Adam was already on his feet, but the other two were struggling to sit up.

The Prefect coalesced into the shape of a man again, then immediately expanded in size until the human form was distorted into something grotesque. Greer recognized a flash of razor teeth. It stalked toward her. "I have waited too long for you. The others were never this difficult. Well, except for my dearest Agatha. You had better be worth the wait." Black liquid dripped from the fangs gnashing in his mouth, sizzling as each drop struck the floor.

Greer heard Adam call to her. She awkwardly scrambled backward from the approaching creature. Fear at how those razors would feel as they tore into her flesh filled her mind even as she raced for a solution. Another prayer? Risk siphoning the others? Greer settled on a distraction.

"Why did you use Jones? Aren't you strong enough to do your own dirty work? Not much of a prefect then are you?" she said, taunting the demon. "Instead, you use a boy."

She saw the murky figure shrug. "He was a convenience," it said. "It took far less energy to inhabit him and manage my affairs than it would in this form."

Greer continued to scramble backward, heading through the chancel toward the altar. She didn't think there was a way out of this end of the cathedral.

"You made Jones mess with the dig. He flooded it."

"Yes," it hissed. "I had hoped you would abandon the effort after that."

"But we didn't. In fact, we discovered your many victims. Your secrets."

The dark creature became more defined as he moved toward her. The mouth was a gash that twitched violently as he spoke, and the eyes were aflame much like the hellhounds that had chased her all those weeks ago.

"You made a real mess of my work. But I will take my time with you. It will be perfection."

The Prefect loomed closer until Greer bumped against the altar itself. She could see Adam and April trying to sneak toward her, outside of the creature's sightline. Hurriedly looking left and right for an escape, she found none. The spirit was right on top of her. The putrid smell of burnt flesh filled her nose and stung her eyes. She threw her hands up in a vain attempt to keep him away, but he transformed into mist again and flew into her chest, straight into her heart.

Greer blinked slowly, feeling like she'd blacked out for a moment. She turned wide eyes to Adam who had frozen mid-step. "Is he gone?" she asked. He slowly shook his head, his eyes bright with fear, as she heard evil laughter rise inside her own head.

"I am here," the voice said in soft purr to her alone. "You, as so many before, are now mine."

Adam's face crumpled as the Prefect's deep, bizarre cackle escaped her lips.

Greer was aware of what was happening but had no control over her own body. The spirit spun her around, smacking her violently into the altar.

"Now let us see what we can work with," he said gleefully. "Ah, here we are."

Greer watched as her own hand grasped the empty crystal wine cruet used for communion and then brought it crashing down against the edge of the stone table. The globe of the cruet shattered all over the floor leaving the neck of the bottle in her hand.

"Yes, this will do," the voice said mockingly.

Adam and April ran to her, yelling the prayer for exorcism at the top of their lungs. Adam's amulet shone, and April's whole body gleamed with her rainbow aura.

Greer raised her empty hand and heard herself utter the unnatural words the spirit was saying in her head. A wave of dark energy left her, knocking her two saviors off their feet once more. Grating laughter threatened to split her mind in two.

As she watched Adam struggle to stand, Greer felt her free hand pull forcefully at her collar, ripping the fabric open down the front. The hand that still held the broken bottle slowly lifted the jagged glass to her chest. She could make no sound, but her tears broke free as the razor-sharp crystal cut the skin just beneath her left breast.

"No!" Adam yelled as he stumbled toward her. He grabbed the small vial of holy water that Tony had left on the altar and dashed it over her. Then, locking eyes with her, he hastily began the exorcism prayer again.

Greer could see Adam praying inches from her, but all she could hear was the voice in her head speaking its own evil curse. The sharp pressure at her chest increased. Warm blood coursed down her ribs as the bottle slowly traced its path under her breast. Greer tried to speak: to plead for help.

Adam saw rather than heard what she said. Gutted, he abruptly stopped the prayer. "What can I do? Tell me what to do!" he cried. He watched in horror as the Prefect forced Greer to cut herself. He tried to grab her hand, but the spirit was stronger than him. He grabbed her arms and tried shaking her. "Greer! Can you hear me? Fight! Fight, damn it!"

She longed to cry out. Struggling, she barely managed a whisper. "Help me," was all she could gasp as the tears flowed.

"Oh, God! Dear God!" He shouted up to the rafters. He looked back down at her shimmering eyes. "I love you, Greer!" He pulled her lips to his own. "I love you," he whispered as he held her.

Her hand was being crushed between them, the crystal digging deeper into her flesh. The momentary pause in her hand's course threw the spirit off guard for a moment. Greer was ready.

She focused her mind on the darkness inside of her, seeking it out as if it was a cancer she could discover and cut from her body. However, instead of cutting it away, she began to siphon it. Her insides began to vibrate with power. This power didn't bring the same warmth and joy she felt when siphoning Adam and April's powers. This was dark, cold, and angry.

Greer didn't care because she grew stronger with each passing second and sensed the demon growing weaker. Her sadness over Liz's death and the fury over her mother's murder were rushing through her in a tidal wave of rage.

"What are you doing?" said the strained voice in her mind.

Greer released her own mad laugh once she understood the Prefect was panicking. As her delirious cackle ricocheted in the crackling air, Adam stepped away from her, uncomprehending, while April watched from the floor, slack jawed.

"I guess your Agatha was never able to do this?" Greer said, mocking the demon as she continued pulling energy from his darkness within her. She didn't notice her wing pendant dimming.

"Stop! How are you doing this?" The Prefect's voice gasped inside her head.

"You may be unfathomably old and evil incarnate, Quintianus, but I know something you don't!" She was growing cold, but her body felt hard and strong as steel. She would've wrestled the Prefect out of her if she could lay a hand on him.

"Stop!" The Prefect's scream echoed through the cathedral as he rushed in a dark mist from Greer.

She reeled backward from the force, but Adam was there to catch her. "Greer! You are ok!" He touched his forehead to hers. "Oh, thank God. We need to run now."

"Let go of me," she said, protesting. "Can't you see I'm winning?" Shoving Adam away, she stood up straight. "I'm not leaving until this bastard is in his grave!"

"But Greer!" Adam objected as he tried to pull her away.

"I said NO!"

She spun from Adam and, spreading her arms wide, focused on the dark form in front of her. He didn't look much diminished, but she knew she'd deeply wounded him. Closing her eyes, Greer stretched her senses out toward the darkness and pulled at the inky thread of his energy once more. The fading glow of her golden wings flickered and died.

Instead of terror, she was met with smugness. "Little human, I have caught onto your trick. Take as much energy as you want. There is plenty more in Hell where that came from. Drink up, little one. I am happy to share."

"Greer, stop!" Adam grabbed her arm, but she shook him off with unusual force.

Greer didn't believe the Prefect had an endless supply of energy. If he did, he wouldn't have left her when she began siphoning him. Calling his bluff, she tried to pull power from him even faster. The more energy she took from him, the worse she felt. She broke into a cold sweat; the chill turned her veins to ice water. Her muscles stiffened until they felt like stone. Unable to move, she screamed in frustration.

"Let go, Greer!" Adam begged.

She refused to listen.

An unexpected pinpoint of light appeared between Greer and the

Prefect. The demon shrank from it, so she pressed her advantage.

"This is not the way," said a voice from the growing light.

Greer faltered. "Mom?"

"Love is the only way, my darling girl." The astonishing music that had accompanied the light before began to sing through Greer's mind. The brilliant speck flew into Greer's angel wings which now radiated again with golden light.

"Love, Greer," came her mother's plea.

Summoning every ounce of focus she had, Greer began the prayerful chant that would connect her to the angels:

Eee Nu Rah

Eee Nu Rah

Eee Nu Rah

Zay

Warm power sparked and began to grow within her, but she needed more. She searched for Adam and immediately found him at her side. Placing a hand to her back, he began to chant with her, and soon his silver light merged with her own.

She quickly built the power of love and joy within her until all the bitter darkness was cleansed from her body. Each of her cells vibrated, almost painfully, with positive energy.

"Now it's your turn, Prefect" she said with a wry smile.

The dark figure had been cowering from the glow. Now, in a true frenzy, it expanded rapidly, roiling and bubbling over and around itself. It grew denser and took on the slickness and odor of burning oil. "Ignorant human! I will crush your body and send your soul into the darkest depths of Hell!" The churning mass began to form six heads and a long tail.

Greer knew she could wait no longer. Focusing on the love she felt for her mother, her father, Adam, and his crazy family, she felt the heat and the energy blaze even hotter within her. It was too much power for one person to contain. She had to release it.

So, she did.

Taking a single step forward Greer reached out and touched the darkness before her. She sent all that light and love into the demon. It cried out in misery while she sang out in joy.

Adam shouted in wonder. "I hear them! I hear them!" He was in sheer bliss as she sang along with the angel choir ringing in their ears.

They could see the physical transformation of the demon Prefect as each atom of his being was turned from darkness to light. When it was complete, the demon continued to shine brighter and brighter.

"Adam, I don't know how to stop!"

"Just let go!"

"I can't!"

The church was filled with so much light that the others were shielding their eyes and turning their faces from the scene below. It rushed toward the sky out of each clerestory window high above. The illuminated demon continued to expand and burn brighter.

"Adam, it won't stop!" Greer said, in the understanding that this was beyond her. Whatever happened next was her destiny. She was not afraid.

Adam jumped between Greer and the transformed Prefect, crushing her to his chest just as the massive orb of light exploded. The stained-glass window above the altar burst in a million shards out into the night. The iron rood screens around the altar and chancel warped. The choir benches were reduced to splinters. Miraculously, the altar and its holy contents were left intact.

When the dust settled, Adam still held onto Greer as if her life depended on it. "Are you alright?" he asked without letting go.

"I think so." She wrapped her arms around him. He winced at the touch, and she was shocked to feel bare skin. "What happened? Are you hurt?"

"Maybe a bit. Do not worry."

"Adam! Let me see." She tried to spin him around, but he collected her under his arm.

"First we need to make sure everyone else is ok. Then we need to get out of here. The police will be here shortly after the light show you just put on."

Joy Comes With the Morning

Greer opened her eyes to the late morning sunlight streaming through the open blinds. She stretched slowly then rolled over to snuggle against Adam. He let out a soft grunt when she draped an arm across his back.

She quickly pulled away, sucking air through her teeth. "Oops. Still sore, huh?"

He'd been sleeping on his stomach and now turned his face to her, not quite ready to open his eyes. "Ayuh. It gets better every day though," he mumbled.

Gently tracing the waves in his hair, she watched him relax back into a light sleep. She propped on one elbow and carefully pulled the sheet down to peek at his back. He'd suffered a first-degree burn across his entire back when he threw himself between her and the explosion. He'd refused treatment at the emergency room. A clean shirt was all he could be talked into as he bounced back and forth between Greer and April's hospital beds checking with staff members on their progress.

April was home now, but they had to monitor her concussion for a few more days. It was hard telling which of her falls had caused the injury; it may have been both. Greer had apologized endlessly for her role in knocking the girl off her feet. April insisted that, since Greer was possessed by a demon at the time, there could be no hard feelings.

Frankie and Tony had been waiting in the nave just out of sight after the Prefect possessed Greer. They gained a few large splinters when the choir benches blasted apart. Mother Rose had plucked their thorns and tucked them into bed with some pain relievers.

Greer had thanked the two of them for doing their best to cover their tracks. Tony burned the remains of the wooden circle and Frankie used her gift to move the ashes and her earthquake debris to the dumpster out back. They left the wood of the shattered benches and twisted iron of the rood screen. The report in the local paper called it a gas leak for lack of a better explanation. Greer and Adam planned to donate whatever time and money they could to the church to make amends.

Greer was extremely thankful everyone had made it through the ordeal alive and relatively intact. She rolled onto her back and tenderly probed at the long line of stitches on her chest. The doctor lost count of how many sutures she'd used and had been apologetic about the inevitable scarring.

Adam pried open one eye and watched her with concern.

She said, "It's really long, right?"

He rolled onto his side and carefully traced a finger just below the healing skin. "I tried so hard. I tried to make it stop."

"You tried like hell. In the end, you saved me from what would've been worse."

When she kept worrying at the stitches he asked, "Are you upset about the scar?"

She sighed. "I'm not thrilled about it." Then she threw him a mischievous grin. "I'll never make money as a stripper now. Good thing I have my archaeology to fall back on."

He started tickling her.

"I can't dance anyway," she giggled.

"I would still come watch you."

Her smile faded. "Does it bother you?"

"That you cannot dance?" he joked as he started tickling her again.

Greer caught hold of his wrist and answered quietly, "No, the scar. Does it bother you?"

"No, Greer, of course not. We have matching scars now," he said running a hand across the claw marks on his own belly. "It would seem we have matching eyes now too."

She rubbed her now bright-blue eyes and blinked a few times. "Has that ever happened before?"

"Not exactly. Mother claims my eyes were a bit darker when I was a child, before my talent presented itself; however, mine did at least start as a shade of blue."

"Do you think they'll go back to brown?"

"I think it unlikely." He moved a strand of hair off her cheek. "Remember, everyone's gifts are different. This seems to be a side effect of yours."

"Like I was zapped with light and it bleached my eyes?" she said sarcastically.

His arms encircled her and locked onto her gaze. "I choose to believe you were filled with God's light, and it stuck around. Your eyes reflect your spirit, the divine joy in you," he said as a promise.

When he kissed her, Greer believed.